I0818605

# THE DEVIL'S POLITICS

The Devil's Politics is published under Reverie, a sectionalized division under Di Angelo Publications, Inc.

Reverie is an imprint of Di Angelo Publications.

Printed in the United States of America.



Di Angelo Publications
4265 San Felipe #1100
Houston, TX 77027

Library of Congress
The Devil's Politics
ISBN: 978-1-955690-03-4
Hardback

Words: Drew Benbow
Cover Illustration: Olga Tereshenko
Cover Design: Savina Deianova
Internal Design: Kimberly James
Editors: Ashley Crantas, Willy Rowberry, Alma Felix, Jessica Warren, Stephanie Yoxen, Elizabeth Geeslin Zinn

Downloadable via Kindle, iBooks, NOOK, and Google Play.



For educational, business, and bulk orders, contact sales@diangelopublications.com.

1. Fiction --- Political
2. Fiction --- African American & Black
3. Fiction --- Thrillers --- Political
4. Political Science --- American Government --- National

# THE DEVIL'S POLITICS

DREW BENBOW

ry "Ace" Glover • Frankie Ann Perkins • Ahmaud Arbery
ames B. Brissette, Jr. • Jordan Baker • Sean Bell • Vincent
monte • Sandra Bland • Michael Brown, Jr. • Eleanor Bumpurs
hilando Castile • Rev. Clementa Pickney • Terence Crutcher •
ald Curtis Madison • Rev. Daniel Simmons • Dannette Daniels
eborah Danner • Amadou Diallo • Patrick Dorismond • Rev. Dr.
rtin Luther King Jr. • Henry Dumas • Timothy Dwayne Thomas,
• James Earl Green • Jordan Edwards • Randolph Evans •
colm Ferguson •George Floyd • Eric Garner • Phillip Gibbs •
ey Goodson • Freddie Gray • LaTanya Haggerty • Nicholas
ward, Jr. • Andre Hill • Cynthia Hurd • Susie Jackson • Michael
ome Stewart • Kathryn Johnston • Jordan Davis • Ethel Lance
argaret Laverne Mitchell • Rita Lloyd • Eula Mae Love • Trayvon
rtin • Depayne Middleton Doctor • Tyisha Miller • Arthur Miller,
• Alfred Olango • Prince Jones, Jr. • Angelo Quinto • Tamir Rice
ad Robertson • Marvin Scott III • Walter Scott • Rev. Sharonda
eman-Singleton • Yvonne Smallwood • Alberta Spruill • Timothy
nsbury • Alton Sterling • Terrence Sterling • DeAunta T. Farrow
reonna Taylor • Myra Thomson • Emmett Till • Tywanza Sanders
rika Wilson • Daunte Wright • Ousmane Zongo • Manuel Ellis
ayshard Brooks • Daniel Prude • Atatiana Jefferson • Aura
ser • Stephon Clark • Botham Jean • Tanisha Fonville • Michelle
seaux • Akai Gurley • Gabriella Nevarez • Tanisha Anderson •
narri Tarver • Tyree Davis • Tina Marie Davis • Brandon Dionte
erts • Kwame Jones • Miciah Lee • Ryan Simms • Albert Lee
hes • Mubarak Soulemane • Samuel David Mallard • Kelvin White
arius Tarver • Andrew J. Smyrna • William Howard Green Jr. •
uyn O'neill Light • Abdirahman Salad • Leonard Charles Parker
• Alvin Cole • Justin Lee Stackhouse • Barry Gedeus • Donnie
ders • Mychael Johnson • Alvin Lamont Baum II • Etonne T.
zymore • Nathan R. Hodge • Tommie Dale McGlothen Jr.
anisha Necole Fuller

# ONE

As a child, Devon had often fantasized about moving away from his hometown. He'd watch movies set in New York, wishing he could transport himself there. He'd commit entire JAY-Z albums to memory—especially the lines about Brooklyn. The music would carry Devon off to that electrifying city, and he'd imagine a life far more exciting than in Macon, Georgia.

After high school, Mama Lee had all but pleaded for Devon to stay nearby for college. She enlisted Butch for help, her brother-in-law and Devon's favorite of his many uncles. Uncle Butch had taken a handful of classes at Macon State College but didn't finish. Devon succumbed to the pressure to stay local and became the first on either side of the family to earn a degree. She again beseeched him to stay and study at Middle Georgia Law School.

The scant market for new grads in Macon gave Devon the perfect excuse to finally leave the town he had long outgrown. Many of his classmates accepted positions in Atlanta, Birmingham, Tallahassee, and other cities in the region. The top third of the class had been offered coveted judge clerkships and impressive jobs at big-name firms as early as the summer before their last year. But since Devon graduated number thirteen from the bottom of his class, no one was exactly knocking down his door to offer him a hundred-and-fifty-thousand-dollar junior associateship. He knew this and didn't waste his time applying.

Devon instead took a position as a legislative aide for a Republican congressman in Washington, D.C., three weeks after graduation. It wasn't New York City, but it wasn't Macon, either.

The job paid exactly $35,620 per year. But most importantly, it was away—with brownie points for being in a metropolitan city outside of the cultural South.

Over the six years since Devon had left Macon for Washington, he'd only returned three times, each for a wedding or funeral.

•••

It was about eleven in the morning. Devon shifted his weight on a wooden pew in his childhood church. The memorial service should've started an hour prior.

Next to him, Uncle Butch sat with legs spread wide, pinning Devon to the bench end.

Devon reclined in a pensive trance, arms crossed over his stomach.

If he could snag a few hours of sleep and hit the road by midnight, he could be out of Macon and back to D.C. in time for the Sunday brunch scene.

But first, he needed to eat. There was a Zaxby's on Zebulon Road, just a mile from his parent's home in south Macon, which was minutes from Interstate 75. To Devon, this fast-casual chain was Macon's only redeeming quality. They had opened one in Chantilly, Virginia, about a year ago, and Devon had dragged Bethany out of bed for the hour-long drive from his Southeast D.C. efficiency to attend the grand opening. They brought back days' worth of chicken strips and crinkle fries. Out of sheer nostalgia, Devon snacked on the cold, stale fries for the better part of a week.

Barely conscious, Devon jumped at the vibration of one of his two iPhones, snapping out of his daydream. He pulled one of them from his inside breast pocket. He tapped the red button to decline the call and sent a text instead.

**Devon:** What's up, Bethany?

Uncle Butch nudged Devon with his bony knee, gesturing for him to put his phone away. The service had begun. A compromise, Devon instead hunched forward, his forehead resting on the back of the pew in front of him.

**Bethany:** What's wrong, babe?

**Devon:** What do you mean?

**Bethany:** You only call me by my full name when something's bothering you.

**Devon:** What's up, Beth?

**Bethany:** Too late, Devon. What's the problem? Are you okay?

**Devon:** I'm good, babe. Just a little tired.

**Bethany:** Well, I know we've only been together for a couple of months, but I'm still upset that you didn't bring me to Georgia with you for your family reunion.

**Devon:** I told you, baby. I need to move at my own pace. It's just not time yet.

**Bethany:** I know, Devon. And I respect that. I don't want to pressure you. But I feel like if I'm good enough to share your bed, I'm good enough to meet your mother. Are you even in Georgia? Are you cheating on me?

**Devon**: Babe, I don't make enough money to cheat on you.

**Bethany:** Touché :)

**Bethany:** Well, did you tell them about me?

**Devon:** Yes, babe. They know all about you.

**Bethany:** You know what I mean, Devon. Did you TELL them?

Devon closed out the text conversation and swiped through

Instagram. Uncle Butch's sharp elbow jab to the ribs jolted him to attention. Butch, with a grunt and puff of halitosis, nodded toward the pulpit. Devon's mom, using the podium for support, managed to control her sobbing briefly to again summon her remaining son forward to say a few words.

He rose slowly, carefully climbing over Uncle Butch, who made no effort to make passing space. As he walked down the center aisle toward the stage, Devon feigned his sorrow. With a bowed head, he embraced his mom. A full foot shorter, she buried her face into his chest, her mascara permanently staining one of Devon's three dingy, off-white dress shirts.

Mama Lee interlocked her arm with his, clutching him at the elbow. He tilted his head back to think about the best way to begin his off-the-cuff speech. Last-minute adjustments to the microphone bought him a few more seconds. He cleared his throat, and in a subdued tone, Devon eulogized his brother:

"Losing a sibling is unbearable. Losing a twin brother is unthinkable. We shared the same womb, at the same time. The same birthday. Part of me is literally gone. And I miss him sorely.

"Don't get me wrong, Damo was no saint. He disappointed a lot of pe—"

Mama Lee's already tight hold suddenly felt like a boa constrictor. He got the hint and backtracked.

"But he was my brother," Devon continued.

"As many of you know, identical twin boys run heavily in the Lee family. Damo and I were the fourth-known generation of twins in this family. Of course, there was Dad—God rest his soul—and Uncle Butch, his twin. Grandad was a twin, and so was his father.

"It was he, Great Granddaddy Lee, who authored a poem a hundred years ago about twin brotherhood, and the bond we share. I recall Dad drilling this poem into Damo and me as kids, requiring that we recite it on demand. Damo and I always thought it was corny. And I haven't uttered these words since Dad was in the hospital, days before he died. Damo and I were barely twenty-one then. I had just graduated from undergrad, and Damo had just finished his first tour in Afghanistan."

Devon swallowed hard, and for the first time all day, true sadness overcame him as he recited the poem:

> I am not my brother's keeper.
> *I know this may seem strange.*
> *Though we have different names,*
> *We are one and the same.*
> *My shortfalls are his,*
> *And his strengths, mine.*
> *We ponder the same thoughts,*
> *Because we share the same mind.*
> *He is I. I am He.*
> *How can you not see?*
> *No, I am not my brother's keeper.*
> *I AM MY BROTHER.*
> *And my brother is me.*

"The poem is called 'I Am My Brother.' And I didn't appreciate these words when Dad and Damion were alive, but they mean so much to me today."

Mama Lee erupted in sobs. Her knees weakened, and Devon ushered her down the stairs to her seat.

He glanced down at the bronze urn that contained his twin brother's ashes. Mama Lee was devastated when she learned that the Army had burned her son's body instead of releasing it to the family for a proper burial. Damion had signed the cremation paperwork from the hospital bed at Fort Leavenworth. She was convinced he had done this to spite the family.

It had been nearly a year since she'd seen him in the flesh. Because of the coronavirus, hospital protocol had prohibited in-person visitation. Mama Lee called the hospital incessantly until she finally got a nurse to facilitate a phone call between her and Damion.

Army unit patches lay at the urn's base. Some of his old Army buddies, all but one dressed sharply in their dress service uniforms, sat stone-faced in the third pew. Two of the soldiers later donned white cotton gloves and presented Mama Lee a crisply folded American flag—although this is typically an honor reserved only for veterans who received an honorable discharge, not a dishonorable one, as Damion had. So, the soldiers weren't there on official orders, but just as friends.

There were two large, suited middle-aged white men standing in the back. Their suits were too nice for them to be cops, not even feds. And they certainly didn't seem like friends of Damion.

With the soldiers, the mysterious men in suits, Uncle Butch, and a handful of other close family members whose attendance was mandatory, the audience count was exactly twenty. That was the church's cap, for social distancing purposes. If anything, the cap did more in the way of allowing Mama Lee to save face. People weren't necessarily breaking down the church door for Damion Lee's memorial service.

•••

Devon ordered fifty chicken strips and negotiated with the drive-thru cashier for thirty packets of Zaxby's special sauce, down from his original request of a hundred.

He savored the first bite and ignored two back-to-back calls from Mama Lee. Surely, she only called to guilt-trip him for leaving for D.C. so soon after his brother's memorial service.

His twenty-year-old Mitsubishi Galant could make it all the way to Florence, South Carolina, before needing a refill. Dad had bought the car for Damion and Devon to share in high school. Nevertheless, it had been Damion who'd always kept the key. Damion would wax the silver paint to shine as if small crystals were in the paint. He'd outfitted it with rims, window tints, a sound system, and a GPS tracker.

He'd claimed it was his car alone. And on the rare occasion he'd allowed Devon to use the car, Devon was considered to be borrowing it. He'd even taken the key with him when he left for basic training at Fort Benning at seventeen. Devon had been forced to pay five hundred dollars to get the dealership to cut him a new one.

Devon drove through his old housing projects. Streetlights flickered. Some were out completely. A plastic bag blew across the street like a tumbleweed in the desert. He passed the intersection near the Splash and Dash laundromat where he and Damion would sell ice-cold bottled water and Gatorade as kids. He merged onto I-75 North, putting the car and his mind on cruise control. Devon resolved to only stop for gas and the number two; he had two empty liter-and-a-half water bottles in the back seat that he would pee in when he needed to.

He toggled between music, podcasts, and audiobooks. At times, he just drove in silence, absorbed in his thoughts.

Windows down a quarter of the way, the crisp air against his face and down his collar kept him alert for much of the ten-hour, overnight drive. By the time he'd reached Richmond, his ears and nose had started to numb, so he rolled the windows up and started the heater. But by that point the sun had already crested the horizon, giving Devon a burst of new energy that would carry him the rest of the way.

Despite the 12-degree January frost, Devon always found warmth in driving north on I-395 and being greeted by the Washington Monument and the Jefferson Memorial, just over the Tidal Basin.

D.C. was home to him. It wasn't New York- or L.A.-big, but it certainly wasn't Middle Georgia, where they rolled the sidewalks up at seven o'clock. Although, in the Black professional D.C. scene, he often grew annoyed that everybody knew everybody. So, in some ways, it wasn't that different.

And what D.C. lacked in Zaxby restaurants, it more than made up for in carry-out spots. Good Hope Carry-Out was Devon's favorite: five wings and fries, ketchup and mumbo sauce on "errything"—that's how the locals would say it. Mumbo sauce was a D.C. delicacy, and Good Hope was two blocks away from his apartment in Anacostia, a neighborhood that was on the slight uptick with gentrification but was still one of the roughest in the city.

Luckily there was a parking spot directly in front of his apartment building. Devon grabbed the drab olive green Army duffle bag that once belonged to Damion and did a once-over to make sure the car was clear of anything inside that might be attractive to crackheads or mischievous kids. And he dragged himself and the duffle bag to his second-floor efficiency, silenced his phones, and slept the Sunday away.

# TWO

Overnight temperatures had plummeted to near zero. The escalator opening to the Capital South Metro stop created a wind tunnel, causing bits of snow and ice to strike Devon's face like miniature darts. He sidestepped Metro workers who were busy covering the platform with rock salt.

Devon kept his loafers in a canvas shoulder bag, a free door item from a Congressional Black Caucus reception three years prior. He'd slung the bag over his black trench, under which he wore a green Patagonia vest, a birthday gift from Bethany, and under that, a middle-of-the-line suit, with which he wore a pair of black suede and nylon Saucony running shoes; he owned two other identical pairs. On nasty weather days like these, he'd cover them in plastic grocery bags, tying the bags at his ankles. Randy, the office chief of staff, chided him more than once about wearing sneakers to hearings and important meetings. A lowly aide, Devon took great satisfaction in Randy's irritation and continued wearing them as a small act of rebellion.

The train cars were empty. On days like this, the Office of Personnel Management would decide on whether to keep D.C.-area federal offices open and impose a one- to three-hour delay for commuting employees, or closed and allow workers to work from home.

Washington had figured out long ago that teleworking was an effective way to keep the ball rolling on inclement weather days. So when the coronavirus first struck, the city didn't skip a beat because most people's jobs were connected to the government. In a few keystrokes, D.C. was up and running as if a well-oiled backup generator had kicked in. Universal telework meant midday naps, cocktails, and unnecessary Zoom calls for everybody.

That is, everybody except the staff of the Honorable Johnathan E. Grayton IV, a thirteen-term Republican congressman from Georgia's sixteenth congressional district.

Congressman Grayton was old school. He was from the era of top hats, washable handkerchiefs, and adding two spaces after a period. For years, he refused to use email, preferring the typewriter, or better yet, the "safer" and more personal touch of the handwritten note.

During snowy days, he grumbled at the thought of any of his staff working from home. When the pandemic hit, it took being mentioned in *Politico* as a corona-doubter to get him to loosen up. He often would say he just liked to see people in the office doing work; it "inspired" him. Devon slumped into his office chair, untied the bags over his feet, and kicked off his sneakers.

Devon was once one of Congressman Grayton's students at the Middle Georgia Law School. Grayton, the school's most esteemed alumni, would travel back to his home district twice per week on the taxpayer's dime to "check in on his constituents" and teach his constitutional law course.

Devon moved to D.C. at twenty-four, shortly after graduating law school, and Congressman Grayton gave him his first job working as a legislative aide out of the Rayburn Congressional Office building, steps away from the U.S. Capitol. After a couple of years, Devon had become well aware of the rumblings among other staffers that the reason he hadn't jumped ship yet was that he hadn't passed the bar after three attempts. Why else would a thirty-one-year-old attorney settle for thirty grand a year in one of the most expensive cities in the country?

A bump against his cubicle wall jolted Devon.

"Sooo, you just weren't going to call me when you got back to Washington?" Bethany's voice pierced the office silence as she leaned over his canvas partition.

Bethany's boss couldn't care less about suits and ties. He was a bearded, hippy congressman from Oregon's seventh congressional district known for his rotation of five or so well-worn Woodstock-era T-shirts, Birkenstocks, and one of many pairs of thick wool socks woven and sent to him regularly by Mrs. Daisy McDonald, a 104-year-old woman from Carlton, Oregon.

So, it wasn't a problem for Bethany to wear her blue-and-gold Berkeley sweatshirt, which she always did on bad weather days. And in case there was ever a question about her physique, her designer jeans fit as if they were made specially for her. Rain or shine, arctic winds or blistering heat, Bethany would run five miles daily, ten if she was stressed, and she had the legs to show for it. She had tucked her slightly-distressed jeans neatly into her L.L.Bean boots—the ones with the brown clamshell rubber toes and the fur on the inside. The cold, sunless D.C. winter took a toll on her complexion, for which her bold, naturally red hair framing her twenty-three-year-old face more than compensated.

"Well, good morning to you, too, Beth."

Bethany shifted her weight and let out an exasperated sigh.

"Look, Beth, I drove overnight. I didn't want to call and wake you. And when I got back to my apartment, I just crashed all day. Give me a break, babe; you know how visiting family takes a lot out of me."

"Well, considering I've never met your family, no, I don't know."

Devon slipped on his sneakers, unplugged his two phones, and nodded toward the large, ornate, oakwood double doors.

"Babe, I have about fifty minutes until my next meeting. Let's go downstairs to the cafeteria. I'm sure we could both use a cup of coffee," he said, gently directing her at the waist.

He led her the long way through the labyrinth of cubicles so as to avoid walking by Randy's office. As chief of staff, Randy ran a tight ship. His desk faced the door to have full view of passersby, and he regularly questioned the comings and goings of the staff.

"I'll be back in a few. If it's important, I have my cell with me," Devon said softly to Kate, the office receptionist.

Devon stepped out ahead of Bethany to hold the door.

The halls had begun to get busier, but still not to pre-pandemic levels. Where before you'd have to guess a person's politics by their hairstyle, or whether they wore an American flag lapel pin, the new clear line was whether they wore a mask.

"So, how was the reunion?" Beth asked as the two made their way to the elevator.

"It was good. It was more like a small gathering, nothing too big."

"Who has a family reunion in the middle of winter, anyway? In a pandemic?"

"Don't judge, Beth. I told you, my family is weird."

"Well, I would have loved to have gone with you, to meet your family, see where you grew up, and at least help you drive. You must be exhausted."

"I got enough sleep yesterday. Last night was rough, because my sleep pattern got thrown all outta whack, but it's nothing a tall, hot cup of black coffee won't fix."

"You're reading my mind, baby. I wouldn't mind skipping out and spending the rest of the day with someone hot, tall, and Black, too," Bethany replied seductively. "Let's blow this joint. I can go grab my things and meet you at the Capitol South Metro in twenty."

"Babe, as tempting as that sounds, I have to get back to work. I can probably wrap up everything sometime shortly after lunch—say, two? I can block off my calendar with fake meetings. We can go to your place and ball up with a bottle of vino and a movie, and see where things go."

"Sounds like the perfect evening to me," Bethany replied.

As they approached the cafeteria's glass doors, Devon pushed the stainless-steel handicap button with his elbow.

He followed Bethany to the coffee bar. She tapped half a packet of Splenda into a double-cupped coffee and picked a lid from the center of the stack.

The short-staffed cafeteria had been forced to transition away from the Starbucks-esque custom orders of caramel macchiatos with oat milk and a little foam to a self-serve coffee station.

They took up seats at a long, wooden, knee-high table in the corner of the cafeteria, Bethany on a leather loveseat, and Devon across from her in a matching armchair.

"Devon, did you really tell them about me?"

"Tell who what?" Devon said, rolling his head, and eyes, back in annoyance.

"Don't be funny, Devon. Your family. Did you tell your family about me?"

"I told you I did. They know you're twenty-three. And they know you're from California."

"You know that's not what I'm talking about. Do they know I'm white?"

"I may have inadvertently omitted that part," Devon mumbled into his cup.

"Really, Devon? You told me you'd tell them. Look, if you're too embarrassed to let your family know you're dating a white woman, then what are we even doing?"

"Sweetheart, it's not that. It's just complicated, and I need a little more time."

Bethany sank deeper into her seat, legs crossed, sipping her coffee as she peered over the table at Devon.

"Wait, have you told your family about me?" Devon asked.

"What about you, Devon? Of course they know about you. They know you're Black, and that you're a few years older than I am. They also know you're from Georgia."

"But do they know I'm a Republican?"

Bethany broke eye contact, watching as the Speaker of the House passed on the other side of the cafeteria's glass wall. "Don't try to flip this on me," she replied.

"Exactly. Listen, babe," he said, switching from the chair over to the sofa cushion beside her. "We've only been together for a couple months. How 'bout we let things evolve organically? Can we do that?"

"I guess so," Bethany replied.

"Sooo, are we still on for our playdate tonight?" Devon asked, hooking his pinky finger into the belt loop of her jeans.

"Actually, I just remembered," she replied, scooting away. "I'm supposed to be linking up with some of the Dem staff from Ways and Means at Off the Record tonight."

"Oh, how convenient, Bethany."

"Well, you know you're always invited," she replied.

"You want me to hang out with a bunch of entitled, fresh-outta-undergrad kids who don't have a worry in the world that their dad's AmEx couldn't fix?"

"Well, I'm one of those *entitled, fresh-outta-undergrad* kids. And unfortunately, my dad's AmEx can't fix you being a jerk to me right now."

Bethany stood up, and so did Devon.

"Listen, Beth. I have a lot on my mind these days. I'm usually game to shoot the intellectual one with your dumb-ocrat friends; I just don't need them busting my chops tonight. Plus, you know I have better things to do with the little money I have than spend it on twenty-two-dollar cocktails. I'm gonna have to pass."

"First, I resent your very original play on my party's name. Second, you know I don't have a problem covering you when we go out. What's mine is yours. Actually, you know what, Devon? How about you don't come, and just call me when you're having a better day?"

"Sweetheart," Devon said, reaching for Bethany's hand. She dodged him, turned around, and took up a power walk to the exit.

Devon didn't want to follow directly behind her and give onlookers an indication that he was harassing her. So, while Bethany had made a beeline for the door, Devon walked the perimeter of the cafeteria. He made it back to the office with about ten minutes to spare.

"Hey, Kate. Any messages?"

"Actually, yeah. Two guys came in looking for you. They said they had a legislative proposal to run by you, and they were hoping to get it in front of the congressman before next session."

"Did they ask for me, specifically? By name?"

"Yup! I think they were lobbyists. But they looked like a couple of Senators," Kate replied.

"Wait, senators or lobbyists? From which states? Why would senators be visiting me?"

"No, silly. The Ottowa Senators—it's a Canadian hockey team. Anyway, the guys were big like hockey players. Nice suits, though."

"But you do realize you work for the *U.S.* Congress, right? And how saying 'senator' to refer to anything but one of a hundred legislators can be confusing? Besides, it's the Caps for us. Never mind that; did the guys leave names? A card?"

"No. They said they'd just try back another time."

Devon returned to his cube and flipped over a laminated sign that read "On A Call." He popped in his AirPods, slipped off his sneakers, and logged in. He was aloof for most of the meeting, though, preoccupied with the thought of the two men.

Who were they? What did they want? He thought back to the two men he had seen at Damion's memorial service. He had half a mind to go to the Capitol Police and ask for video footage. But what would he tell them? There were two men in suits in a congressman's office, requesting a meeting with his legislative aide? There was nothing suspicious about that. He'd sound ridiculous.

# THREE

Off the Record was a warm space with luxurious red velvet, dark wood chairs, and matching walls with tufting. The light fixtures, made of tarnished-looking, antique bronze, held glass faux candles. The carpet was lush and intricate. Stepping into the speakeasy-type bar in the basement of the Hay-Adams Hotel gave the feeling of being transported back in time, as if Abe Lincoln himself could walk in at any moment. In fact, it wasn't that uncommon to spot high-profile political elite closing out their busy days there.

The hotel sat directly north of the White House, only separated by Lafayette Square Park. On the way inside, Devon had paused to admire the famous pastel yellow St. John's Episcopal Church. Dwarfed and surrounded by imposing concrete blocks of edifice, this little sanctuary stood out and didn't care. The early nineteenth-century building sat directly across Black Lives Matter Plaza, a street separating the hotel and church. He recalled the day Trump posed in front of it in 2020 for a photo-op, using federal police to violently clear away peaceful George Floyd protestors with tear gas, smoke canisters, and pepper balls.

Bach or Beethoven played at a level just loud enough to snuff out the sound of a private across-the-table conversation to an eavesdropper's ear, but soft enough for a table of lively young staffers to draw contemptuous eyes from the other patrons.

"Whoa! Is that Devin Lee?" a wiry, tipsy Gen Z-er shouted, his N95 mask over his forehead.

"So much for trying to make a stealthy entrance," Devon muttered under his breath. "Beth, dear, can you tell your friend Seth that my name is 'De-*von*'?" he asked, drawing out the soft *o*.

"I think you just did, baby," Bethany said with a chuckle. "I'm glad you decided to come out tonight. Come have a seat."

"Well, I felt pretty crappy about earlier. Plus, I could use a stiff drink," Devon said into Beth's ear as he leaned over her from behind, and he gave her a peck on the cheek.

"I felt bad, too. And I could also use something stiff tonight," Beth playfully whispered back.

They both smiled. Devon stepped around and sat next to her. She clutched his arm. He caressed her bare knee through the hole in her distressed jeans.

As she worked on her third cab, he ordered a Heineken, but she switched his order to a dirty martini. He shot her an approving eye. The tension from earlier had subsided.

Bethany and Devon shared a cozy booth with Tim, Seth, and Makeba, three first-year Democratic staffers of one of the most powerful committees in Congress, the House Committee on Ways and Means. Seth had moved to a chair at the end of the table to make room for Devon in the booth.

Tim's dad owned a massive farm in North Carolina and a vineyard in Virginia that pumped out thousands of barrels of the east coast's most popular wine, and he was a sixth-generation Tar Heel.

Seth's mom was a federal judge, and his dad a retired Navy admiral and Academy grad. Seth was a military brat who bounced around from Japan to San Diego, to Hawaii, to Norfolk, never in any one place long enough to plant roots.

If the term "Black elite" exists as a concept, Makeba embodied it. She was from Prince George's County, Maryland, said to be the wealthiest Black county in the country. Her mom was a psychiatrist and had her own practice in the County, with four offices and an impressive team of people working under her. Her dad owned a contracting company. He got contracts for plumbing and electrical work at federal buildings throughout the D.C. metro area.

Makeba's parents were able to send her and her younger sister, Malika, to the prestigious Sidwell Friends School, also known as "the Harvard of Washington's private schools." The Obama girls went there—so did Biden's grandkids and Chelsea Clinton. So, it was no small wonder when Makeba got accepted into actual Harvard—Cambridge Harvard. She worked hard, double majoring in economics and finance, and decided she wanted to go to law school. With Harvard Law, Yale, UPenn, Georgetown, and dozens of other law schools clamoring for a Black woman with her talent, she instead chose historic Howard University for her Juris Doctor degree. There, she became president of the law review, graduating number one in her class.

With Makeba's perfectly smooth, youthful complexion, she could expect to be carded for the next twenty years. But being the only other person there whose skin was as mahogany as the table, and who could rent a car at the regular rate, Devon found himself naturally drawn to her.

Squarely on brand for the political capital of the world, when two or more D.C. policy wonks got together, it could always be expected for them to solve all the world's problems over a three-hour cocktail session. Devon dove right into the group's already spirited debate. Despite almost categorically disagreeing with virtually every point they'd make, Devon lived for these sorts of high-level, intellectual discourses on how the world should work. They all did.

"So, Devon, how's life on the right side of the aisle?"

Devon, attempting in futility to resist Seth's bait, quipped, "You mean the *bright* side of the aisle? All is well."

While Bethany and Makeba side-barred, Seth studied Devon, savoring a sip of his craft IPA and shaking a fistful of wasabi nuts and pretzels as if he was about to roll a lucky seven. He set his beer down on the cardstock coaster, which was decorated with caricature portraits of historical political figures. And with a mouthful of nuts and a belly full of liquid courage, Seth smugly reclined and blurted, "So, nobody's gonna ask the question?"

Makeba and Bethany paused their discussion. The table was Seth's.

"Ask what question?" Devon asked, fully loaded, cocked, and eager to fire back at what was clearly about to be a philosophical pile-on.

Devon, being the only Republican at the table, was prepared for a fight on all fronts, even if that meant ideologically slaying his own girlfriend.

"Okay, then I'll do it," Seth said, leaning forward. "What's it like being a Black Republican, Devon?"

Tim turned beet red with discomfort, digging into his rocks glass for the Luxardo Maraschino cherry buried beneath the ice. He wanted no part of this discussion.

Beth rubbed her knuckles into Devon's knee, a desperate plea for him to not engage.

But Devon couldn't if he wanted to. He was stunned to silence. He'd had this conversation with other Black people more times than he could count, but never with a white person, especially not in such a setting. Seth had some nerve!

Before Devon could respond, Makeba retorted, "What's it like being a white Democrat, Seth?"

And suddenly, the scales were a little more balanced. Devon had thought he'd be on an island, having a circular debate on abortion, guns, maybe even Black Lives Matter. He had mentally prepared for that. What he didn't expect was a topic much more sensitive—racial politics, more specifically Black politics. In Devon's experience, white people had stayed far away from that topic for fear of being labeled racist.

Devon grew instantly closer to Makeba. She had abandoned, or at least tabled her identity as a Democrat, and chose her Blackness, just as she did when she chose Howard over an Ivy for law school.

Seth didn't relent. He doubled down. "I mean, I don't mean to be offensive. I just don't understand how you're Black *and* a Republican. That's like, uh, an oxymoron. I mean, what has the Republican Party done for Black people?"

Devon collected himself. He quickly thought of all the ways he could mount a counterattack. He considered a debate on values and policy ideas. But that was just like running on a treadmill—it's an exercise that gets you nowhere. He could've gone down the "Blacks aren't monoliths" path. But the fact is, for decades, over 90 percent of Black Americans have voted for the Democratic presidential candidate. No other major voting demographic had turned out almost exclusively for one party in this way. So at least by that measure, the monolith argument was a failing one. But in that vein, Devon decided to stick to the numbers.

"If thirty percent of Black people voted Republican, Trump would never have been elected president," Devon asserted.

The table was unified in their confusion.

Devon continued, "More than half of the U.S. states have closed or semi-closed presidential primaries. That means that in order to vote for the Democrat in the primary in those states, you have to be a registered Democrat. And to vote Republican, you have to be registered as Republican."

"We know what a closed primary is, Devon," Seth interjected.

"Okay," Devon replied, ignoring Seth's snark. "So, because Black people aren't registered as Republicans in any meaningful numbers, we don't get the chance to participate in the Republican primary. Trump never would have made it to the general election in November if Black people had voted Republican in significant numbers in the primary. It's like playing full-court basketball, but one team only gets to play on half the court. You can't win.

"So, what you have is Democratic candidates taking the Black vote for granted, and Republicans not caring about the Black vote, because they know they won't get it anyway. In both instances, neither party courts our vote with actual policy. Imagine if there were only one smartphone maker; there wouldn't be an incentive for that company to make a better camera, or improve processing speed. But when they have to fight for market share, they constantly have to improve their products and cater to the market. In the same way competition is good for the economy, it's also good for politics."

Seth nibbled at the end of his thick, brown eyeglass frames in contemplation, then inhaled loudly through his nose.

"I get that, buddy," he said. "But what's the big deal? It doesn't look like Blacks have it that bad to me anymore. I mean, sure, slavery was bad, but that was a long time ago. So was Jim Crow. I don't see anybody siccing German Shepherds on you guys for trying to sit at the front of the bus. You had Obama, and now the VP. Dems gave you the Civil Rights Act of '68, MLK Day, and Juneteenth. I look at you and Makeba here. You both have fancy law degrees and work for powerful members of Congress. Sounds like the Democratic Party has served you pretty good."

Devon and Makeba looked at each other with raised brows to determine which of them would set Seth straight. With a nod, Makeba yielded to Devon.

"Seth, my guy," Devon started, shaking his head, "Did you know that just shy of twenty percent of Black people in this country live in poverty? That's one in five. That number is worse than for any other race. For whites, it's about seven percent—not even one in ten. Do those numbers sound *pretty good*?"

Seth started to speak, but Devon cut him off.

"This country has continuously moved the goalpost for Black people each time we managed to make inroads. Jim Crow supplanted slavery. And mass incarceration replaced Jim Crow. Did you know that Black people represent almost forty percent of the federal prison population, despite being only about thirteen and a half percent of America's total make-up?"

The table focused intently on Devon.

"You see, Seth," Devon continued, "Black people in this country *are* still at the back of the bus. Yes, we're doing better because America is doing better. Just like when the bus goes faster, so do the people on it. But Black people are still at the back of the bus."

Tim finally chimed in, spitting a cube of ice into his glass: "So, what you're saying is, your argument is not on policy, but strategy. It's a numbers thing for you."

"Well, ballots are about numbers, Tim. But the policy is what matters. What's the point of having Black people in office who don't care about issues affecting Black people?"

"I see. But what about unity?" Tim asked. "Surely, Black voters can pack a bigger punch if they stick together."

Everyone's eyes bounced between Devon and Tim as they spoke.

"Unconditional party unity disenfranchises unconditionally," Devon said. "So, when I talk about Black people voting Republican, I don't mean a mass exodus. Then we'd be in the same situation, where one party holds the Black voter monopoly.

"Don't get me wrong, unity is important. But what has party unity done for us in this country? It's still more expensive to be Black than any other race. For example, mortgage interest rates are higher for us. And when we happen to get the loan, our house is going to appraise for less than our white counterpart but be taxed at a higher rate. Our schools, which property taxes supposedly pay for, are under-resourced, and our people are over-policed. So, yes, the Democratic Party gave us the Civil Rights Act. But my question is: What have you done for us lately?"

"The point is, to move the equality needle, I'd like to see Black Americans unify under policy instead of party. We need people on both sides of the aisle who care about issues that affect the Black community, people who won't bend to white supremacy, and who are not afraid to take it head-on."

Seth pushed away from the table, leaning back onto two chair legs. "Is it me, or does this guy sound a lot like any one of us?"

"Basically, I'm the most liberal Republican you'll ever meet. How's that for an oxymoron, Seth?"

The group shared its first laugh of the night together.

Devon glanced at Makeba and noticed her studying him with raised eyebrows and the corners of her lips turned downward. She looked away quickly. Devon's eyes then darted to Bethany, who didn't try to conceal that she had noticed Makeba's stare, too.

Bethany climbed over the back of the couch and snuck off to the bar. Minutes later, she returned with a server who carried a silver, antique-style tray of eight chilled shots of extra añejo tequila. She slid in the booth on the opposite side of Devon than before, in between him and Makeba.

Bethany distributed the shots. Raising her glass high, she announced, "To Monday nights—*salud!*" The group replied in unison: "*Salud,*" each downing their shots with ease.

Tim slipped a platinum AmEx into the textured leather bill sleeve without checking the damage.

Makeba called her Uber and walked to the restroom.

While Makeba was in the ladies' room, Devon heard Seth and Tim having a not-so-private chat about walking to a gentlemen's club of sorts, a nearby establishment called "Alastair's." Many a wholesome politician had been known to visit this place—for the wings and great drinks, no doubt.

Makeba returned to the table minutes later to grab her coat and scarf.

"Hey, guys," she said. "Great catching up, but I gotta run—Uber's waiting." She rushed out the side door, up the stairs, and to the curb.

Devon thanked Tim for the drinks and idly promised to return the favor next time.

As he stood up, Devon saw the backs of two large men, half the room away in identical black, calf-length wool coats. They were heading toward the door. He grabbed his bag and coat and started after them, hoping to get a glimpse of their faces.

"Devon, where're you going?" Beth asked.

"Oh, I thought I saw someone I knew," he replied, turning back to help Bethany with her coat, eyes still fixed on the exit. "But it's nobody."

They were just two men in black coats and dark suits in a city full of men in black coats and dark suits.

# FOUR

Being from Macon, Damion was accustomed to hot weather. But this was different. The stifling 105-degree heat, compounded with strong winds, assaulted all his senses.

When he had first arrived in-country, he gagged on his first breath of the rank air, which carried powder-like sand and particulate fecal matter from a manmade pond the size of two football fields. Situated in the center of Kandahar Airfield, the "Poo Pond," as it was referred to, was a collection point for sewage and other waste produced by tens of thousands of troops and workers on the U.S.-Afghan military base.

Kandahar was one of the main three military bases in Afghanistan, deriving its name from the province in which was located. Compared to the stories Damion had heard about other, smaller bases throughout the south of the country, he understood the base to be relatively safe—although from time to time, large, bullhorn-looking sirens atop wooden utility poles would sound from all directions, drowning out everything else and signaling for everyone to take cover in one of the many concrete bunkers, or some other hardened structure. But the Taliban mortars would rarely reach the base, and after a while, Damion had come to expect the "God voice" to announce the all-clear across the base-wide intercom system. He'd emerge from his shelter with the others and continue about his daily business—a minor inconvenience at most.

Corporal Damion Lee's job was to lead a group of ten soldiers, ranked specialist and below, to the front gate every morning at 0500 hrs. to meet, credential, and escort local Afghan workers onto the base. At twenty-one, Damion was the oldest on his team.

The soldiers' job was to ride around base for twelve hours a day with the Afghan local drivers, who sat in the passenger seats of their jingle trucks. The three-axle vehicles were old, often barely functioning, but beautifully decorated. The custom art included intricate calligraphy, paintings, ornaments, beads, and chains that hung from the front bumper and "jingled." And, of course, they had no air conditioning.

The duty was simple: ride shotgun with the Afghan drivers as they covered a route of hundreds of portable toilets on the base. The drivers would travel from base to base for weeks, seldom showering, except for washing their feet five times per day for prayer. But their body odor was Chanel No. 5 compared to the fumes the Poo Pond emitted.

The soldiers had orders to stand guard with a loaded M4 Carbine rifle while the Afghan workers inserted a firehose-like tube into the toilet, sucking the contents into the truck's tank. They'd drive from latrine to latrine until the tank was full. Then they rode with the Afghanis to the Poo Pond, pumped out the sewage from the tank into the pond, and continued along the circuit. Another Afghan-soldier pair would come behind them to clean. They repeated this three times per day.

This highly coveted job was reserved for the lowest-ranked and the screw-ups. A literal shit detail.

Damion's occupational fate came about after being labeled a troublemaker by his platoon sergeant, who Damion believed singled him out for some reason. Though naturally an early riser, Damion would consistently arrive to formation a few minutes late just to get under his sergeant's skin. He was also blamed for instigating several fights. This earned him a series of Article 15s—a form of administrative punishment.

The catalyst, however, was when his platoon leader and first sergeant showed up at his living quarters at 0100 hrs. for a health and welfare check. They discovered Damion with his battle buddy, Corporal Zapata, a Dominican from New York, and two Italian soldiers all drunk off Centerba, gambling in Spades, which Damion had taught them, and blasting Biggie Smalls' "Mo' Money Mo' Problems" through a Bluetooth speaker.

The Italian military allowed their troops to drink while deployed in-country. They even shipped the booze in along with their military rations. For Americans, however—even the contractors and civilians—alcohol was strictly prohibited by General Order Number 1.

As punishment, Damion was demoted from sergeant to corporal, and Zapata from corporal to private first class. Both were immediately assigned to the shit detail "until further notice."

The smell was pervasive, its pungency increasing the nearer you got to the center of base. Soldiers on the detail often lost five to ten pounds within the first two weeks of duty, as the inescapable stench clung to their camouflage uniforms, making it impossible to keep food down, even after several showers and double laundry. Eventually, those on the detail would get used to it. But nobody else did.

The residual odor repelled others. Standing in the chow line, Damion and his crew were afforded a six-foot bubble by other soldiers who wished to preserve their appetites. Inside the dining facility, or DFAC, a single, rectangular cafeteria table was set off in the corner and unofficially reserved for the detailees.

On a particularly hot, humid, and dusty evening, Damion and Zapata sat down for dinner chow a few minutes before the DFAC closed, their M4 rifles propped on bipods at their feet. Each Friday was surf 'n' turf night—succulent, well-seasoned steak, corn on the cob, fried butterfly shrimp, king crab legs the size of little league baseball bats, and sometimes even lobster tail. Their plastic compartment dinner trays overflowed. The food in Afghanistan was the only thing that brought Damion and his guys pleasure.

Zapata tore off a piece of steak with a fork and his fingers. He sandwiched the meat between a dinner roll and moaned as he bit into it.

With a cob of corn held between his middle finger and thumb of one hand, Damion scrolled through Instagram on his phone with the other, catching himself up on trashy celebrity gossip and snickering at memes.

The DFAC was starting to clear out. A few clusters of soldiers remained, eating, chatting, and watching TV. They were allowed to stay for as long as they wanted after closing, but no one new could enter.

A DFAC worker in a white uniform and white paper boat hat passed, pushing a pile of trash with a dry mop. Once the DFAC was closed and cleaned, and everyone else had cleared out, the workers, all Indian, would enjoy the space for themselves with their own traditional food.

"May we join you gentlemen?" a large, bearded man asked, but only after sliding his tray onto the table and knocking it against Zapata's.

"Do you, man. It's a free world," Damion replied.

Another man of a near-identical build showed up and slid his tray onto the table, too. Both men stepped away to the refrigerators, then each returned with three Beck's Non-Alcoholic beers.

Damion scooted to the end of the long table as if the two men were the ones who reeked. Zapata followed suit.

"Why the fuck do they wanna sit wit us?" Damion muttered under his breath.

Zapata shrugged, holding a crab leg between his teeth. Juice squirted as he bit and twisted, exposing three inches of orange and white meat.

"We don't bite, bro," one of the men said to Damion and Zapata. Both men moved closer to them, half the distance of the bench. "I'm Jim. And this is my colleague, Jon."

"You mean, like, Jimmy John's," Zapata said, and erupted in open-mouth laughter, a whole dinner roll stuffed in one cheek like a squirrel.

The men feigned amusement.

"Well, I guess so, huh?" Jim replied. "Never thought of it that way. But it's 'Jim,' not 'Jimmy.' And his name is 'Jon,' J-O-N, no 'H.'"

Jim and Jon were two linebacker-sized men, both wearing sharply pressed tan camouflage uniforms, the old ones that the Army had long since retired and replaced twice with new patterns. "CONTRACTOR" was stitched in block letters over their right breast pockets, and their first names over their left. Their sleeves were rolled over their forearms to just below their elbows. They would have had to cut them to roll them any higher. They were each at least mid-forties, more salt than pepper in their beards.

"So, who are you guys with?" Jon asked.

"It's right here," Damion answered dismissively, pointing with a steak knife to the subdued black and green patch Velcroed to his left sleeve.

"We're not up on all our patch insignias," Jon replied.

The DFAC worker passed their table again, pushing the dry mop in short, quick pumps.

"It's the transportation brigade," Damion answered.

Jim and Jon exchanged subtle looks.

"Yeah, our unit is in charge of the airfield and all the cargo trucks that come on and off the base," Zapata added. "Our real job is doing cargo manifests for the planes, but we're not doing that for the time being. We both slipped up and got hit with a couple of Article 15s. So, we're just ridin' in the shit trucks all day now."

"Ya don't say," Jon said, raising his upper lip to his nose as he sniffed the air in Zapata's direction.

"I damn sure don't miss those days," said Jim. "We used to be in, too. Seven years for me."

"I did five," Jon added.

"So, who are you guys with now?" Zapata asked.

"Oh, we're contractors with ZinCorp," Jim replied. "It's a public health company. You know, keepin' you guys safe from pathogens and stuff, while y'all keep everybody back at home safe."

"Public health? So, y'all just two big-ass nurses or somethin'?"

They all laughed.

"We're definitely not nurses. We're what you call 'air pollution analysts'," Jim said. "We collect air samples and take them back to the lab for testing, to make sure the air everybody's breathing is safe."

Jon cut one of his three steaks in half and forced it into his mouth. He washed it down with a Beck's, finishing off the can in three gulps.

"How can y'all stomach your food, sittin' over here by us?" Damion asked.

The worker passed again, this time hitting Zapata's foot with the dry mop.

"Yeah, we smell like shit," Zapata added, ignoring him.

"Oh, it doesn't really bother us. We've spent our fair share of time testing the air around the Poo Pond. So, we're used to it," Jon said.

"Yup, don't even faze us anymore," added Jim.

Jim slid a cold Beck's over to Zapata. Jon gave one to Damion. Jim led the toast, each raising their cans to the center. "To a shitty day!"

They shared a hearty laugh.

"So, is it?" Damion asked.

"Is what?" Jim and Jon asked together

"Is the air clean?"

With raised brows and averted eyes, Jim sucked his teeth and inhaled deeply.

"We plead the Fifth," Jon said.

"I guess I didn't need anybody to tell me that," Damion said.

"Risking our health for a bullshit few extra hundred bucks a month in hazard pay," Zapata said.

Damion wrapped four slices of white bread in table napkins and tucked them into his bag.

Jim gestured toward the snack section of the DFAC. "This place is full of all the junk food anybody could want, and you're squirreling away Wonder Bread?"

"It's not for him," Zapata said. "It's for the birds. He has a weird obsession with them."

"Hey, everybody has a thing, I guess," Jon said. "Anyway, you guys should come work with us. Our company pays a lot better. If you're gonna be here anyway, you may as well get paid well for it."

Damion noticed Jon jolt in his seat as if Jim had bumped him under the table to silence him.

"Shit, I wish, man," Damion said. "We're active-duty Army. We'd have to get out first, or at least go Reserve if we wanted to come back over here as contractors like y'all. I know for me, I still have two years left on my enlistment contract. You see these letters on my uniform? 'U-S-A-R-M-Y.' That shit stands for 'Uncle-Sam-Ain't-Release-Me-Yet."

"Or backwards, 'Y-My-Retarded-Ass-Sign-Up,'" Zapata added. "Plus, we don't know anything about being a nurse."

They all laughed.

"They tricked my dumb ass with an eight-thousand-dollar enlistment bonus. What they don't tell you is that it ain't even eight racks; you get half after Basic Training, and they tax the shit out of that. And then they chop the other four up over the next couple of years," Zapata complained.

"Just out of curiosity, how much do you guys make anyway?" Damion asked.

The DFAC worker passed for the fourth time in ten minutes, pushing the same pile of trash.

"We just met you guys. I don't want to hurt your feelings," Jim said with a smile, crow's feet forming next to his eyes. "But it's a pretty penny. Even prettier than your pal here," he said to Damion, aiming his fork at Zapata.

"Hey, guys. Listen, great chatting, but we have to break away and head back to the office. Let's meet up tomorrow for dinner chow and talk about it, same time," Jon said. The two piled the crushed near-beer cans on top of the crab leg shells, steak bones, and empty cobs. They then stood up and collected Damion's and Zapata's trays, too.

As Jim and Jon walked off, emptying then stacking the trays on their way out, Damion and Zapata remained seated.

"Cool dudes, right?" Zapata said, his voice elevated to overcome cheerful Indian music that had gotten progressively louder. They ignored the DFAC worker, who had begun to wipe the table between them.

The workers began to congregate around a table across the dining hall that had three large metal communal trays of rice, naan, curry chicken, and lamb in the center.

"Yeah, they seem cool as shit," Damion replied.

# FIVE

The daily routine was grueling and monotonous, but Damion had begun to settle into it. Though physically demanding, it was simple, and nobody bothered him.

Each morning, there would be dozens of drivers at the front gate, hoping Damion and his team would select them to go on base and work for the day. There was only a need for ten. The other drivers would have to either wait in their trucks where they'd sleep until the next day, or drive over one hundred miles to the next U.S. base. Most waited, as the trip could take days or even weeks depending on weather conditions. The roads were mostly unpaved, too, so navigating the mountainous areas was dangerous. There were also fuel costs to take into account and a good chance of breaking down. And the war.

For Damion, the worst part of the work was having no one to talk to, as the Afghan drivers didn't speak English. To remedy this, Damion always picked the same driver each day. He called him Rambo because of his long, black hair and the black bandana that he'd fold into a headband. Despite the language barrier, the two were fond of each other. They'd figured out their own ways to communicate simple things like lunch time, break time, quitting time—the important things. Damion had even begun to pick up words in Pashto; he seemed to have a knack for the language. Rambo would show Damion photos of his family, and Damion would bring Rambo packs of beef jerky and cans of Rip It, an energy drink.

But mostly, Damion listened to music, no longer bothering to get out of the cab of the truck during the stops like he was supposed to.

He and Zapata met every day at the DFAC for lunch and dinner—breakfast was grab-and-go, due to work. They preferred eating at the end of mealtimes, a half hour or so before the DFAC closed. The line was shorter then, and you could get as much food as you wanted on the first pass.

Jim and Jon started joining them for dinner, occasionally. Their dinner meetups soon turned into an unofficial standing calendar item. Each Friday, after the four had gotten their fill of steak and crab legs, they'd all hop in a decades-old Land Rover Defender, owned by the Army and loaned to civilians and contractors for them to get around base.

In a quick ten-minute drive, they'd pull up to a large, wooden deck, not too far from the base's post office. Strings of large, clear light bulbs and a breathable camouflage netting draped tall poles surrounding the deck. The woodwork was impeccable, the product of years of so many men deploying to the base and leaving their marks.

A wooden, door-sized plaque nailed to the deck's railing depicted a camel with an oversized cigar hanging from its mouth. Next to the camel, in large writing, read "Kandahar Koughars."

Anywhere from ten to three dozen men, a mix of soldiers and civilians, would gather, blowing plumes of cigar smoke and laughing loudly. The men would order their cigars online and bring them to the deck to trade and smoke. They played poker, talked shop, listened to music, and ragged on each other. "The Koughars" was a cigar club that allowed them to unwind after a long week.

"I've driven by this place a million times in the shit truck," Damion said to Jim and Jon. "Saw the lights, but never knew what it was until you guys brought us here."

Damion and Zapata enjoyed the comradery and the atmosphere at the deck. But the kicker was that the pungent smoke would smother their Poo Pond odor. It was the only place they could go where people didn't dry-heave around them.

Damion, Zapata, Jim, and Jon took up seats in four canvas folding chairs in the corner, a large standing ashtray in the middle of them. "Hotel California" played from the other corner.

Damion loosened his boot laces.

"We shoulda been coming here all along; it's the only thing we can do on this base that's halfway fun and won't get us in trouble," Zapata said as he bit off the end of his Romeo y Julieta.

"Bro, that's a fine Cuban cigar, not one of those cheap sticks they sell in the PX. Don't disrespect the stick like that. Here, use this." Jon handed him a stainless-steel cigar cutter with his name engraved on it in fancy script.

"Well, we have a fifth of a Johnnie Walker Blue back on our compound, if you guys want to partake properly," Jim offered.

"Oh, hell no," Damion replied. "I'm not going down that road again. If we mess around and get in any more trouble, we'll get put out of the Army. Our platoon sergeant already has it out for us."

"I hear that," Zapata added, leaning forward as Jon torched the end of his cigar for him.

"It's Friday, we have good cigars and good company, and it's payday. The only thing missing besides a bottle of Henny is women," Damion said as he reclined and took a pull.

"Tell me about it," Jon replied.

Summer nights in Kandahar were a comfortable seventy-five degrees. The air was still, allowing the smoke to linger around their heads.

From his thigh cargo pocket, Damion pulled a napkin with white bread he'd taken from the DFAC. He dropped pieces onto the bench beside him. Two small brown birds pecked at the crumbs. A third ate straight from his hand.

As the birds gathered around Damion, Jon struck fire to a wooden matchstick and flicked it at Damion's birds. They all scurried.

"What the—Why would you do that!" Damion shouted, ready to retaliate before Zapata cut in.

"Yo, don't touch his birds, bro," Zapata said, shaking his head.

"Okay, okay!" Jon replied, hands up in mock surrender. With a clenched jaw, Damion stared hard at Jon.

"Speaking of payday," Zapata interjected, changing the subject to ease the tension, "y'all never told us how much you guys made as nurses out here."

"Oh, it'd make you sick," Jim replied. He and Jon shared a laugh.

"Tell us," Damion said, his jaw still clenched and eyes fixed on Jon. "How much are they paying y'all to hold a pole in the air all day and run it through a computer?"

"Just let us put it this way: our biweekly salary is more than you make in a few months out here," Jon replied. The two laughed again.

Jim pulled out an iPhone in a thick, rubber protective case. He opened his pay statement and passed Zapata the phone. Zapata hung his head and passed the phone to Damion.

"Damn," Damion said. "You guys pay more in taxes than our whole salary."

"This is bullshit," Zapata said.

"Oh, it's real," Jon replied.

"No, I mean it's bullshit that we're all out here. You guys don't have to deal with half the shit we have to deal with, and you make enough to buy a new Honda every month," Zapata said.

"We all make our choices," replied Jim. "Plus, remember, we used to be in the Army, too. So, we know the struggle."

"I've never seen that many zeros in my life," Damion said, still stunned.

"But that's beans, compared to our real hustle," Jim said.

"Your real hustle?" Zapata asked.

Jim and Jon looked at each other.

"Eh?" Jim said to Jon.

Jon studied Damion and Zapata, mouth curled downward as he stroked his beard.

"Listen," he said. "We like you guys. We do. We just need to know that you can keep your fuckin' mouths shut."

Jon scooted his chair toward the center. Damion and Zapata moved in, too. Jim reclined and coolly glanced around for eavesdroppers.

Jon took a pull from his cigar and blew hard into Damion's and Zapata's faces, indifferent to their coughs.

"Now, what I'm about to tell you cannot leave this deck," Jon said in a low voice, just above a whisper. His eyes were serious. So were Jim's.

"You two're nurses," Zapata quipped. "What are you gonna do, give us a prostate exam?"

Jon reached across with the speed of a cobra snake, his large hands gripping a handful of Zapata's collar.

Zapata's eyes bulged and his face grew fat as blood rushed to his head. He gagged. Jim stood and turned his back to the group to block the view of potential onlookers.

"Chill, bro," Damion pleaded, grabbing Jon's forearm. But it was massive, and solid like a log. It was clear he wouldn't let go until he was ready.

In one quick motion, Damion then pulled a folding knife from his belt and flicked out the three-inch blade. "Let him go or lose the arm," he said to Jon, pointing the sharp tip in Jon's direction.

Jim turned and tapped Jon on the shoulder. Jon released Zapata into a gasping slump.

"You know what? Fuck this. These kids aren't ready," Jon said. The two men extinguished their cigars and started collecting their things.

Damion folded the knife and returned it to his belt. He then helped Zapata sit upright.

"And what were you gonna do with that little butter knife, help me with my ingrowns?" Jon laughed.

"Listen, forgive my friend here," Damion said with a stiff forearm to Zapata's shoulder. "I know he can be a little childish sometimes. But he's still my friend and I gotta look out for him. I'm sure you two can understand that. Either way, we still wanna know how to make some extra bread."

"Yeah, my bad, man. Let's...Let's talk business," Zapata said, still wheezing.

Jim and Jon stared at the two for no less than ten seconds. Then they looked at each other. Jim gave Jon a nod. Jon leaned in closer. Damion and Zapata did, too. Jim lit another cigar.

"No hard feelings?" Damion asked, his eyes bouncing between Zapata and Jon.

"Water under the bridge," Jon replied.

"Now that we got that outta the way," Jim said, "we are about to offer you both the business opportunity of ten lifetimes. You have the chance to become wealthier than you or anyone you've ever met could imagine."

Damion and Zapata exchanged a nervous look.

"I'm going to offer you a deal. But there's one catch," Jon said with raised eyebrows. Damion and Zapata were silent with curiosity.

"The catch is, we need you to agree before we tell you about the opportunity."

"But how are we supposed to—" Damion started.

"I know. I know," Jon interjected, "but that's the catch, gentlemen. You take it or leave it. This is some sensitive stuff. It could cause some serious ripples."

"More like tidal waves. Tsunamis, even," Jim added.

"Now either you both say 'yes' right now, and we can make some serious money together, or you stay broke shit-peddlers, and we can keep smoking these stogies," Jon said.

"Just one thing," Zapata said, "I'm in as long as this ain't one of those things where you want me to steal military secrets or something. I ain't with that shit."

"Are you kidding me? You guys ride with the shit-man all day. Even if that was the offer, the Indian dude who served me my meal earlier would be in a better position to have that sort of information than you two assholes," Jim said.

"And no terrorist shit either," Damion added.

"Right, none of that either," Zapata agreed.

"Don't worry—we're patriots like you. It's not either of those. So, are you two in or out? We don't have time to be going back and forth all night. We've been here for three years and have been running this operation for two and a half. Each time you military guys rotate out, we have to find new ones to bring into the fold and train up. And those guys went back to their families set for life. So, last fucking time: in or out?" Jim asked.

Damion and Zapata exchanged one last look.

"Fuck it, we're in," Damion said.

# SIX

Devon stood in a line that extended out the double doors and down the stairs of the Cannon House Office Building. Before the January 6 Capitol insurrection, as a Hill staffer, he could bypass the magnetometer screening with the flash of his ID and a chummy greeting to the guards.

In the days since, however, everybody underwent a thorough check. Before, congressmen and senators were allowed to jump the line, but even they now had to be screened.

Ahead of Devon was a middle-aged man with a sweatshirt and cap that read "FBI." His wife and grade school-aged kids were all wearing matching gear, purchased from one of the hundreds of souvenir stands throughout downtown.

There were at least a dozen other tourists ahead of him in line.

It was 9:13 a.m. when he finally made it into the building. It would take another seven minutes for him to walk to the office. Were it not for the line of tourists, Devon would've made it into the office on time at nine.

Twenty minutes late, he'd have to sneak the long way around to his desk to avoid passing Randy's open door.

"Morning, Kate," Devon said softly.

"Morning, Devon." Her high-pitched voice carried throughout the office, ruining Devon's attempt at a stealthy entrance.

"I left a sticky note on your computer and sent you an email. The boss wants you to meet him for dinner after his four o'clock."

"Thanks, Kate," Devon replied, waving his iPhone. "I got your email twenty minutes ago, and I'm sure I'll see your sticky note when I get to my cube. And I appreciate the verbal reminder, too."

"No problem. You know me! I'm a belt and suspenders type of gal," Kate replied as she dismissed Devon's sarcasm without looking up from her monitor, her fingers owning the keyboard.

Devon sighed and started toward his cube. He passed Randy's office, relieved he wasn't there.

Flopping into his seat and logging in without removing his coat, he opened Congressman Grayton's private schedule. The Congressman's four o'clock was with Aisha Jennings, the interim president and CEO of the Congressional Black Caucus.

The meeting was at The Yard, a restaurant popular with Black professional millennials in the city. After work, hundreds of slim-suited and stilettoed twenty- and thirty-somethings converged on the Black-owned, four-story building. Happy hour drinks were top-shelf and six dollars, undercutting everywhere else in the city. The music was always perfect—R&B and hip hop, the DJ flawlessly transitioning between old school and new; it was always loud enough to vibe to, but low enough to carry on a conversation.

The meeting was scheduled to be forty-five minutes long. Doors didn't open until five. Devon arrived at four thirty that evening, and he could see Congressman Grayton's unmistakably wide torso through the glass panel toward the back of the restaurant, totally eclipsing Aisha Jennings.

Devon took up a seat on a park bench directly across the street and called Bethany to pass the time.

"Hey, babe."

"Hey, Beth."

"I poked my head in your office and didn't see your coat on your cube. Did you slip out early and not tell me?" Bethany asked.

"I'm actually sitting outside The Yard, waiting for a meeting with my boss."

"The Yard? Like the restaurant? Isn't that the place you took me a while back, where that girl confronted me and said I was taking all the good Black men?"

"That would be the spot," Devon replied.

"What's a white Republican from Georgia doing at The Yard?" Bethany asked.

"Your guess is as good as mine. And get this! He's meeting with Aisha Jennings."

"*CBC* Aisha Jennings?"

"Yup! The meeting was set up for four, an hour before The Yard opens," Devon said.

"Interesting. What do you think is up?"

"I couldn't even begin to speculate. But something's up."

"Do you think he's trying to switch parties?" Bethany asked.

"I don't know. And I know he and I go way back to when I was his student, but he's never invited me to coffee in the cafeteria, much less to join him for dinner and drinks."

It was ten till five and a line had already begun to form.

"Hey, babe. They're about to open up. I'll call you when it's over."

"Sure thing."

"Oh, and Beth?"

"What's up?"

"Keep this hush-hush."

"That goes without saying, babe," she replied.

"Gotta go, babe," Devon said. "Don't wanna be late."

Devon hung up and slid his phone into his messenger bag. He then darted across four lanes of stop-and-go traffic.

When he arrived at the doors, he found a large bouncer had emerged with a tablet and a clear spiral earpiece.

"The line starts back there," he grumbled.

Devon flashed his congressional ID.

"That's my boss right there. He's a member of Congress, and I have a meeting with him," Devon said, pointing through the window.

The man in black inspected Devon's credentials closer, then took another look toward the only white person he'd see that night. He then raised the red velvet rope.

"Enjoy your evening, sir," the bouncer said with more enthusiasm than before.

Devon passed through the opening of the heavy curtain, walking by a pretty, young hostess whom he politely greeted with a nod.

Aisha Jennings was nowhere to be seen, but Devon had been watching the main entrance for the better part of a half-hour and never saw her leave.

Devon approached Congressman Grayton from behind. There were four small plates stacked in front of him. The top plate had about a dozen bones, clean to archaeological standards; he'd even cracked them open to suck out the marrow.

A perky server, even cuter than the hostess, approached with four more small plates.

There were no misses on the menu. But, on a busy night, you could look around at almost every table and instantly know the fan-favorite—the jerk chicken and macaroni and cheese. The small, meaty, fall-off-the-bone wings were seasoned to perfection, though not at all spicy. The mac-n-cheese was ranked second, only to his mother's. And it was made in an oven.

"Congressman, good evening, sir!" Devon said, with a squeeze of the congressman's shoulder.

"Why didn't you tell me about this place?! I could eat a whole pan of this mac-n-cheese. And these wings!"

"Well, I'm glad you like them, sir," Devon replied, taking the seat opposite of the congressman.

Facing the door, Devon could see over the congressman's shoulder as the first couple of small groups filtered into the restaurant, each claiming one of the tall, round standing tables.

"So, Devon, you've been with me here in D.C. for some time now. I regret that it's taken this long for me to have a one-on-one with you outside of that stuffy Hill setting. How're things going for you?" the congressman asked with earnest eyes.

"All is well, sir. I think I've settled in just fine. I love this town," Devon replied.

"Oh, forget the 'sir.' Right now, we're just two dudes catching up over drinks and a meal. What is that—water you have?" He raised his arm straight up and gestured downward toward the table, never looking around to see if the server he was summoning had even acknowledged him.

Nonetheless, the same bubbly server from before emerged from thin air.

"More mac 'n' jerk, Congressman?" she asked.

"Just a coupla' scotches, rocks in a separate glass. And bring him two," he said with a jolly wink towards Devon.

"I'm not much of a scotch drinker. I'll do a vodka soda, if you don't mind. And the mac 'n' jerk," Devon said.

"Right away, gentlemen," she said, carefully collecting the used plates from the table.

"So, how're you really doing?" Congressman Grayton asked. "Do you like the job? Do you have any issues with my positions on policy matters? Tell me your gripes."

"Everything's going great from my vantage point," Devon replied.

"You don't have to sugarcoat shit with me, son. You can be candid. I called you here so you can be just that with me," the congressman said.

The owner of The Yard, an early fifty-something bald Black man with kind, sleepy eyes and a burgundy velour sweatsuit came to the table. He brought with him a bottle of Cîroc vodka in a plastic ice bucket with the brand printed on it, and a half-carafe of ginger ale. "This is on the house, gents. Thanks for coming to The Yard," he said.

Congressman Grayton dug three of his thick, Ninja Turtle fingers into the bucket, grabbed some ice cubes, and dropped them into the heavy rocks glasses, not the custom, disposable plastic happy hour cups that they served to everyone else. The restaurant owner cracked the seal and poured generously.

"Let me know if you need anything else," he said before stepping away, the original server behind him.

"Wow. I've always wanted the VIP treatment here," Devon said, doing his best to ignore the attention his table was attracting.

"Well, it comes with the territory. You'll see when you become a congressman or better," Congressman Grayton replied. "Now, where were we, Devon? That's right—this is a safe space. Complete amnesty. You can tell me anything."

"Okay, sir. Can we start with why you just had a secret meeting with Aisha Jennings from the CBC? Seems like quite the odd couple to me—a serious mismatch," Devon replied.

"Ah, straight for the gusto, huh, Devon?"

"I'm just saying, if you want to keep meetings like that quiet, I don't think having them in public places is the best way to do it. Respectfully, that is," Devon said.

"I've been in this game since before you were squeezed outta' your mama's love box, son; I know what I'm doing. This wasn't a secret meeting. I just wanted people to think it was a secret meeting. If it was secret, you think I would have put it on my calendar, even if it was my personal calendar? This way I get free press coverage. People like to talk about things they think are salacious. Just wait; by tomorrow, they'll be 'twittering' about me."

"That's 'tweeting,' sir."

"Twittering, tweeting, twatting, whatever—you know what I mean. And stop with all the formalities. Tonight, it's just Johnny."

"Okay...Johnny. So, why are you, a white Republican member of Congress from one of the most conservative states, meeting with the CEO of the Congressional Black Caucus at the Blackest restaurant in town?"

The congressman dropped chunks of ice into his second drink, stirred it with his index finger, and leaned forward onto his elbows.

"Because I'm gonna need Black support at the polls," the congressman replied.

"Black support? You won the last three elections with over sixty percent of the vote. Over ninety percent of those voters were white conservative Republicans. You need Black voters like I need more fast-food restaurants in my neighborhood." Devon paused in bafflement. "Unless..."

The congressman's eyebrows rose an inch higher as Devon started to get the picture.

"You're running for president?" Devon asked.

"Not quite. U.S. Senate. And I want you to be my spokesperson here in D.C."

"Me? Oh, no, no, no. I'm flattered, sir—I mean, Johnny. But I'm not qualified to be the public face for your campaign, or anything for that matter."

The congressman signaled to their dedicated server, who was on standby. She was tableside seconds later.

"A coupla' waters, please, hun."

"Absolutely!" she said as she bounced away.

He turned to Devon with a deep, frustrated sigh.

"You know what I don't get about you people? And don't give me that 'you people' bullshit. You know me, and you know my heart. We're speaking frankly here, right?"

Devon took his first sip of the evening.

"What I don't get is: why do Blacks always talk about not having opportunities, but I'm sitting here dropping the opportunity of your career smack dab in your lap, and your first thought is to pass it up? I've worked with some brilliant Black folks—brilliant—back when I was in the Marine Corps, teaching at the law school, and certainly on the Hill. I've seen too many highly capable Blacks forego chances to get a leg up, because they're 'not ready,' or they 'don't have the qualifications,'" the congressman said with appropriately placed one-handed air quotes. "Meanwhile, some little white fucker with half the qualifications, a quarter of the skills, but ten times the confidence will come behind you and snap this same job right up without blinking."

Devon refreshed his glass. Neat, this time.

The congressman continued.

"What, are you just going to be a can't-pass-the-bar law school grad working as a legislative assistant all your life? Trust me. That cute, young redhead I see prancin' in and out of my office ain't gonna keep her wagon hitched to a sick and dying horse for long."

The congressman had accessed some of Devon's deepest insecurities. These words stung. Devon winced down his shot and mustered up an argument.

"Well, shit, Johnny. Why don't you tell me how you really feel? First of all, you—this right here—is why Blacks are repulsed by the Republican Party. You don't get it. You continually dismiss the racist history of this country as if slavery never existed. Ever heard of the Black Wall Street Massacre? Jim Crow? Racial discrimination in housing? Emmett Till? Trayvon Martin? Shall I continue? Not only that—you are ignoring the fact that despite every barrier placed in the system specifically designed to hold us back, many of us nevertheless thrive and prosper."

"Yes. But not enough," the congressman interjected. "Listen, Devon, I've heard it all before. I know all the arguments. I teach constitutional law for God's sake; so, obviously, I know the history of racism and discrimination in this country. Better than you. But here's the thing: sometimes there's racism, and sometimes you may be having delusions of racism. You have to look for the difference. And in any event, you can't let either keep you from moving forward. I'm offering you a chance to move forward, son."

In the distance, over the congressman's shoulder, Devon was briefly distracted by a familiar physique who had just sat down with another person at a booth near the window.

He returned his attention to the conversation.

"I don't know, man. Another thing is, this just seems so transactional. You've never invited me out for drinks or anything like this before. Now that you're running for Senate, and you think you need to put a Black face out there, I'm your guy. I just don't know how I feel about that. When we're needed, Black people get used, exploited, and then thrown away like garbage."

"Ah, shit. Give me a break, Devon. 'Transactional'? This whole goddamn city is transactional. Life is transactional. Nobody is giving you anything. You think I was talking to the head of the CBC because I like her? I can't stand that woman—all the things she's said about me in the media. I met with her because I needed something from her. And if I get elected, she'll be expecting something from me."

"Hell, you're a nice guy and all, but the main reason I have you working in my office is because I need your Black face to counter the race-baiters. Of course I'm using and exploiting you. But you have to stop thinking of those as bad words. What you need to learn to do is use and exploit circumstances to your benefit. And this is one of those circumstances. Want my advice? Don't be so emotional. Be more transactional, more calculating—that is, if we're being honest."

Devon focused on his glass, spinning it slowly on the table.

"But I still don't get it. Why do you need the Black vote? There is no Republican in the country who wins on the Black vote. Normally, the Republican game plan is to do whatever they can to keep Black voters home. You never needed Black people to win any of your elections. What's different?"

"The difference is that my opponent, the incumbent Senator Cumberland, has strong support throughout Georgia. White support. Polls do show that support waning a good bit, but not enough to put me over the top if I were to mount a conventional challenge—you know, going for his same white voters. But if I could get just twenty percent of Blacks to come over to me, I could win. Numbers show by something like ten points. My record is moderate enough that I can make a reasonable appeal to the Black people in the state who are conservative thinking, but nevertheless vote Dem. You know, the DINOs."

"DINOs?"

"Yes. 'Democrats In Name Only,'" the congressman replied. "You know, I never understood how there could be so many Blacks who love guns, love Christ, and hate abortion, but nevertheless vote for people who won't allow good, honest, hardworking Blacks to protect themselves, use science to try and stamp out religion, and who want to kill babies."

"I'm not even gonna touch that one," Devon said. "So, Johnny, what's the job description? Because right now, you're about to talk me right out of the Republican Party."

"I know that was harsh, son. I'm just trying to make a point. I hear the racist rhetoric that Republicans spew; I get it. But they do it because they can. They do it because they don't need Blacks to get elected. Their specific objective is to keep Blacks out of the party. But it's time to change that. And you can help," the congressman said.

"I'll need you to talk. I'll need you to work as my main surrogate, appearing on news segments, political ads, things like that, voicing your full-throated support for my campaign. You've been with me for a few years now, so you know my legislative record. And most of these events are virtual nowadays; you can do them right from your living room. You'd occasionally have to take trips back home to Georgia, but mostly, you'd be right here in D.C."

"And you need me," Devon said smugly.

"Now you're catching on," the congressman said. "Yes. And I need you. You're part of my staff. I trust you. And the narrative works for perception; it won't be like I just grabbed any African American off the streets and made him do my bidding for the Black vote."

The congressman noticed Devon's eyes straying, and turned around to see what had captured his attention.

"No. Don't look. She's going to think I'm talking about her," Devon said.

"She? She who?" the congressman said with a surprised, but approving grin.

"Nobody," Devon answered.

"Oh, so it's like that?" the congressman said. "Right now, we're just two schmos getting drunk. And I'm old and married; may as well let me live a little through you."

"Okay, fine," Devon said. "But don't turn around again." Devon pulled up Makeba's profile on Instagram and handed his phone to the congressman. "Here, take a look. She works for Ways and Means—the Dem side. Super smart. Harvard undergrad. A lawyer, too."

"Not bad. Not bad at all," the congressman said. "She's gorgeous, accomplished. Now, she's the one for you. Trust me. I've been around the block. She's your Michelle Obama."

"What, 'cause she's Black and I'm Black, we should be together?"

"That's it, exactly," the congressman replied. "You can't be a Black Republican *and* have a white wife. That's the Uncle Tom starter pack. You'd never have credibility with Black people whenever you do run for Congress."

"Who said I was ever going to run for Congress?" Devon replied.

"Whatever. That's a conversation for another time. At the very least, though, she could help you pass the bar. She's clearly smarter than you," the congressman said with a disarming wink. "Remember: be more transactional, more calculating. Go say hello to her."

"She's with someone," Devon replied.

"Here we go again. Opportunity falls smack dab in your lap and you wanna piss it away. Don't worry about me; I have Kate on the way to pick me up. Just go."

With the courage provided by several shots of vodka, Devon removed his tie and collected his things.

"Okay. I'll do it."

"Attaboy."

"See you in the office tomorrow, Johnny."

The congressman raised his glass. "It's 'Congressman' to you," he said. His smile was jolly, but Devon read something different in his eyes.

"Oh, and Devon."

"Yeah?"

"Forty-eight hours. You've got forty-eight hours to give me an answer."

Devon nodded. "Yeah—forty-eight hours. Got it."

Devon's confidence diminished with each step. Halfway to Makeba's table, he decided to abort, changing course for the exit.

In the nanoscopic space between the DJ's transition from Jodeci's "Come & Talk to Me" to JAY-Z's "Song Cry," the sound of shattering glass drew the attention of everyone within a thirty-foot radius. As it turned out, that bubbly server from before was also quite clumsy, and she had dropped her tray of Hennessy and a half dozen short glasses near Devon's feet.

The owner dashed to her rescue.

"Devon?" Makeba's voice pierced the hum of the crowd.

Devon ignored her and kept toward the door. He then remembered that the congressman was almost certainly watching, and he responded to her second call.

He turned and saw her waving him over. He then weaved through the tables to where Makeba and her associate were seated. "Join us," she said.

"Fancy seeing you here," Devon said while lifting the strap of his messenger bag over his head.

"Perfect timing." Makeba introduced Devon to Martin, a thin and uptight-looking gentleman whom she called her mentee. Martin's necktie was still wrapped snugly under his Adam's apple. He sat with perfect posture, both feet planted flat on the floor. When Devon was close enough, he sprang up, found Devon's eyes, and extended a firm, professional handshake.

"Martin just graduated from Georgetown, and does congressional affairs for the VA around the corner," Makeba said. "He was just heading back to the office to close out some work stuff."

Martin produced a business card from thin air like a magician and handed it to Devon.

"Nice to meet you," Devon said, inspecting the card. "Martin Jones, BA, MPA" the card read. His title was "Program Analyst."

Devon took Martin's seat as Martin slung his leather messenger bag across his body and bid his farewell.

"Fancy seeing you here, and with your boss?" Makeba said to Devon.

"This place was actually his idea," he replied.

"Oh? Pray tell?"

"Don't ask, don't tell," Devon countered.

"Fair enough."

She flipped over an unused wine glass and pushed a marble chiller of Sauvignon blanc across the table.

"No thanks," Devon said. "I might've overserved myself already with the congressman."

"Oh, come on. A gentleman never makes a woman drink alone."

"Is that a rule?" Devon replied.

"If it's not, it should be," she answered. "Come on—Martin was a stiff and only had water. If another man turns me down for drinks tonight it might mess with my self-esteem. Sip with me. I know the owner; he comps all my drinks."

"Well, if it's free, it's for me," Devon replied, surrendering, but pouring himself far less than the standard five ounces. Makeba took the bottle and filled his glass halfway.

Holding the glass at the stem, Devon took small sips, barely wetting his lips. "So, how's Ways and Means?" he asked. "What's at the top of your guys' legislative agenda for next session?"

Makeba served herself the last of the wine and turned the bottle upside down in the chiller.

"This is my safe place," she replied. "Can we not talk shop here?"

"Fair enough," Devon replied, echoing her.

There was silence between them. Makeba absorbed herself in the music, mouthing the entire last verse of the JAY-Z track that was playing.

"Wait—you're a JAY-Z fan?" Devon asked.

"Um, *yeah*," she replied. "He's only the best rapper—dead or alive."

"I knew there was something about you," Devon replied with a smile, wink, and finger gun.

"Rap music isn't appreciated for its true literary value," she said. "When you dissect it, it's brilliant."

"All facts," Devon replied.

Devon and Makeba spent the next two hours and the next bottle debating JAY-Z's best lyrics and his best album.

Her favorite was *The Black Album*.

# SEVEN

Jacob and Belinda Lewenberg's Gulfstream G600 taxied off the runway at Reagan National Airport, a ten-minute drive from the Washington Monument.

Devon was awed that airport security had allowed Bethany to drive her Tesla Model 3 right onto the tarmac to greet her parents. They pulled up behind a larger Tesla SUV, and a driver standing on the passenger side. The SUV's rear butterfly doors were spread as if it, too, had just landed.

"No fucking way," Devon said, marveling at the shiny white and navy luxury private jet. "I knew your folks were loaded, but I didn't know you were *loaded* loaded!"

Bethany buried her face into her palm in embarrassment.

"They don't always travel like this. They're just still paranoid about the coronavirus. We don't even own that plane," she tried to explain. "It's rented."

"Must be nice," Devon murmured, still in wonder.

The door retracted into the plane's hull, and stairs deployed to the ground. An unusually tall, thin woman emerged first, ducking out of the doorway and down the stairs with assistance from the driver. She had three feet of bone-straight ruby hair, the lenses on her round shades custom-made to match, and a flowing blue, ankle-length dress; she boasted no makeup or jewelry.

Jacob Lewenberg stepped down behind her. The top of his head met his wife's shoulders at most. His hair and beard were completely white, and his oversized Baja hoodie swallowed him. He had something in his mouth that first appeared to be a cigar, but turned out to be a licorice root stick that he enjoyed chewing.

The pair stood out, not for conspicuous affluence, but sheer quirky eccentricity.

Unbothered by the biting wind, Mrs. Lewenberg extended her arms, and with her wingspan nearly matching the jet's, she glided toward Bethany.

"Bethany, baby, I've missed you!" Mrs. Lewenberg said, cradling her daughter's face with both hands. "And you're glowing! No doubt due to this handsome young man here." She pulled Devon into a threesome hug. "I've heard so much about you. It's so great to finally meet in person!"

"It's my pleasure," Devon said, angling his head for a glimpse inside the jet.

"All right. All right. Don't be greedy. You can't have both my girls," Mr. Lewenberg chuckled with a pat to Devon's beltline to break up the hug.

"Mr. Lewenberg, sir, welcome to D.C. Nice to finally meet you."

Devon extended his hand for a standard shake. Mr. Lewenberg, though, went to dap Devon with an awkward slap to the palm. Devon played along and they released the clasp with a pulling-back of the fingers until they made the popping sound. Mr. Lewenberg beamed with satisfaction.

"Great to meet you, too, my soon-to-be son-in-law," Mr. Lewenberg replied.

Devon and Bethany exchanged uncomfortable looks.

"Well, it's a bit brisk out here, and I know you're both exhausted from your flight. How about you guys head back to the hotel, freshen up, and we can meet for a late dinner and drinks in the city?" Bethany suggested.

"Oh, we slept and showered on the jet. As Three Stacks would say, 'We're so fresh and so clean, clean.' So, how 'bout we do something right now instead?" Mr. Lewenberg countered. "Our driver can just take your car, sweetie, and park it at the Mandarin where we're staying, and I can drive us all in the Model X into the city."

"I'm afraid not, Jake," Mrs. Lewenberg replied. "This isn't one of those self-driving cars you're used to testing. The last time you tried to drive a real car, you almost drove us off the Golden Gate."

"But it has autopilot," Mr. Lewenberg replied.

"That doesn't mean you get to close your eyes and fall asleep. I'm driving. It's settled," Mrs. Lewenberg said. "Bethany, dear, give your car key to this nice gentleman and he'll take it to our hotel. It'll be in the garage when we return from dinner."

The driver, who had already collected their bags from the plane, held the door for Mrs. Lewenberg with one hand. He extended the other to her, and she climbed behind the wheel. He then loaded the Lewenbergs' two pieces of luggage into Bethany's car and drove away.

Bethany and Devon got in the back of the SUV. The interior was snow white. Devon sniffed audibly, filling his lungs with the HEPA-filtered air of the brand-new car. The leather seats were firm, yet supportive.

Mr. Lewenberg tapped a button on the automatic door. It lowered and closed.

"Where to?" Mrs. Lewenberg asked. She touched an icon on the oversized screen to pull up the GPS.

"And no place fancy. We want something with a little character, some soul. You feel me?" Mr. Lewenberg added.

"I defer to you," Bethany said to Devon, ignoring her dad's dialectical overreach.

"Sure. Let me think...Okay, there's this little place in Adams Morgan called Bukom," Devon suggested. "It's a West African spot. About this time, they always have a live band playing. The drinks are great, and the food is even better."

"Bukom it is!" Mrs. Lewenberg replied. "B-U-K-O-M," she mouthed as she set the GPS.

Men with lighted signal cones directed the SUV to the exit.

"So, Devin. Is it just 'Devin,' like the rapper?" Mr. Lewenberg asked.

"It's De*von*. Short O, stress the 'on'. And my last name is Lee. The rapper is Devin with an I. But I'm incredibly impressed that you even know about him."

"Are you kidding me? That *The Dude* album is a classic. What's the song about him sitting on the toilet? Hilarious," Mr. Lewenberg replied.

"Oh, Lord, Jake," his wife interjected. "I guess I have to drive the conversation, too."

"Oh, don't be so rigid. I'm just trying to be relatable," Mr. Lewenberg said.

"So, Devon, do you have any siblings?" Mrs. Lewenberg asked.

"It's just me," he replied. "I always wanted a brother, though—someone to play with when I was a kid, and maybe stand up for me on the playground."

"I know the feeling," Bethany said.

Mr. Lewenberg took a call, and from his tone, it sounded like work. His wife found the local NPR station for background noise.

Bethany texted Devon.

**Bethany:** Sorry about my dad. He can be a bit wacky sometimes.

**Devon:** That's all parents.

**Devon:** No need to apologize. The real question is: why didn't you tell me you guys were this rich?

**Bethany:** I told you my dad owned an AI tech company in Silicon Valley.

**Devon:** For some reason, that didn't translate in my head to private-jet, my-daughter-gets-to-drive-on-the-tarmac rich.

**Bethany:** I figured you would've Googled him already.

**Bethany:** I don't see why it matters anyway.

"Listen, Zuck," Mr. Lewenberg said into the phone. "We're gonna have to table this discussion. I'm getting another call." He switched lines.

Devon continued to type, but Bethany didn't see the three dots on her phone to indicate that he was typing to her. She sent him a text as she bumped his knee with hers.

**Bethany:** Don't look him up right now!

The Google search field auto-populated "Tim Lewenberg" after only typing "Lew." The first search result, a Wikipedia page, put Mr. Lewenberg at the helm of Cintotech, a company that made software for autonomous cars. Belinda was his second wife, and the company's CFO.

**Devon:** Five billion dollars?!

**Devon:** Your dad is worth five billion dollars?!

Bethany snatched Devon's phone, turned it off, and then pressed it back into his chest.

"So, Mom. How was the flight?" Beth asked, redirecting her attention.

Devon sat in silence, trying to hear the radio over the voices of the three Lewenbergs.

•••

When they arrived at the restaurant, the band hadn't begun playing yet. The four took up seats in a sunken dining area in the rear. Devon ordered a Tusker. Mr. Lewenberg followed suit. The women shared a bottle of Prosecco.

"So, Mr. Lewenberg—"

"Jake. Just call me Jake."

"Okay, Jake. How's the autonomous car business going these days?"

"Oh, we only do the software. Maybe someday we can do cars, too. Either way, it's going quite smoothly—the company pretty much drives itself." Mr. Lewenberg then erupted into a hearty laugh.

"I see what you did there," Devon replied with a polite chuckle.

"That joke was funny the first ten thousand times. Now, it's just offensive," Mrs. Lewenberg said. "We're actually in the final stages of deploying software that can call your car to you from up to six blocks away. Imagine when we're done eating here, at the same time we ask for the check, we're able to open an app, tap a button, and summon the car to the front door. It's basically done. We already have buyers; we're just waiting on the U.S. Department of Transportation to clear it."

"Think KITT, from *Knight Rider*," Mr. Lewenberg added.

"You're showing your age, dear," Mrs. Lewenberg said. "Neither of them was born yet when that show was running."

"Either way, that's some cool, futuristic stuff," Devon replied.

"We're calling it 'DirectValet,'" Mr. Lewenberg said.

"You know, if you're having trouble with DOT, I can talk to my boss. He's the chair of the House Committee on Transportation and Infrastructure. Maybe he can look into it," Devon offered.

"That's very kind of you. But we pay lobbyists a fortune to do just that for us," Mr. Lewenberg replied. "Wait. Did you say your boss is the chair of a House committee?"

Devon noticed Bethany sink in her seat beside him, as if she was hoping it would swallow her.

"Sure. Congressman Johnathon Grayton, from Georgia," Devon replied.

"Well, I don't know Grayton. But I do know that Republicans hold the House right now. And if you work for a committee chair, that makes you..."

"A lowly, overworked, underpaid, sleep-deprived staffer," Devon answered.

The table went silent. On cue, the band began to play a Burna Boy cover, a song called "Dangote."

"A Republican?" Mr. Lewenberg shifted his weight and turned to Bethany as if she had made the revelation.

"A card-carrying member," Devon said matter-of-factly. "Beth didn't mention it to you?" he asked, eyeing Bethany.

Suddenly, Devon had an appreciation for the evening he had spent a week prior with the Ways and Means Democrats. It was preparation for just this moment.

"No. *Beth* did not mention that little factoid," Mr. Lewenberg said, peering at his daughter. "You'd think she would have, though. Right, hun?" He turned to his wife, who raised her eyebrows.

"Dad, it's not that serious. You have to be able to separate the person from the politics. And Devon is a good person."

"How many times have we spoken since you first told me you two were dating? At no point in any of our little chats did you think I might be interested in knowing that my daughter is dating a Black Republican?"

Bethany's voice grew stern. "Wait, what does him being Black have to do with this conversation?"

Mr. Lewenberg's face instantly flushed.

At this point, Devon had decided to let this play out and quietly watch the father-daughter verbal slugfest. He tipped his beer to his mouth, his eyes ping-ponging between the two as they spoke.

"Don't try and flip this on me, young lady. It's not about him being Black; that's just an observable fact. And I resent the implication that this is in any way about his race. Some of my closest friends are Black. And you know this."

Devon continued to fight the urge to chime in, while Mrs. Lewenberg searched for an opening to redirect the discussion.

"This is about values. You can sit on your utopian perch all you want, but the reality is that you cannot take the politics out of the person. They're both inextricably intertwined." Mr. Lewenberg gestured with crossed fingers. "And Republican politics go against everything I stand for. Personally. Everything we taught you!"

"Is that so? And what exactly are those things?" Bethany asked, to Devon's pleasure.

"Over the years, your mom and I have donated millions of dollars to progressive candidates and organizations all across this country, including Black Lives Matter," Mr. Lewenberg explained, emphasizing the three words while looking at Devon, turning to address him.

"Our money goes to giving women the right to choose what happens with their bodies," Mr. Lewenberg said. "Meanwhile, your boss and his Republican pals want to force unwanted pregnancies, but don't want to give the woman any support once the child is born. *We* want to get guns out of the hands of criminals, so your pick-up basketball games aren't getting shot up. *You* want to make it easier for these murderous thugs to get guns. *You guys* have Big Oil in your pockets, so you cling to fossil fuels, knowing full well the destruction it's causing to the Earth. *We*, on the other hand, are investing in clean and renewable energy sources to leave the world better than how we found it."

"I take it that Gulfstream private jet you flew in on was solar-powered?" Devon, said, no longer able to resist.

Just then, the band's trumpet blared, as if to punctuate Devon's zinger.

Mr. Lewenberg pushed away from the table in a huff.

"Did you vote for Trump?" he asked Devon.

"I don't—" Devon started.

"Did you, or did you not vote for Trump?" Mr. Lewenberg repeated. "It's a simple 'yes' or 'no' question."

In desperation, Bethany looked to her mom for help.

"Jake, dear?" Mrs. Lewenberg interjected. "How about we give it a rest?"

Bethany closed her eyes and massaged her temples.

"Not to be rude, but I think it's best if you all enjoyed some family time," Devon said with a cracking voice. "You haven't seen each other in a while. Maybe we can all get together after you've had the chance to catch up. And you seem to have a lot you need to talk about."

Devon stood and pulled out his wallet from his jacket pocket.

"Oh, please no," Mrs. Lewenberg said. "We'll cover the bill."

"No, by all means, let him pay. Republicans don't like handouts," Mr. Lewenberg grumbled.

Devon opened his dad's decades-old leather wallet and removed all the cash. "By the way, not all Black people play basketball," he said while sliding a five-dollar bill and four ones onto the table. He then walked off to a slow Bob Marley number.

# EIGHT

The temperature had dipped by double digits since the airport run earlier in the day. What was only an annoying drizzle when Devon and the Lewenbergs had entered Bukom Cafe was now ice. Belligerent winds threw the stinging little shards into Devon's already-numb face.

He had initially regretted letting go of his last nine dollars before storming away from the table, but decided it was a small price to pay to preserve his dignity. Payday was tomorrow, anyway. What he regretted more, however, was leaving before the food had arrived. Aside from the instant oatmeal he had eaten that morning, his last proper meal had been the evening prior with the congressman at The Yard.

His Mitsubishi was parked at Bethany's. He was unsure of his gas level situation, but he'd get it after work the next day. The credit card connected to his Uber account was maxed out at the moment.

Devon's only way home was to catch the bus. He wasn't sure how much money he had left on his Metro SmarTrip card. If it turned out to not be enough, he planned to appeal to the bus driver for a little grace. That usually worked, especially on a cold night.

The fifteen-minute wait felt like an hour as the air grew even more bitter. The digital marquee signs of the first two buses that passed read a demoralizing "NOT IN SERVICE." Devon began to think about how nice it would be to have a warm car, equipped with DirectValet, pull up to rescue him.

Finally, a third bus, this one in service, arrived. The bus driver was heavyset and well bundled. At first glance, she could pass for Mama Lee. He had an evanescent thought of calling his mom for a bridge loan, but decided against it—though she'd do it in a heartbeat.

"Come on, baby," the driver said, waving him on after his SmarTrip declined. Devon was grateful that she'd shown him mercy and hadn't made him ask.

He thanked her, then took up a seat at the back of the bus. Mentally inventorying his refrigerator and cabinets, he recalled having a few tins of sardines, maybe some pasta noodles, Cheerios, a couple of bottles of San Pellegrino, and a carton of oat milk that Bethany always kept there for when she stayed over. He could raid his coin jar for some change to pick up a couple of packs of Top Ramen from the twenty-four-hour store if he didn't like any of his other menu options.

What he wouldn't do for some Zaxby chicken strips and Texas toast.

Devon needed a distraction to take his mind off of his empty belly. He opened Instagram and mindlessly scrolled. Several of his Insta-friends were flooding his feed with posts of their lavish vacation to sunny Tulum, Mexico; that was apparently the trendy new travel destination for young professionals in the city. These online friends were mostly other Hill staffers with trust funds, who called Devon "bro" in the halls and hearing rooms. They were nice enough, but outside the office, Devon couldn't keep up with their penchant for off-dry Rieslings and sushi at The Hamilton, and weekend excursions to Virginia wine country. So, Bethany was his circle of one. And with his southern training, he only seldomly and begrudgingly allowed her to cover tabs.

Images of his colleagues enjoying margaritas next to the infinity pool of their luxury AirBnB made Devon sick.

Just as he went to close the app, he noticed Makeba's profile picture, a pink and green "1908" graphic. He started viewing the stories. There were three or four Black Lives Matter-related posts and a couple of relationship advice memes from several hours prior. And then there was a thirteen-second video of a wooden, long-handled cooking spoon turning over in a massive pot of chili. At the top of the frame, he could see just the corner of what was unmistakably a pan of cornbread.

He held his phone's speaker to his ear to listen for any audio. It was

Makeba narrating that this was her grandmother's half-century-old recipe. She had only swapped out the beef for lean ground turkey. He could hear the gleeful chatter of others in the background.

Devon replayed the video until he could practically taste the savory dish. Or maybe hers was a little sweet?

He noticed the video's timestamp was thirty-three minutes ago. If Makeba was a real-time poster, that meant that this little chili dinner gathering was happening as he sat there drooling.

Devon replied to the video with a private message—"Looks delish!"—adding staring eyes and drooling smiley face emojis.

He had a fleeting and admittedly far-fetched fantasy that his message would prompt an invite. But at this point, he didn't even have enough money to stop off for a box of crackers to bring with him. He'd just be showing up with two hands swinging.

The app showed that she had read the message almost instantly, but hadn't started a reply. His steaming hot chili and warm, buttery cornbread dreams faded away completely.

The bus stopped on Fourteenth and M to collect a half-dozen new passengers—some loud teenage boys playing mumble rap from a Bluetooth speaker. Angel, the name Devon had given the kind bus driver in his head, chided the boys to turn the speaker off so as not to disturb the other passengers.

Devon's phone buzzed with an Instagram notification. It was Makeba.

> **Makeba:** You and Bethany should come by! There's more than enough chili!

This was music to his soul. He sang the polite, but obligatory "I don't want to impose" song and prayed she didn't get distracted before sending her address, or worse, agree with him.

> **Makeba:** Don't be silly.
>
> **Devon:** What can I bring?
>
> **Makeba:** Just bring yourself.

**Makeba:** When you get here, type 1-1-2-7- # on the keypad and I'll buzz you up.

Makeba lived on Twelfth and Massachusetts Ave. A quick GPS check put her apartment building about four blocks away. He rang the stop signal and moved to the front exit, thanking Angel again on his way out.

As he stepped off the bus, back into the freezing cold, shivering, he remembered the background chatter he had heard in Makeba's video.

**Devon:** Who's all there?

He texted while he could still use his fingers. Her answer didn't matter, though. That chili had his name on it.

**Makeba:** You remember Tim and Seth from the other night, right? And a couple of my old roommates from Howard are here, too.

**Devon:** Cool. See you shortly.

Just then, a gust slammed into his chest. By the third block, the cold had pierced his layers and was working its way to the bone.

Smelling the chili from a block away, Devon picked up a jog once her building was in sight.

He keyed in her access code. The seconds felt like hours until he heard a buzz and the click of the locks on the vestibule doors. He pushed through both sets of double doors.

The warmth of the building's lobby was welcomed, but Devon wouldn't fully thaw until he had something hot in his system.

He reached Makeba's level and counted down to her apartment. The door opened just as he was about to knock.

"Hey, Devon!" Makeba greeted him. "Come on in! You can put your coat on the chair with the others. Oh, and no shoes, please."

Devon untied the wet grocery bags from around his ankles and left them in the hallway. He stepped inside, removing his long wool outer layer, but not the Patagonia vest underneath. He placed his sneakers neatly with the other shoes and shook off the chill with a "Brrr."

He scanned the apartment over Makeba's shoulder.

Her one-bedroom was modern and neat, with tasteful souvenirs from all her travels thoughtfully placed throughout. "Hank" was the name she had given the ninety-year-old, four-foot, wooden statue of an old man crouching; she had taken a gap year between high school and her freshman year of college. She spent the time visiting fifteen African countries, and had shipped Hank home from Uganda.

Devon had recognized the art from one of her Instagram posts a hundred or so photos deep in her feed.

There was a large, framed portrait print of Michelle Obama watching over the living room. This piece hung across from an even larger original work of the Notorious B.I.G. in dark shades, exhaling a cloud from an oversized cigar, his image set on a background of real one-dollar bills.

Four people stood already chatting, two of whom Devon realized were Tim and Seth. Across from them were two women Devon didn't recognize. One wore a navy, red, and white Howard University hoodie over a set of green scrubs. The other had on a pair of faded black jeans and a dressy pink silk blouse—Zoom meeting attire, no doubt. Both sported long, neat braids. The four seemed to be getting along.

"You look miserable. Did you walk here?" Makeba asked Devon.

"Parking was no bueno. I had to hump it for a couple of blocks," he replied. "It's frigid out there!"

She led him down the short, narrow hall to the restroom and took the opportunity for a brief chat out of earshot of the others.

"By the way, I meant to tell you that I felt terrible about the way Seth ambushed you at Off the Record that night," she said almost in a whisper. "I talked to him after. You shouldn't have to worry about that happening again."

"I appreciate that. But I'm a big boy. I can handle it."

"Well, just so you know," she replied, then turned back down the hall toward the kitchen and living room.

Although Seth wasn't at the top of the list of people Devon wanted to see at the moment, the cheerful banter coming from the living room was welcoming, considering his recent outing with the Lewenbergs.

Devon joined the group after freshening up.

"Cheese and chives?" Makeba asked Devon, as she prepared a colorful plate with a steamy ceramic bowl on top, and a square of warm cornbread on the side.

"Please, both," Devon said.

"There's homemade hot cocoa on the stove, too," she said.

*God bless her*, he thought.

"Where's Bethany?" she asked. "I thought you two would be together."

"Her parents flew in from San Francisco today. I thought I'd give them some alone QT to catch up. I'm supposed to be meeting them tomorrow."

"Nervous?"

"Not really. Well, a little," he replied.

"I'll bet," she said.

They both laughed.

Seth, whose back had been turned to Makeba and Devon, finally turned around to notice that Devon had arrived.

"Devin!" Seth announced. "Good to see you again, brother. No hard feelings about last time, right?"

Makeba shot Seth a warning look.

"Once again, it's De-*von*. And no hard feelings at all. It's politics. Sharp elbows get thrown from time to time," Devon answered.

He flopped onto the couch, foot under thigh. Makeba served him on a wooden tray.

Devon ate.

"Sweet baby Jesus, this cornbread is perfect," he said, words muffled.

"Thanks. It's from scratch. I got the recipe from Pinterest, but the chili is my grandma's," she said. "So, Devon, you already know Tim and Seth; this is Ebony and Donita. We all went to Howard together. Ebony and I were in the same section in law school. And Donita was at the dental school. We shared a three-bedroom dump in Petworth."

"You're making it sound nicer than it actually was," Donita replied.

The girls laughed.

"Girls, this is Devon, Bethany's beau."

Devon wasn't completely resuscitated yet. He politely nodded and smiled. They understood.

After about twenty minutes, he was ready to join the group. The debates shifted seamlessly from Cuban-American policy to the best Tarantino movie, to human cloning, to recreational drug legalization, to the best part of the chicken: drums or flats.

Meanwhile, the game of Phone Stack was in full effect. Everyone had piled their phones in the center of the coffee table; each time someone grabbed theirs, they had to take a shot. Tito's was the liquor.

Donita had argued that she should get a pass, because she was co-parenting a five-year-old daughter and needed to check in on her from time to time.

"Everybody's got something," Seth said. "You touch, you drink. Plain and simple."

They were each roughly four shots in, except Seth. He wore an Apple Watch, which he surreptitiously checked throughout the night. He just nursed a couple of black labels.

As the night drew on, blood alcohol levels increased and energy waned, until finally, Seth conceded to Ebony's argument that members of Congress should be term-limited. *Seth* conceded. That was cue enough that the night had come to an end.

The consummate host, at some point, while everyone was quibbling over MJ or Prince and Bieber versus Timberlake, had readied and lined up five uniform brown bags with handles. Inside each was a generous serving of Grandma's chili in quality Tupperware, and a cube of cornbread wrapped in aluminum foil.

The falling ice droplets must have gotten bigger than when Devon had arrived. They tapped on the sliding glass door as if to taunt him. He'd known this time would come. It was nearly eleven. After ten, the intervals between buses would stretch from fifteen or twenty minutes to forty-five minutes or more. And at that late hour, the online bus schedules served only as loose recommendations to the drivers. Even if he managed to time one just right, it was possible the driver wouldn't be an Angel and let him ride for free.

He needed to think of something fast. Last he'd checked, he had missed thirteen calls from Bethany. Calling her for a ride was not an option.

They each thanked Makeba for the hospitality, donned their layers, and shuffled to the door. Devon was last in line. He jingled his car keys on the five-floor elevator ride down.

"Oh, snap," he said, between second and first. "I think I forgot my phone." He frisked himself Macarena-style and then tapped the button back to Makeba's floor. "Can one of you call up and let Makeba know I'm coming back?"

"Sure thing," Tim replied, and fired off a voice memo to Makeba.

"Tim, Seth, great catching up with you again," Devon said. "See you fellas in the hearing room. Nice meeting you, Ebony and Donita. We should all do this again. I had fun."

The elevator doors opened and discharged four. Devon rode back up.

When Makeba opened the door, she was already in her bonnet and had traded her contact lenses for a pair of tortoiseshell Warby Parkers.

"Where'd you leave it?" she mumbled over the hum of an electric toothbrush.

"It's probably in the couch cushions," he replied.

"Come on in and have a look for yourself," she offered, on her way back to the bathroom.

He went to the coffee table, straight for an old ACLU magazine under which he had planted the phone.

"Find it?"

"Yup!"

"Great. Lock the door behind you. Thanks for coming. Tell Beth we missed her!"

The falling ice tapping on the sliding glass door got louder.

"Um, Makeba."

"What's up?" She poked her face, now covered in a teal cream, out the bathroom door.

"It's late," he said. "And my head is still spinning like a DVD from all the shots. I shouldn't drive home right now. Do you mind if I crash here on the couch for a bit, just until I feel up to driving? I promise I won't disturb you, and I'll let myself out."

Makeba walked into the living room in a vintage Howard sweatshirt and leggings.

"I don't know if I'm comfortable with that, Devon. I barely know you. You could be an ax murderer. Plus, you're Bethany's boyfriend."

"Makeba, one: I don't have my ax on me. Two: it's not like we're doing anything. I'm just catching a few winks. That's all."

"Seriously," she said. "How would that look—everyone leaving and you coming back up to spend the night?"

"Never mind. Thanks for the chili," he replied, moving toward the door.

"No. Wait, Devon. You seem nice enough. And Beth always talks about how gentle you are. Plus, it's starting to snow now, too, and I'd hate for anything to happen to you out there tonight. I'll let you stay here on my couch. *But* if you try *anything*, I'm warning you, I sleep with a machete, and I know how to use it."

"I'll be gone before the sun comes up," he replied.

He set his alarm for 4:00 a.m. and laid down.

Makeba tossed him a blanket, commanded Alexa to turn off the lights, and walked to her bedroom.

"On second thought," she said, "I probably wouldn't need a machete. Pretty sure I could take you with my bare hands."

"Pretty sure you could," Devon muttered. "Good night, Makeba."

Makeba shut her bedroom door, and jiggled the knob more than needed.

•••

Devon awoke startled when the pillow was yanked from under him, his head hitting the couch. He looked up to see Makeba standing over him.

"What's the problem? Everything okay?" Devon asked, hands over his eyes.

"I can't sleep when strange men are sleeping in my apartment," she replied, "which means you can't sleep either. So, coffee or tea?"

Disoriented, Devon sat up, dropping both feet onto the floor.

"I'm not strange," he said groggily. "You know me. We've had drinks together. Twice. Now, can I get back to sleep?"

"Coffee or tea?" she repeated.

He yawned while rubbing the sleep from his eyes, then sighed in resignation.

"You win." He groaned. "Got any more of that hot cocoa?"

"Cocoa it is," she replied. "I'll have chamomile."

She turned on the kettle and leaned forward with her elbows on the kitchen island, her palms to her chin.

"So, Devon Lee, Black Republican Georgia man, working on Capitol Hill. What's your deal?"

Devon peeled himself from the couch and made his way to the opposite side of the island.

"You have a knack for summing up a man's entire existence in a few words, I see," he replied as he climbed onto the barstool.

"Well, tell me what I missed."

"What do you want to know?

"I want to know what you're about. What makes Devon Lee tick?"

She whisked some sugar, salt, and milk into the cocoa, and reduced the heat under the saucepan.

"Please, I hope you're not about to ask me if I voted for Trump. Because that question is played out."

"Well, did you?"

"The ballots are secret for a reason."

She chuckled as she shook her head and retrieved two cups from the kitchen cupboards. "If you say so," she replied.

She turned off the burner beneath the kettle just as it had begun to scream, then pinched tea leaves into a single-serve infuser.

"So, the only other thing people seem to care about, besides me being a Black Republican, is the fact that I'm dating a white woman."

"Okay. So, let's talk about that," she replied.

"Well, I don't date for skin color. If I like a woman and she likes me, and she happens to be a good person, that's all that matters to me. I don't understand why people are always so fixated on race."

"*You* brought it up. Not me."

"I just know how you think. That's all," he replied.

"By 'you,' do you mean *me,* or 'you' as in Black women in general?"

"Do you have any more marshmallows?" he asked in a futile attempt to deflect.

"No."

Devon took a long sip of his cocoa and braced himself.

"First of all," Makeba started, "you don't know me enough to tell me how I think. And for you to even go there with me means, apparently, you don't know much about Black women, period. Second, you know as well as I do that there is a population of Black men out there who specifically seek out white women as a sort of status symbol—to show that they've made it. Meanwhile, they use Black women like doormats until they need them.

"Now, I've never been a stick-to-your-own-race person. I agree with you—if you love him, her, or them, you should be with that person. And I can't even front, I've been hurt so many times by Black men that I have PTSD symptoms sometimes just looking at y'all. But what I also know is that people are dynamic human beings. We're all different. So, I can't try to predict how one person will treat me based on someone else.

"The bottom line, though, is that Black men who date white women because they are white need to take a good hard look at themselves, and maybe see a therapist. Now, if the shoe fits, you can wear it or go barefoot. I honestly don't care. What I won't do is sit here and tell you how you think. You know, the way you just did me," she said with a smile.

Devon let out a shaky laugh.

"What's so funny?" Makeba asked.

"You just gave me Claire Huxtable vibes. That's all. But I wasn't trying to offend you," Devon said, alert and fully awake now.

"No offense taken. Just stating my position. If we *are* being honest, I'll also tell you that Bethany's not the one for you, though."

"Oh, really?"

"Yes. Really."

"What makes you say that?"

"I can just tell you don't like her like that. I can see it in the way you look at her. I'd even venture to say you don't trust her."

"How do you figure all that?"

"Well, first, because you didn't disagree with me. And second, because you're here and not with her. Last I recall, she has a car. Why didn't she just come get you? I'll tell you: it's because you didn't feel comfortable calling her. Am I right? She clearly doesn't know you're here with me, or else she would've at least called me—by the way, I'd like to keep it that way."

"It's not that I distrust her. I just don't feel comfortable telling her certain things."

"And why do you think that is?"

"I don't know. I guess we just don't connect all that well."

Makeba added more hot water to her mug.

"So, again, why are you with her?"

"We're being honest here, right?" Devon asked.

"I know *I* am. Are *you*?"

Devon slurped the last of his cocoa and placed his mug near Makeba, silently asking for more.

She pretended she didn't notice.

"If I told you that you might have been onto something earlier, would you be angry?" he replied.

"Wait. Are you telling me it *is* because she's white?" she asked. "Because if *that's* what you're telling me, I might just put your ass out in the white snow."

"Hear me out," he said. "In Macon, where I'm from, it's still segregated. All the whites are in the north, and the Blacks are in the south. There's a white mall up north, and the Blacks have a mall down south. There's a white Walmart, and a Black Walmart.

"Everything up north is nicer. Cleaner. Safer. I always wanted to know what it was like to live in that part of town. Life seemed happy there. Free. I guess I saw dating Beth as my gateway to all that."

Makeba raised an eyebrow and took a sip of her tea with both hands while peering through the steam over her mug at Devon.

"What you need is a therapist," she said as she refilled his mug.

She pulled a bag of miniature marshmallows from the cabinet above the refrigerator and added some to his cocoa.

"Listen," she said, "I didn't have a hard life like I imagine you did growing up. We were solid upper-middle class. But my neighborhood was mostly Black, too, *and* it was nice. I say that to say this: being Black doesn't mean we can't live in nice, clean, safe communities. It doesn't mean we can't be happy and free.

"You need to understand that neighborhoods like where you grew up are the product of a racist design. Policies existed—*and still do*—for the purpose of depriving Black people of earning a livable wage, voting, buying property, and providing for their families. So, it shouldn't be any surprise when folks feel hopeless and depressed.

"Now, I don't have the time or energy to give you a full-on history lesson on racism in America. I'll just say this, and I'll let it go: you can be Republican if you want. And you can date who you want. None of that will necessarily make you happy and free. It's far deeper than that. You need to wake up."

Devon pushed the marshmallows down into the cocoa with his spoon, then scooped them out into his mouth.

He broke a half-minute of silence as he reached over, placing his mug into the sink.

"I actually just got into it with her parents—well, her dad—over dinner tonight, right before I came here."

"Wait. So, you lied to me about meeting them for the first time tomorrow?"

"You lied to me about not having any more marshmallows," he answered.

"Whatever. Let me guess: she didn't tell them you were Black, and they freaked when they met you."

"Actually, that's not it at all—at least, her dad seemed to be thrilled that I'm Black."

"Then what is it?"

"They hate that I'm Republican, working for a Republican member."

"That would've been my third guess, right after poor," Makeba said.

Devon directed his gaze away from Makeba and to the falling snow through the glass door.

"Can I be honest with you?" Devon asked.

"Well, that's up to you, isn't it?" Makeba replied.

"You saved me tonight."

"Oh? How so?"

"I was fresh out of cash, and like an idiot, I stormed away from the table with Beth's family before the food came. I was freezing and starving. When I saw your post on Insta, I wanted to reach through the phone. Had you put me out tonight, I wouldn't have known what to do."

"Well, the Lord works in mysterious ways, huh? I guess He was working through me tonight," Makeba replied. "I think it's a shame how little they pay staffers on the Hill. These are powerful jobs that come with tremendous responsibility and opportunity. They require a lot of time and skill, and staffers can't even afford to feed themselves."

"It's by design," Devon replied. "They do it to keep a certain segment of the population out of policymaking. We all know that it's the staffers who do the real behind-the-scenes work. The members just take their recommendations. The exceptional kid from Southeast D.C. who made it out and went to college has bills to pay and family to help out; he could never survive on what we get paid. Meanwhile, I walk through the halls and see twenty-three-year-old trust-fund babies who use their salaries as tip money at restaurants. That's why I'm not going anywhere. My representation is needed."

"Is that honestly why you're still with Grayton? Word is, you're having trouble passing the bar."

Devon broke eye contact again.

"I'm not making fun of you. What I'm trying to say is I can help you pass the bar. In my free time, I work with recent UDC law grads who failed the bar at least once. My kids have a one hundred percent pass rate after I work with them."

"Well, I don't want to be one of your *kids*."

Makeba sat next to Devon.

"Lose the ego, Devon. I'm trying to help you."

"Speaking of Grayton," Devon said, changing the subject, "he offered me a new position yesterday. He's making a political pivot. He's running for Senate, and he wants me to be his spokesperson. I imagine it comes with better pay."

"Congratulations."

"Well, I haven't given him an answer yet."

"Well, what are you waiting for?"

"Wait. You're not gonna try and talk me out of it?"

"Why would I do that? The question that you need to ask yourself is: would you be able to look at yourself in the mirror at the end of the day? If the answer is 'yes' and it works for you, then take the job."

"Another thing is that I've never done anything like that, on such a large scale. I don't know if I'm the right guy for it."

"Devon, if you're scared, say you're scared. Being scared doesn't make you less of a man. But passing up an opportunity because you're scared does. In fact, it makes you weak. And I don't keep weak people around me, so..."

"I hear you. I'm just nervous about putting myself out there and getting dragged by Black Twitter and Instagram for being an Uncle Tom. You know how brutal *we* can be. Black Dem staffers on the Hill already treat me like a pariah."

"Then don't be an Uncle Tom. It's just that simple. Don't allow yourself to be used. Don't go out there saying wild things you don't believe in and can't defend. Contrary to popular belief, Democrats don't have a monopoly on wokeness. You're about to have the opportunity to speak publicly on behalf of an influential member of Congress. He wants our vote? Make him earn it. Make him understand our issues. Make him speak to our issues. Most importantly, make him act on behalf of us."

"'Democrats don't have a monopoly on wokeness,' huh? Don't be surprised if that ends up in my talking points."

"It's all yours. Just don't attribute it to me," Makeba said.

They laughed.

"Well, I have about fourteen hours left to give him my answer, and you gave me a lot to think about. Thank you. By the way, he hasn't announced yet. So, keep that on the low."

"My lips are sealed."

Devon's phone vibrated.

"Great—payday," Devon said. "My direct deposit just hit. It's not much, but at least I can get home now."

"Well, that's good. I'm actually getting tired now anyway. I'll let you at least get a bit of rest. Thanks for chatting. I feel like I know you a little better now," Makeba said.

"No, really, thank *you*. I don't know what I would've done without you tonight. I owe you one."

"Well, you can pay me back by answering this one last question truthfully."

"Shoot away."

"Promise to tell the truth?"

"Promise."

"Okay. You didn't vote for Trump. Did you?"

"No, I didn't, Makeba."

Makeba smiled and started down the hall to her bedroom.

Just then, Devon's alarm sounded. He silenced it.

"Makeba?"

"Yes, Devon?"

"Are you serious about helping me pass the bar?"

"Of course I am."

# NINE

A set of large oak double doors seamlessly set in the matching walls around them opened. The judge appeared, took no more than four steps to his oversized leather chair, and spun around to his bench.

"All rise!"

A stocky, pissed-off-looking Black man with a polished bald head, thick mustache, and a pressed tan uniform announced the judge's entry. The bass of his voice reverberated in chest cavities throughout the courtroom.

"The Honorable Judge Lemuel A. Murray presiding."

"Thank you, Bailiff," Judge Murray said in a much softer, almost labored voice. "All may be seated."

Damion's eyes were as big as a child's who had just gotten in trouble. He was no stranger to the courtroom. Yet, this time was different.

He had spent the better part of two months awaiting trial and sentencing in a juvenile facility. But on this morning, he had been separated from the other juveniles and brought to the courtroom on a bus with fifty grown men. The bus had smelled of metal, B.O., and ammonia.

His seatmate had been more than twice his size. He had had a long goatee that ended in a point, unkempt, loose cornrows, and a tattoo of a cobra that extended up the side of his neck, the mouth opening around his right eye. The man had been at Reidsville, and was thirteen years into a life sentence for murder, as he'd explained to a silent Damion on the ride, and was being sentenced for another murder, which he had admitted to committing while in prison. His name was Fang, the self-identified snake—or snitch—hunter.

Damion trembled at the defense table next to his attorney. In pew-style benches set away from the court audience were Fang and the other forty-odd men in jumpsuits, all chained together.

Judge Murray was seventy-five, and a thirty-year veteran of the bench. He had retired two years ago. As a retiree, he was considered a senior judge, and Bibb County Court rules allowed senior judges to continue on the bench even after retirement, to the extent they were fit to do so.

Scattered liver spots covered a third of his sagging face. He had egg-in-the-nest hair, teeth the color of the coffee he'd been drinking for decades, and a wattle of skin that extended from his chin to between his collarbones like a boat sail.

Judge Murray patted at his chest for a pair of readers. He unzipped his robe some, exposing a silver and gold crucifix necklace, and pulled the glasses from the breast pocket of his suit. They slid to the tip of his nose as soon as he put them on.

"Mr. Damion Corey Lee, has your attorney explained to you your rights and entitlements under the laws of Bibb County, the laws and constitutions of the great state of Georgia, and of the United States of America?"

"Ye-ye-yes, she did, Your Honor," he stuttered. His voice was shaky, soft, and octaves higher than normal.

Damion's orange jumpsuit draped over him, the short sleeves almost reaching the end of his forearms. A chain wrapping his waist connected to the cuffs around his wrists in front of him, and another extended to the shackles on his ankles.

The angry bailiff moved from his position near the court reporter next to Damion. He gripped Damion by the bicep. Damion jerked in pain. The grip grew tighter.

Mama Lee sobbed next to her husband, Percy Lee. Damion was the reason they both had become familiar with the Bibb County Juvenile Courtroom over the last five or so years. Devon never wanted to go to court to see his brother, despite Mama Lee's emphatic pleading.

Percy Lee was always stoic. He never showed emotion at these proceedings, barely even comforting his wife.

The trial had lasted six hours over two days. The third day, today, was set for Judge Murray's decision and sentencing.

"Mr. Lee, you have elected to exercise your constitutional right to a bench trial by me, forgoing your right to trial by a jury of your peers. Now, I understand the prosecution has offered you a plea deal. I also understand that it is still on the table. Has your attorney explained the details of this offer?"

Damion looked over at Fang. He was paralyzed by the thought of spending years with the likes of him. Fang winked, and clicked his tongue at Damion, snapping him out of his trance.

"The judge is talking to you," the bailiff said, his grip tighter still.

"Yes, Your Honor," Damion replied.

"Well, I'll give you one last opportunity to consider, accept, and/or reject that offer before I render the court's decision. Mr. Lee, do you wish to accept the State's offer?"

A numbing calm suddenly came over Damion as he began to accept his fate. He had seen the imposing eyes of people like Judge Murray look down at him many times before. In his experience, those were not the eyes of compassion, empathy, or kindness. He felt he was simply a passenger in the car that was his life, the accelerator weighted down by a cinderblock that was his Black skin. And they were fast approaching the cliff's edge.

Damion and his attorney briefly exchanged whispers. Damion was inclined to take the deal and serve only four years, which meant he'd definitely become more acquainted with Fang; rejecting it, however, there was a 50/50 chance at acquittal. Damion quivered at the thought of another second with him. He followed advice of counsel.

"My client does not wish to accept the State's plea offer, Your Honor."

"Is that true, Mr. Lee?" Judge Murray asked.

"Yes, Your Honor," Damion replied. His heart pounded. The neck of his stretched undershirt was soaked with sweat.

"Very well. Then I'll get right to it. Mr. Lee. On the one count of armed robbery, after observing all the evidence, the State of Georgia deems you guilty as charged. The State has carried its burden of proving, beyond a reasonable doubt, that on the date in question, you produced a .38 caliber revolver handgun, and with force, the threat of force, and intimidation, you demanded the contents of the victim's pockets with the intent to permanently deprive him of those items."

"Oh, Jesus Christ!" Mama Lee belted. "Son of the Lord God, Almighty. I pray for your mercy. Because I know that my son's life lays in your hands, O Lord, and not the hands of man."

A sheriff's deputy started to approach Mrs. Lee.

"It's all right. Let her finish," Judge Murray said to the deputy.

Mama Lee rose to her feet and continued her prayer, swaying side to side with her head bowed and hands and arms stretched to the ceiling.

Percy Lee eventually guided her by the waist back down into her seat next to him. They interlocked fingers and waited to hear the judge's sentence.

"Mr. Lee, you are sixteen years old and ten months. You're certainly old enough to appreciate the potential consequences of your actions. You have nearly a dozen charges on your juvenile record, ranging from petty theft under five hundred dollars, to grand theft auto."

Damion's jawline flexed. He pressed his clammy palms together.

"But this is, by far, the most serious of them all," the judge continued. "Mr. Lee, in my over thirty years on the bench, I've learned that patterns like yours get progressively worse, until, eventually, you end up killing someone. In fact, you could've killed that man you robbed. Because of this, I'm not inclined to give you any leniency."

"Sit up, boy. Back against the chair," the bailiff said to Damion, who had now placed his forehead on the table.

Mama Lee sobbed louder.

"In the case of a juvenile, aged sixteen or seventeen—which you are—who commits an inherently dangerous felony—which armed robbery is—the laws of this state authorize me to choose between sentencing you as a child, or an adult. *If* I decide to sentence you as a child, any sentence I give you will expire by law the day before your eighteenth birthday. An adult sentence carries with it not less than one, and not more than twenty years in the state penitentiary."

"Oh, Father Lord Jesus!" Mama Lee yelled. Percy Lee caressed the back of her hand while still holding it with his other.

"Now, because of your rather extensive record, and the seriousness of this offense, it is in the people's best interest that you be charged as an adult. You are a high school dropout. You don't have a job. You have not shown that you have any potential to be a positive contributor to society, Mr. Lee. In fact, you have demonstrated the opposite—that you are, and will likely continue to be, a menace to society."

Tears dropped from Damion's eyes for the first time. His attorney placed her hand on his.

"I am sentencing you to ten years at the Georgia State Prison in Reidsville."

Percy Lee raised his and Mama Lee's clasped hands to his chin and began to cry.

The bailiff pulled Damion by the arm from behind the defense table.

"Hol' on, bailiff. I'm not done yet."

The bailiff loosened his grip.

Judge Murray leaned forward, peering over the top of his readers directly into Damion's eyes.

"Mr. Lee, now, I want you to listen closely. What I'm about to say to you will be the most important words you've ever heard in your short life thus far."

With the exception of Judge Murray's voice, the courtroom was quiet.

"Georgia state law also authorizes me to suspend any sentence I render, so long as certain conditions are met. Now, I've had cases similar to yours in the last few years, where offenders, without an adult record, but clearly headed down the wrong track, joined the military and made something of themselves. They each have families now and are serving their country proudly," Judge Murray said, gesturing toward the American flag. "The military allows you to join at seventeen with parental consent. Now, I can't condition your suspended sentence on military enlistment, but I can evaluate that as a factor in addition to your good behavior and obtaining your high school equivalency. And I tend to look favorably upon those who serve their country. I'm offering you this option in lieu of prison time. Mr. Lee, do you accept?"

"Yes, he does! Oh, Jesus! Yes, he accepts!" Mama Lee shouted.

"I hear ya, Mama. But I need to hear Damion say it," Judge Murray said with a slight smile.

Damion's chin dropped to his chest. Not used to second chances, he was in disbelief, weeping in short uncontrollable sniffs and huffs.

"Yeah, I accept," Damion said between breaths. "I mean, yes, Judge—um, Your Honor." His shallow breathing became deeper. He raised each shoulder to his eyes to wipe away his tears.

"Good, son. Now, these are the conditions. One: you need to obtain your GED. Get in a class. Do whatever you need to do to get it. And like I said, I can't condition anything on you joining the military, but if I see a signed enlistment contract with your name on it before your eighteenth birthday, I'll look favorably on that."

"I understand, Your Honor."

"No, you don't understand, because I'm not finished."

Damion's attorney tapped his hand.

"The clock strikes twelve on your eighteenth birthday. If these conditions are not met by then, you are headed to Reidsville, young man. And by the time you get out, *if* you survive, your twenties will be almost over. Now, if you meet these conditions, your adult record will be wiped clean, as if none of this ever happened. Needless to say, you cannot get into any more trouble between now and then."

"Hallelujah, God of all Gods, King of all Kings. Oh, hallelujah. Bless His name!"

"I am offering you the chance to change the trajectory of your life. Reidsville is not a place for you, son. It's a maximum-security facility that houses hardened rapists and murderers. You do not want to ever step foot in that place. Now, I believe you can be better than you are. But I need you to believe it for yourself. Do you believe you can be better, Mr. Lee?"

"I do, Your Honor."

"I do, too!" yelled Mama Lee.

"Then I want you to be better, and I'm giving you one chance to prove it. Don't make a fool out of me."

"Thank you, Your Honor. You won't regret it," Damion said, no longer attempting to wipe the tears that flowed down his cheek onto his jumpsuit.

"Don't thank me. Thank that praying Mama you've got behind you. She's the one who changed my mind about you."

Judge Murray turned to the court reporter and announced: "In the case of *the State of Georgia v. Damion Lee,* enter the decision of guilty, with a suspended ten-year prison sentence pursuant to the fulfillment of the aforementioned conditions."

"So ordered."

The bailiff walked Damion to a bench directly opposite of Fang and the other prisoners. Damion avoided eye contact with him.

•••

Percy Lee arrived after his shift at the warehouse.

He emptied the contents of his pockets into a plastic bowl and stepped through the magnetometer, then through the steel turnstile gate. A county officer passed him the bowl from the belt on the other side.

It had been two days since the sentencing.

"I'm here to pick up my son," he said to the desk officer.

"Inmate's name and your I.D.," the officer said without looking up from her computer.

"Damion Corey Lee is his name. And he's being released today. So, I'd appreciate it if you didn't call him 'inmate.'" He pulled his old leather wallet from his back pocket, found his driver's license, and slid it across the counter.

"As long as he's in our custody, he's our responsibility, which makes him an inmate. When you two step out that door, *then* he's your son," the officer said, aiming a pen at the turnstile. "Now, what I need you to do is have a seat. When the *inmate* is here, you'll sign, because he's a minor, and then you two will be free to go."

A corrections officer escorted Damion out. He was wearing the mesh basketball shorts and white tank top undershirt that he had been arrested in during the summer. It was now December and 50 degrees.

The officer uncuffed Damion.

"Here. Put this on." Percy Lee took off his corduroy jacket and handed it to Damion.

He signed the paperwork, Damion collected a Ziploc bag with his personal effects, and the two walked out of the Bibb County Jail in silence.

"What, no Mickey Dee's?" Damion said as he climbed in the passenger seat of his dad's '90 Impala. "I've been in jail for almost five months, and I can't even get a 'Welcome home'?"

"Getting out of jail is nothing to celebrate," Percy Lee grumbled.

"Well, I've never known you to celebrate nothin'," Damion replied.

Percy Lee ignored the comment and reached on the floor behind Damion for a massive canvas book of CDs. He flipped through the pages and carefully removed one by Luther Vandross. Damion cracked the window and savored the fresh, crisp air.

They stopped at the red-light intersection of Mason Street and Anthony Road. Three bucket boys converged onto the Impala. Two of them squeegeed and dried the windshield with the speed of a NASCAR pit-stop crew, while the other displayed a box of Snickers, Twix, M&Ms, and Skittles for a dollar.

Percy Lee didn't wave them off before the service as most people did. Instead, he allowed it, and when the light changed, he eased into the acceleration.

"Bruh! You ain't gonna tip us?!" one of the boys yelled. "Cheap ass!"

Fifteen minutes later, the Impala turned into Langston Homes, a public housing complex. This was a sprawling, three-hundred-unit project of uniform two and three-bedroom duplex homes. During the summer, little boys played with foam footballs in the patchy yards, and girls jumped rope in the parking lots.

On every other corner was a Lincoln, Cadillac, Chevy, or some other old, boxy, big body car. Some were restored with pristine candy paint, opaque, black window tint, shiny rims the size of hula hoops, and a trunk full of speakers capable of causing seismic activity. And some were clunkers that belonged at the junkyard. Each had no fewer than five young men between the ages of thirteen and twenty-five posted in, on, and around them. They shot dice, rated women, and debated sports and rap music to pass the time. All this, while distributing crack cocaine to the all-Black community, and the occasional white person who'd sneak down from North Macon.

It was the drugs that caused the feuds among crews, and the inevitable violence that followed.

As a result, Langston Homes was more commonly known as "Alphabet City," because the drugs and violence made sightings of "Alphabet Boys" familiar to the residents—that is, men from the FBI, ATF, and the Georgia Bureau of Investigation, GBI. It also happened to be that all the streets were named for letters of the alphabet.

The screen door creaked open and slammed behind them. The smell of collard greens, macaroni and cheese, and ham embraced Percy Lee and Damion.

"Now, that's what I'm talkin' 'bout," Damion said, inhaling deeply, his nose to the ceiling.

Devon was on the couch, reading.

"Sup, Dev? You ain't happy to see your twin brother? Stand up and gimme some love," Damion said.

"Sup, Damo," Devon said with only a slight upward nod. He continued reading.

"Whatever," Damion muttered with a shrug, turning his attention to the kitchen. "Hey, Mama!"

"Hey, baby. It's so good to have you home."

Mama Lee wiped her hands and squeezed her son for over a minute, rocking side to side.

"I've missed you so much."

"I've missed you, too, Mama. I've missed you, too."

Damion went for a fork to sample the mac and cheese.

"Aht, aht, aht!" Mama Lee said, popping his hand. "You need to go take a long, hot bath. You smell like the whole jailhouse. And pour a couple of caps of rubbing alcohol in the tub. And some Epsom salt. It's under the sink. Dinner will be ready when you're done."

"I told you not to do nothin' special for him," Percy Lee said to Mama Lee.

"What, this?" Mama Lee said. "This ain't nothin' special. I was just in the mood to make my family a nice home-cooked meal."

Damion went to his room where he unpacked his Ziploc bag and arranged the contents carefully on his dresser: an iPod, wallet, cell phone, a miniature Bible, and notepad.

He was obsessive about his twin bed. The pillow was smooth and flat, and perfectly centered at the head, just as he had left it. The cover was pulled tightly, folded at right angles, and tucked between the mattress and box spring.

On top was a thick GED book. Damion opened the cover and a receipt fell to the floor. The back of the receipt read:

*Damo,*

*If you're serious about this, I'm here to help.*

*-Dev*

•••

Mama Lee's prayer had started to draw long.

"Amen. Let's eat," Percy Lee cut her short.

Their round table of pressed wood and woodgrain plastic sat in the corner of the kitchen. The refrigerator, sink, stove, and back door were all within five feet of it.

Damion savored the spices in the stuffing and the richness of the cheese in the macaroni. In jail, he'd had only ten minutes to eat. So, he'd mix the barely edible slop together and scarf it down.

Aside from the sporadic "Mm-mmm," they ate in silence for the first five minutes.

"You really scared us this time," Mama Lee said to Damion, breaking the silence.

"I know, Mama. This is the last time. I promise. I've got my head on straight, and I'm gonna do right this time," he replied in between chews

"How 'bout we talk about something else? Anything else," Percy Lee said.

Damion gulped down half his grape-flavored Kool-Aid from a repurposed spaghetti sauce jar. He breathed in deeply with a renewed appreciation for the slightest of details he thought he wouldn't get to see again for the next few years. He noticed the dead bugs collected at the center of the ceiling light cover, chipped paint on the wall exposing several layers of different colors, the hum of the refrigerator.

Percy Lee fixated on his plate, while Mama Lee watched her boys.

Devon and Damion were elbow to elbow. Both still had slender, youthful builds, but Damion had put on some muscle. A vein ran the length of his biceps. His forearm flexed when he cut into the ham. He had gotten a new tattoo—a bird of some sort. The wings, spanning the width of Damion's chest, were visible under his tank top undershirt.

Though the boys were identical and not yet seventeen, Damion's eyes were much older than his brother's. The innocence was gone.

"Okay," Mama Lee said. "I watched the debate yesterday. Hillary did good, but I like that Obama guy."

"You honestly think America is going to elect a woman *or* a Black man president? Gimme a break," Damion said.

"When I said we can talk about anything else, I didn't mean politics," Percy Lee said.

"Well, you said 'anything,' didn't you?" Mama Lee replied.

Percy Lee sighed with pursed lips.

"I don't know why y'all love the Democrats so much anyway," Devon said. "They ain't never done much to help us. I mean, what is Obama offering us? Hope? Change we can believe in?"

"When I was young, I remember seeing pictures of LBJ and Martin Luther King. You didn't see no Republican presidents meeting with MLK, did you? Democrats gave us Blacks the right to vote. They made it so we have a place to live. They fight for us," Mama Lee said.

"You mean a place to live like Alphabet City?" Devon said. "They *give* us welfare, food stamps, and Section Eight housing. Then they tell us, 'Oh, by the way, if you want to keep getting this *free stuff,* you have to live together over in this corner of the city. Your kids have to go to these schools.' It's legal segregation all over again."

"Watch it, boy. Your Mama and I work hard to keep a roof over your head," Percy Lee said.

"No disrespect, Dad. I'm just saying, we can't even go up to North Macon without being harassed by the cops. Everything up there is better. Their movie theater, the grocery store. Everything. If you ask me, it seems like the Republican Party is where it's at. They have the money, and they own stuff."

"Those Republicans don't mean Black folks no good. They are the devil. What they are practicing is the devil's politics," Mama Lee said. "This household is Democrat. Christian and Democrat. That means as long as you live under this roof, you're a Christian and a Democrat."

Percy Lee put his fork down. "All right. That's enough politics. Give it a rest."

No one spoke for the rest of the meal.

Damion had nothing to say anyway, as he was still absorbing his environment outside of cold metal and cement. He stood, went to the counter, and returned with a second plate that was larger than the first.

When dinner was over, Mama Lee began washing the dishes.

"Go have a seat, Joan," Percy Lee said to Mama Lee. "You have two grown boys here to do that for you."

Percy Lee stood up from the table, leaving his plate. Then he took an orange from the refrigerator. He sliced it in half with a dirty steak knife from the sink and brought one of the halves into the living room, where he kept a pair of blue and green parakeets in a cage.

He spoke tenderly to them. His voice would raise several octaves higher than his deep speaking voice. He carefully opened the cage door and slid the orange half onto a stick for the birds to feed from.

He adored the birds. Only he was allowed to feed them, clean the cage, or even speak to them.

Damion looked on as his dad tended to them.

Growing up, when no one was around, Damion would sit in his dad's metal folding chair next to the cage. He'd watch the birds. Sometimes, he'd close his eyes and just listen to them chirp. He understood the peace they brought his father. Damion felt connected to him through them.

Percy Lee pulled a cheap cigar from his work uniform pocket, grabbed his jacket, and went outside to have a smoke on the front porch.

"I guess you two do have some catching up to do," Mama Lee said as she went into the living room to watch *Family Feud*.

Damion tossed a hand towel at Devon, hitting him in the head.

"I wash. You dry."

Damion could hear Mama Lee yelling answers at the TV. Percy Lee would smoke for at least an hour while reading *The Macon Telegraph.* That ritual brought him peace in the evenings, rain or shine.

"You know you're destroying this family, don't you?" Devon said. "You're stressing Dad out, and you're breaking Mom's heart."

"Don't start with me," Damion said. "You've always been the favorite. You know that. You did good in school. You were always a little 'yes, sir,' 'no, sir' goody-two-shoes. You can't tell me Mom and Dad didn't treat you better than me our whole lives."

"Oh, please. We are identical twins, Damo. We were born three minutes apart. If Mom and Dad treated us differently, it was because we behaved differently. I never went looking for trouble like you."

"You ever stop to think, maybe I wasn't lookin' for trouble? Maybe I was lookin' for attention? Maybe I was looking for love? I didn't have perfect one hundred scores on my homework to bring home like you."

"That's a cop-out. You're making excuses for yourself. There're a ton of other things you could've done for attention, instead of getting in fights and stealing from the corner store."

"Oh, yeah? Like what? You want me to play the cymbals in the marching band, like you?"

"How about not getting in fights and stealing, for one? How about that, Damo?"

"You know what? You're a weak little punk, Dev. You never could've done five months in juvie like I just did."

"Oh, you think five months in jail makes you strong, huh? You think that makes you hard? That makes you dumb. You can't think for yourself. So, you become a sheep and let those idiot dudes on the corner tell you what to do. 'Go beat up that guy for me. Go rob that man.' You think robbing someone with a gun makes you strong? That makes *you* the weak one."

"Whatever, man," Damion replied.

They each quieted, and began washing and drying with intensity.

Damion scrubbed the steel wool against the cast-iron pots. Plates clinked as Devon stacked them in the cupboard.

"So, you're gonna do the military thing, huh?"

Devon flung the towel over his shoulder.

"I got no choice."

"Which branch are you gonna pick?"

"I don't know yet. I was thinking about the Army. But I heard the Air Force has the best girls."

"I heard that, too. Whatever you do, just don't be on the front lines. You already worry Mom and Dad enough."

"Oh, say less. I ain't riskin' my life for a country that wanted to lock me in a cage for ten years."

"I hear that," Devon replied. "For what it's worth, I think it'll be good for you."

Damion took the towel from Devon's shoulder and wrapped it over the end of a long-handled wooden spoon to dry the inside of a mason jar.

"Hey, 'member that one time when we were walking home from school, and the UPS man left the back of the truck open?" Damion asked with a smirk.

"Don't remind me," Devon said, shaking his head and smiling.

"You didn't say nothin'. You just jumped right on the truck, grabbed a box, and pitched it to me," Damion said. "You grabbed another one and we hauled ass."

"That UPS man went after you," Devon said. "And as soon as we hit the corner, those two fat cops—what did we used to call them? One was Black and one was white."

"Rolie and Polie!" they said in unison, both with a hysterical laugh.

"Rolie and Polie came waddling after me," Damion said. "We split up. I ran down that grassy hill by the barbershop, and Rolie fell down it, rolled into Polie. And when they reached the end, they both had dog shit all over them. I think it was on one of their faces."

Damion laughed tears, leaning against the refrigerator, while Devon laughed hunched over the back of a chair.

"The hood still talks about that," Damion said, collecting himself. "I heard the UPS driver came back to an empty truck."

"Man, I had forgotten about that," Devon said. "Those were fun times."

"Yeah, and when the cops came to question us, you were a rock,"

Damion said. "We were thick as thieves back then."

"Literally," Devon replied.

They each let out a high-pitched sigh, collecting themselves.

"You see, you've done your dirt, too. You just ain't get caught," Damion said.

"Oh, please. We were kids. And that's completely different from sticking a gun in someone's face."

Damion stacked the last plate inside the cupboard, while Devon wiped down the stove.

"By the way, I'm serious about helping you with the GED," Devon said. "I'm not very good at standardized tests, but I'll do what I can. But listen here, Damo. This is it. This is your last straw with me. If you get in any more trouble, that's the end of the line with you and me. We're done. You follow?"

"'Preciate it, Dev," Damion said, snapping Devon with the wet towel.

# TEN

It had been three days since Damion and Zapata had heard from Jim and Jon. They hadn't seen them in the DFAC. And they hadn't seen them near the Poo Pond.

That Friday at the cigar deck had ended in confusion for them. Jim and Jon had kept them in the dark about the details of the opportunity; Damion and Zapata knew nothing.

They felt bullied. Jim had told them that their decision was irrevocable—whether they'd said "yes" or "no" to the deal, there was no backing out, no "flip-flopping," as Jim put it.

Damion and Zapata were beginning to have second thoughts. They questioned whether Jim and Jon were even who they'd said they were.

They each carried a loaded M4 carbine with a full combat load of 210 rounds everywhere they went, even to the latrine. They had qualified on the marksmanship range as experts, the level above sharpshooter. And they could pick off a soup can at three hundred meters. Taking out Jim and Jon would be like shooting a dead fish in a bucket.

Still, they got the sense that these men had a mean side to them. And they didn't want to test them.

...

The guard returned Damion's military ID card to him, clipped to a red ID badge that read "VISITOR ESCORT REQUIRED." Damion unclipped the cards and handed the red one to Rambo. They each waited as the gate guards swept the truck with dogs and mirrors for explosive material. Once cleared, they each hopped in, and Rambo put it in gear.

The day was as ordinary as any other, except Rambo had been late. He hadn't been late the entire time he and Damion had been working together—about six weeks at this point. During that time, Damion had mastered his routine. He had a good idea of when he'd be at certain places on the daily circuit, and most importantly, when it was time to get off and go to chow. Rambo being late had thrown off the schedule.

For most of these truck drivers, being late meant you didn't get to work for the day. No work, no pay. But not for Rambo. Damion liked him.

When they got in the truck, Damion nonetheless scolded him with several harsh points to his own wrist, the universal sign for "You're late."

In case Rambo didn't understand that, Damion said, "Late, late. Don't be late again. Do you understand?" in a loud voice, as if Rambo could suddenly understand English if Damion spoke louder.

Rambo lifted his right hand from the wheel and placed it on his boney chest, nodding in humble contrition.

The two rode in silence. The workday passed unremarkably.

It was just before 1800 hrs. when they pulled up on their last set of Porta-Potties for the day. Damion had dozed off.

The truck came to an abrupt stop. Damion briefly came to, instinctively bracing himself against the dashboard. Then he resumed sleeping.

"Hey! Hey!"

Damion felt a rough shove on the shoulder.

"Up! Up! Get up!"

"What the fuck, Rambo?!"

In a mental fog, Damion awoke to the sight of the headlights reflecting off of the cloud of sand the truck had kicked up.

"Get out!" Rambo said. "Get ass out truck!" he repeated in broken, but passable English.

"Get your fucking hands off me!" Damion shouted. "Are you crazy?! Don't you ever touch me!"

"I'm charge tonight! I'm boss!" Rambo shouted as he reached his left arm out the window to open his door. He leaped to the ground in front of three Porta-Potties. Damion grabbed a fistful of his top, but the brittle fabric ripped.

Damion opened his door and jumped to the ground. On instinct, he jerked the charging handle of his M4 to the rear and let it slam forward to chamber a round in the barrel, and moved the selector switch from "Safe" to "Semi-automatic" in one quick motion. He cautiously moved around the rear of the truck, his weapon at high ready. He panned wide around the Porta-Potties, nervous, but alert.

He found Rambo squatting down behind one of the Porta-Potties, scooping away loose earth with his hands.

"Put your goddamn hands up!" Damion ordered. "Stop what you're doing!"

Rambo continued as if Damion hadn't said anything. Damion charged toward Rambo and landed a boot to his shoulder. He stood over Rambo as the man lay flat on his back, hands over his head.

"What the fuck are you doing, Rambo?!"

Rambo said nothing. Damion pressed the muzzle of his M4 into Rambo's clavicle, causing him to whimper in pain.

"Jeemjone!" Rambo blurted. "Jeemjone!"

"What the fuck is a 'jeemjone,' Rambo?"

"Jeemjone. You know Jeemjone, no?" Rambo said. "Jeemjone! Big, white man. Jeemjone!"

"Wait. Are you saying 'Jim and Jon?'"

"Yes! Jeemjone!" Rambo replied.

Damion clicked the selector switch on his M4 from "Semi" back to "Safe" and slung the rifle over his back. He easily lifted Rambo's slight frame and sat his back against the Porta-Potty.

"How do you know 'Jeemjone'?" Damion asked.

Rambo reached for the spot where he'd been digging. "Don't fucking touch it!" Damion ordered. "Sit over there!" Damion directed him with a knife-hand motion.

Rambo scooted away from the spot, toward the last Porta-Potty.

"Don't move!" Damion ordered.

Damion knelt over the spot, eyes fixed on Rambo, and began to sweep the sand away. He lifted out an object the size and shape of a cereal box, the weight of a brick, wrapped in dark green duct tape.

"What is this, Rambo?"

"It's from Jeemjone. But I don't know what is it. Jeemjone tell me to tell you bring to DFAC tonight. You and you friend must leave in Porta-Potty outside DFAC tonight. You must meet Jeemjone inside DFAC after," Rambo replied. "Do not open."

"Get up and get in the truck!" Damion ordered as he climbed into the driver's side and over to the passenger's seat. Rambo climbed up behind him. Damion examined the package, smelling it and putting it to his ear.

"Let's go to the gate," Damion said. Rambo put the truck into gear. He removed his shemagh scarf from his neck, handed it to Damion, and motioned for Damion to wipe the package clean and put on his gloves. Damion pulled a pair of hard-knuckle tactical gloves from his assault pack and began to dry-scrub the package thoroughly.

"So, wait. You mean to tell me that you spoke English all this time?!" Damion asked.

"English, not very good," Rambo answered.

"It's good enough. Better than my Pashto," Damion said.

"You no ask never about my English," Rambo said.

"How do you know Jeemjone?" Damion asked again.

"I know Jeemjone two years. We business partners. Good two man. You can trust Jeemjone. Do as Jeemjone say and we all make big money together," Rambo replied.

"Well, seeing as I've been riding with you for almost two months and I'm just learning that you speak English, I don't know if I can trust you, Rambo."

"You no ask never about my English. You can trust me," Rambo said, earnestly touching his chest.

The brakes squealed as Rambo brought the truck to a stop. Rambo handed over his red visitor badge to Damion. Damion grabbed his M4 and assault pack containing the box, and hopped out of the truck.

"Remember, do what Jeemjone say tonight," Rambo reminded

Damion.

"You just remember to be on time tomorrow. Five o'clock sharp!" Damion replied.

Damion walked to the base circuit bus stop, where Zapata was waiting as usual. They got on the next bus. Zapata followed Damion to the back row.

"You're late, bro," Zapata said.

"Yeah, fuckin' Rambo was late this morning. Threw my whole day off," Damion replied. "Yo, look at this." Damion lowered his assault pack onto the floor between his legs and unzipped it.

"What is that?" Zapata asked.

"I have no idea," Damion answered. "Rambo pulled it out of the ground today while we were doing our routes. He said he knows Jim and Jon, and that they want us to put it in one of the Porta-Potties outside the DFAC tonight."

"Well, open it."

"Rambo said we can't."

"So, you're taking orders from fucking Rambo now?"

"He said Jim and Jon said not to open it."

"Well, I'm not planting no suspicious package outside a DFAC with hundreds of troops," Zapata said.

"Rambo said for us to meet them inside the DFAC right after. If it's a bomb or something, why would they be anywhere near it?" Damion reasoned.

"How do we know they'll be inside? I mean, really, how well do we know these guys? Let's go to the military police and tell them what we know. We can just say we were trying to help out by gathering information," Zapata said.

As the bus came to a stop, Damion spotted Jim entering the DFAC.

"We're not saying anything to the MPs. There. See, look. There's one of them going inside right now," Damion said, pointing in Jim's direction. "Stop being a pussy and let's get this money."

The two exited through the rear doors of the bus. Zapata trailed several feet, while Damion walked toward the Porta-Potties, about one hundred feet away from the DFAC building.

"Stand here and cough loud if somebody walks up," Damion

whispered to Zapata.

Zapata stood guard, pretending to use his smartphone. Damion entered one of the Porta-Potties. Two minutes later, he emerged with a noticeably lighter assault pack.

The two walked inside the DFAC without a word to one another. They each selected the fried chicken, rice, and green beans. They found their table where Jim was already seated. Jon showed up minutes later, sliding his tray onto the table.

"What the fuck? Y'all got us doing some shady shit!" Damion said in a low voice.

"If I were you, I'd be shoving my chow down my throat," Jim said, mouth full, eating quickly himself.

"What do you mean?" Zapata said.

"Just fucking eat," Jon ordered.

Two soldiers with leashed German Shepherds entered the DFAC, each wearing Velcro patches on their left shoulders that read "MP."

"Listen guys, don't be alarmed at what's about to happen. It's all a part of the plan. We don't want to draw attention to ourselves. We need to just blend in, okay?" Jim said calmly to Damion and Zapata.

Damion pressed his fist against his chin, cracking each knuckle, while Zapata fidgeted with a torn piece of napkin. They exchanged looks with wide eyes.

"Listen up! I need everyone to stop eating, stand up, and leave the building through the rear exit," one MP ordered in a loud, but composed voice. "Everyone, evacuate the building now." She pointed toward the exit with all her fingers extended.

"Stand up and let's go," Jim said.

"Don't forget your rifles," Jon reminded them.

Damion and Zapata followed Jim and Jon to the Land Rover.

"Get in. Don't say a word until we get to the deck," Jim ordered.

They rode in silence as Jon drove.

When they arrived at the deck, there were only three cigar smokers seated in a huddle. Jon plugged in a Bluetooth speaker and aimed it in their direction.

"What the fuck was that?" Zapata said.

"Calm down, guys. You did great," Jon said as he thumbed open the latch to his humidor. "This was a test, and you passed with flying colors."

Jon held out the humidor. Damion and Zapata declined. Jim picked a mild Torpedo and clipped the end.

"Are you going to tell us what the fuck just happened?" Damion asked.

"That was a test, but more importantly, it's our insurance," Jim said.

"What the fuck do you mean 'insurance'?" Damion asked.

"Just shut your mouths and listen one fucking minute, guys," Jon hissed through gritted teeth. "We needed to know that we could trust each other. I know your guys' word is good, but that's not enough. We needed something in our back pockets just in case you started having second thoughts."

Damion and Zapata peered at Jon as the take-cover sirens sounded in the distance over the base intercom system.

Jim leaned back, torching the end of his Torpedo. He took several successive puffs to get a good smoke going.

"You guys just planted a bomb," Jon said.

"Oh, hell no," Zapata said. "I thought you told us we weren't going to be doing no terrorist shit!"

"Lower your goddamn voice and listen!" Jim said, leaning forward again. "It was a dud, a prop—no more dangerous than this box of cigars. There was C4, but we left out the igniting components, not even a blasting cap. There was no way it could have exploded."

Damion palmed his face, elbows resting on his knees.

"Relax, brothers. Like I said, this was just insurance for us." Jim reached into his cargo breast pocket and pulled out a smartphone. He handed it to Damion. Damion didn't reach for it. Jim placed the device on the wood table in front of the two, and they both hovered over it. Jim tapped "Play." A video of Damion entering the Porta-Potty with the package began. It was dark and grainy, but Damion's face was visible enough.

"Oh, my fucking god," Zapata said as he sank deeper into his seat.

Damion swallowed hard. "So, what are you going to do with this?" he asked.

"Nothing," Jim replied. "Look, we are about to make some serious cash together. We can't take you to court if you don't keep your end of the bargain. Before tonight, if you guys wanted to go to the MPs and tell them about us, Jon and I would be up shit's creek, sailing one-way to Leavenworth Penitentiary. Now we can sleep comfortably knowing that if you guys decided to get cute on us, with one tap of a screen, we could make you movie stars."

"How could we tell something we don't fucking know?" Damion asked.

"You guys are stressed right now. And rightfully so. I would be, too," Jon said. "Hey, Jim. Whaddaya say we put their minds at ease?"

"My pleasure," Jim replied. "What do you boys know about crypto?"

Damion's brow furrowed. "You mean the stuff Superman was afraid of?"

"No, cryptocurrency," Zapata said. "Yeah, I know a little bit. My cousin put me on to it before I left to come over here. I've been investing in it for a few months."

"Explain it to your friend here, then," Jon said.

"It's like money, but not like dollars. But you can turn it into dollars," Zapata said to Damion.

"Way to go, Obama," Jim said. "You are the shittiest explainer ever."

"Here, allow me," Jon interrupted. "Crypto is a secure, digital currency. It only exists online; there's no paper money. But like your friend here so eloquently stated, with a touch of your screen, you can sell your crypto at market rate and convert it into dollars, or euro, or dinar. Mexican peso if you want. The best part is that it's untraceable. The government has no way of tracking your transactions or interfering with it in any way. And the only way someone can take your money is if they have your private key. Bitcoin is the most popular type of cryptocurrency. It's also the most stable."

"Okay...?" Damion said, still confused.

Jim pulled another smartphone from his other cargo breast pocket.

"Are you about to show a video of me rubbing one off in the shower last night?" Damion said.

"I already uploaded that one to Pornhub. You'd be happy to know you got almost a hundred likes and twenty comments in under an hour," Jim retorted. "Here, Zapata, show me your Bitcoin digital wallet."

Zapata pulled an iPhone from a cargo pocket on the side of his calf just above his boot, unlocked it, and opened an app.

"Set it on 'Receive,' and hand it here," Jim said.

Zapata tapped a button and a square QR code opened up. Jim held his phone over Zapata's. Both devices dinged like old cash registers in less than a second.

Zapata looked at his iPhone and lit up with excitement.

His screen read, "You have received ☒3.2. Swipe up to accept."

He swiped and his account increased to ☒3.2097. He turned the phone to Damion, who was unimpressed.

"So what? He just sent you three dollars?"

"Bro, that's not a dollar sign. That's a Bitcoin symbol. Do you know how much this is?" Zapata asked, eyes bulging.

"Keep your voice down," Jon cautioned. "Let him do the math for himself. Damion, I want you to open up Google and search 'Bitcoin to USD conversion.'"

Damion pulled his phone from a Velcro pocket on the shoulder of his uniform, unlocked it, and began typing. The others sat in silence.

"Hold on. I must've done something wrong," he said after entering the figure.

Jim and Jon reclined with smug countenances. Jon crossed his legs at the ankles and blew smoke to the purple sky.

"You got it right," Jim said.

Damion looked at his phone, then at Zapata, then at his phone again, then at Jim and Jon. His eyes grew as large as golf balls.

"That's over thirty—!"

"Shhhh!" Jim interrupted.

"That's over thirty grand," Damion said in an elevated whisper.

"That's right. Thirty grand for one night's work," Jon said. "How much did Uncle Sam pay you tonight?"

"So, wait, you want us to go around base and plant fake bombs?" Damion asked, the initial excitement subsiding.

"Like we said, gents, that was just insurance—an expression of goodwill, if you will. And the thirty grand is just us returning that goodwill," Jon said.

"Damion, set yourself up a Bitcoin wallet account, and your friend here will send you over your half," Jim said. "From here on out, that's how you'll be receiving your compensation."

Jim pulled two brand new iPhones from a canvas bag and gave them to Damion and Zapata.

"These are your new work phones. Keep them with you at all times. They have enhanced encryption and are virtually impenetrable, so only do business on these phones, not your personal ones. If things ever go awry, they'll be wiped remotely. If you lose them, Jim or I need to know immediately. Got it?"

"Got it," Damion and Zapata said together.

"And don't worry, no more fake bombs," Jim added. "Just stay ready and you'll be hearing from us soon about the details of our partnership. But no more shoptalk tonight. Now we celebrate."

He passed Damion and Zapata two Cuban Montecristos, then flicked open a large, black pocketknife and used it to lift up a false bottom in the humidor. Underneath was a plastic bladder with a clear liquid inside. He emptied a plastic water bottle and motioned for everyone else to do the same. Leaning low, he filled the bottles about a third of the way each.

"This had better be what I think it is," Zapata said.

"Oh, you better believe it," Jim replied. "Gran Patrón Platinum Tequila—two hundred a bottle. We're disrespecting it by drinking it from water bottles, but it is what it is."

"Fuck yeah. After today, I need a drink," Damion said.

They reached their drinks to the center, but did not raise them. Jon led the toast.

"To partnership!"

"To partnership!" the rest replied.

# ELEVEN

The Army called it the Morale, Welfare, and Recreation center, MWR for short. And on any given evening after the workday, the building buzzed with troops. It was a community center, a place to unwind. Soldiers could take off their camouflage uniform tops and play pool or foosball in just the beige undershirt. There was a video game room, a soundproof music studio, and a place for troops to record themselves reading books for their children back home in the States.

Damion had been in the MWR's computer lab for three hours learning about cryptocurrency. The more he read, the more he realized that the fifteen thousand dollars worth of his portion that Zapata had sent him was real. He found it exciting and equally unnerving.

Damion had learned as much as he was going to that evening, and was getting ready to leave. Just as he started to log out, a black message box popped up on the screen with a ten-second countdown clock.

The box read: "C5RW72330."

Damion initially thought nothing of it, dismissing it as an error, or some programming process. But he had received so many Army briefings about terrorist hacking in the past and the ten-second timer seemed odd enough that he decided to jot down the code to pass along to the computer lab attendant.

The physical act of writing down the code forced him to take a closer look. His mind began to decrypt it. He added slashes so that it read: "C5/RW7/2330."

This wasn't an error or hacking attempt; it was a message. And the message was for him.

Because he was a logistics specialist with an airfield management unit when he wasn't on punishment detail, he understood "C-5" to be the name of a military aircraft. "RW7" meant "Runway #7." Damion was to meet someone at 2330 hours on the airfield at the seventh C-5 runway. That was in forty-five minutes.

He looked around nervously. Someone must have been watching him. He was on a community computer, in a computer lab; there was no way for anyone to know he'd be there, or which of the two dozen computers he'd choose to use.

Damion caught the twenty-four-hour base circuit bus to the airfield. After 8:00 p.m. the bus began to arrive every thirty minutes instead of the fifteen-minute interval schedule kept during regular working hours. The ride was another thirty minutes. Damion arrived at the airfield just after midnight. Runway #7 was the last runway, and from a distance, with several bulldozers, forklifts, and other large machines, it appeared to be under construction.

Damion posted up next to a tall, gas-operated generator light. He opened the hood, plugged his phone in to charge, and waited. After twenty minutes, he pulled out the gum wrapper in his pocket that he had used to jot down the meeting instructions.

As minutes went by, he began to think. Maybe they weren't meeting instructions after all. Maybe the code *was* just some programming process. Maybe it *was* a hacking attempt.

Fifty minutes had passed. Damion was exhausted. Between waiting for the circuit bus and the trip itself, it would take him about an hour to get back to his B-hut. With his day starting at 4:00 a.m., that would give him about two hours of sleep.

He unplugged his phone from the generator and started back. Just as he did, he heard hands clapping slowly.

The silhouettes of two large figures grew larger.

"Good job following instructions," Jim said.

"You guys are late," Damion replied.

"No, *you* were late," Jim said. "The instructions said to be here at twenty-three thirty hours. You showed up at zero zero zero five hours. We were watching. But the important thing is you demonstrated critical reasoning skills by decoding that message. That quality is going to serve us well this year. You see, Zapata got the same message on the TV while he was playing his little video games. You know where he is right now?"

"In his B-hut, sound asleep. Exactly where I should be, instead of freezing my nuts off with you two assholes. So maybe *he's* the smart one."

"You have to trust us, Damion. There's a method to our madness. We had to figure out who was the leader between the two of you, and you clearly beat him out. So, congrats. And rest assured that with greater responsibility comes greater reward. How's that fifteen grand working out for you?" Jon asked.

A reminder of the largest lump sum of money Damion had ever seen slightly disarmed him.

"That was pretty sweet. But listen, guys, from here on out, you have to bring me in the loop on all the ins and outs of the operation, whatever it is. And stop all this mind-fuckery," Damion said, still agitated.

"You're right. You're right," Jim said. "After tonight, you're a full-fledged member of the team. No more feeling around in the dark. You have our word."

"We know you have to get a couple winks in, so we'll make this short and sweet," Jon said. "Tomorrow, when you pick Rambo up, where's your first stop on the route?"

"Pick-Up Point One, over by the DFAC," Damion replied.

"Wrong," Jim answered. "It's right here. As soon as you credential Rambo in a few hours, you are to escort him right here to Runway Seven. Got it?"

"Didn't we just talk about filling me in on the details?"

"Reach out to Zapata in the morning; I want you both to meet us at the cigar deck at eighteen hundred hours. Pick up your chow from the DFAC to-go, and meet us there. We'll fill you both in at the same time."

"Whatever. Can I at least get a ride back?" Damion asked.

•••

Rambo and his jingle truck were first in line. Credentialing took a fraction of the time that it usually did, and the K9 screening was noticeably perfunctory.

"Sup, Ram-Ram," Damion said as he climbed into the cab and handed Rambo his red badge.

"Morning, morning," Rambo replied.

"It's gonna take me some time to get used to hearing you speak English," Damion said.

Rambo smiled, nodded, and ground the truck into gear.

"Listen, Rambo. This morning we have to stop somewhere different than usual first."

"I know. Already, I know," Rambo replied.

"Of course, you would know more than I do," Damion muttered under his breath.

They rumbled over the dirt and gravel lot onto the paved road, and twenty minutes later, they pulled up at Runway #7 to a crew of five soldiers waiting.

"You get out. Just don't ask no question," Rambo said to Damion.

Damion jumped out of the truck while Rambo stayed inside.

Two of the soldiers had shoulder-length rubber gloves and were using a long wooden pole with a hook attached, to fish large black plastic bags out of the truck's tank, where the waste was stored.

Damion counted forty black bags.

Another soldier stood by with a hose, spraying down each bag. The last two soldiers unpacked the rinsed bags, removing brown bricks sealed in clear plastic.

They placed the bricks inside footlocker-sized boxes, all labeled "RETROGRADE EQUIPMENT." They loaded the boxes onto a metal pallet designed for transporting large amounts of heavy cargo by plane. Then they piled identical boxes onto and around them.

One soldier strained to lift an industrial-sized roll of plastic wrap from the ground. He attached the loose end to the cargo on pallets, then raced a lap around it and passed the plastic wrap off to his colleague like a relay baton. After ten trips around, another soldier ran a thin steel band under the pallet and around the top of the cargo, sealing the ends on the other side. Another soldier produced four shipping labels from a handheld printer gun and slapped one label on each side of the cargo.

The destination was Fort Hood, Texas.

The stop took less than fifteen minutes. And with the smooth credentialing earlier at the front gate, Damion hadn't lost any time with his route.

Damion climbed back into the cab.

"What the fuck was that?" Damion asked Rambo, who was finishing up his breakfast of brown rice and some sort of meat wrapped in naan bread.

Rambo chuckled. "That? That make us rich mens," he replied with full cheeks. "Don't worry. Jeemjone tell you everything. Later he tell you everything."

They drove away.

Damion's exhaustion was stronger than his nagging curiosity. So, he listened to his music and passed out for most of the day, while Rambo drove the route and did the pumping and dumping, as usual.

•••

Damion and Zapata were fifteen minutes early. They each had a stack of three Styrofoam takeout containers on the wooden table in front of them.

They had begun to eat their dinner when Jim and Jon pulled up in the Land Rover. At the same time, Damion's phone chimed like a cash register, the way Zapata's had when they'd received their first payment.

As Jim and Jon approached, Damion checked his Bitcoin account. His eyes grew as large as saucers. Jim placed his large hand on Damion's shoulder and roughly massaged it.

"Excellent work today," he said.

Damion, still stunned by the figure on his phone, was too busy running numbers in his head to respond.

"Let me save you the headache of doing the math; that's the equivalent of one hundred K," Jon said.

Damion and Zapata exchanged looks.

Jim leaned in, his beard brushing Damion's shoulder and cheek, "That's a hundred thousand dollars for fifteen minutes of work. Now, how's that for a shit detail?"

"Wait, is that a hundred per, or do we bust that down?" Zapata asked, grabbing Damion's phone to confirm the figure for himself.

"That's one hundred for Damion," Jon said. "You didn't do anything but play video games and sleep in. You got the same message as Damion last night. And don't lie to us about that."

"But I..." Zapata started.

"We'll leave it up to Damion to decide if he wants to give you a cut," Jon interrupted, "but as far as we're concerned, Damion did the work. So, it's Damion's money. But don't worry; there's gonna be plenty of opportunities to make much more than that. Just follow instructions next time."

"We'll work something out," Damion said to Zapata.

Zapata sat back in a pout.

"So, what's the deal? What's the operation?" Damion asked.

"Ah, yes. The operation," Jim said, snapping open his humidor. He passed cigars around. Damion and Zapata placed theirs on the table, while Jim and Jon lit theirs. "I told you that I'd fill you both in. And I'm a man of my word. But first, I have a question: have you ever been outside the wire? You know, off base?"

Damion and Zapata looked at each other. "Yeah. We took a chopper a couple times to one of the other bases when we first got here. Does that count?" Damion said.

"Absolutely. Matter of fact, that's even better," Jim replied. "When you looked down from that Black Hawk, what did you see?"

Damion and Zapata gave him a blank stare.

Zapata threw up his hands. "Why does everything have to be a riddle with you guys?"

"Hang on, hang on. We're getting there," Jon said. "Do you remember seeing white fields? Miles and miles of them?"

"Come to think of it, yeah, I do. The view was dope," Damion answered. Zapata agreed.

"Well, that's one way to put it, but we don't care for that term. Those flowers that you saw swaying back and forth from the chopper are opium poppy plants," Jon said. "And they are what's making us rich."

"You mean opium—like the drug?" Zapata asked.

"We prefer the term 'therapeutic medication,'" Jim answered. He and Jon shared a chuckle.

Damion folded his arms across his chest and sat back. "So, we're drug dealers—is that it?"

"Don't think of it like that. You're not some punks on the corner selling nickel and dime bags to pregnant teenage girls," Jon replied. "Here, let me explain: our company, ZinCorp, has several other subsidiary companies."

"Sub-what?" Zapata asked.

"'Subsidiary.' In other words, ZinCorp is an umbrella company that owns other companies," Jim explained. "Keating Pharmaceuticals is one of the companies under that umbrella. And their bread-and-butter is pain meds—stuff like codeine, morphine, oxycodone, hydrocodone. You get into a car accident and break your leg? Your doctor will prescribe you Percocet or something for the pain. Get a tooth pulled? Your dentist gives you Tylenol with codeine," Jon explained. "And the main active ingredient in these meds is opium—the same opium found in those pretty white fields you guys were looking down on from that helicopter.

"The global market for opium and the medications that it makes its way into is in the hundreds of billions worldwide. And guess where ninety percent of the global opium demand is met? You got it—right here in beautiful Afghanistan. Afghanistan is the largest producer of opium in the world. Myanmar, Mexico, and Colombia trail far behind."

"But wait. Opium is also in heroin, right? Doctors don't prescribe that, huh? That's just on the streets," Damion replied.

"You're right—opium is in heroin," Jim answered. "But we aren't supplying heroin to street dealers. We are working for a legit pharmaceutical company. The service we provide makes countless people feel better. Now, is it possible that some of the opium we move makes it on the streets? Sure. There's no doubt about it. With an operation as large as ours, it's impossible to completely control for leaks. But that's not our mission. We ship to Keating Pharma. That's it. What happens after that is out of our hands. If some of it makes it on the street, that's too bad. But nobody is telling people to shove a needle between their toes either."

"If Keating Pharma is so legit, why are they transporting it underground through us?" Damion asked.

"Because pharmaceutical companies are greedy. Just like the four of us. If they went about it the above-board way, they would be subject to a million regulations, and import and export fees to both the Afghan and US governments. They're using military planes, provided by taxpayers. Plus, it allows each country to avoid potentially bad press—you know, plausible deniability. Not to mention, it's faster through us," Jim explained.

Zapata smirked. "Fast like Jimmy John's?"

"Fast like Jimmy John's," Jon replied, reaching over to torch Damion's cigar.

"You guys good so far?" Jim asked.

Damion and Zapata exchanged looks.

"We're good," Damion replied.

"Good deal. So, let's get down to brass tacks," Jon continued. "We have Afghan workers throughout the Kandahar and Helmand Provinces who minimally process the opium. They work the fields, package it all up, and get it ready for your drivers to pick up. Now, each week the drop days will be different. But there's a pattern. There will be Monday, Wednesday, and Friday weeks, and Tuesday, Thursday weeks. The weeks will alternate for each of you. For example, Damion, this would be your Monday, Wednesday, Friday week, and Zapata, this is your Tuesday, Thursday. Next week, the drop days will flip for each of you. The idea is that you two will never have the same drop day. You guys still with me?"

"Yup. We're tracking," Damion replied, while Zapata sat, squinting and rubbing his forehead.

Jon continued, "On drop days, credentialing your drivers will be as smooth as it was this morning. Your drivers will be first in line. And when you get on base, you drive directly to Runway #7—no other stops, whatsoever, no PX runs, no nothing. You gotta take a shit, too bad; do it after or do it on yourself."

"Wait. What about the canine search at the front gate?" Zapata asked.

"Don't worry about that. We've already greased those skids. The gate guards and everyone else are all taken care of," Jim replied.

"Besides, the dogs are only trained to sniff out explosives, not drugs," Jon added.

"You mean 'therapeutic medications,'" Zapata said, using finger quotes.

"Don't be cute," Jon replied with steely eyes. "Every Friday at eighteen hundred hours, we'll all rendezvous here at the deck to discuss the next week's shipments. Payday is every third Friday. We'll do the settling up here, too."

"Speaking of settling up, what's our take moving forward?" Damion asked.

"Ah, yes! It's all about the Benjamins, innit, fellas?" Jon replied. "Here's the deal: there's some sweet and sour in each of your packages. Compensation will be different because of the different levels of responsibility each of you will be taking on. Damion, you will get the equivalent of one hundred K in Bitcoin per delivery that you and Rambo make; Zapata, you will get twenty-five for the deliveries you and your driver make."

"I think the fuck not!" Zapata replied.

"I'm only going to say this once—lower your goddamn voice," Jim warned.

"Listen, Damion will be taking on significantly more risk than you, or any of us, for that matter," Jon explained.

"I'm listening," Damion said.

"If things ever go sideways, there will be a need for a scapegoat. And, Damion, that's you," Jon explained. "All evidence will point in your direction. I'm just being honest here."

"Wait. I am not cool with that. I thought you said everybody was taken care of?" Damion replied.

"They are. But in the very off chance sunlight ever does get shined on our little operation, everybody, from the governments to military officials to Keating Pharma, will need to have plausible deniability. And that's you. You will be fingered as a mastermind, kingpin drug trafficker," Jon said. "No great reward without great risk, right?"

"But, don't worry," Jim interjected. "You'll get the best criminal defense attorneys that money can buy. Money also buys judges. And when you do get free, all your money is still your money. Because it's in Bitcoin, there's literally no way for the government, or anybody else, to seize it if they don't have your private key."

"But I wouldn't dwell too much on that. It hasn't happened yet, and it's very unlikely that it will anytime soon. There's just too much money being made, and everybody's fat and happy, from military brass to politicians," Jon added.

"And you," Jim said to Zapata, "you're gonna be making over a quarter mil a month, just riding around with your thumb up your ass. Be quiet and be happy. You're going home a millionaire."

Damion sat back in a deep sigh and a seconds-long blink. "Is there anything else we need to know?" he asked before reopening his eyes.

"I assume that means you two are comfortable with the arrangement?"

"As comfortable as a concrete pillow. But you still gotta sleep, right?"

"Well, after this tour is up for you two, you guys will be sleeping on a bed of money," Jim replied. "And trust me; that's way more comfortable."

They all laughed.

"Just one last thing," Jon added. "It should go without saying that discretion is the name of the game here. A life-or-death game."

Jon locked eyes with each of them individually to ensure they understood.

"Well, now that all the shoptalk is done, let's have a couple," Jim said in a low, but enthusiastic voice.

He pried the false bottom of the humidor up and filled everyone's empty water bottles.

"Hold up. We're not done just yet. What about my cut from today?" Zapata asked Damion.

# TWELVE

It was between four and five in the morning—payday for Devon. He had withdrawn forty dollars from a nearby ATM and hailed one of the few still-existing taxis home. The chili-party-turned-overnight-life-coaching session he and Makeba had the night before had left him exhausted.

He removed his thick knit hat to form a pillow against the taxi window and slept the twenty-minute ride from Makeba's Northwest D.C. flat to his efficiency in Southeast. He secured his leftover chili close to his chest, protecting it the way a good running back protects a football.

Devon felt his body jerk back and forth against the seat as the taxi braked hard three times in a row.

"We're here!" the driver called.

Barely awake, Devon started to gather himself and his things.

"Thanks a lot, man." Devon put on his knit cap, secured his chili, and stepped one foot out the car door.

He noticed a long, black, late-model Chevy Suburban on the side of his apartment building with the engine running and only the parking lights on. It wasn't the type of car you'd normally see in the neighborhood.

He immediately got back in the taxi.

"This isn't the right place, man. I need you to take me down the street." Devon scooted low in his seat.

"What are you talking about? This is the address you gave me. I put it in my GPS," the driver said in a thick Nigerian accent. He showed Devon his phone.

"Can you just drive?"

"You were about to get out without leaving a tip. Now you want me to drive you someplace else?"

"Please, sir. I'll tip you. Just go."

He pulled off slowly. "Where are we going, sir?" the driver asked.

Just then, the SUV drove up behind them, feet away from the bumper.

Devon hadn't seen the two mysterious shadow men in a while, but this looked like the sort of vehicle they'd drive.

The Suburban's headlights blinded the taxi driver from behind. He pulled over.

Devon's heart raced. He shrank as small as he could.

"I need you to get out of my taxi!"

"Sir, please."

"Out!"

Just then, as the Suburban pulled around on the taxi driver's side, Devon heard a woman call his name.

"Devon, is that you?"

The voice was familiar. He looked closer and realized it was Kate, Congressman Grayton's receptionist. He got out of the taxi.

"Kate, what are you doing here?"

"No time for that. Hop in," she said. "I'll explain on the way."

Devon thanked the driver and shut the door.

"What about the tip?!" the driver shouted through the open passenger window.

Devon waved him off.

"Fucking asshole!" The driver accelerated hard and disappeared down the street.

"On the way where?" Devon asked Kate.

"Just get in! We have to go now," she said.

"Okay, okay. But first I need to go inside and freshen up. I'm still in yesterday's clothes. Give me twenty minutes."

"Go grab a suit, razor, and toothbrush and meet me back here in five. You can clean up when we get there. Hurry!"

Devon darted up the stairs, three at a time. "Shit!" he said as he unlocked his apartment door, realizing he had left his chili in the back seat of the taxi.

He ran to the closet and pulled from a wire hanger a dingy white dress shirt with a black stain on the front. He snatched a pre-knotted tie from the back of a chair. He then stuffed them both in a Walmart bag, grabbed some grooming essentials, and rushed back downstairs to the Suburban.

As Devon skipped down the porch steps to the Suburban, the driver hopped out to get the door for him. But Devon beat him to it.

Devon snatched open the rear door and felt around on the ceiling for a place to hang his clothes.

"What is going on, Kate?" he asked. He climbed inside, glistening with sweat.

"*This* is where you live?"

"Not everyone still gets an allowance from their parents, Kate."

"Never mind that; I've been calling you all morning."

"I turned my phones off because I thought you were Bethany."

"I actually thought I saw her leave your building just before you showed up," Kate said. "Relationship on the rocks, I take it?"

"Never mind that, too," Devon said. "Where are we going?" He looked around and tapped on the dark, three-inch-thick windows. "And why do you have a driver?"

"He's not my driver; he's U.S. Capitol Police. He's part of the congressman's security detail."

"Congressman Grayton doesn't have a security detail," Devon replied. "Only congressional leadership gets a detail. So, unless he's the new Speaker of the House, you wanna tell me what this is all about?"

"Members and their senior staff get temporary twenty-four-hour protection when there's a specific, credible threat against them," she replied.

She passed him an iPad. There was a black-and-white group photo of seven white men, a white woman, and a Black man, all dressed in black judge's robes.

"Okay. What is this?"

"Look closer," Kate said. She minimized the photo and pulled up an AP article.

Devon and Kate braced themselves as the driver made a hard left turn onto Eighteenth Street, barely touching the brakes.

"They're saying the African American pictured is Congressman Grayton in blackface," she said.

"Hence the security," Devon replied.

"Yup, the death threats have already started rolling in. I even got some hate mail. Can you believe that? Little old me?"

The Suburban approached the red-light intersection at Minnesota Avenue and Good Hope Road. The driver activated bright red and blue lights and blew through the traffic signal.

"Well, congratulations, superstar."

"Thanks," she said. "I actually just got an email from *Politico*. They want to interview me about staffer security..."

"Kate, I need you to come back to me. Is it him?"

"Huh?"

"Is the man in the photo Congressman Grayton in blackface?

"Oh, right. Well, that's a question you need to ask him."

"*Me*? Why do *I* need to ask him?"

"Well, you *are* his new spokesperson. Aren't you?"

"Spokesperson? He asked me Wednesday if I wanted the job. I was supposed to give him an answer by six this evening."

"Well, it looks like he's answered for you."

"Where is the congressman?"

"He's holed up in a hotel. We're on our way to him now."

"Wait, so if only the congressman and his senior staff get a security detail, how do you have one? You're just a receptionist. I mean, no offense, but, you know..."

"None taken. This detail isn't for me; it's for you. Spokesperson is senior staff, right under chief of staff. Exciting, isn't it?"

"I guess."

Devon checked his congressional email. There were 210 unread messages. Half were from the big cable news networks: *CNN, Fox News, MSNBC,* and every Post, Times, and Tribune in the country. The other half were from Bethany.

He checked his text messages. There was one from Makeba. It read: "Heard the news. It's do-or-die time. Remember, don't Uncle-Ruckus out on us."

The Suburban rounded Thomas Circle and stopped in front of the Westin, formerly the Vista International Hotel, the same hotel where the beloved mayor of D.C. was set up in an FBI drug and prostitution sting in the '90s.

Kate and Devon got off on the third floor. There was a single officer in a navy-blue tactical uniform guarding the door.

Devon's guard stood at his post at the end of the hall and radioed to the door guard using his clear spiral earpiece.

"Sir, ma'am." The door guard greeted Devon and Kate. He turned and knocked using a coded pattern.

Randy Russo, the congressman's chief of staff, opened the door. It was the first time Devon had seen him in something other than a suit and tie with the top button undone to accommodate his wide neck. Randy's red and black Rutgers Rugby jersey hugged his beer belly, which still showed the vestiges of a six-pack.

Congressman Grayton wore slacks and an old congressional baseball game t-shirt. He was barefoot, his legs on the chair across from him. He was hunched forward over a table with a magnifying glass an inch from his eye, inspecting a page from a thick book.

Papers were strewn over the two queen beds. *Fox News* was muted on the mounted flat screen, while the voices of *CNN* talking heads on an iPad competed with those of *MSNBC* on a laptop.

"Johnny boy! I heard you needed my help." Devon said, using sarcasm and artificial energy as a decoy to hide his exhaustion.

"Just because you got a promotion doesn't mean you're on a first-name basis with the congressman," Randy chided.

"First of all, Randy, I haven't accepted the job yet. Second, and more importantly, everybody's job here seems to depend totally on my presence and participation at the moment, including yours, and including Johnny's here. But pardon me. I interrupted you. Please continue."

"All right," the congressman said. "Enough. Now's not the time, gents. We have a problem. Let's focus on the solution."

"Again, *we* don't have a problem," Devon said.

"Listen, are you with us or not?" Randy said. "If you're not, you should leave right now."

Devon started for the door.

The congressman held up his hand to Randy. "It's okay, everybody. Let's all just relax. Devon, please, have a seat. If there's anybody in this room who deserves an explanation, it's you. Forget the formalities. First names are fine."

Devon stood, arms and legs crossed, leaning against the bathroom doorjamb.

"Ask me what you want to know, son."

"What is it you think I want to know, Johnny? Is it you?"

"Do you believe it's me?"

Devon shot the congressman a piercing look.

"Listen," the congressman said. "In the court of law, the question is never 'Did he do it?' The question is whether they can prove it. I taught you this when you were my law student." The congressman held up the book that contained the questionable photo. "Now, I've been examining this book for the last half hour. There's not a single caption or anything that lists my name or references me in any way. It's a grainy, black-and-white picture in a 1984 law school yearbook. It's impossible to tell if it's me."

"Are you done?" Devon said.

The congressman turned away from the table and leaned forward, elbows to knees, slicking back his few remaining hairs.

"First of all, this is not a court of law, and I am no longer your student. If I decide to help you—*if* I decide to help you—you need to tell me the truth, the whole truth—and as they say in the court of law—nothing but the truth. The burden is on *you*. Now, I'm going to ask you one more time: Congressman Grayton, is that a photo of you with blackface makeup in that photo?"

"Yeah. It's me," he mumbled.

"I'm sorry? I didn't catch that."

"Yes. It's me. It was taken at a Halloween party. I didn't think it would end up in the yearbook. More than that, I certainly didn't account for it going viral on Tweeter and Insta-whatever. This book should be collecting dust in attics and basements. In fact, it took my wife two whole days to find it and overnight it to me. She hurt her back digging for it in the garage."

"It's Twitter and Instagram, sir. And they didn't exist way back then," Kate said.

The men scolded her with their eyes.

The congressman continued, "Me and eight of my classmates dressed up as Supreme Court Justices. We wanted to make it as realistic as possible, and we didn't have a Black man..."

"So, you were Clarence Thomas, the first Black person on the Supreme Court," Randy interjected. "It's all starting to make sense to me now."

Devon, Congressman Grayton, even Kate, the twenty-three-year-old receptionist who was raised in Canada, all looked at Randy in shock and disbelief.

"What?" Randy said with large eyes.

"Randy, you're chief of staff to a member of Congress who sits on the House Judiciary Committee. Yes, I dressed up as the first Black man to sit on the Supreme Court. And his name was Justice Thurgood Marshall, *not* Clarence Thomas. Thomas came over two decades after Justice Marshall took the oath."

"Oh," Randy said.

"Anyway, so, you couldn't find a single Black man in your whole class who wanted to dress up as Thurgood Marshall?" Devon asked while eyeballing Randy.

"No. That's not what I said. What I said was: 'We didn't have a Black man.' In other words, in all three classes—about one hundred and forty students to each class—at the Middle Georgia School of Law in the eighty-three to eighty-four academic year, there wasn't a single Black male student enrolled. There were two Black women, but no men."

The congressman flipped to the back of the yearbook and inserted a pen as a bookmark. "Here." He passed the book to Randy. Randy passed it to Devon.

Devon thumbed through the small black-and-white headshots of the 1984 class. "I see two Black women in your class alone."

"Yes. They were the first Blacks accepted to MGLS. The other two classes didn't have any at all. And none before them either, all the way back to 1896, when the school was founded. When we were deciding who'd dress up as who, I got Marshall only because I happened to be carrying a few extra pounds like 'em."

"I hear you, Johnny," Devon said. "You guys were training to be lawyers and wanted to dress up as Supreme Court Justices. That's actually flattering. And there were no Black male students at the school in eighty-four. I think people can swallow that pill. It's a big pill, but people can get it down."

"Wait, Devon. You're not planning on admitting to the public that that's me in the photo—are you? I thought this was just us talking candidly in the room, you know, strategizing in confidence."

"Johnny, if I do this for you, I have conditions. The first of which is that I will not put myself out there and end up looking like Boo Boo the Fool for you. Sure, your face is impossible to make out in the photo, but the other eight are as clear as day; they aren't wearing any makeup. One of those faces I just happen to recognize as the current lieutenant governor of Alabama. Another bears an incredibly curious and rather uncanny resemblance to you, at least in the face."

The congressman pinched the bridge of his nose, with closed eyes and raised brows. "He's my younger brother, Charles. He was a 1L that year."

"Ha! Your brother! Say it ain't so," Devon said. "It keeps getting better and better. That's probably how you got caught. Needless to say, *The Associated Press* broke this story at two a.m. Don't you think they'd have their ducks in a row before publishing something like this? Don't you think they have concrete proof it's you in the photo? Do you know how easy it is for the media to get in contact with a lieutenant governor, your blood brother, and the other six?"

"As much as I hate to say it, he's right, sir," Randy said. "If you deny this, the media will have a field day with us."

The Congressman swiveled back around to the table. "I know he's right, Randy."

He looked at Devon. "And that's why you are our only hope to get us out of this. You're smart and..."

"And Black?" Devon finished the Congressman's sentence. "Go ahead and say it. Don't blow smoke up my ass."

"Yes, Devon—and being Black gives us credibility."

"Thank you for being honest," Devon replied. "By the way, what is this 'us' and 'our' and 'we' I keep hearing? I don't understand," Devon said.

"I don't get it. I thought you were on board," the congressman replied.

"What I said is: *if* I do this, I have two conditions. And on those conditions, I will not bend."

"Okay—you don't want to be made a fool of. What is your other condition?" the congressman asked.

"I'm serious about this," Devon said. "I'm a Black Republican about to go on the record defending a white southern Republican for wearing blackface. Blacks are already going to fire me up about this. But if I can't thread this needle perfectly, I'm going to get skewered and roasted by them. You don't understand the extent to which I'm putting my neck on the line for you, Johnny."

"I get it," the congressman replied.

"No, you don't get it. That's my point," Devon said.

"You're right. I mean, I don't get it," the congressman said.

"This leads me to my second condition: I run this show."

Randy held up his hands. "Hold on, sir," he said. "I'm your chief of staff. Devon works for me."

"No. Devon works for me. And so do you. You're my chief of staff, and you will remain so, but on this issue, I need you to take second chair. Let Devon drive on this. Otherwise, we're all gonna be out of jobs. This is a private and temporary arrangement only on this issue until it blows over. Right, Devon?"

"Between the four of us and these four walls," Devon answered.

"So, do we have a deal?" the congressman asked.

Devon connected eyes with Randy. "I don't know. Do we have a deal?"

Randy confirmed with a nod while clicking his tongue and exhaling audibly.

"Good, then. And one last thing," Devon added. "This isn't necessarily a condition. But what's a chief of media relation's salary look like these days?"

The congressman gave a knowing smile. "The salary is double and a half that of a legislative assistant."

"Wait, that's almost more than I make," Randy said.

"You're my chief of staff, and you control my office budget. I'm sure you can make it work."

Devon calculated the figures on the ceiling.

"I know *I* can make that work," he said.

# THIRTEEN

"All right. It's quarter to six. Time to get ready. Chop, chop!" Randy said.

"What do you mean 'ready'? I thought that's what we were doing right now, 'getting ready,'" Devon replied.

"No, I mean it's time to shave, shower, and get dressed. Do that fast enough, and maybe you'll have time to brush your teeth."

"Where are we going?"

"We aren't physically going anywhere. You and I are going to take interviews with the networks from right here in this hotel room. Kate brought your laptop from the office, and I have mine. I'm sure you've received hundreds of media queries by now, as have I. It's time to get on TV and defend our boss."

"TV? But we're not ready for that yet. We still have a lot to plan," Devon replied.

"Well, six o'clock ain't gonna wait for us. The East Coast wakes up at six, and we need to be gettin' out of bed with her if we expect her to fix us breakfast. Otherwise, we'll be on the menu. The media will report whatever it wants, with or without our side of the story, and that'll mean the end of the Honorable Johnathan E. Grayton IV, Congressman from Georgia.

"Look, Devon, we got lucky that this story broke in the wee hours on a Friday morning. If we handle this right, it'll be part of the Friday news dump, and it'll get buried faster than Jimmy Hoffa. If we botch it, and this thing carries over into Monday, he can kiss his congressional seat goodbye, and we all will be saying 'Hello' to the unemployment line. *Capisce*? Now, I'll be honest, as chief of staff, I'm not in love with our arrangement, but the congressman is right—you at the helm is our best hope."

"I understand all that. Only thing is, I've never been on TV before, much less live, national news," Devon said.

"It's a piece of cake. I'll give you a few pointers in the shower. Let's go," Randy said.

"I don't care what time the East Coast or anybody else wakes up; I *am not* taking a shower with you."

"I'll take a shower—*in* the shower. You can wash up at the sink."

"How about I just wait for you to shower, and I'll go in after you?" Devon said.

"No time. Let's go now. We'll start you off with something local. How's *FOX 5 Atlanta*? I'll go first so you can watch and get a feel for it."

•••

It was 6:03 a.m. Kate turned on *Fox News*. The lead story was about China closing in on ambitions to land humans on Mars.

"Bless their hearts," Randy said. "They're trying to buy us some time. Switch to *CNN*."

They all waited through a Volvo commercial.

"And now for some disturbing news," an anchorwoman said, starting the segment. "People are shocked and appalled at an image that appears to show a Republican member of Congress from the state of Georgia, Johnathan Grayton, in blackface."

There was a side-by-side image of the yearbook photo next to one taken at a hearing the previous year of the congressman, mouth open, questioning a witness.

"We've reached out to Congressman Grayton's office for a response to the allegation, but we haven't heard back. We'll follow this story closely and keep our viewers posted with new developments," the anchor continued.

"I'm glad they took the time to find a flattering picture of me," the congressman said.

"Kate, I need you to call and set up interviews with the following networks right now," Randy said, combing his wet hair back with one hand and smoothing it with the other. "I'll take *NBC4*, here in D.C. I want you to give them no more than five minutes with me. Devon will take *FOX 5 Atlanta*. His should be five minutes, too. Make sure his interview is after mine. After that, on to the big networks; Devon will take *CNN*, and I'll take *FOX*. And we'll recalibrate after that first batch. You good with that, Devon?"

"Um, no. You're not about to set me up for the okey-doke. I'll take the conservative network and you'll take the liberal."

"I don't think—" Randy started to protest. "It's your show," he grumbled instead.

Within minutes, Kate had arranged the first interview.

"I have you set up with *NBC4* now, Randy."

"Now? Okay, perfect. Forward me the link to their feed," he replied.

"Stand by. Link's O-T-W!"

Randy opened the link to a black screen and the voice of a producer. They had a brief chat, then the producer counted him down: "And we're live in five, four, three, two, and..."

After an introduction and standard pleasantries, the reporter, in her late twenties at most, started the interview: "So, let's get straight to it. I hope you don't mind my bluntness, but there's just no other way to put it: is this a photo of Congressman Grayton in blackface?"

The reporter's boldness straight out the gate caught Randy off guard.

"Well, what the photo depicts certainly appears to be the congressman," Randy said. "Although, it hasn't been authenticated just yet. In this age of modern technology and digital manipulation, it's always best to not rush to judgment. We simply need to wait for all the facts to—"

The reporter interrupted with a follow-up: "But is this the congressman?"

Devon mouthed "Yes!" with big hand gestures, three feet from Randy's face, the laptop between them.

"That's not what I'm saying. I'm simply saying we should not rush to judgment. Things are not always as they seem at first blush. In situations like these, you have to allow space for all the facts to come out."

"All due respect, that's why we have you on the show, sir—to get all the facts out," the reporter said.

"Listen, we're going to have to fall back off this purity standard for politicians. Sure, we should hold them to a higher standard, but we can't hold them to an impossible standard. They're fallible people just like you and me. They make mistakes just like the rest of us. This photo was taken in the early eighties, before Twitter, before Instagram and Facebook. Before even the internet. There's no way anybody would expect a photo taken at a party almost forty years ago to resurface."

"So, Mr. Russo, did I hear you just admit that this is, in fact, Congressman Grayton in the photo?"

"That's not what I'm saying..."

"So, it's not him," she interrupted.

"What I'm saying is we should all calm down and let all the facts come out."

Congressman Grayton began signaling to Randy to cut the interview.

The reporter continued to press, and Randy held his position until time expired.

"Well, that didn't go too bad. Did it?" Randy said, dabbing his neck under the collar with a hotel napkin.

"Didn't go too bad?!" Devon said. "I thought we agreed that we wouldn't deny the photo. What was that?"

"Did you hear me deny anything?" Randy asked, holding up an index finger. "I never denied it; I only questioned it. The name of the game is 'cast doubt.' We don't have to prove or disprove anything. All we have to do is inject a little skepticism in the minds of an already skeptical public and we can survive this. We'll be bruised, but we'll stand to fight another day."

"Hey, listen. Randy could be onto somethin' here," the congressman said. "He damn near fumbled the ball at the end there, but I think his strategy is at least worth a try."

"That is not what we agreed on," Devon said. "Why would you want to confuse people, anyway? You see, this is the problem with our party. Whether it's birtherism, voter fraud, or coronavirus vaccine conspiracy theories, instead of being forthright with the people, we've been deliberately injecting doubt into their minds about things that matter. And it's not right. And it's not happening under my watch. Be a man; take your lumps and let the chips fall where they may. Now, we all agreed that we were going to handle this my way. Did we not?"

"Yup! Sure did!" Kate said.

"So, we're not going to lie, obfuscate, or otherwise muddy the waters about this thing. We are going to speak the truth, and issue an unqualified, full-throated apology."

"You're on with *FOX 5 Atlanta* in about forty-five seconds, Devon," Kate said.

"Me? Now? Live?"

"Yup! Hop on the laptop there, click the link I just sent him, and say all the stuff you were just saying to us."

Kate cleared the congressman's table and spun the laptop around so that the background was a black-and-white wall portrait of the D.C. subway. She plugged two AirPods in Devon's ears.

"Can you hear anything?" she asked.

"Testing, one, two, three," said a voice over the laptop.

"Yeah, but I can only see myself," Devon replied.

"That's fine," Kate said. "You don't need to see. They can see you."

She turned to the congressman. "Sir, the TV—mute it," she commanded.

Devon rubbed his clammy hands together.

"And we're live on 'Good Day Atlanta' with a breaking story that we told you about at the top of the hour—Congressman John Grayton of Georgia's sixteenth congressional district is being accused of having worn blackface in a 1984 law school yearbook photo," started the anchorwoman.

Damion palmed away beads of sweat from his forehead.

"Hands down!" Kate whispered loudly. "You're on TV."

"There still seems to be a question—or at least no one from his office has confirmed—that this is actually him in the picture," the reporter continued. "Well, we happen to have the congressman's chief of media relations, Devon Lee, ready to clear things up for us. Welcome, Mr. Lee, and thanks for coming on the show."

Devon sat frozen, holding onto the sides of the laptop.

"Mr. Lee?" the reporter said.

"Say something," Randy and Kate whispered.

Devon slipped two fingers into his damp collar and tugged. His nervousness had paralyzed him. His mind emptied. He had always been only a cocktail conversationalist. Sitting two feet from a video image of himself, and knowing the interview was being broadcast far and wide, was different from sitting at a restaurant table debating drunk hill staffers.

"Yes," Devon said with a dry throat.

"Oh, good. You can hear us," the reporter said. "Have you spoken with the congressman about this photo? What does he have to say about the allegations that he posed in blackface?"

"What we have to do is put this in context," Devon said. "I mean, this is not birtherism. It's voter fraud—no, um, I mean, Congressman Grayton is not injecting doubt. Um, excuse me. We have to fall back from this purity standard, um."

Randy leaped from his seat and slammed the laptop closed. "Interview is over. What in hell was that?!"

"I, I—"

"You were a bumbling fool," the congressman said.

"Take it easy on him, sir," Kate said. "He was nervous."

Randy watched the *FOX 5* reporter on his tablet.

"Mr. Lee?" the reporter called out twice, before announcing to her viewers that there was a connection problem, then cutting to an Atlanta United soccer commercial.

"I'm sorry. I just didn't expect it to happen so fast. My mind went blank, and suddenly, all my thoughts came crashing in at once."

Elbows on the table, Devon rested his head in his hands and looked down at the closed laptop. From the side of his eye, he could see Kate prompting Randy to say something.

"Uh, um—don't worry, Devon," he said. "It was bad, but you didn't tank us. This was your first time. For all anyone knows, your audio could've been out. Let's focus on what's next. We have about twenty-five minutes before I go on with *CNN*; we're gonna use that time to go over some interview techniques and talking points because you're on with *FOX* right after."

"Hold on. You don't expect me to do that again, do you? I don't think I'm the right guy for this. I'm a laughingstock."

"Actually, no, you're not," Kate said, swiping up on her tablet. "Early Twitter traffic seems to be sympathetic. People are feeling sorry for you."

"That's even worse," Devon said.

"Not really," Randy said. "At the very least, it's taking the heat off of the congressman here. People like you. And if they like you, they'll like him."

"Hold on. Wait. What do we have here?" Kate said. "You just became a meme. *Now* they're laughing."

"That's not helpful, Kate," the congressman said.

"Sorry."

"Devon, I didn't mean it when I called you a fool a minute ago," the congressman said. "I was angry. Now, I thought about what you said earlier about not misleading the public and owning up to my faults and all. I want you to know you're right. Not only is that in line with Republican values, but it's how I was raised, too. *You* reminded me of that. So, you had a little snafu. So what? You're going to get it together and we're gonna fight this thing. If you're still willing to be my chief of media relations, I still want ya. We'll put up a fight and let the chips fall where they may. How's that sound?"

Devon sat back in his chair. "You guys really have faith in me, huh?"

Randy scratched his neck and looked away. Kate jabbed him with her elbow. He snapped his head forward. "Sure we do," "You got this," they said, stepping on each other's words.

"Of course, we have faith in you, son," the Congressman answered after them. "The question is: do *you*?"

"I ordered a few vegan omelets, bagels, and some coffee for us from Bars Bread and Books," Kate said. "I'm sure you're all starved. I know I am. I'm gonna run down to the lobby and grab it."

"Thanks, Kate," Randy said.

"Oh, by the way, I found something interesting on Google. Check your inbox, Devon. I think you'll like it. Be back in a jiffy!"

The men hovered over Devon's laptop. Devon clicked the link.

"What's it about?" Randy said.

"Here, let me sit down, Devon," the congressman said.

His eyes darted left to right over the page.

"I forgot all about this."

"What is it?" Devon asked.

"It's an article I wrote for the *Virginia Law Review* that September, a month before the photo was taken."

Devon pulled the article up on the iPad and studied it, while Randy went over his talking points.

Kate entered with both arms full. The men were so focused, they didn't acknowledge her return.

"Miss me?" she said. "It looks like I'm just in time for Randy's *CNN* spot. Link's already in your inbox."

This segment was different from the others. This time, instead of only being grilled by a network reporter, Randy was set to face off in a split-screen debate style against a professional talking head. His opponent was Marshanda Williams, a witty and fierce Black woman who had come to notoriety after serving as spokesperson for a prominent, ultra-liberal former presidential candidate.

"Here's the question everyone seems to be asking this morning," the reporter started. "Is it him?"

"First off," Randy said. "I want to thank you for giving me the opportunity to address this important matter. I empathize with the African Americans who may be hurt by this photo—"

"Let me go ahead and cut you off right there, Mr. Chief of Staff," Marshanda said. "Here's a little vocabulary lesson: the word 'empathize' means that you understand and share the feelings of someone. Sitting there as a white man, who has never been discriminated against a day in his life, it's impossible for you to *empathize* with Black people. Oh, and by the way, it is okay to say 'Black people.'"

"Excuse me, Ms. Williams. In case you didn't notice, my last name is Russo. I'm a first-generation Italian American. So, I know a thing or two about prejudice."

"Listen, I'm not about to sit here and play 'Oppression Olympics' with you. Do you ever worry about being murdered while running outside? No. When you have an encounter with the police, do you ever think that you might end up on the ground with a cop's knee on your neck? No. So cut the B.S. and answer the lady's question. Is the blackface picture him or not?"

Kate stood Devon up. She removed his tie from his neck, unfastened his top button, and gave him a head-to-toe once-over.

She then signaled to Randy to tag Devon into the debate.

"Um, I'd like to bring on my colleague. Is that okay? He's the congressman's chief media guy, and he'd like to say a few words."

"Get in there," she whispered to Devon like Cus D'Amato to Tyson.

Randy yanked the earbuds from his ears and slapped them into Devon's hand. Devon took Randy's seat.

"Thank you, and good morning, Ms. Williams."

"You ought to be ashamed of yourself, *brother*," she replied.

This time, Devon could see his opponent—an attractive, fair-skinned Black woman. Her hair was pulled back into a ponytail, which rested over the shoulder and onto the lapel of her red blazer.

"Listen, I'm not here to play in the mud with anybody. I'm here to speak the truth on behalf of the congressman. And that's exactly what I intend to do," Devon said to her. "So, to answer your question, Ms. Williams: yes. The man in blackface in that photo is Congressman Grayton, in costume as the first Black person on the United States Supreme Court, Justice Thurgood Marshall. It was flat-out wrong. There's no two ways about it. The congressman recognizes this, and he's deeply regretful and remorseful..."

"Then why aren't we hearing this from him right now?" Marshanda interrupted.

Devon controlled his hands by holding the ends of a pen beneath the table.

"Allow me to finish, ma'am," he replied. "I just want to contextualize this for you: the congressman likely would not have made this mistake if there had been a Black male law student enrolled at the school. You see, in 1984 at Middle Georgia Law School, there was not a single Black man enrolled. Now, if you know anything about Thurgood Marshall, you know that he dedicated most of his early legal career to achieving equality in education. In fact, in the groundbreaking case of *Brown v. Board of Education,* he famously said that 'separate is inherently unequal.' There's something tragically poetic about a white man dressing as a Black man who fought against discrimination in schools, *because* of discrimination in schools."

Devon held up the iPad.

"Now, this is an article Congressman Grayton penned a month before the photo was taken. In this article, he lauded Justice Marshall's work in *Brown v. Board.* You see, he wasn't mocking him. As off-color and flat-out wrong as it was, the congressman was showing that he revered him."

Devon's words disarmed Marshanda Williams, who again pressed Devon about why they weren't hearing from the congressman himself. The reporter ended the segment with an invitation to Congressman Grayton to appear on the show.

"Bravo!" Kate said.

"No, bravo to you," Devon replied. "If you hadn't found that article, we would've been toast."

"Way to go to the both of you," Randy said.

The congressman rocked back and forth in a rolling chair.

"Thank all of you. I mean it. I'll admit, I was nervous at first. But I think we can beat this thing now. And Devon, I knew you had it in you."

"I'm glad he did," Kate said. "'Cause Randy sure didn't. That woman was about to rip him a new one."

"I've had about enough of you," Randy said, smiling and tossing an empty plastic water bottle her way.

"Now, where're those vegan omelets?" the congressman said.

# FOURTEEN

It had been nearly thirty-six hours since Devon had had a proper night's sleep. His performances on the cable news shows were solid and had taken on lives of their own. The networks would play his sound bites once an hour for the rest of the weekend. And for the next two days, the talking heads on each side would quibble over stylistic insignificancies, and pontificate about the congressman's future in politics.

Congressman Grayton was pleased with his team's work. They all left him alone in the makeshift situation room in the early evening.

Devon connected with his security on the other side of the hotel room door. On the way downstairs, he checked his personal phone for the first time all day. Bethany had called twenty-one times; Mama Lee, five; Uncle Butch, once; and Makeba called once as well. He had texts from all the holiday mass-texters, who he'd otherwise never typically hear from.

In the four years that he'd had an Instagram account, he had only posted two times. The first was three years ago when a butterfly had landed on his shoulder at Malcolm X Park. The other was a nature picture, taken just after he'd met Bethany. She'd wanted to go on a five-mile hike at Annapolis Rock, and he'd wanted to impress her. That was also the last time he had intentionally exercised.

Opening Instagram and scrolling through others' curated lives was a mindless routine that happened whenever he looked at his phone. Twelve hours ago, he only had three followers: Bethany, Makeba, and, oddly enough, Mama Lee. When he opened the app that evening, his follower number had increased by 213,000. And he had over 21,000 new comments—15,000 comments under the butterfly photo, the rest under the nature picture.

He reached out to Bethany for the first time since dinner at Bukom a day ago. She answered on the first ring.

"I feel honored. *Devon Lee,* celebrity fixer, finally found time to call little ol' me."

"Listen, after the day I've had, I just need to be comforted. Please cut me a break."

"Oh, I know all about your day. I watched you on television, defending your disgusting, racist pig of a boss. My parents saw it, too. They flew out this afternoon, by the way. Three days early. And they happen to not be speaking to me at the moment."

"I'm sorry about that, Beth. But that's not my fault. You should've told them I'm a Republican."

"Oh, like you told your mom I'm white?"

"Okay, sure. You got me on that. But I certainly would never spring it on her by turning up on her doorstep with you on my arm. Listen, I haven't slept in a while, and I'm pooped. I don't have the mental energy to process more drama."

"I know, I know. But you could've called..."

"Aht, aht, aht," Devon interrupted. "That's drama."

"Where are you?" Bethany asked.

"I'm at an undisclosed location."

"Don't be a smartass, Devon. You're already in the doghouse."

"Okay. If I tell you, will you come?

"Of course."

"With a bottle of that Perrier-Jouët that I like?"

"Two."

"And no drama?"

"Scout's honor."

"Good, then. I was just leaving the Westin on Thomas Circle; that's where I've been taking interviews from all day. I was headed home, but now that you're coming, I think I'll just get a room here, and we can celebrate my promotion and the hell of a day I had. I'll leave a key for you at the front desk and text you the room number."

"Okay, but how about we celebrate just the promotion, and not that you defended white supremacy today?"

"Aht, aht, aht. Drama."

Devon keyed his hotel room door and said goodnight to his bodyguard. The guards would change shifts twice throughout the night.

Eager to catch himself on television, he kicked off his shoes, flopped on the bed, and found the remote. He cringed and quickly clicked away from a channel that was airing his first interview of the day.

Mama Lee called again.

"Hey, Mama."

"Don't 'Hey, Mama' me. If you hadn't answered this time, I was on my way to Hartsfield to catch a flight to D.C."

"I take it you saw the news?"

"My whole church saw the news. With all the calls I've been getting, if I wasn't expecting a call from you, I would've turned my phone off. So, when were you planning on telling me?"

"Telling you what, Mama?"

"Don't you play simple with me, boy. You know exactly what I'm talking about. You told me you work in politics, but I always assumed you were on the right side."

"I am on the *right* side, Mama."

"Get smart with me again, and I'll reach *right* through this phone and yank those lips *right* off your face. You know good and well what I mean. When were you going to tell me you were with the Republicans? I have to learn by seeing my son on T.V., going to bat for a racist white man? Don't you think we have enough good, Black folks out there who could use your voice, and you go give it to a racist who hates us?"

"I'm sorry you had to—"

"I didn't raise you that way, son. I raised you to be Christian and Democrat. The Good Book says to train up a child in the way he should go, and he will not go astray. Well, son, you are as stray as an alley cat. What next? You gonna turn up on my doorstep with a white woman on your arm?"

"Mama, just hear me out."

"Oh, I heard you. I heard you all day. And I saw you. And I'm upset. And you know what else I am?"

"What's that, Mama?"

By this point, he had put her on speaker and placed the phone on the nightstand nearest him.

She paused, then spoke again in a much softer tone.

"I'm so very proud of you, son."

He picked up the phone. His eyes began stinging with tears.

"Really, Mama? I thought you were going to say you were disappointed in me."

"How could I be disappointed? I mean, I'm shocked, and I wish you wouldn't fight for those devils. But I could look into your eyes and tell you were speaking your truth, from your heart. And your father and I taught you that, too. My only other wish is that he was alive to see it, God rest his beautiful soul. I could never be disappointed in you. Lord knows, your brother, Damion, God rest his soul as well, gave me enough disappointment for ten people and twenty lifetimes. But watching the passion in your eyes today could not have made me happier. You were smart, articulate. And I'm no big-time politician like yourself, but what I can tell from down here, it looks like you won. Listen, son. You just keep doing what you think is right. And whatever you do...Are you still there?"

"I'm here, Mama."

"Whatever you do, just make sure to always take God with you."

"Always."

"All right, son. I won't talk your ear off. You get some rest. I love you to the moon and back."

"I love you, too, Mama."

•••

Devon winced as sunlight lit up his vision, and he blocked his eyes with his hand. Peering through it, he blinked and looked up to see Bethany sitting on the bed beside him, the curtains pulled open behind her.

"What time is it?" He felt around for his phone.

"It's quarter to ten. You were passed out by the time I got here last night. We didn't even get to share a single celebratory toast."

"My bad. I was so out of it."

"No worries, I figured you'd probably be too tired to play. Anyway, I picked up a couple of croissants and some fresh-squeezed OJ and coffee from that French spot across the street."

"Sweet. Thanks." He felt around under the sheets and pillows. "Have you seen my phone, babe? My personal one."

"Yeah, it's right here." Bethany passed it to him from the nightstand nearest her.

"Thanks, babe."

"Sure thing. Oh, by the way, Makeba called."

Devon sat straight up.

"Um, why are you going through my phone?"

"*Um,* I didn't go through your phone. She called and her name showed up. Now, the real question is: why is *my* friend calling *you*?"

"It's not what you think, Bethany. If you recall, after your dad accosted me, I left before the food came. So, I was starving. I'd left my last bit of money on the table for the beer I had and didn't even have enough for the bus ride home. Luckily, a kind bus driver looked out for me."

"That's nice, but what does any of this have to do with you and Makeba?"

"I'm getting there. Well, like I said, I was hungry, and she posted on Insta a pot of chili she'd made."

"So, you DMed her and you guys ate chili together on a cold night? How romantic."

"Relax. It wasn't just the two of us. Tim, Seth, and two of her ex-roommates were there, too."

"You don't have any friends of your own. So, you're stealing mine—is that it?"

"Now you're just being mean. Bethany, you have no reason to distrust me or Makeba."

"Except the fact that I was calling you all night. I even stopped by your place. Why didn't you answer your phone if it was just a friendly gathering?"

"We were playing Phone Stack. And I won."

"Obviously."

"So, where did you sleep?"

"That's the other thing."

"Devon!"

"Nothing happened. It was late, and I didn't have money to get home, so I stayed there."

"Why didn't you call me?"

"Because I knew how it looked, and I'd have a hard time explaining it to you."

"So, you slept there?"

"Well, we didn't exactly sleep. Wait. That came out wrong. Nothing happened. We just stayed up talking politics, you know, until my direct deposit hit and I could get home. I didn't want to ask her to get me an Uber, because I was embarrassed, okay? But trust me." Devon cradled Bethany's face. "Nothing happened. I'm a stand-up guy, and Makeba is a good friend to you."

Bethany searched his eyes for the truth.

"I do trust you, but I don't like this at all. I'm going to have a chat with Makeba."

Devon reached for her hands.

"Beth, babe. I don't want this to be a thing. Just leave it alone. Nothing happened, and there's nothing going on between Makeba and me. I'm with you. End of story."

"So, you want me to just pretend nothing happened, Devon?"

He held her hands to his chest. "No, you won't be pretending, because nothing did happen."

Bethany sighed. "Okay," she said. "But please do me a favor and don't spend any more alone time with her. It makes me uncomfortable."

"Um, that's the other thing," Devon said, with a wince.

"What's the other thing, Devon?" Bethany said, snatching her hand away from his.

"She said she'd help me pass the bar."

"Devon, out of all the lawyers you and I know, why is Makeba the only one qualified to help you study for the bar? I've even offered to pay for your bar prep class."

"Bethany, you know I hate it when you throw your money in my face. I hate it even more, now that I know you're a billionaire."

"I'm not. My parents are."

"Anyway, I've taken those classes before. They don't work for me. Plus, she says that in her free time she helps people like me, who have trouble passing. Babe, trust me, I'm not interested in her. And I don't even think she likes me generally—as a person—like not even in a platonic way; I think she was just offering to be polite. But if she does end up helping me, I promise, it'll be just that." Devon reached for her hands. "Are we good?"

"I still don't like it. But if it helps you, I'm on board."

"You're the best, babe." Devon leaned in for a hug. She dodged him and stood.

"I went down and asked for a late checkout, so we have until one," Bethany said. "Although we should probably get back to my place soon, because it's starting to come down out there, and you're parked on the street in an emergency snow route. I don't want you to get towed. I can just get you a parking pass, and you can use the garage in my building."

"What did you just say?"

"I said you're parked on a snow route."

"No. The other thing."

"You can use the garage?"

"Fuck!" Devon said, palming his forehead. "Oh, hell no!"

"What is it?"

"With all the chaos happening yesterday, I missed it."

"Missed what?"

"I got played! He already knew about the story. He's known for days at least!"

"Babe, I need you to calm down and explain."

"Look, today is Saturday. *AP* broke the story at around two on Friday morning. Johnny and I met for drinks on Wednesday evening."

"Who's Johnny?"

"Grayton, Congressman Grayton. Follow me, here. He and I met at The Yard on Wednesday, which is when he offered me the spokesperson job. Are you with me?"

"Yeah."

"When I showed up to the hotel room early yesterday, he was already looking at his old copy of the yearbook."

"Well, maybe he kept it at his place here in D.C. I don't see why, but it is possible."

"No, no, no, no. That would be possible and maybe even marginally plausible, except yesterday, he mentioned that it took his wife two days to locate the yearbook and overnight it up from Georgia. He also said that she had hurt her back digging for it in the garage. It clicked for me when you said we should move my car to the garage in your building. I was just so distracted yesterday by all the commotion—the bodyguard, the bulletproof SUV, the secret hotel room, the reporters—to pick up on it then."

"Not to mention exhausted, considering you were up all night chatting with Makeba."

"Exactly," Devon said, refusing to breathe life into Bethany's snark. "Two days, plus a day for shipping. That's three days. And congressman or not, nobody receives deliveries before five a.m., so he must've had it delivered on Thursday. Three days back from Thursday is Monday. That means..."

"He knew about the story before it broke," Bethany interrupted.

"Right. Three or four days before, at least."

"Okay, but he is a congressman. You can expect him to have advance notice on things like this."

"Sure, but follow me, here, Beth. The problem isn't just that he had advance knowledge; it's that he knew *before* our little Wednesday evening 'bro sesh' at The Yard. *Before* he asked me to be his spokesperson. That means the whole point of the meeting was for me to be his front guy for this blackface thing all along..."

"Because he knew it was about to break, and he needed a Black person to vouch for him," Bethany added.

"Bingo. And who better than a Black guy who was his student—someone who has been his staffer for years? Not some strategist from a boutique PR firm. It's brilliant, actually. Now that I think of it, he never had any intention of running for Senate. That was just a fat-mouth fib of a story to get me to agree to take the spokesperson job."

"And he knew you'd never sign up if you had known from the beginning that it had something to do with him in blackface."

"I'm such an idiot! Why would I allow my ego to make me believe that he'd pick me, a peon, a lowly legislative assistant, who he barely acknowledges, to speak for him in a Senate race? Plus, he's been a congressman for a quarter-century and has never run for Senate. Suddenly he wants to make a bid for another Republican's seat? How did I not see this?"

Bethany massaged his shoulder with one hand. "Don't be too hard on yourself, babe."

"He planned it all out, all the way down to having us meet at The Yard, of all places."

"Well, it must've caught him at least a little flat-footed, since he gave you forty-eight hours to take the job and it broke twelve hours sooner."

"Yeah, but all that means is some ambitious editor over at *AP* wanted to get ahead of everyone else and took a five percent chance of being wrong, so they could be first. *Or* Grayton wanted to use the element of surprise and ambush me so I didn't have time to process. And now that I know how slimy and calculating he is, I'd put my bet on the latter."

Devon began to get dressed.

"Where are you going?"

"I'll be back. He's probably still in the hotel. I'm headed down there to talk to him."

"Just hold on a moment. Let's think about this."

Bethany guided him down onto the bed beside her.

"Grayton is a shrewd politician," she said. "He's been doing this for as long as you've been alive. He has to know that after a good sleep and a cup of coffee, you'd figure this all out. He's waiting for you to act impulsively. Don't fall into his trap."

"So, what do you think I should do?"

Devon flopped his back to the bed, both feet flat on the floor. Bethany lay back beside him. Both stared at the ceiling.

"I don't know yet," she replied. "But for now, do nothing. Spend some time with it. Enjoy the newfound fame. After all, you are one of the few people in this divided country right now who both Republicans and at least a chunk of Democrats like. Your best advantage right now is that he doesn't know that you know; keep it that way until you're ready to strike. If you give that up too soon, you've lost. Let him think you're dumb. Lie low in the grass. And when the time is right, pop up and bite his head off."

"Okay, you're kinda scaring me right now," he replied. "But you do have a point, I guess."

Bethany laughed. "I was raised by parents who rose to the top in a cutthroat business environment. Don't you think I picked up a few things along the way? This is a game of chess, and you're playing a grandmaster. You have to be strategic. Put him in a corner and force his moves."

"Chess, huh?" Devon replied, finding her hand.

"Yeah. My dad taught me. Anyway, don't be scared, babe. I generally only use my powers for good. You'll know when you need to be scared. Or maybe you won't," she said with a playful chuckle.

"Noted."

# FIFTEEN

Damion had become obsessed with Bitcoin. He had an incessant urge to check his account. It dominated chow discussions between him and Zapata. They could spend a whole evening talking about market prices, support and resistance points, bulls and bears. Damion was officially a millionaire now, a couple times over. And Zapata was well on his way.

"Bro, this can't be real," Zapata said. "I'm sittin' on bread—like real money, man. What am I doing? I don't even know why I'm boastin' to the big dog, Damo, here. You probably have, like, ten times my bread."

"I am sittin' pretty, man. I can't even lie," Damion said.

"How pretty?"

"Prettier than all the women in your family put together, plus Beyoncé."

"But you ain't got Beyoncé bread, yet."

"After a few more deliveries, and if Bitcoin keeps jumping in market value, I just might."

"Seriously, bro, how much you got?"

"You know how many drops we've done—do the math. I don't ask you how much you have."

"That's 'cause you pay me. You know exactly what I have."

"How 'bout you stop counting my pockets and worry about your own? Here, pass me that torch."

Zapata took a pull from his cigar, propped his feet up on the wooden bench, and reclined against the deck wall, Damion beside him.

"Just to think," he said, "four and a half months ago, I was arguing with Ma Dukes, 'cause she was asking for my whole check. Fast forward to now, I just moved my whole family out of that cramped apartment in the Bronx to one of those brownstones in Harlem. Paid the rent up for a whole year. I even bought my sis a new car. She wanted a Lexus."

"Are you fucking stupid, Zapata?!"

Damion sat straight up and landed a swift backhand to Zapata's chest. Zapata coughed hard. His cigar fell to the deck floor.

"What the fuck is your problem, man?!" Zapata replied.

"How many times did we talk about keeping a low profile until we made it back stateside? Once you get back home, you can do whatever the hell you want to do with your money. But we all agreed—you, me, Jim, and Jon—right here at this cigar deck, that you and I would be smart and invisible. Shit's supposed to be too easy. All we have to do is ride around all day, get paid, keep our goddamn mouths closed, and go home rich."

"You're making it seem like I told someone what we're doing."

"You may as well have. When people start seeing new money, they get nosey. If the wrong people get nosey enough, they start looking for trails. The point of not spending until we got home was to make sure that the trail ended far away from this place, and far away from our thing here."

Zapata found the cigar on the floor and wiped the dirt from the tip onto his uniform pant leg.

"I was careful," he said. "The car is in my cousin's name, and we didn't buy the house, just rented; that's in my mom's name. The only reason I paid a year out was because she couldn't qualify with her credit."

"I don't give a shit about your mom or her credit. Zapata, I need you to hear me loud and clear: Do not spend any more money. No more cars, no rent, no furniture. I don't care if the baby needs diapers, and your little sister needs tampons. They can shit and bleed all over each other for all I care. If the money doesn't come from your Army paycheck, it doesn't get spent. You trackin'?"

"I'm trackin', man. I just—"

"I don't want to hear it, Zapata."

He smacked the cigar from Zapata's mouth, off the deck onto the ground.

"What did you tell them when they asked where the money came from, anyway?"

"I told them it was an enlistment bonus. None of them have ever been in the Army, so they don't have a clue."

"I take it they don't have the internet either. Damnit, Zapata. I thought you were smarter than this."

"Look, I'm sorry, man."

Damion stood and started to leave.

Zapata grabbed Damion's sleeve. "Hold up. I gotta tell you somethin'."

"What?"

"They're takin' me off the shit detail."

"At this point, I can't say I'm mad about that," Damion said, as he sat back down. "Your stupidity is about to get us all canned."

"I said I was sorry."

"Yeah, tell that to the MPs. But seriously, so what—you're off the detail? You don't have to walk around smelling like asshole all day. Congratulations. Everything comes to an end—sometimes, sooner than you expect. It's a detail, and details are supposed to be temporary. They could call *me* back tomorrow."

"Yeah, but they haven't. I want to keep earning. You're still making money; I want to, too."

"Bro, you're rich already. Do your job, and in a few months, we'll all be going home. Serve out the rest of your enlistment contract and live your life. Don't be greedy."

"That's easy for you to say."

Damion sighed deeply.

"Okay. So, you want to keep earning. Let's think about this. They'll probably send you back to work on the airfield. Just show up early and you can work with our crew packing and wrapping on Runway Seven. You probably won't get paid as much, but it's still a lot more than Army pay."

"Nah, man. They're short-handed in the DFAC."

"What does that have to do with you? Contractors serve the food in the DFAC, not soldiers."

"Yeah, but Army green-suiters supervise and make sure everything is sanitary."

"And they picked you, of all people."

"Yeah, because my secondary specialty is in food services. Went to school for it and everything, eight weeks at Fort Lee."

"Then get in trouble again and get back on the detail."

"That's a no-go, too. My commander told me that if I got in trouble one more time, they'd send me home and chapter me out of the Army with a dishonorable discharge."

"Well, I'm fresh out of ideas, brother. All I can tell you is to save what you made already and invest it. It's still a lot of money. You'll be fine."

"Come on, man," Zapata said. "Don't do me like that."

"What—you expect to get paid without working?"

"I mean, we are battle buddies, right?"

"Yeah, but I ain't your sugar daddy."

"Don't look at it like you're giving me money."

"Then tell me how I should look at it, Zapata."

Zapata crossed his arms over his chest, turned his back to Damion, and then turned back around.

"Like you're paying for a valuable service?"

"And what exactly is that service?"

"My silence."

"You can't be serious, man. Are you threatening me? Last I checked, you were just as involved as I was. So, if you tell on me, you're telling on yourself."

"No, *you* are the fall guy. Remember? All signs point to Corporal Damion Lee, not me. I seem to recall a certain video of you planting a dud bomb. You didn't see my face on that video, did you?"

"You are a piece of shit. You know that? You have more money than you probably ever would've seen in your entire miserable life, because of me. And now you're trying to shake me down? All because you're greedy and jealous. You need to get out of my face and get a life. You're lucky I'm not a snitch. If I went to Jim and Jon with this, you'd be done."

"Tell them what you want. I'm not afraid of Jimmy John. They're all bark, no bite."

"Give me your work phone," Damion said, gripping and yanking Zapata at the sleeve. Zapata jerked away.

"I ain't givin' you shit. You think you're a boss. You're no boss."

"No problem. Since you're big and bad, we'll see what the fellas have to say."

Damion pulled his work phone from his sleeve pocket.

"No, please." Zapata covered Damion's hand with his. "Here. Take the phone," he said, digging it from his breast pocket. "I was just kidding about snitching, man. I'm no snitch. I'm not greedy either. I just..."

"Just what, Zapata?"

Zapata put his hands to his nose as if he was praying, both thumbs under the chin. He teared up. Damion stared, unaffected.

"My cousin. My fucking snake of a cousin. *¡Serpiente!*" Zapata pounded his own forehead with his palm.

"Tell me why I should care about your cousin, Zapata."

"I gave my cousin the private key to my Bitcoin wallet so he could manage it and pay small expenses. He was doing just fine for a couple of months. Now, nobody's seen or heard from him or his girlfriend in two weeks. And when I checked my Bitcoin wallet three days ago—empty. Nada."

"Yeah, and how's that my problem?"

"I just want you to know that I'm not greedy, man. I was just going to set up a new Bitcoin wallet and write the money off that my cousin stole. I figured I had at least another five months to earn. I would've been happy with that and never even said anything to you, but then they took me off the detail, and I'm broke. Back to square one."

"Just out of curiosity, what do you want me to pay you? Because you do realize that *if* I paid you, it would be coming out of my end, right?"

"I know you're a good dude, man. This would mean so much to me and my family—when I get back home, of course. I figure I was making 25K per shipment. I don't even need half of that. How about just ten per?"

"You want me to give you a hundred stacks a month? You are out of your damn mind, man."

"Okay—cut that in half."

Devon calculated the math in his head for the five months.

"I'll give you one hundred thousand. One time. And I'm holding on to it for you for the rest of the deployment. I'll get it to you when we get back stateside, not a minute sooner. You're just going to have to trust me."

"Come on, man. A hundred is nothing to you. You can at least do one hundred fifty."

"When do you start working at the DFAC?"

"They want me there Friday Morning."

"Today is Monday. That means you have two more runs. That's fifty K. So, that's your hundred fifty right there. Look, I'm doing you a solid, take it or leave it. It's not my fault you fucked your money up. You can't say we didn't warn you."

"You're right, man. You're a stand-up dude, bro."

Zapata dapped Damion.

"When are you planning on telling the guys about your move to the DFAC?"

"I was thinking about telling them at our Friday meet-up. What—do you think I should've given them two weeks?"

Zapata laughed. Damion turned and walked away.

•••

Badeed had worked for the Americans since the war had begun in 2001. First, he was an interpreter. For four years, he'd worked on Shindand Air Base, an austere compound in the Herat Province. He'd interpreted for U.S. Army units stationed there who needed to procure equipment and supplies from the local economy.

Once, a young first lieutenant, who had started studying Dari a year before his deployment, caught Badeed cheating the Americans in a deal. It turned out Badeed had been colluding with the Afghan merchants to negotiate a price much higher than the actual value of the items. The scam was simple: he'd identify the requirements, go out into town to "find" a vendor, and then bring the American soldiers into town to make the connection. He'd return to the same Afghan merchant later in the day, without the Americans, for his cut of the profit.

The U.S. military consequently blacklisted Badeed from doing interpreter work for them anywhere in the country. So, he became a driver.

Zapata was fond of Badeed. And Badeed liked Zapata, because he didn't mind pitching in with the work; he didn't just sleep all day like the other military escorts. Zapata would feed the hose into the Porta-Potty reservoir, and Badeed would start the pumping, or vice versa. They were a team.

On drop days, they worked together like a well-oiled machine. Zapata would sling his rifle across his back, and they'd both help the crew with packing and wrapping the drugs onto the pallets.

•••

It was just above freezing on Thursday. The sun wouldn't rise for another ninety minutes.

Badeed had brought Zapata a small container of sheer pira, a popular Afghan sweet.

"You know I love these, man. You're gonna have to give me the recipe so I can have Ma Dukes make these when I get home."

"No problem," Badeed said. "Anything for you, brother. You've been so kind to me."

"And I make you a lot of money," Zapata said.

"That, too," Badeed replied.

They both laughed.

After credentialing, they drove to Runway #7 for the drop.

"Let's rock," Zapata said.

They prided themselves on the speed with which they could finish the drop and get started on their route. Zapata would often even time them. The clock started when Zapata opened the cab door and didn't stop until they were back inside, doors closed. Their fastest time was nine minutes, thirteen seconds, with the help of the on-site pack-and-wrap crew. They were aiming for sub-nine.

Badeed's jingle truck screeched to a halt. Zapata set his timer, and the two jumped down from the cab. One of the crew members had already started fishing bags from the tank. Another had stood ready to rinse them. Zapata and Badeed formed a chain, where they passed each bag along until it reached the wrappers.

Zapata checked his watch. They were at 8:19 a.m. and had just passed along the last bag.

"Badeed, let's go! We're about to beat our record."

Zapata darted toward the truck, and Badeed started after him.

While running, a soldier chased Zapata down from his blind side and drop-kicked him to the shoulder and head. Zapata hit the ground, then popped up immediately, and another larger soldier tackled him back to the ground. Two more soldiers struggled to control his arms and legs. His boot connected with the face of one of them, knocking him out cold.

The others flipped Zapata to his stomach, his rifle still slung to his back. A soldier knelt on his ear. Another straddled him, pinning down his arms.

"*¡Hijo de puta!* Get the fuck off me!" he yelled. He jerked and squirmed, but he couldn't break free.

They waited for him to tire, and then tied his ankles and wrists with 550 cord, a thin but strong, multipurpose rope used for Army parachuting. They tied his wrists so tightly behind his back that his hands bulged, then turned purple.

"Badeed!" he yelled. "Badeed, brother. Help me, please!"

Badeed said nothing. He turned away and walked to the cab of his truck.

Two soldiers tried to carry Zapata the twenty feet to the wrapping station. He bent at the waist and kicked out hard, knocking one to the ground. The soldier got up and the other one dragged him by the collar the rest of the way. Another soldier searched Zapata's pockets and removed both his phones. They then began wrapping him in the plastic, industrial-grade shipping wrap, starting at the calves.

"*¡Mamá!*" he cried. "*Ayúdame, mamá, por favor. Ayúdame.*"

They wrapped him tightly three times, along with his rifle, all the way up to the mouth, leaving his nose, eyes, and ears exposed. Then they laid sandbags on his legs, using more plastic wrap to attach the full bags to him. Then they wrapped his whole body several more times.

Jon emerged from behind a large tractor that had been used to build the landing strip. He sat next to Zapata on the ground, pulling a thick cigar from his cargo pocket. He bit the end, and lit it. He took a long pull and blew the smoke to the sky.

"I hate that it had to come to this, man. I do. Ah, who am I kidding? I never liked you from the start. But what does that matter? You don't have to like a fella to make money with him, right? Anyway, do you remember what I told you the day you guys accepted the offer? If my memory serves me, I think I said, and I quote: 'Discretion is the name of the game. A life-or-death game.' A *'life-or-death game,'* I said to you."

He tapped his ash on Zapata's forehead. Zapata flinched, then squirmed. Tears rolled from his eyes, down the side of his face.

"From day one, I pegged you as a liability. Too dumb and immature to play this very simple, but high-stakes game. And as sure as shit stinks, I was right. You were too eager to spend. Your motives were noble, I'll give you that. You wanted to help out your family, so you sent them some money. That's virtuous—stupid, but virtuous. And Jim and I could've gotten over that. In fact, we were ready to clean up after your little mess with your thieving cousin, and cut our losses with you. The transfer to DFAC duty? That was us. We called in a favor. We were planning to give you a modest severance package, and wash our hands of you.

"And then you showed your true colors. Didn't those Bronx streets teach you anything about what happens to snitches? Jim and I were putting more money in your pockets than you ever would've seen. And this is how you repay us? By threatening to rat us out?"

Jon turned to a soldier. "Hand me the phone." The soldier obeyed, and Jon held it to Zapata's eyes.

"You didn't think we'd bring you into this operation and not keep tabs on you, did you? No. We put spyware on the phone we gave you guys. We monitored every move you made. We read all your texts, listened to all your conversations. We remotely accessed your microphone. So, on Monday evening when you had your little chat with your battle buddy? Yeah, we heard that, too. You know what that makes you? A rat? No. You're no rat. You're lower than a rat. You're shit. And you, of all people, know how we get rid of shit here on Kandahar Airfield."

As Zapata lay on his back, Jon palmed his forehead and pressed down into the ground. He then ashed his cigar just under Zapata's right eye. His cries were muted.

Jon nodded to two of the soldiers.

The soldiers lifted Zapata waist-high and carried him to the truck. One climbed into the cab and hoisted while two others lifted Zapata's mummy-like body from the ground. They dragged him into the sleeper behind the driver's seat.

Badeed took the driver's seat. Another soldier climbed into the cab with him to replace Zapata as his military escort for the day. Badeed put the truck into gear and drove away, Jon following at a distance in the Land Rover.

It was still dark when they arrived at the far end of the Poo Pond. Badeed and his new escort pulled Zapata from the sleeper by the torso, dragging him to the ground and then to the edge of the pond.

They attempted to swing Zapata into the pond, but Badeed wasn't strong enough to lift his end of the body.

"Move out of the way," Jon said to Badeed.

Jon and the soldier lifted Zapata. Jon held him by the head, and the soldier by his feet. They swung twice on Jon's count and released on the third.

"Motherfucker!" Jon exclaimed as a splash of brown liquid spattered on his face and neck. He jerked away, hocked, spat, and wiped away the gunk.

Badeed erupted in laughter.

"Shut up, or you're next," Jon barked.

The sandbags wrapped at Zapata's lower legs caused him to sink slowly at the feet. The pond wasn't deep enough. So, he stood straight up, the waste coming to his shoulders.

"Go get the pole," the soldier said to Badeed. "The pole–you know, the stick!"

Badeed ran to the cab and returned with the wooden pole with the hook at the end that they used to fish out the bags of drugs from the tank.

The soldier used the pole to push Zapata's head under. Zapata's eyes grew large, and his muffled cries louder. His entire body was soon completely submerged until tiny bubbles appeared on the surface.

Jon returned to the Land Rover in a swearing fit.

Badeed and the soldier returned to the truck.

"Have you ever tried sheer pira?" Badeed said to the soldier.

# SIXTEEN

The Army considered a soldier's personal arms to be a sensitive item, especially in a combat zone. Your rifle was an extension of yourself. A soldier wouldn't forget his firearm any more than he would one of his two actual arms.

So, on the very rare occasion a rifle turned up missing, that was a major problem, requiring the stoppage of all nonessential work. Punishment for losing a weapon ranged from a mere counseling statement to dishonorable discharge.

The platoon sergeant and lieutenant did one more pass through the ranks. "Rifle 1027719. That's the missing rifle," the lieutenant said. "Whose rifle is 1027719?"

Every Friday morning, by 1000 hours, the soldiers in Damion's platoon had orders to text a photo of their rifle's serial number up the chain of command, to verify that they hadn't lost it. This was the lieutenant's way of circumventing the weekly in-person inspection requirement. Most soldiers simply recycled the same photo week to week. Once the lieutenant received the "All green" from the platoon sergeant, he recorded the metric and sent his report to his higher command.

But when a photo for Rifle 1027719 wasn't received, this triggered the lieutenant to have to recall all the soldiers from whatever they were doing to show up in person.

"Squad leaders, report!" the platoon sergeant ordered.

The soldiers stood at attention, rifles to their sides. Each of the four squad leaders reported their personnel status.

"All present and accounted for, sar'nt!" each squad leader said as they saluted and reported in sequence.

"Open ranks, march!" the platoon sergeant commanded. The formation of soldiers expanded. He and the platoon leader, a young first lieutenant, passed through the ranks.

The platoon stood erect, now with their M4 rifles held diagonally across their chests. The two leaders passed each soldier to inspect their rifle's serial number. And each soldier recited his seven digits from memory. The platoon sergeant verified visually, and the lieutenant checked off the number in a green canvas notebook.

"Close ranks, march!" the platoon sergeant commanded.

"How in hell can all the soldiers be present or accounted for, but we're missing a fucking rifle?" the platoon leader said.

"We'll get to the bottom of this, sir. Don't worry. I'll handle it," the platoon sergeant said.

Damion cut his eyes left and right. He didn't see Zapata, who was assigned to the squad directly in front of him.

He and Zapata hadn't spoken since the confrontation on Monday.

"Permission to speak, sir!" one of the soldiers in the first rank requested.

"What is it?" the platoon leader replied.

"Well, who does the rifle belong to? Shouldn't you have that in your little green book there?"

"Shut up and stay in your place," the young platoon leader answered.

The platoon sergeant released the formation with orders to turn Kandahar upside down to find the missing rifle. They'd reconvene in one hour.

Damion immediately ducked off inside one of the large concrete bunkers. He called Jim. No answer. He then called Jon. No answer.

His phone dinged, as he received a text from Jim: "Meet at DFAC now."

Damion began power-walking the quarter-mile to the DFAC. Halfway there, Jim and Jon pulled up in the Land Rover.

"Get in."

Damion hesitated, then climbed into the back seat. The three drove away.

Jim and Jon looked straight ahead and didn't bother to address him or each other on the drive. With every silent passing moment, Damion felt a pit in the bottom of his stomach growing bigger. His hands gripped his rifle.

"Where's—"

Jon turned to face Damion, his index finger to his lips.

They pulled up at the cigar deck, the hard stop kicking up a cloud of brown dust. The deck was always empty during midday hours. Today was no different. The camouflage tarp that draped above the deck for shade was also perfect cover in case Jim and Jon had planned to harm Damion.

"Where's—"

"Shhhhh. Just wait," Jon said.

They hopped out of the car and took a seat in a corner of the deck opposite their normal corner. Jim checked around, running his hands under the bench and chairs.

"Goddamn splinter!" he suddenly cried out. He picked a shard of wood from his finger and sucked the blood.

"I know what you're going to say already: 'Where's Zapata?'" Jon said.

"Then where is he?" Damion replied. He sat on the edge of the bench, poised to pop up and run if Jim and Jon had made any sudden moves.

"That was our question to *you*. He missed his drop yesterday morning. And we put you in charge of him. So, *you* tell us," Jim said.

Damion studied their eyes for the truth.

"I haven't seen him since Monday after we got into it about..." he said slowly, now looking at them from the sides of his eyes.

"About what?" Jim asked.

"It was nothing. He just borrowed something of mine and returned it damaged. And when I brought it up to him, he said it was damaged when I loaned it to him."

"What did he borrow?"

"Nothing."

"What did he borrow?" Jim asked, leaning in, a foot away from Damion's face. Damion scooted away to the end of the bench.

"It was just a Bluetooth speaker," Damion said, now with most of his weight shifted to his feet, rather than the benchtop. "My speaker is better than his little one."

"Oh, that's it? Well, you're a millionaire now. You can buy as many Bluetooth speakers as you want," Jim said.

"It's not the speaker," Jon said. "It's the principle. Right, Damion?"

"Right, 'the principle,'" Jim repeated.

"We understand principles very well, Jim and I. A man's gotta have his principles. And he must be willing to kill for them. Isn't that right, Jim?"

Damion grabbed the pistol grip of his rifle. "What did you do to my friend?" he asked through gritted teeth.

"What did *we* do to him? Absolutely nothing. And we resent the accusation," Jon said. "You're the one who had a falling out with him. We should be asking you that question."

"Why would I hurt him over a speaker?"

"I know *I* wouldn't hurt anyone over something like that. But each man has his own set of principles. Who am I to judge?" Jon replied.

"Listen, I didn't do anything to Zapata. He's my friend."

"He was ours, too," Jim said.

"'Was'? What do you mean, 'was'?" Damion replied.

"Freudian slip, my boy," Jim said. "Annoying as he *is*, we still like the kid, and we're going to do whatever we can to help find him."

"Seriously, you wouldn't think we'd hurt our friend, would you?" Jon asked.

Damion didn't respond.

"Would you?" Jim repeated.

"I don't know at this point," Damion replied.

"The answer is 'no,'" Jim said. "I want to hear you say it out of your mouth: 'I don't think you'd hurt Zapata.'" Jim and Jon stood over Damion. "Say it," Jim said.

"*Okay*. I don't think you'd hurt Zapata," Damion replied.

Jim and Jon sat.

"Good. Glad to hear you say that. After all, what's a business relationship without trust?" Jon said.

"Tell, me, Damion," Jim said, "if you two weren't on speaking terms, how'd you know he was missing?"

"He's in my platoon. They had a rifle inspection and one of the M4s was missing. I looked around and didn't see him. So, I assumed the rifle was his."

"And nobody in your platoon figured out he was missing but you?" Jim asked.

"I guess. Not yet."

"Did you say anything?" Jim asked.

"No. As soon as they released us from formation, I called you two."

Jim and Jon exchanged looks.

"Sounds about right for the Army," Jon said. "They'll realize a rifle is gone before they realize the man it's attached to is gone along with it. Man, I sure don't miss being a soldier."

Jim and Jon laughed.

"Listen, we'll do our best to locate him," Jim said. "And you let us know if you hear anything on your end."

Damion tapped the side of his rifle with his fingers in a wave motion. He glanced over his shoulder toward the exit. "Will do."

"Knowing Zapata, he probably slipped and fell into the Poo Pond," Jon said.

Jim and Jon laughed. Damion forced a chuckle.

"Well, I have to get back to my unit, guys. I have about fifteen minutes before I have to be in formation again."

"We'll give you a lift," Jim said.

•••

It took several hours for Damion's unit to realize that Private Zapata was missing along with his rifle. Because he and Damion were normally already out working in the mornings, they were typically excused from appearing at first formation. So, Zapata's absence from the inspection formation didn't ring any alarm bells.

The initial presumption, considering his previous bad conduct, was that Zapata had simply gone AWOL. After about a week, his status was upgraded to MIA. The Americans sent drones and military search teams out into the Kandaharian towns and villages.

The story that had started to gain traction, and would eventually stick, was that Zapata had become very close with his driver, Badeed, and was disgruntled because of his detail duty. The two left the base one day, and neither was to be seen again. They presumably joined the Taliban somewhere in Helmand Province.

Zapata's status was changed from "MIA" to "Deserter."

# SEVENTEEN

After Zapata's disappearance, the practice of texting photos of serial numbers ended for the duration of the deployment. The commander ordered that all future inspections be conducted in person. Damion's platoon leader and sergeant were relieved and replaced.

"Corporal Lee!" the new platoon sergeant called.

"Yes, sergeant!" Damion replied.

"Front and center!"

Damion broke ranks and double-timed to the front of the formation, then snapped to parade rest to await further instructions.

"I need you to report to the personnel shop, ASAP, and then go pack your bags."

"Uh, pack my bags? Roger that, sar'nt."

When Damion snapped to attention, he and the platoon sergeant exchanged salutes, and Damion double-timed off to the personnel shop at company headquarters.

There, he met the young female captain who ran the shop. She invited him to sit and left the office, then returned with the battalion's chaplain. She handed Damion a brown clasp envelope and waited as he read the letter inside.

The document was from the American Red Cross. Damion began to read:

"With deep condolences, we regret to inform you that your father,

Germaine Percy Lee, has died..."

He crumpled the paper, without finishing, and rested his head on the captain's desk. She stood and placed a hand on his shoulder. The chaplain offered a prayer, to which Damion declined.

"We're sorry for your loss, Corporal Lee," she said in a subdued tone.

After a brief pause, she continued: "We're gonna need you to contact your family as soon as possible. They're expecting a call from you. Soldiers are ordinarily authorized two weeks of emergency leave to their home of record, before having to return to duty in-country. But since we are under two months away from end-of-tour, the commander has authorized you to stay stateside—no need to return to Afghanistan. You'll just have to report to Fort Benning to link up with our rear element. How does that sound?"

"Thank you, ma'am," Damion said. He un-balled the letter, smoothed it out, and folded it before putting it in his pocket.

He found an empty corner inside the MWR, connected to the building's Wi-Fi, and plopped down on a beanbag. He pulled his uniform cap from his cargo pocket to cover his face. And he sobbed for a half hour. The white noise of the world around him concealed his cries.

•••

Damion called his brother.

"I've been trying to reach you, man," Devon answered.

"I know, bro. Things are super busy out here, and with the nine-and-a-half-hour time difference, it's hard to keep up."

"Yeah, it's two a.m. here in Macon right now. But you know you can call any time, man. I take it you got the Red Cross message?"

"Yeah, about a half-hour ago. How's Mom holding up?"

"She's a wreck. She's been wanting to speak to you. I'd put her on the phone, but she's been a crying mess all day and just finally lay down about an hour ago. She could use the rest."

"What about you? How're you doing?" Damion said.

"It hasn't hit me yet. I've just been focused on making sure Mama's okay. It is weird being in the house without Dad, though—you know, seeing his things and all. Mama used to fuss at Dad about not dumping the little tin bucket that he'd ash his cigars in. I went to dump it today and she had a fit."

"She's still in shock. Just look out for her. Do they know what happened?"

"He had a stroke from high blood pressure. You know how Mom loved to cook; I guess all the salty greens, fried chicken, and pig's feet over the years just caught up to him. The stress, too. He always tried to play everything cool, but he bottled a lot of stuff in. So, I'm sure that played a role."

"Well, they're sending me home. I don't have to come back out here, though. After two weeks, I just have to report to Fort Benning. It's only about two hours away from Macon."

"That's good. It'll be good to see you, brother. Mom certainly needs to see you.

"It'll be good to see you, too. By the way, how's law school?"

"You see why you need to keep in touch? You miss things when you don't. I graduated back in May and moved up to Washington, D.C., shortly after. Got a small apartment, a job on Capitol Hill. Been there for a month. I'm still trying to figure things out, and I don't have any friends yet. I drove down to Macon when I got the news that Dad was in the hospital."

"Man, congratulations! I can't believe it. The Lees have a lawyer in the family. My bro, Dev, a whole lawyer—an ashy-ass boy from Alphabet City. Now you're big time in D.C. That's awesome, man. I'm sorry I missed the graduation."

"It cool. You know Mama was hoopin' and hollerin' the whole time. She had signs, balloons, the whole nine."

"I know she did. I would've been hoopin' and hollerin' right there beside her, though. That's a big deal. You're a lawyer now and I'm proud of you."

"Well, I'm not a lawyer yet; I still have to pass the bar. I took it back in July and missed it by a few points. I'm getting ready for the February exam now."

"You'll blow it out of the water this time, I'm not concerned about that. Either way, I'm still proud of you."

"No, I'm proud of *you*. It's been a long time coming for you—all those run-ins with the law. We thought for sure we'd be either talking to you from the other side of the glass, or the other side of the grass by now. But you proved us wrong and turned your whole life around. I remember when you had just gotten released from jail that one time, and I told you that that was the last straw for me. I guess that was the tough love you needed, huh?"

"To be honest, it was. That, and I was tired of going in and out of the system, anyway. I saw what it was doing to Mama and Dad. But I have you to thank for getting me on the right track; I would never have passed the GED without your help. Hey, maybe I can help you pass the bar!"

They laughed.

"It was my pleasure. Now look at you—a decorated combat veteran."

Damion looked down at the desk where his work phone that Jim and Jon had given him was. He covered the phone with his uniform hat.

"Man, aside from mortars landing here and there off in the distance, I ain't seen a lick of combat."

"That's good. But I'll bet that's not what you're going to tell the women when you get back, old Forrest Gump ass."

The two laughed.

"When will you be home?"

"Probably in three or four days. It's a long trip."

"All right, bro. You be safe."

"You, too. Keep your head up, and take care of Mama till I get there."

"And you just keep your head down till you get home."

"You got it, bro."

•••

Jim sent Damion a text that read: "Outside."

Damion had been at the passenger terminal, waiting for a Space-A flight for seven hours. Even though soldiers traveling on emergency leave were a priority, he could expect to be waiting for another half-day.

Outside the terminal were Jim and Jon in the Land Rover. Damion hopped in the back. He still didn't trust Jim and Jon, but in front of the terminal with dozens of passersby, he felt no immediate threat to his own safety.

"Sorry about the bad news, brother," Jim said.

"Thanks, man," Damion replied, handing Jim the work phone.

"You've made us a lot of money. We're gonna be sad to see you go," Jon said.

"We aren't the sentimental type, but we just wanted to give you a token before you left. Just a little parting gift from us." Jim passed Damion a package.

"Oh, great—another fake bomb."

Jim and Jon laughed.

"Not this time, my friend. It's three dozen Cuban Montecristos."

"Oh, so the feds can arrest me as soon as I touch down in Atlanta for smuggling Cubans? I'll pass. Thanks, though."

"Take the cigars. You'll be fine," Jim said. "They're not searching for Cuban Cigars. Plus, we removed all the labels. It would be impossible to tell they're Cubans unless the cops smoked them themselves."

"Well, thanks," Damion said.

"I guess this is it, then," Jim said.

"I guess it is. You guys gonna live without me?"

"Rule number two in this game, right after discretion, is: everybody's expendable," Jon said. "Turnover is expected. Anyway, we've been grooming a new guy for the last month to take over your route. We think he's about ready."

"Good luck with that."

"And good luck to you," Jim said. "Just remember: don't draw attention to yourself by spending too much too fast. And discretion is still the name of the game."

"For sure," Damion replied. "Peace out."

"Peace," Jim and Jon replied.

They all bumped fists, and Damion climbed out. Jon put the Land Rover in gear, and the two drove away.

Damion opened his package on the curb, removed a cigar, bit the end, and had a smoke.

Within a few hours, he had boarded a U.S. Airforce C-5 jet, configured for passengers and cargo. The passengers strapped themselves into net seating along the plane's walls, and two fifteen-ton MRAP tactical vehicles the size of elephants were chained down to the center of the plane.

Damion inserted his earbuds and zoned out to JAY-Z. Four hours later, he touched down in Kuwait. After an overnight at Camp Arifjan, a relatively plush American military base, he boarded a shuttle bus to Kuwait International Airport, where he caught a commercial nonstop flight to Hartsfield-Jackson Atlanta International Airport.

•••

It had been eleven months since Damion had left for Afghanistan.

He had once flown to Fort Lee, Virginia, for some training when he'd first joined the Army. Besides that, he had never left the state of Georgia, much less the country.

When the plane's wheels touched down, his heart palpitated, partly due to flight anxiety, but mostly because he was excited to be home. He thought of the spread Mama Lee was sure to have ready when he got home.

Damion checked his account. He had earned nearly seven million U.S. dollars in Bitcoin from making drops for Jim and Jon. He'd watched the market balloon over the months, and by the time he made it home to Georgia, the value had more than doubled, worth over seventeen million. His heart pounded harder.

He still had just over a year left on his enlistment contract but had thought daily about ways to get an early discharge for some medical condition he could invent for himself.

A volunteer patriot group had tracked all the military flights coming in from overseas. Dozens of them cheered with signs, balloons, and mini-American flags that they waved for the troops as the escalator carried them from the terminal.

Damion scanned the crowd. He soon heard the sound of Mama Lee's voice slicing through the airport hum and crowd cheers.

"Yea, though you walked through the valley of the shadow of death, you feared no evil. Hallelujah!"

She stood between Devon and Uncle Butch.

The volunteers had laid down a twenty-five-foot red carpet for the troops to walk as they exited the terminal. A sparkling red, white, and blue "Welcome Home Troops" banner extended half the length of the carpet above the exit doors. The crowd stood on the other side of a velvet rope. Two speakers on tall stands began to fill the space with Lee Greenwood's "God Bless the U.S.A."

Small kids sat on parents' shoulders holding personalized signs for their soldier. Wives cried. Siblings, children, and friends shouted the names of their returning veteran. A boy gave a young, Black soldier his mini flag. In return, she ripped a subdued Velcro American flag patch from her right shoulder and gave it to him, making his day.

As Damion walked the red carpet, he was moved by the big smile on Mama Lee's face and her teary eyes. He had seen that expression many times before—but only for his brother, never him. Damion had made his mother proud.

He video-recorded as he approached his family at the end of the carpet. Devon videoed Damion, too. Mama Lee extended her arms, while Uncle Butch stood in a Superman pose, wearing a "Vietnam Veteran" hat and a pair of dark aviators.

A jolting bump from behind almost knocked Uncle Butch to the floor.

"Make way! Step aside! I need everyone to step aside!"

No fewer than fifteen police in tactical gear had suddenly parted the crowd. Some had "ATF" and others "DHS" printed on the chests of their armored vests. They all carried assault rifles and pistols.

Damion moved to the side to allow the officers to pass. His eyes grew large when they continued straight towards him.

An officer snatched Damion by the sleeve and shoved him to the wall. With a forearm to the back, he bent Damion's arm behind him until he could touch the nape of his own neck.

From the speakers now played Irving Berlin's "God Bless America."

Another officer pulled Damion's bag away and passed it off.

The music stopped. The crowd froze and looked on in disbelief. It was now so quiet that everyone watching could hear the sound of the plastic zip ties clicking as they tightened around Damion's wrists.

"They're just cigars!" Damion shouted. "All this for some goddamn, motherfucking cigars?"

"Corporal Damion Lee?" a female officer asked.

"And y'all gonna do this in front of my family?! My Mama?! All these people?! I'm a veteran! I just got home from Afghanistan! I've fought for this country!"

The officer pulled Damion's wallet from his back pocket to find his I.D.

The crowd buzzed, then booed and hissed. Half recorded on their smartphones. A mother buried her son's face into her thigh. The boy's Velcro American flag patch fell to the floor.

"Is all that even necessary?!" shouted an older Black man.

"Let go of my son!" Mama Lee unhooked the velvet rope.

With one side of his face pinned to the wall, Damion watched helplessly with one eye as an officer restrained his mother from moving to the scene.

The female officer read Damion his Miranda rights, while two large, muscular officers handled him by the biceps, walking him off.

"Y'all could've waited," Damion sobbed, his chin pressed hard into his chest. "This ain't right. Y'all didn't have to do me like that in front of my family."

"Not again, Damion!" Mama Lee cried. "Not again. We believed in you!" She stomped with one foot, driving her tan orthopedic into the floor repeatedly.

The officers moved him within feet of Mama Lee. He could hear Uncle Butch say to her, "It's time to go, Joan. Let's get out of here."

He watched over his shoulder as Uncle Butch ushered her away by the hand, with consoling pats to the back.

Devon trailed behind. He watched as his brother grew smaller in the distance.

# EIGHTEEN

It had been seven months since Damion had left Afghanistan. He never thought he would be returning. His unit had long since finished its yearlong tour and gone back to Fort Benning, Georgia.

This time, Damion was on Bagram Airfield, northwest of Kabul and about 650 miles from Kandahar.

The C-5 landed just before four in the morning. Damion's wrists and ankles were shackled. A chain wrapped his waist and was secured to bolts on the plane's wall and floor, such that Damion could only sit upright for the nineteen-hour flight. He wore an Army camouflage uniform with no patches, nametag, or rank, and a pair of grimy Reeboks with no laces. Three sizes too big, the sneakers were wrapped with duct tape around the tongue and sole by his guards to keep them on.

A black hood covered his head and face.

He only briefly felt the crisp mountain air, as guards guided his short steps onto an up-armored military ambulance that they had backed onto the plane's ramp to minimize Damion's exposure.

The ambulance, repurposed as a paddy wagon, transported him to yet another detention facility, where he'd sit in confinement for weeks.

Damion had spent the previous seven months, following his arrest at Hartsfield-Jackson Airport, hopping around from solitary confinement cells in various federal prisons while three-letter agencies quibbled over jurisdictional issues related to the investigation. The Secretary of Defense prevailed over the DHS, CBP, DEA, and FBI. Since Damion was still on the Army's payroll, they'd finally transported him back to Afghanistan to stand trial by military court-martial.

Having a trial 7,500 miles away from American soil allowed the Army to control any negative press coverage, or exposure, altogether. Although some media outlets would station their journalists on the base, the chance of a full-on media frenzy there was zero.

Such was the case for Damion. His press coverage amounted to a two-inch block in the *Stars and Stripes* newspaper, probably ghostwritten by some Army public affairs officer.

Damion's court-martial ended after only two and a half days, with the presiding judge, a two-star general, convicting him with one count each of wrongful introduction, with intent to distribute, and wrongful importation of opium. He was sentenced with a dishonorable discharge and fifteen years total at the Fort Leavenworth maximum-security military prison in Kansas.

It turns out, just as Jim had promised, transporting the three dozen Cubans hadn't been a problem for Damion after all. In fact, the corrections officers at the various prisons he'd been housed at even allowed him to smoke the cigars during his one-hour outdoor recreation time.

After the trial, military guards transported Damion in the same patchless uniform that he'd arrived in downstairs through a damp, dimly lit underground tunnel, back to the detention building, which connected the nondescript court building. There, he would have to wait. Maybe for days, maybe for weeks, or longer.

Damion welcomed the long wait, however, because at least he wasn't in solitary confinement anymore. He had a cellmate, a Black private first class from Baltimore. He was awaiting court-martial for allegedly shooting his lieutenant during a skirmish with the Taliban.

The underground detention facility was dungeon-like. There were no windows, so there was no way to tell the time of day, except by the meals they were served. The gray, unpainted cinder block walls were rough and cold to the touch. There was poor ventilation, so the air was stale. Fluorescent lights flickered and shut on and off automatically when it was time to sleep or wake, or whenever they wanted.

Damion found the twin mattresses, however, to be surprisingly comfortable. He slept for much of the first three days following his conviction, while his cellmate read.

•••

Damion executed a series of perfect bridge shuffles. The cracking of the playing cards eased his anxiety.

"Do you mind, bro? I'm trying to read, and that's kinda distracting," his cellmate, Oni, said.

"Oh, my bad, man. Just bored," Damion replied. "Do you know how to play Tonk?"

"I'm from *Baldamore*—of course I know how to play Tonk," he replied, looking over the top of his *Bikes and Beauties* magazine. "Me and my cousins from D.C. used to play all the time."

"I have a twin brother who lives in D.C." Damion slid a metal chair between their bunks to use as a playing table, scraping the concrete floor. "What type of name is 'Oni' anyway?" Damion asked as he dealt out five cards each.

"It's my name," his cellmate replied.

"I mean, where's it from?"

"My father is from Nigeria."

The two began to gamble for each other's desserts from future meals. Brownie, chocolate chip cookies, or pound cake seemed to be the options for lunch and dinner. Glazed donut or banana nut muffin was the breakfast sweet. Oni was up by three.

Oni kept score on the back of a letter envelope. When he ran out of writing space, he rifled through a stack of magazines and newspapers before eventually just ripping the blank page from the front of a paperback novel.

A passport-sized headshot photo printed in one of the old newspapers caught Damion's eye.

"Hey, hand me that paper," he said.

Oni passed Damion the three-month-old newspaper. Damion grabbed it and started reading.

Oni's shuffle wasn't as crisp as Damion's. He slid the deck across the chair and waited for Damion to cut it.

"What the fuck!"

"What is it?"

*Soldier Found Dead After Accidental Drowning in Waste Disposal Repository*

This was the headline of the below-the-fold article. The photo was a three-year-old Basic Training picture of Private Omar Zapata.

"Oh, that?" Oni said. "Yeah, that was some trifling shit, literally."

"I know this dude," Damion said. "He was my battle buddy—we were deployed down in Kandahar together."

"Aw, man. Sorry to hear that," Oni replied. "I was stationed on Kandahar, too, a few months ago. Matter of fact, I was there when they found the body. I'm an MP—well, I *was* an MP. Anyway, I was there, and heard the original dispatch come over my police radio."

Damion had begun carefully folding and ripping the photo from the newspaper to keep.

"And, let me tell you, bro," Oni said. "That wasn't no damn accident."

"What do you mean?"

"First of all, who goes anywhere near the Poo Pond voluntarily?"

"Well, he was on the shit detail with me, so he had to. But that is a good point. Even we didn't get close to the edge, not enough to fall in, anyway."

"Right. And, not only that. Hear this." Oni leaned in over the chair. Damion leaned forward, too.

"When the call first came over the radio and they were fishing him out, I swear they said he was wrapped in plastic, with his feet and hands tied up. He even still had his weapon slung on his back," Oni said in a throaty whisper. "I'm not crazy. I know what I heard. But when I looked at the official report, none of that was in there. It just said 'Accidental drowning.' But that wasn't no accident. Somebody killed that man, and it's being covered up. I'm sure of it."

Oni sat back on his bunk. "But what do I know?" he said no longer whispering. "I'm just a private about to get a dishonorable discharge and probably twenty years in prison."

"Motherfucker!" Damion shouted. He pounded the mattress with his fist. The thin bedding barely gave. "I knew it! I fucking knew it!"

Damion sprang to his feet and paced the six-foot length of the cell, from the iron bars to the cinderblock wall.

"It's messed up, right?"

"Keep it down in there!" the military guard yelled from the end of the hall.

The same guard, a corporal, returned fifteen minutes later with a stainless-steel cart carrying a few dozen trays of food.

Oni popped up and grabbed both trays through the opening in the bars. He placed Damion's tray on the mattress beside him, swiped the donut wrapped in cellophane, and flopped down on his own bed.

Remaining on his tray were eggs, grits, sausage links, fruit medley, and a plastic cutlery packet. There was also a mini box of plain Cheerios, and a small, plastic container of 2 percent milk. There was no bowl. The idea was to pour the milk over the cereal directly in the bag inside the box, and eat from that. Damion normally saved the dry cereal to snack on later in the day.

The guard would return in twenty minutes to collect the empty trays.

Damion finished in five. He gulped down the milk and grabbed the cereal box to store under his bunk.

He shook the box, held it to his ear, and then shook it again.

"What is it?" Oni asked.

"I don't know. Something's in the box."

"Yeah, it's cereal. If you don't want it, give it to me. I'll use it as a topping on my extra donut," Oni said with a chuckle.

"No, I mean, there's something else in here. The weight is off."

"Well, open it."

"Hell no. You open it."

"All right. Give it here."

Damion placed the box on the chair. Oni picked it up.

He dumped the contents on his tray. "Oh, shit. It's a cell phone," Oni said. He picked it up and blew the cereal crumbs away.

The phone was small and basic—no touch screen, only actual buttons.

"Well, give it back," Damion said.

"Nope. Finders, keepers."

"What are we, seven? Hand it over. It's for me." Damion was getting agitated.

"How do you know it's for you? I know people in high places. It could be for me."

"Give me the fucking phone," Damion said.

Oni powered it on.

"Wait, there's a text message," he said.

Quietly, Oni read the message aloud in a low voice: "DL, call ASAP. JJ."

"You see? 'D-L.' Stands for 'Damion Lee.' That's me." Damion passed Oni one of his court documents so he could confirm the name.

"Lucky mofo." Oni tossed the phone to Damion, who fumbled the catch and then picked it up. "I got next," Oni said.

Damion waited for the guard to return for the empty trays. Once the guard left and Damion heard the steel door slam at the end of the hall, he made the call.

He scooted back on his bunk, into the corner of the cold walls. He covered his head with the green wool blanket.

"Let me know if someone comes," he said to Oni.

Jim picked up on the first ring.

"Welcome back to beautiful Afghanistan! I bet you thought you'd never hear my soothing voice again," he said.

"Let's cut to the chase. Whatever happened to nobody getting caught? You guaranteed that this was an easy operation—just make the drops, and get paid. That's what you told me."

"Whoa, whoa, brother. First of all, I need you to mind your mouth. This is an unsecured line," Jim replied. "Second of all, neither me, nor my partner guaranteed you anything. What I said was: nobody has ever *gotten caught,* which was true at the time. There was a one in a million chance that you would. Well, I guess you're the lucky one. But listen, we told you on Day One that you'd be the fall guy, and you agreed—you went into this thing eyes wide open. This was your choice. We even gave you an out."

"And what happened to my lawyer? You said that if things went south, I'd get the best legal representation there was. I was stuck with some brand-new JAG from a poo-putt law school, who never even objected to anything."

"Yeah, man, sorry about that. They threw a monkey wrench in the plan. We didn't expect them to send you back over here to stand trial; we thought if you ever got caught, they'd try you stateside. Even though you had the right to a civilian lawyer, there aren't many private attorneys willing to pack it up and fly to Afghanistan. Even if one was willing, there'd be a mountain of red tape to cut through. That was totally unexpected and out of our control."

Damion heard Jon's voice on the line.

"Listen," Jon said. "Okay, so we dropped the ball a little by not planning for this, but it's not over. You still got an automatic appeal left, and our lawyers are all over it. They say you've got a good shot, so you're in good hands now. But no guarantees. Even if, by some turn of events, you lose on appeal, you're still young. It's fifteen years; keep your head down, your mouth shut, behave yourself, and you won't even do half that. You're a strong kid. The most important part is that you were a stand-up man in the courtroom. We followed the situation since the day you got pinched in Atlanta, and you never folded. So, to that, me and my partner here say bravo, brother. *Ben fatto!*"

"'Pinched'? This ain't some episode of *The Sopranos,* and you ain't Tony. This is real life," Damion said. "It's my life."

"Just out of curiosity," Jon replied, "have you checked your Bitcoin balance recently?"

"Yeah," Damion replied. "We have high-speed fiber-optic cables, two hundred megabytes per second, running through each cell. Are you kidding? No, I haven't checked it lately."

"Fair point," Jon said. "Well, you'll be pleased to know that the market has quadrupled. What you earned with us is now worth almost forty million. And that's in USD. As long as you don't forget your private key, you, and only you, will still have access to it. It'll be there waiting for you when you get out. Who knows? It could be worth a hundred million by then."

"Yeah, that sounds nice and all, but I might not even survive the first year at Leavenworth to spend a nickel of it. While we're on the topic of not surviving, what did you do to Zapata?"

"Zapata? I don't know what happened to your shoe," Jon said.

"What are you talking about?" Damion replied.

"Don't know why you're speaking Spanish to me. But I heard that your *Zapata* was laced up tightly and thrown away. It was cheaply made and had started to fall apart. When shoes start to fall apart, that's what happens to them, right? They get thrown away. We will search and find them anywhere—under the bed, behind the sofa—and when we find them, we tie them up, and we throw them away. Now let me ask you this: is the other *shoe* starting to fall apart?"

"First of all, Spanish for 'shoe' is *zapato*. And fuck you. Fuck your partner. And fuck your threats."

"Careful, brother. You've been doing great so far. Don't poo in the pond of goodwill now—pardon my pun. I need you to follow me here: your *favorite shoe* is the only reason the other shoe was put away in a box. It started leaving footprints. And those footprints led all the way back to its mate. Get my drift?"

"He didn't deserve what you did to him. You are evil. I think there's a lot of other loose *shoes* that need to be stored away in their boxes."

"You don't mean that," Jon said.

"I'm not afraid of you."

The line went dead.

# NINETEEN

"I thought you were supposed to be one of the best law firms money could buy. It's been seven years. I'm rotting away in here."

Winston Nightingale Esquire was a slight man. His shoulders were narrow, and his shiny, black, Superman-style hair matched his thick plastic frames. His navy-blue suit was tailored to fit every slope and contour. His Super 150 thread count suit almost shimmered in the fluorescent white lighting. Exactly forty, he appeared no older than twenty-five.

He sat with perfect posture on the edge of the folding chair, both his Salvatore Ferragamo loafers flat on the floor beneath him.

"Corporal Lee..."

"I'm no longer a corporal. Remember? *Dishonorable discharge?*"

"Forgive me," Winston said, sliding his glasses up a pointy nose. "Mr. Lee, you can be assured that we're doing everything we can over at The Arcum Firm. We have committed four attorneys to your case, including a senior partner; appeals are just notoriously slow. We submitted the brief within three months of your sentencing. The Army Court of Criminal Appeals affirmed the court-martial decision. Now, we're just waiting to see if the U.S. Court of Appeals for the Armed Forces will review your case. And, honestly, there's no guarantee. If we're unsuccessful there, it's the U.S. Supreme Court, which is a long shot."

"You aren't telling me anything you didn't tell me two weeks ago. Or two weeks before that."

"I'm sorry, Mr. Lee. This is just where we are for the time being. Hang tight. We still may have some legal tools at our disposal."

"So, if you don't have any news for me, why are you here? You work in Washington, D.C., right? Why fly all the way out here to Kansas every two weeks to feed me spoonfuls of nothing?"

"Mr. Lee, Arcum sends me here to put your mind at ease—so you know we're working for you, and that you're not just a file on our computers. It's our policy to give our clients regular updates, even if there aren't any updates to give."

"You know what I think?" Damion said. "I don't think they put you on a private jet twice a month to the middle of nowhere to put *my* mind at ease. I think they send you here to keep *their* minds at ease. You're not here to give me updates; you're here to update them. I think your only job is to keep an eye on me. To make sure I don't crack and expose your little black market pharmaceutical operation. Don't worry, I haven't let the cat out of the bag. Not yet, anyway."

"Mr. Lee, I need to caution you against saying anything incriminating. They could be listening."

"I thought anything I said to you wouldn't be admissible in court. The whole '*attorney-client privilege*' thing," Damion said with finger quotes.

"That's exactly right. But just because they can't use it in court, doesn't mean they can't use it. Look, Mr. Lee," Winston said, capping his Montblanc pen. "Is there anything I can do for you? Are they treating you okay? Are you getting enough to eat? Trouble with any of the inmates? Guards? We can request to have you moved to another pod, if so."

"Unless you can somehow shrink me and smuggle me out with you in that briefcase of yours, I'm good. You can go report back to your people that I haven't ratted them out."

Winston flipped forward the pages of his legal pad and closed his personalized leather portfolio over it. He stood, collected his briefcase, and started for the door.

"Actually, there is something," Damion said, just as Winston had knocked for the guard. Winston signaled the "Never mind" through the reinforced strip of glass.

"Yes, Mr. Lee?"

"You have a D.C. area code, right? My brother lives there, and I've been trying to reach him, but he won't accept calls from here. Can I use your phone? Maybe if he sees a local number, he'll answer."

"I'm not supposed to—"

"You asked how you could help me. I need to use your phone."

Winston frowned and threw up his hands. "Okay, but make it quick." He pulled his iPhone from an inside coat pocket and placed it on the stainless-steel table, turning his back against the window to block the guard's view.

"Privacy?" Damion said, gesturing for Winston to leave the room.

"But I—"

"I need you to leave."

Winston begrudgingly turned and tapped his pen against the glass. After an emphatic exchange with the guard, he said, "Three minutes," to Damion. The heavy door closed and locked behind him.

Damion googled the current Bitcoin price. He did some quick mental math. Forty-five million, plus or minus a few hundred thousand.

"Crazy," he said to himself.

He dialed his brother. The call went to voicemail. He tried again.

"Hello?" Devon answered.

"Dev, brother. Thanks for taking my call."

There was a pause. "I don't have a brother," Devon said. "I see you're still breaking the rules. Do I need to change my number?"

"Don't hang up, man. I just wanted to call and apologize."

Both of them barely recognized the voice of the other. Their voices were tired and raspy, as if they'd aged thirty years.

"That ship has sailed, Damo. Your apologies mean shit to me. I told you when you beat that robbery charge years ago that that was the last straw for me, and I meant it. I can't believe you tricked me. You tricked Mama and Dad. You had us all believing that you'd changed, that you'd turned over a new leaf. You are a lost cause, do you know that? When we were kids, I used to wish I was an only child because of all the stunts you'd pull. I once prayed you'd get hit by a bus 'cause of all the bullshit you put our family through."

"Listen, Devon. I know. I know. I deserve this. You have no idea how shitty I felt that day at the airport."

"How shitty you felt?! How do you think we felt? Do you know I stopped telling people I have a brother? Nobody knows that here in D.C. You don't exist, as far as I'm concerned. I hope you die in there."

"Devon, I am your brother, no matter what you tell people." His voice cracked and grew hoarse.

"Do you know what you did to Mama that day at the airport? She was so excited to see you. You broke her heart."

"I know, brother. I know."

"No, you don't know! She had a nervous breakdown. We had to take her to the hospital. She spent thirteen days there."

"I'm sorry, brother. I'm sorry."

"Stop fucking calling me that!"

"Okay," Damion said, his voice quivering.

"You're the reason Dad died. Years of stress killed him. Stress that *you* caused. I hate you, Damion! Don't you ever contact me again!"

The line went dead.

Just then, Winston reentered the room. Damion quickly blotted his wet eyes with the sleeve of his khaki jumpsuit.

•••

The United States Disciplinary Barracks at Fort Leavenworth, Kansas, were different from civilian federal penitentiaries. Fights were rare, due to the collective discipline of the population and the fierceness of the military guards; food quality was much better; the cleanliness of the facility was remarkable. In other civilian prisons, it was not uncommon for inmates to fall ill or even die from salmonella or E. coli because of undercooked food or unsanitary conditions, if they didn't kill each other in a shank fight first.

Inmates at Leavenworth served out their sentences in regimented boredom. The military guards tolerated nothing more than low-level gossip. These guards were in charge completely, unlike in civilian prisons, where inmates formed their own hierarchy and dispensed justice on their own terms.

"'Sup, D." A passing inmate greeted Damion while carrying three rolls of Charmin, which was the max allowed for toilet paper, and a brown Ziploc bag of candy.

"'Sup," Damion replied with a slight upward nod.

He was standing in the commissary line. Damion's inmate ID number was 2921-1726, which he printed at the top of the commissary form. He checked off the following items:

Little Debbie Nutty Bars
Cajun Chicken Ramen (x4)
Tang Orange Powdered Drink Mix
Composition Notebook
Toothbrush (MEDIUM)

He slid the form and his commissary card to the attendant through the opening under the thick plexiglass window.

The attendant passed the form off to a runner and then swiped the card. She paused for a moment, and swiped it again. Her long, acrylic nails then struck the keypad with speed and aggression. The runner returned with a cart containing the items Damion had ordered.

"Put it all back," the attendant said to the runner. "I keep telling these inmates not to come down here if they know they don't have nothin' on their books. Y'all are wasting my damn time."

She slid the form and card back under the window to Damion. "Your account is empty."

"Can you swipe it again?" he said. "I come here every week, Ms. Lawson. I always have money on my books. There must be a mistake."

"Well, I guess you musta pissed somebody off on the outside, 'cause it shows here that you don't have enough for a stick of gum."

"Just one more..."

"Back away from the window, inmate. Move along," a guard said.

Damion's routine included visiting the prison commissary every Thursday at 1500 hours. In the six years of confinement, he never had to question whether his balance could cover his snacks and toiletries.

Someone had deposited the eighty-dollar maximum on his books every month, without fail or delay.

He suspected it was Mama Lee. Or maybe Devon didn't hate him as much as he led on.

Another part of Damion's routine was his biweekly Friday visits, usually from Winston, but occasionally from another attorney at the firm. When an Arcum lawyer didn't visit for the first time in six years, it didn't take long for Damion to deduce who the mystery commissary benefactor had been.

During rec time, he attempted to phone Winston. He had to search his footlocker for the business card because typically he would just wait a few days for the in-person visit.

The line was no longer in service.

•••

Normally, rec time was outside in the yard, but it had been raining all day. So, according to protocol, the inmates were moved to an inside gym with a basketball court. While one half of the gym was used for basketball, on the other half, inmates played chess, cards, and dominos. A mixed-race group of Christians had formed a prayer circle, and next to them were three lines of a dozen Black Muslims wearing kufis, standing, kneeling, or bowing in prayer.

Seven phones were mounted into the cinderblock wall. A line of inmates half the periphery of the basketball court stood in line to use them.

Out of sheer routine, during rec time on Fridays, Damion always tried Mama Lee's line. As usual, there was no answer. He tried his brother. Same result.

Damion placed the receiver on the hook.

Just then, he felt a poke in the ribs.

"What, you don't have guards bringing you cell phones in cereal boxes anymore?"

"Oh, shit!" Damion said, turning around, delighted to hear the familiar voice. "What the hell are you doing here?!"

Oni had gotten noticeably thinner. His afro was linty and unkempt. His beard was patchy. His teeth were yellow and covered in plaque.

"You look good, brother," Oni said.

"Three to five hundred push-ups a day does a body good," Damion replied, refusing to return the compliment.

"Well, you need to do some squats while you're at it—beef up those chicken legs."

Damion and Oni dapped, making a loud clapping sound, and embraced each other firmly.

"Bro, I thought you had beat your case when I didn't see you around here after the first few months," Damion said.

"Nah, bro. Far from it. They threw the fucking book at me—gave me all twenty, a shot at parole in seven," Oni replied. "They just had me in the other wing with the lifers. We got moved over here 'cause there was a coronavirus outbreak."

"Don't be bringing y'alls germs over here on our side," Damion said. He gave him a playful jab to the shoulder. "Just playing, man. I'm glad you're here. Say, break out the cards; I haven't had a good game of Tonk in a minute."

Oni looked around for a place for them to play.

"Are you sure you want to play me again?" Oni said. "You still owe me thirty snacks. But I'll wipe the slate clean since it's been a while—give you a fighting chance. What do you have to trade?"

"I have a whole footlocker full of snacks in my cell—Oatmeal Creme Pies, Skittles, Oodles of Noodles, you name it," Damion replied. "It's not like it matters, though. I'm about to run this table. I see that box of Nutty Bars under your arm, and you can never have too many of those. Let's get it poppin'."

"Let's do it, then."

Oni grabbed a rubber-banded deck of worn playing cards from a milk crate. He led Damion to a pair of orange plastic chairs in the corner of the rec room, and Damion slid a metal table between them.

"Twenty years, huh?" Damion said, while Oni placed each card onto the table to confirm a full deck.

"Yeah, man," Oni replied. He dealt five cards each. "I'm going crazy in here, bro. Same shit, day in and day out."

"Look on the bright side, man—at least we're not in the civilian feds. I hear that shit is a zoo."

"I guess you're right, man. But, still, I'll do anything to make parole when my number gets called next year."

Damion was already up by one Nutty Bar.

"How did they get you anyway?" Damion asked. "I never heard your story."

"A couple of months before I met you, my platoon was escorting some cargo trucks to a FOB in Helmand. We got into a gunfight with the Taliban. My LT got hit in the back. They tried to pin it on me when there were ten other guys firing his direction, too. He was an idiot, though, trying to win a Silver Star. Who in their right mind runs in front of a platoon of blazing M4s?"

"Well, was it you?"

"What do you mean?"

"Did you shoot him?"

"I plead the Fifth," Oni said with a smirk. "Sure, I couldn't stand that asshole, but that doesn't mean I wanted him dead. Whoever hit him got him center mass, right in the back. His armor absorbed the whole round. He might've had a bruise for a couple of days after, but he would live. If *I* had been gunning for him, I would've gone for the neck, right under his helmet, maybe even the thigh—you know, hit that femoral artery."

"Bro, you've thought about this way too much," Damion said, scooping the cards into a pile. "That's two packs, by the way."

"I've had nothing but time to think in here," Oni replied. He broke the seal of the Nutty Bars box and dumped two twin packs onto the table. "You've been sharpening your game, I see."

Damion shuffled and dealt. Oni played an Ace of Clubs and plucked from the deck. Damion opened a pack and bit half a Nutty Bar.

"You sure you want to eat them right now?" Oni said. "I'm just about to win them right back."

"Then you can dig them out of my commode later tonight," Damion replied, biting the other half.

"Oh, you're talking shit?"

"Literally," Damion replied.

The two laughed.

Damion cleared his throat, spreading three kings onto the table.

"Damn, bro. You won again," Oni said, extending the box to offer Damion another pack.

Damion began to cough.

"You good, bro?"

Damion's eyes suddenly grew large as panic set in. He leaned forward with his elbows on his knees.

Oni patted his back. "You okay, man?"

"Get help," Damion said in a labored, breathy voice. "Please," he added, now wheezing and clutching his throat.

Damion collapsed face-first onto the table, then rolled and dropped to the floor.

"Guard!" Oni yelled. He stood up, pointing down at Damion.

Three soldiers converged on Damion. One radioed a lockdown order, while another called for a medic.

The lockdown horns sounded, and all the inmates in the rec room scurried against the wall.

The medic arrived within minutes to relieve a soldier who had begun performing violent chest compressions.

# TWENTY

"Hey, Kate," Devon said to the unresponsive receptionist.

Ever since the team had shuttered the Grayton-Blackface Response Center, Kate had been buried under a mountain of media inquiries and constituent calls. Devon and Randy had worked up four pages of canned talking points for her to use to respond on their behalf.

She managed to find five seconds between calls. "Hey, Devon. If no one's told you, your chariot turns back into a pumpkin this afternoon. So, be careful out there," she said, and returned to the phone lines.

"Yeah, what?" he replied, tapping the top of her laptop to get her attention again.

"You're losing your bodyguard," she sharply replied.

"Thanks for the heads-up."

"Oh, and by the way, you also have a two o'clock with WAMU. And Randy wants to see you."

"W-A-M-what?"

"NPR," Kate snapped.

"Thanks."

Devon made a beeline for Randy's office.

The office door was already open when he arrived, and Randy was busy chattering away on the phone inside.

Without a word, Devon stood in the doorway, leaning on the frame, arms crossed over his chest.

Randy appeared to be on a personal call, but from the bit that Devon had heard, it seemed Randy had just finished taking full credit for leading the office through the blackface scandal.

Randy looked up to notice Devon standing there and quickly changed the subject to his niece's wedding plans.

"Sit down," Randy mouthed, covering the phone receiver.

Devon settled into the plush sofa and checked his phone. As he waited, Devon marveled at his Instagram follower count: it was at 310K, and he now had the little blue check. He was official.

"Devon, great morning to ya, bud," Randy said, spinning around in his chair.

"Kate says our security is going away today," Devon replied.

"Well, yours is going away. The congressman and I will keep ours for a few more weeks."

Devon stood, all ten fingertips pressed onto Randy's desk. "Wait, I no longer get security, but you get to keep yours?"

"Relax, man. It's a rank thing. Outta my control," Randy said with a shrug.

"But am I not still considered '*senior staff*'? I thought that was the rule. I'm more recognizable than you right now; if anybody needs to keep their security, it's me. I'm still getting death threats."

"Again, not my call, brother. Just know that you saved us, man. You got us through this. Security going away is a good thing—it means that we are coming out of the dark. Make sure you continue sending any threats you receive to the Capitol Police. And watch your back out there."

Devon put his hands on his hips in a huff.

"Really? Watch my back? That's all you got for me?"

"I don't know what else to tell ya, man. It is what it is."

Devon sat on the sofa's arm, glaring at Randy, who had turned his attention to his laptop screen.

"Is that all?" Randy asked, typing harder than necessary.

Devon wiped away his scowl, replacing it with a devious smile. "You know what? It's no biggie. Anyway, now that this is basically behind us, I have some ideas about the direction of the campaign. I sent Johnny a text, but no answer. I need to get on his schedule this afternoon."

Randy leaned back in his chair, fingers interlocked behind his head.

"So, um, about that," he said, "we're pumping the breaks on the Senate run for the moment. This whole controversy was unexpected. It set us back a bit. We have a lot of rebuilding to do before we can even think about such a move."

"Rebuilding? Are you kidding me? This is the perfect time for him to run. Nobody even knew who he was before this; now, everybody knows him. White Georgians love him, and because of me, now Blacks are okay with him, too. Strike while the iron is hot!"

"I'm not saying he's not running. Just not this go 'round."

"Are you saying wait another six years? That's absurd. I need to talk to Johnny."

"That's another thing, Devon. We dispensed with all the formalities because of the exigency of the situation, but we're back to normal now. Back to normal, back to formal. I'm going to need you to refer to him as 'sir' or 'Congressman' from now on, even when it's just us in the room. Also, all meetings go through me. I don't want you meeting with the congressman without me. We appreciate your help, but there is still a pecking order. I'm still the chief of staff."

"Appreciate my help? If it weren't for me, you, me, Johnny—all of us—would be looking for jobs right now. Now I'm on the outside again? Did you call me in here to demote me back to legislative assistant?"

"No, that's not it at all. You're still chief master press advisor general, or whatever. We just need to get back to the business of the people."

"It's chief of media relations," Devon replied.

"Yeah, that's it," Randy said. "Just make sure you run all media interview requests through me, too. It's time to start paring those down. I want to put this blackface thing to bed as soon as possible."

Devon narrowed his eyes at him. "All right, Randy. I mean, *sir*. Whatever you say, boss."

"It's not like that, man. You're still part of the team," Randy said.

"If you say so. I'll just go back to my cube."

Devon turned to leave Randy's office for the front desk.

"Kate, I need you to cancel my two o'clock with NPR," he said, his elbows resting on her partition.

He started for the door.

**Devon:** Hey, babe. If you're free, meet me in the cafeteria. I'm headed down now.

...

Devon ordered a large, black coffee, sat in their usual spot near the glass wall, and waited.

"Hey, you!" He felt a poke on the shoulder from behind.

"Oh, hey, Makeba."

She had changed her hair. Her once elbow-length braids had been cut to barely touch her shoulders, the ends curled toward her jawline. Her navy blue, just over-the-knee dress was professional, yet revealed her athletic figure in a way Devon hadn't noticed before.

"Do you mind?" she said, taking the seat across from him.

As she passed around him, a pleasant and subtle floral scent trailed with her and then disappeared.

"Sure, have a seat. It's actually good to see you."

"You've had quite the couple of weeks, huh?"

"I suppose I have," Devon replied. "My fifteen minutes of fame are over now, though."

"What do you mean, 'over'? You guys are just getting started. You killed the media circuit, and now, your guy is about to jump into a Senate race. The iron is white-hot, pun intended."

"Yeah, right? That's what *I* thought, too."

"So, what makes you think it's over?"

"Grayton played me. He used me."

"What do you mean? I thought we talked about this."

"He only needed me to get him out of the mud with the blackface thing. He tricked me into the spokesperson job by convincing me that he needed me for a Senate run. Now that the controversy is basically behind us, I can't even get a meeting with him."

"What are you saying—he's not running for Senate?"

"Not this term anyway—probably never."

"You're something else, you know that, Devon?"

"What do you mean?"

"Your loyalty is admirable. But it will sink you if you're not loyal to yourself, first."

His phone buzzed on the table with a new text message. "One sec," he said, picking it up.

> **Bethany:** I'm on my way down.
>
> **Devon:** No need to break away from your work.
>
> **Devon:** I'm actually headed back to the office. Let's link up later.

"What makes you think I'm not loyal to myself?" he said to Makeba.

"You took a job that you didn't want to take, under false pretenses. Then you defended a man on a national scale for wearing blackface; you were a lightning rod for him. And now you're allowing them to discard you like garbage after you saved the day. Doesn't sound like self-loyalty to me."

"Are you saying I shouldn't have taken the job? Because I seem to recall you encouraging me to do just that."

"What I said was: 'you should take the job if you can look yourself in the mirror at the end of the day.' Sounds like you're not liking what you see these days."

"I hate it, actually," he replied.

Makeba reached over, palming Devon's knee. "I also said you should *make him* earn our vote. *Make him* understand our issues. *Make him* act on behalf of us."

"Make him, huh?"

"Yes. Make him."

Makeba took her hand off Devon's knee when she spotted Bethany entering the cafeteria in the distance. She alerted Devon with a slight nod, and they both smiled and watched as Bethany approached.

"Hey, guys. I hope I'm not interrupting anything," Bethany said, her eyes fixed on Makeba.

Bethany had a new hairdo, too. Her usual work style was a loose updo with hair sticks holding it in place. It now looked redder, shinier, and fell over her shoulders in feathered layers. She wore lipstick today.

She smelled good, too.

"Oh, hey, Bethany," Devon replied.

"Hey, Beth," Makeba said. "You're not interrupting at all. I was just leaving. Let's all do drinks again soon."

Makeba collected her coffee and stood to leave. Their shoulders brushed together as Makeba negotiated the narrow space between Bethany and the couch, Bethany making no effort to get out of the way.

"Looks like your little bar exam study sessions are going well," Bethany said to Devon. "Oh, and never mind the fact that you told me not to come meet you here, just for me to come anyway and see *her* caressing your thigh."

"First, it wasn't my thigh, it was my knee, and she wasn't *caressing* it. I bumped into her right after I had sent off that text to you."

"Well, I still don't like it."

"We've already had this discussion, babe. There's nothing between us," he said in a dismissive tone. He looked at his phone and pretended to have gotten an urgent message. "Hey, listen, sorry to break away like this, but something just came up. I've got to get going. Get together after work?"

"Sure. Whatever," Bethany replied.

•••

Devon entered the office in a rush. The door slammed against the doorstop.

Kate fiddled with the tangled coils of a corded office phone, the receiver she had balanced between her shoulder and ear, while two iPhones rang simultaneously. She answered each in sequence, putting whoever was on the other end on hold.

"Hey, Kate. Kate? Kate!" Devon said, snapping his fingers a third time.

"What is it, Devon?" she replied, agitated.

"Did you cancel my two o'clock with NPR yet?"

"No, I didn't. Cut me some slack, I'm slammed here. I'll get to it in a minute."

"No," Devon replied. "Don't cancel it. I want to take the call. Put them through to my cell."

"Okay. Whatever you want."

"And Kate?"

"Yes, Devon?"

He leaned in. "Randy doesn't have to know about it."

She puckered her lips and looked at Devon from the sides of her eyes. But then the phone rang. "Congressman Grayton's office," she said into the receiver, giving Devon the thumbs up.

Devon left the office. He walked a couple of blocks down to Folger Park, where he found an empty bench beneath a tree.

The NPR reporter was polite, with a calm, soothing voice and a slight accent, which Devon couldn't place. He had done enough of these interviews by now, however, to know that a polite and calm voice didn't necessarily mean softball questions. Often, it was just the opposite.

The interview started not much different from all the others: pleasantries, and then they got right into it.

"Can you tell me, Mr. Lee, what was the congressman thinking *in 1984*, dressing in blackface? That was just plain wrong, wouldn't you say? Even if it was—as you say—to celebrate our nation's first Black Supreme Court Justice. I mean, this wasn't the fifties or even the sixties; this was the post-civil rights era. He should have known better. What do you say to that, especially as a Black person yourself?"

Devon had gotten to the point where he could rattle off an answer to this question in a coma.

"I think you're right, and I think I've spent enough time on the networks answering this same question. It was wrong, full stop. And the congressman recognizes this. I think it's time to move forward. To heal. Now, you say this was after the civil rights era; I would offer to you that it wasn't. I would argue that the civil rights era in this country hasn't ended, and that we are squarely in the middle."

"What do you mean by that?" the reporter asked.

"What I mean is when a Black man can't go for a jog. When he can't exercise his body in the street without fear of being hunted down because of his race, that's a civil rights issue."

"Of course, you're talking about Ahmaud Arbery, the twenty-five-year-old Black man who was killed by a white father and son while jogging in your home state of Georgia in early 2020."

"Yes. And not just him. I'm talking about George Floyd. Those cops killed him for sport. And Breonna Taylor. The list goes on and on. People have the *civil right,* not to mention the *natural right,* to live their lives in peace, without fear of being hunted and slaughtered in the streets—not by the police, or anyone else. So, no, the civil rights era in this country isn't over."

"You have no argument from me there," the reporter replied. "Now, you say 'it's time to heal and move forward.' Elaborate on that; what does moving forward look like for Congressman Grayton?"

"First, I want—I mean, the *Congressman* wants to help empower the Black community. He wants to encourage Black Georgians and across the country, frankly, to participate in every aspect of the political process. We are let down daily by our system of laws. Can you blame us if we want to wash our hands of it all? But even though we are let down, we can't let up.

"When the officer shot and killed Michael Brown in Ferguson, Missouri in 2014, the Black population there was sixty-four percent. The mayor was white. The police chief was white. The police force was ninety-four percent white. And of the six city council members, only one was Black. There's something wrong with that picture. That's what it looks like when we don't participate."

"Hmm," the reporter said as he listened.

"What we need is actual policy change—changes in the laws—starting at the federal level, to go after these racist people, bad cops included. And beyond that, we need policies that help uplift the Black community, so that we can buy homes, own a piece of this country, leave our children an inheritance so they don't have to start from negative nothing—so that we can have a piece of the American pie, not just the crumbs."

"Can you give us a sense of what some of that policy change looks like?"

"By all means," Devon replied. "Did you know that the cumulative endowment of all HBCUs is around four billion dollars? We're talking about over one hundred schools. Emory University alone, a Georgia school, has an endowment of almost double that. This needs to be addressed."

"Those are staggering numbers," the reporter replied.

"Exactly," Devon said. "And addressing these issues is at the top of the congressman's legislative agenda when he becomes a senator. He wants to even the scales. Because right now, there are two separate Americas. There's a white America, and there's everybody else. And as our late, great Thurgood Marshall taught us: separate is inherently unequal."

"Hold up, wait just one moment, sir. You buried the lead. You can't just breeze by a bombshell statement like *that*. Did I just hear you say, 'when he becomes a senator'? Does the congressman have senatorial ambitions this term?"

"The congressman has ambitions to further equality in this country. And he believes the best place from which to do that is a seat in the United States Senate. So, yes, he will be running for Senate this term."

"Correct me if I'm wrong, but there are already two Republican senators in Georgia, both of whom are running for re-election. Is the congressman changing parties?"

"The congressman is a conservative. He's a Republican—always has been. So, no, he's not changing parties."

"So, he's challenging from the right?" the reporter clarified.

"No, he's challenging his party to do *what's* right. And basic equality for all is what's right. Period. Listen, Democrats don't have a monopoly on wokeness, plain and simple. There are unfair things happening in this country, and whoever doesn't see that is willfully ignorant, party notwithstanding. Change can't happen from only one side of the aisle. You need Republicans, too. You have no chance of winning a game of full-court basketball if your team can only go to half-court."

"'Democrats don't have a monopoly on wokeness,'" the reporter repeated. "I like that. You certainly have a way with words, Mr. Lee. Well, listen, you heard it here first: Congressman Johnathon Grayton from the state of Georgia is mounting a same-party senatorial challenge in the State of Georgia this upcoming Senate race."

No sooner than when he hung up did the calls and texts begin to flood in. Seven calls from Kate, thirteen from Randy...And twenty-one from the congressman himself.

"MY OFFICE NOW" was the last message the congressman had sent him.

Devon's heart pounded with adrenaline. He turned off the work phone and opened his personal one. He had two texts: one from Bethany, and one from Makeba.

**Bethany:** ♟️👍

**Makeba:** You did that! 😊

He opened Instagram. His follower count was increasing by twenty each time he refreshed. He could have a half million by day's end.

He stacked both phones on the bench next to him and enjoyed the park view. Small kids from a nearby daycare played duck, duck, goose.

He took the long way back to the office, stopping for pizza in Eastern Market.

•••

Devon spotted the congressman's large frame standing in the corridor outside his office thirty yards away, waiting for him to arrive.

"Who do you think you are?" the congressman said, arms folded, as if chastising a child.

Devon said nothing. The congressman stormed ahead, leading the way to his office. Devon sauntered behind him.

Kate took a break from her calls to watch the action.

The congressman waited for Devon, and slammed the door behind him. "Sit down," he said, pointing at the couch.

Devon, instead, took a seat on the deep windowsill, knocking over a photo of the congressman's wife. He didn't pick it up.

Randy entered and stood at the door as if to prevent Devon from leaving.

"Who in the hell gave you the authority to speak on my behalf and announce a Senate race?! You were out of line!"

"You did, Johnny. You don't remember?"

"I should have you brought up on charges."

"For what? Doing my job?" Devon replied. "At this point, you can't even fire me. Think about how that would look in the media:

'Congressman Johnny Grayton Fires Black Media Chief After Blackface Scandal.' No bueno, buddy."

The congressman looked to Randy, who reluctantly nodded in agreement."

"Listen," Devon said, "I didn't ask for this. I was content at my cubicle, silently making sausage for you. *You* asked me to do this. In fact, you insisted; you basically forced me to be your spokesperson for a Senate race that you had no intention of running in."

"That's not it," the congressman replied. "The circumstances changed, and it's just not the right time..."

"You're damn right they changed," Devon replied. "You knew the blackface thing was coming out, and you picked the one Black person you knew to help get you out of hot water. And when it was all over, your plan was to use the scandal as a reason to can the Senate plans that you never had in the first place. How am I doing so far?"

The congressman sunk into the couch and folded his hands together.

"You made me take a job that I didn't want. Now, I'm making you do the same—*if* you win, that is. Anyway, whatever happened to all that 'opportunity' stuff you were talking about at The Yard? I'm sitting here dropping the opportunity of your career smack dab in your lap, and your first thought is to pass it up? Remember that? Oh, and here's the classic: 'you have to learn to exploit circumstances to your benefit.' Certainly, you remember that. Those are *your* words, Congressman—I mean, Johnny. I learned from the best. That is, if we're being honest."

Devon's personal phone had been vibrating so much that it was hot to the touch.

"Here's the deal, Johnny," Devon said. "You're running for that Senate seat. And I'll continue to be your front guy. I'm in charge of the campaign messaging. Randy, your post is here, in this office. I will not answer to you. Ever. I'll have a direct line to the congressman at all times. Who knows? We might just win!"

Congressman Grayton and Randy looked at each other, mouths open.

"Excuse me," Devon said to Randy as he snatched open the door, startling Kate, who had been eavesdropping from the other side.

# TWENTY-ONE

Damion arrived at Saint John Hospital two weeks before Christmas without a pulse. His heart and lungs had stopped functioning.

A young nurse intercepted him between the automatic doors of the emergency room entrance. She paused his gurney and activated a portable defibrillator, ordering a soldier to unbutton the jumpsuit and rip open his undershirt.

"Clear!"

Damion was still unresponsive after three shocks.

The team of EMTs and two military guards followed the nurse. They dashed inside, where they found an empty treatment station. A doctor yanked back the curtain. The nurse briefed him in shorthand medical jargon while another nurse prepared an epinephrine injection and handed it to him.

Within seconds of the adrenaline entering his system, Damion gasped deeply. He sprang upright, nearly headbutting the young nurse, but was snapped back by the handcuffs connecting him to the gurney railing.

He had been clinically dead for nearly three minutes.

After the initial jolt, Damion returned to a glassy-eyed and confused slump. He was in and out of consciousness. Doctors gave him atropine injections to keep his heart rate above sixty beats per minute.

•••

He was in the hospital for the coronavirus, even though he had tested negative four times, and the sudden onset and nature of some of his symptoms were inconsistent with the respiratory disease.

Nonetheless, within the first week, Damion's vitals stabilized. He had begun breathing on his own, no longer requiring the assistance of a ventilator, and he was able to speak and walk, albeit slowly.

Nurse Toni had been caring for him since he had arrived. She'd found him handsome, and far too young to die. So, she took particular interest in his recovery, sometimes staying hours beyond her twelve-hour overnight shift. She even postponed her acceptance of a much higher-paying traveling nurse position to see his care through.

She was petite. Barely over thirty, she took the traditional approach to her work attire: instead of the popular scrub pants, shirt, and Crocs, she opted for the white scrub dress, opaque white tights, and the classic white leather Anni Lo shoes. She kept her hair pulled back into two French braids, that came together into a bun that rested on the nape of her neck.

Damion had never seen the lower half of her face, but he could tell she was stunning under the mask. Her eyes were almond, her skin, dark chocolate. She reminded him of Lupita Nyong'o.

Nurse Toni bathed him and changed his clothes. When he was able to chew and swallow, but not hold a fork, she fed him. She held his hand as he walked slowly from one end of the hallway to the other, once having an intense argument with his two military guards for them to remove the cuffs and leg irons for this purpose. "He can barely walk. Where's he gonna go?" she'd say. When he asked, she'd look up and tell him the current market price of a Bitcoin, even though she had not a clue what it meant.

Nurse Toni was passionate and quite influential when advocating for small comforts on his behalf. The guards often found it easier to simply acquiesce. So, when Mama Lee called the hospital for Damion and found Nurse Toni, the guards didn't even attempt to stop it.

"Can you ask him to just keep it to five minutes?" one of the guards requested of Nurse Toni. "If our sergeant does a spot check on us, we could get in trouble."

Nurse Toni nodded with a grin.

Both guards returned to their corner of the room. They donned large, over-the-ear headphones and returned their attention to their own smartphones.

"No problem," she replied, handing Damion the phone with a wink. Nurse Toni had received Mama Lee's initial call on the hospital landline but had her hang up and call back on her personal phone.

On the cellphone screen was a sticky note that read "Click over in a minute."

"Be back soon, guys," she said to Damion and the guards as she left the room.

"Mama!"

"Oh, praise the Lord!"

"Hey, Mama," Damion said to her. His voice trembled. Hers comforted him. Feelings of guilt, embarrassment, and sadness started to collide within him.

"It's so good to hear your voice, son. I've been calling around for days ever since they told me you were conscious again. I wanted to come to Kansas, but they said I wouldn't be able to see you in the ICU if I did. Oh, praise God for making a way."

"It's good to hear your voice, Mama. I've missed you so much. I'm so sorry for—"

Damion swallowed a lump and closed his eyes in a futile attempt to hold back tears. They rolled down the side of his face onto the white linen.

"Damion, you're my son." Mama Lee's voice quivered. "You might have made a few mistakes in life. But I will always be in your corner. More than that, I will always love you. Until the good Lord calls me up to be with Percy, I will always love you and your brother. You just stay strong. You come from good stock," she said between sniffs.

She changed the subject in an attempt to regain her composure. "How're they treating you? Are you eating okay?"

"I'm surviving. But boy, what I wouldn't do for a plate of your collards, ham, and macaroni and cheese. I had a dream about it the other night."

They both laughed.

Mama Lee invited Damion to a compulsory prayer. Just then, another call came through from a "913" area code. Damion glanced at his guards. Both were just as absorbed in their phones as Mama Lee was in her prayer.

Damion switched lines.

"Pretend I'm your mom," Nurse Toni said in a low voice, just above a whisper.

"Yes, Mama. I'm feeling better now," Damion replied.

Nurse Toni continued: "We don't have much time. Listen, you didn't have the coronavirus. You were poisoned."

"Yes. They're treating me fine, Mama."

"When your blood sample that I sent off came back clean, I drew another sample and hand-carried it myself to a friend of mine in the lab. It seems you were poisoned by a nerve agent, something called Novichok."

"Is that right, Mama?"

"Yes. And I don't think it was a mistake. Someone deliberately swapped your blood sample with someone else's. And when I flagged it, it was swept under the rug. I tried to point it out again and was threatened with reprimand. Listen, do with this information what you please. I just thought you should know."

Nurse Toni hung up.

Damion switched over just as Mama Lee was finishing her prayer.

"In Jesus' name, amen."

"Amen," he replied.

"That's enough, inmate," one of the guards said, standing over Damion's bed.

"Just one more minute. I'm talking to my mother. Cut me a break," he said, attempting to block the guard with his other arm. "They're telling me I gotta go now. I love y—"

The guard reached over and snatched the phone away.

"You didn't have to be an asshole about it," Damion hissed.

Just then, Nurse Toni returned with chicken noodle soup for Damion and coffee for the two guards.

"Everything okay?" she asked, eyeing the guard.

He put the phone on a table near the door. "All good. Are those coffees for us?"

Every night, near midnight, one of the young guards would go on a McDonald's run, while the other would doze off with a roaring snore.

The runner took his partner's food order, a large Number 9, and Nurse Toni dimmed the lights when he left. Within minutes, the lone guard had loosened his bootlaces and reclined in his chair, forehead to the ceiling and mouth wide open. His breathing grew heavy, almost labored. Soon he began to saw logs. Nurse Toni covered the sleeping guard with a thin, wool hospital blanket.

"Looks like our friend here has taken well to my special blend," she said with a wink. "It's decaf with a scoop of melatonin."

"Good. Now, listen, you have to help me," Damion said in a panicked whisper. "They're trying to kill me."

"Who?" she replied, returning to his bedside.

"The people who put me in prison. They don't think I'll stay quiet any longer, so they're trying to kill me off."

"Well, whoever it is, they're not small time. They're sophisticated."

"What do you mean?"

"What I mean is, that nerve agent they gave you—Novichok—it isn't just something you buy on the streets. I did some research, and it's highly toxic."

The guard let out a loud snort. He rubbed his nose, then returned to a garbage disposal-like snore.

"I need you to help me get out of here," Damion said.

"You want me to help you escape from prison? I like you, but you're crazy. I'm a nurse!" she whispered. "I could lose my license. Hell, *I* could go to prison!"

"Listen, they're releasing me back to the prison in the next couple of days. If I go back to Leavenworth, I won't survive a week."

"I just can't take that risk. I have a five-year-old daughter. If I got caught, I could lose my job, not to mention my license. I'm sorry. I just can't do it."

"Nurse Toni, you know how I ask you the Bitcoin price every day? That's because I have a lot of it. Like a *lot*. I can make you an instant millionaire if you do this for me. Here, give me your phone."

She did so, and Damion logged into his account.

"You see this number?" He held the screen eye-level to her. "That's in Bitcoin. It's worth over forty million dollars—like George Washington dollars. You help me pull this off, and I can send you a million dollars' worth within the day. You could quit your job and care for your baby girl full-time."

Nurse Toni studied Damion's face, and her expression softened.

"C'mon, Nurse Toni. We don't have much time before the other guard comes back. I need an answer. Will you help me? If not for me, think about your daughter. Do it for her."

"One million dollars?"

"Yes. One million."

"Make it two."

"Done."

Nurse Toni took a deep sigh, her now trembling hands together at her lips as if she were praying. "Okay. Think, Toni," she said to herself. She rocked left to right.

"Okay," she whispered. "But if it doesn't work, you have to promise me that you'll leave me out of it."

Just then, the door opened. Nurse Toni turned around quickly.

The cleaning lady poked her head into the room.

"Come back in an hour, Debbie." Nurse Toni whispered to her with a shrug, gesturing to the sleeping guard. Debbie rolled her eyes but acquiesced. She shut the door behind her.

She turned back to Damion. "I can't do this."

"You can do this. You just got a little spooked. I'll leave you out of it; you have my word. If this doesn't work, play dumb. I'd be done for either way, so I'll have no reason to throw you under the bus."

"Shit," Nurse Toni replied, pacing back and forth. "Okay. Okay. But two million dollars?"

"Two and a half," Damion replied.

Nurse Toni considered that.

"I got it," she said. "You're going to die tonight."

Damion's brows drew together as he scratched his head. "Not exactly what I meant when I said I needed to get out of here."

"No, that's not what I meant. We're going to fake your death and get you out of here."

His forehead relaxed. He canted his head and nodded. "That could work," he replied.

"That's what it's going to be. I'm going to disconnect you from your ECG now. When the sun rises, you're going to have to play dead—and I mean you need to play dead, like your life depends on it. Now, I'm going to bring you something to help you out with that. When I do, wait until I leave the room and take three of them. They will put you in a deep state of relaxation, and help you to slow your breathing. Just lean into it. If you feel like someone's looking at you, hold your breath. I'll try and distract them as much as I can.

"I'll come in and make the announcement in the morning, and I'll bring the death pronouncement paperwork to the doctor. I'll say you've been dead for hours, no chance of resuscitation."

The sleeping guard shifted in his chair. Nurse Toni paused. The guard resumed a whistling snore.

"Now, here's where it could all fall apart, Damion. When I hand the doctor the death pronouncement document, he can do one of two things. He can take my word for it and sign the paperwork, which I've seen him do for inmates many times before. Or he can come verify for himself. There's a sixty-forty chance he'll do the first."

"Well, if the doctor is in on it, that means he wants me dead anyway. So, that would be good news to him."

"Let's hope so. Next step: cremation. I'll be back in a bit with the cremation consent paperwork. Fill it out and backdate it a couple days. Check the 'Cremation' box and initial above it. I'll sign as your witness. If all goes well, you'll be transported in a container that looks like a hospital bed down to the morgue in the basement; that's how we move dead bodies discreetly, so people don't get freaked out. Are you sensitive to cold?"

"I'm from Georgia."

"Well, you'll be naked in a thirty-six-degree refrigerator, so mentally prepare yourself. I'll get you out of there as soon as possible and swap out your toe tag with another dead man's. I'll stop at the gift shop and pick you up some sweat clothes, and you'll be free to go. In the meantime, don't eat anything from anybody, except me."

"Have you done this before?"

"Only in my head."

"You're my guardian angel."

"And you're my ticket to a beach house in Maui," she said with a playful smirk.

"Wait, so if this Novichok poison stuff was so deadly, how did I survive?"

"I'm pretty sure it was the atropine; you needed it to get your heart rate up. Coincidentally, the atropine happens to be a nerve agent antidote, so you're a lucky man. Now, about this two and a half million: how are you planning to get it to me?"

Just then, the door flung open and slammed against the stopper.

The other guard had returned from the McDonald's run to find his partner passed out. He kicked his boot, causing him to snort, choke on his spit, then cough violently. "Wake up, man!" he said. "You can't keep falling asleep if I'm not here."

"How about a little consideration, fellas? We have a resting patient here. Keep your voices down," Nurse Toni scolded.

Damion didn't move, but his heart hammered while Nurse Toni pretended to be recording his vitals.

"Sorry about that, ma'am."

•••

"Oh, no! What did you do to yourself, Mr. Lee?!"

Damion felt weak and groggy, but coherent enough to remember the plan and hear what was happening around him.

He felt Nurse Toni's cold fingertips touch his wrist to check for a pulse, the back of her hand over his mouth and nose to feel for air, and finally her hand on his forehead. "He's cold," she said.

"How did you let this happen?" she said to the guards. "You didn't notice the ECG was no longer beeping? You didn't see the pills? Of course you didn't, because you were so focused on your damn phones! Your inmate—my patient—is dead!"

"I thought he was asleep," one of the guards said.

"Well, he wasn't!"

Devon heard Nurse Toni's footsteps as she walked around the bed, then the rattle of pills in a bottle.

"He OD'd on oxycodone. This bottle belongs to Mr. Walker next door. I thought you were supposed to be guarding him. You let him wander off?"

"You idiot!" one guard said to the other. "You fell asleep again, didn't you?! We're in a fuck-ton of trouble! Let's go. We gotta let the captain know."

Both guards exited the room, leaving behind their things.

Nurse Toni pulled the white bed sheet over Damion's head. She, too, left the room, returning minutes later.

Damion heard an unfamiliar man's voice.

The man identified himself to the guards as officer Reynolds, a sergeant with the Leavenworth Police. "But you can just call me Ray."

The lackadaisical sounding officer performed a perfunctory investigation. Damion heard the digital shutter as Officer Aristide snapped photos with his smartphone. He got a statement from Nurse Toni. "Seems pretty cut and dry to me," he said. "Some people just can't handle the time. Be good or be good at it—that's what I always say."

Nurse Toni left the room again and returned twenty minutes later.

"Quick, while the guards are out," she whispered in Damion's ear. "This is my assistant. He's here to help. By the way, the doctor signed the death pronouncement form. We're in the clear."

Damion felt a bump and heard a metallic clink against his bed.

"This is the transport container," she whispered. "We gotta get you inside it. Do us a favor and make it easy on us."

Damion braced himself on his elbows, raised his hips and started to scoot. Suddenly, one of the guards entered the room. Damion fell limp.

"Need some help with that?" one of the guards said.

"We're good," Nurse Toni said. "You've done enough. You just stay over there." She closed the transport container bed, once Damion was inside, and started for the door.

"You can't leave with him right now," the guard said to her. "We have to wait for our commander."

"This is a dead body," Nurse Toni replied, "no longer your inmate.

We're required to get him downstairs to the morgue within an hour of death. And because of your incompetence and inability to stay awake, who knows how long he's been dead? Now, do you want me to stick around to tell your commander that?"

"No, ma'am."

"Then get out of my way."

She and the assistant rolled Damion out of the room, down the halls, and directly to the staff elevator.

They hustled inside and the elevator doors closed.

"Oh, my God!" Nurse Toni said. "I'm a nervous wreck! My heart is pounding! I can't believe we pulled that off."

"You deserve an Oscar," the assistant said to her.

"You okay in there?" She banged on the side of the container bed. "This is Mateo, my assistant. He's cool. You owe him 50K, by the way."

"Okay. Whatever," Damion replied. "Just hurry up and get me out of here. I'm feeling claustrophobic."

"This box is taking you to freedom. This is your freedom box. Think of it that way," Nurse Toni replied.

# TWENTY-TWO

For the first time in over seven years, Damion was a free man.

In the meantime, another Damion Lee, a sixty-one-year-old white man from Olathe, Kansas, who had succumbed to pancreatic cancer earlier in the day, was on his way to the crematory, while the dead body of a Walker Theodore Clement Jr. seemed to have gone missing.

Damion tried to suppress the excitement on his face, despite wearing a surgical mask, which Nurse Toni had left in the pocket of his Fort Leavenworth-logo sweatpants along with a crisp fifty-dollar bill with her cell number written on it.

The cold, dry wind cut through the cotton fabric, giving him a chill. This was a welcomed sensation, as it had been a long time since Damion had felt a strong wind. At Leavenworth, the outdoor recreation area was in the center of the prison facility surrounded by prison buildings on all four sides. Inmates could only see the sky. The gale caused a parachute effect in his sweatshirt as he walked into it.

He had passed two hospital security officers in the lobby, and a pair of Fort Leavenworth policemen in the parking lot. He had contemplated running each time, paranoid that they would somehow have sensed that he was an escaped convict.

After about a mile, Damion found a 7-Eleven, where he purchased two bowtie donuts, a large black coffee, a burner phone, and a copy of the *Leavenworth Times*.

He looked for the best place to rest out of the cold. In the distance, he spotted an old man entering a Wells Fargo. It was after hours, but the ATM area was accessible twenty-four hours with a bank card. He jogged across the street to the bank and stood against the wall. He pretended to read the paper, waiting for his window to enter, when the old man exited. The man fumbled with his wallet and cane at the door. Once he pushed the door, Damion politely pulled it to allow him to pass.

"Thanks a lot, young man."

"You're welcome, sir," Damion replied as he walked inside.

He sat in the corner, where the glass door and the wall met. He pulled out his burner phone, powered it on, and texted Nurse Toni.

**Damion:** Call me from another phone.

He sipped coffee and flipped through his newspaper while he waited for her reply.

Jumping off the page was the headline of a baseball card-sized article: "Inmate Murdered in Fort Leavenworth Prison, First in Twenty Years." And there was a jail mugshot of his former friend, Ndulue Oni. Damion found the news both satisfying and chilling—satisfying because it cleared up any residual doubt that Oni was responsible for the poisoning, and chilling in that it demonstrated the reach and lethality of Jim, Jon, and whoever else might still be hunting him.

The phone rang.

"Don't say my name."

"I take it you're in the clear?" Nurse Toni replied.

"Not quite yet. I need cash."

"Cash? What do you mean *you need cash*? What happened to the millions in Bitcoin?"

"Listen. Just listen," Damion replied. "I said I need cash—like physical dollars. I'm using a dumbphone right now, so I don't have a way to access my Bitcoin account."

"Well, where are you?" Nurse Toni replied. "I can come to you, and you can use my phone."

"No. Someone could be following you."

"Following me?! Who's following me? Listen, I don't know how I allowed myself to get wrapped up in whatever you have going on. I just want my money, and I want out."

"You'll get your money. Trust me. You have no idea what you did for me. You saved my life," Damion replied. "Here's the plan: it's late in the day, and everything is closed. Tonight, I need you to download a Bitcoin wallet to your phone, and text me the public key—it's like an email address for your account. Never share your private key with anyone else. Within an hour of you sending the key, I'll send you half the money."

"Half? That wasn't the agreement," Nurse Toni replied.

"I know. I know. I just need one more favor. Just one last time. I'll send the rest after. You have my word."

"Don't you think I've done enough for you? I've risked my reputation, my job, my freedom for you."

"You're right," Damion said. "You held up your end of the bargain. Forget about what I just said. Tomorrow morning, I'll send you the whole amount, and the extra 50K for your guy."

Nurse Toni sighed. "What do you want me to do?"

"No. You were right," Damion replied. "You've done enough already."

"I'm not going to ask you again," she said.

"Okay. If you're really up to it, when I transfer the Bitcoin, I need you to transfer nine thousand of it to your bank account, go to the bank, and withdraw the cash for me. Can you do that?"

"Well, it's against my better judgment, but I've been going against that ever since you were well enough to talk again. So, what's one more stupid—and I mean *stupid*—favor?"

"Thank you so much. I owe you everything."

"Just a couple million dollars."

"Right. And you'll have it in the morning. You should send the 9K through your assistant. Send me his phone number, and I'll text him my location by ten thirty in the morning."

"Why do I have to send it through him? I'd like to see you at least one last time."

"Like I said, I don't know if you're being followed."

"Who'd be following me?"

"I don't know. We just have to be careful," Damion said, carefully tearing the article from the paper. "Listen, those drugs hit hard. I was in and out and don't really remember everything. Did anything happen during the breakout?"

"No. Everything went off without a hitch. But after the standard questioning by the Office of the Medical Examiner, I did have a couple guys ask me some questions."

"Two guys? What did they look like? Big, white, with black hair?"

"Yeah. That's right. How did you know?"

"What did they say to you?"

"They said they were with the Federal Bureau of Prisons, and they were asking about your death."

"Did they show you ID?"

"I didn't think to ask. Should I be worried?"

"No. Don't worry. They were looking for me, not you. As long as you kept with the story, we should be okay. And if you put on the same Academy Award-winning act that you did earlier, I'm sure you were convincing."

"What are you going to do for the night?"

"Don't worry about me. After being in Afghanistan for a year, and in a cage for another seven, I think I can survive a night on the streets."

Damion followed a car into an apartment building garage, where he curled up at the bottom of a stairwell until morning.

•••

The sun hadn't yet risen. It was just before 5:00 a.m., three hours before the library and bank would open. Damion returned to the 7-Eleven for a coffee, donuts, two bananas, another burner phone, matches, and a pack of Black & Mild cigars.

"Thanks a lot," an officer said to him for holding open the plexiglass door to the donut case.

"Not a problem. Hey, sir," Damion added in a bold temptation of fate, "could you tell me where the public library is?"

The officer took a bite from the donut for which he hadn't yet paid.

"You must not be from around here, huh?" he said with a full mouth.

"I'm from Georgia. I'm just here for a few days, visiting a friend."

"All right. Well, look: you just go north on Fourth, and make a quick left on Spruce. It'll be on your left. Big building with the columns. Can't miss it."

"Thanks."

"Sure thing."

Damion paid, left, and began walking north on Fourth.

The same officer then pulled up next to him in his cruiser.

Damion cut his eyes left and right in search of the best direction to run.

"You're not walking, are you? It's about three miles away."

"Yeah, I'll be fine. I was in the Army. A 5K is nothing to me."

"You were in the Army? I'm a retired master sergeant. I spent my whole twenty with the one hundred and first Screaming Eagles. Airborne, hooah!"

The officer continued slow-rolling alongside Damion.

"What was your MOS?" the officer asked.

"Eighty-eight November, nothing sexy," Damion replied, slowing his pace.

The officer stopped the car.

Deciding that continuing to walk would be suspicious, Damion stopped, too, and approached the cruiser. He leaned into the passenger side window.

"Well, if it ain't Eleven Bang Bang, then I don't have a clue what that means," the officer said.

"I wasn't airborne infantry like yourself. Just boring old logistics."

"Well, the infantry can't do our jobs without loggies like you getting us the beans, bullets, and Band-Aids, so, your job was just as important as mine."

"You know what they say about us loggies: 'nothing happens until something moves,'" Damion replied.

The officer let out a hearty laugh.

"Hey, I can't see a fellow vet huffin' it down the street. Hows 'bout I give you a lift?"

"Oh, I'm just fine walking. The library doesn't open for another couple hours. I'm just gonna find a place to sit and have a smoke."

Damion pulled his pack of Black & Milds from the plastic bag.

"Here, lemme see that," the officer said.

Damion handed the officer the pack.

"You don't want to smoke that," the officer said.

He reached under the passenger seat and pulled out a rugged plastic humidor, similar, if not identical, to that which Jim and Jon had carried around in Afghanistan. He popped the latches and gave Damion his choice of three.

Damion's heart pounded when he saw the humidor, remembering the men who killed his friend and sent him to prison.

"There ya go," he said. "One of these'll last ya about an hour and a half."

"Thanks a lot, sir."

"Are you sure you don't want a ride? Rubber wheels are better than rubber heels," the officer said, pointing to Damion's refashioned feet.

Damion waived one of the cigars to redirect the officer's eyes. "Now that I have these, I'm just going to find a spot next to the river and enjoy it. Thanks again, but I'm okay on foot."

"All right, brother. Be safe out here. Hooah!"

"Hooah!" Damion replied.

The officer drove away.

A text came in from Nurse Toni. It was her public key, a salad of numbers and letters—a code that Damion was to use to send the Bitcoin.

Damion pulled his Black and Milds from the plastic bag, then ducked out of the wind, behind a building, to strike a match.

Damion found a park bench with a view of the Missouri River in the distance. He finished two more Black and Milds, decompressed from the cop encounter, and waited, breaking off pieces of donut for the pigeons.

•••

Damion was the first inside the Leavenworth Public Library.

"Excuse me. Where are your computers?" he asked one of the attendants.

"Upstairs to the right. But you need a library card to access them. Do you have one?"

"No, Ma'am. I don't."

"That's not a problem at all," the attendant replied. "We can set you up quickly. Do you have a driver's license with a local address?"

"I'm in the Army and I just moved here. My phone and wallet were stolen, and I need to get in touch with my girlfriend, but I can't remember her number. I just need to use a computer so I can contact her on Facebook or something."

The attendant looked him over.

"Well, I'm not supposed to do this, but you seem polite, and I support our troops."

She directed him to step behind a counter and remove his mask for a photo.

"Here, just fill this short form out, and you'll be good to go."

Damion completed the form and handed it back to the attendant. Minutes later, he had a laminated library card, still warm from the machine.

"Okay, Mr. Devin, is it?"

"De-*von*," Damion replied. "Thanks a lot, ma'am."

Once upstairs, he picked the computer in the far corner. He logged on to his Bitcoin account and initiated the transfer transaction. Once finished, he texted Nurse Toni from his new burner line.

**Damion:** Done.

**Nurse Toni:** This can't be real!!!!!!!

**Damion:** You'll see how real it is when the bank opens. And hurry. I'm broke now."

**Nurse Toni:** OMG

**Nurse Toni:** 👍

**Damion:** I'll be at the place I told you I'd be last night. Just have your assistant come. Stand by for further instruction.

Damion took up a third-story window seat with a wide view of Spruce Street and of the sidewalk leading to the library entrance. He watched the street over his newspaper.

**Nurse Toni:** OTW

**Damion:** ETA?

**Nurse Toni:** ?

**Damion:** How long?

**Nurse Toni:** No more than 10 min.

Within a few minutes, a navy-blue Volkswagen pulled into the dollar store parking lot across the street. A man in blue scrubs got out and started in the direction of the library. Damien recognized him as Mateo.

**Damion:** Tell him to stop 10 ft from the door and check his phone.

Mateo did as instructed.

**Damion:** Tell him to find the book "The Alchemist" by Paulo Coelho. Put the envelope in the book's place. Check the book out.

Damion watched as Mateo paused near the periodicals to text Nurse Toni.

**Nurse Toni:** He doesn't have a library card.

**Damion:** I know a great place where he can get one.

**Nurse Toni:** Oh, 👍

Damion passed by Mateo as he posed for his library picture. He made a beeline for the fiction literature section, where he found the thick envelope. He pulled it from the shelf along with another book for concealment.

Damion ditched the book on a cart, tucked the envelope, and made for the exit. Through the glass double doors, he spotted two unmistakable figures in long, black coats approaching. His first thought was to turn around, but it was too late; that would draw attention to himself.

Damion adjusted his surgical mask, and prayed that it, along with the mini fro he had started to grow, was enough of a disguise.

He passed Jim and Jon in the vestibule by mere feet, close enough to catch a whiff of cigar smoke as they focused on putting on their own masks.

Unnerved, he still resisted the instinct to look over his shoulder while pretending to talk on the phone in a fake deep voice.

Damion went inside the dollar store across the street and shopped only the aisle with a straight-line view to the library's main entrance. He watched Mateo leave, and Jim and Jon minutes later.

Over the course of six years, Jim and Jon seemed to have doubled in age. It was them, all right, but not the same Jim and Jon that Damion had remembered. They looked angry, menacing even.

A minute later, a black Chevy Suburban passed in the same direction Mateo had driven from.

Damion picked up a canvas shopping bag, a bottle of water, and trail mix, breaking a crisp one-hundred-dollar bill at checkout. As he left the dollar store, his eyes cut every direction.

He needed to leave the City of Leavenworth.

# TWENTY-THREE

**Damion:** I'm out ✌

**Damion:** Thanks for my new life.

**Nurse Toni:** And thanks for mine! ♡

He dropped the phone to the asphalt and stomped it, but his rubber soles were too soft to even crack the screen. He picked it up. He'd fling both burner phones over the Centennial Bridge into the river on his way east.

Devon relaxed in the back seat, his back against the door and one leg on the seat.

He dozed off, and after about forty-five minutes, he heard the breaks squeak as the taxi came to a stop. He found himself in Kansas City, Missouri, in a Walmart Supercenter parking lot.

"That'll be seventy-six twenty-five," the taxi driver said.

Damion dug into his canvas bag. Off of his stack of hundreds, he peeled four twenties from the bill he had broken earlier and handed them to the driver.

"Three dollars and seventy-five cents?" the driver said to him. "I drive you from Kansas deep into Missouri, and you tip me three dollars and seventy-five cents!"

Damion got out of the cab and slammed the door shut. "You know what, I'd like my change back," he said through the open passenger window.

"Fuck you!" the driver said, and peeled off.

"Asshole," Damion muttered.

Once inside, Damion searched the aisles for the essentials, ditching his canvas dollar store bag for a backpack, and changing out of his hospital gift shop sweats and prison flip-flops into a pair of straight-legged Wranglers, Skechers, a graphic tee, and a puffy coat.

Using his brother's social security number, a Leavenworth Public Library card as identification, and a Visa gift card, he also bought himself a smartphone, for which he paid a hefty deposit, due to Devon's bad credit.

Damion chatted up another taxi driver to ask where he could get a cheap used car, no questions asked. The driver knew just the spot, and took him to a seedy, glorified junkyard, complete with thickly chained Rottweilers, a flaming burn barrel, and a ginger-bearded, potbellied redneck named Slim Jim. This was apparently the place to go if you wanted a used car with "good papers," and no identity verification at all. Two thousand dollars and thirty minutes bought Damion a 1999 Hyundai Elantra. It cost him another three hundred for the temporary tags and registration and four hundred for a Smith & Wesson .38 Special revolver and twenty hollow-point rounds. Slim Jim even threw in half of a fifth of Uncle Nearest Whiskey.

On the day he escaped from prison, Damion felt a rush of liberation. But pulling out of the dirt lot in his car—no parents, judges, platoon sergeants, or correctional officers, and with more money than he could have ever imagined, Damion now felt truly free for the first time in his life.

•••

Damion picked the largest lobster in the tank. He devoured a mountain of coconut shrimp and a half-dozen cheddar bay biscuits, washing it all down with the half bottle of Uncle Nearest that he'd pour under the table. A wink and flashing his library card weren't enough to get the young server to bring him booze.

He felt the world differently than he ever had before. He watched families enjoy themselves. The elderly pair across from him shared a tender kiss. The TV mounted above the bar showed the football game. The Chiefs were in the playoffs against a team he didn't immediately recognize—apparently, the Redskins were no longer the Redskins. Everything seemed to be moving in slow motion. Or maybe it was the whiskey.

Damion stayed until last call, then dragged himself to his car. He dug out one of the cigars the Leavenworth cop had given him, bit the end, lit it, and blew a plume to the purple sky. He plopped on the hood of his car, pulled the Uncle Nearest from his bag, and poured a little on the pavement.

"Here's to you, Zapata. Keep watching my back, man," he said.

He took a swig, then poured the rest to the ground.

"Dad—Percy Lee—I know I worried you to death. Literally. But I'm good now. I'm real good."

Damion stood, cocked the empty bottle back, and launched it as far as he could toward the tree line.

He then balled up on his back seat under his coat and passed out.

Around noon the next day, Damion awoke, found a small diner, then set off east. He took his time driving, observing speed limits and stopping for rest when he was tired and food when he was hungry. It took him just over three days to make the seventeen-hour trip.

# TWENTY-FOUR

At the end of his trip, Damion had found Strawberry Banks, a budget motel five minutes from the Washington, D.C. line. Guests could pay by the hour, or by the day. A little under $500 cash got Damion a week in the "best room I got," as the motel manager put it.

Out of Damion's second-story window were two side-by-side tobacco stores and a drive-thru liquor store that was connected to a laundromat, across from a kid's skating rink. The manager did not require Damion's library card, but he did require an extra one hundred dollar "non-refundable security deposit" since Damion was paying in cash.

The room had seen better days. The faux wood wall paneling was chipped in some areas and missing entirely in others. The high-traffic parts of the carpet were dark and thin, and the bedspread had cigarette burns.

His cell at Leavenworth was cleaner, but nothing was better than having the freedom to come and go as he pleased.

Uncle Butch had posted the link to the ceremony on his Facebook page. Damion had propped his smartphone up in the corner of the shower and watched while he took his first hot shower in days.

"Losing a sibling is unbearable. Losing a twin brother is unthinkable. We shared the same womb, at the same time. The same birthday. Part of me is literally gone. And I miss him sorely."

Damion felt a chill up his spine as he watched his own memorial ceremony. He mouthed every word of "I Am My Brother" as Devon recited it. He swallowed a lump seeing the tears spill from his mother's eyes and knowing the pain he had caused her.

He dried himself, moving the phone from the shower to the sink. Then he changed into some new underwear and sweats that he had picked up at a Walmart in a small town outside of Indianapolis.

Damion ordered a large pizza. He ate a third before nodding off into the deepest, most recuperative sleep he had had in over seven years.

•••

Damion was hiding under the bed in the dark.

After about an hour, he heard the jingling of keys at the door. It opened, and the light flicked on. Damion blew softly at a dust ball that the closing door had kicked up. The wood floor creaked as he watched a pair of black Saucony sneakers pass a foot from his nose. The tail of a wool coat thrown to the bed obstructed his view. He heard the keys crash to the table. Then there was the sound of liquid on liquid, followed by a long sigh, a voice he knew well.

When he heard the toilet flush, he slid from under the bed. He stood and leaned against the wall, his arms crossed, and he waited.

Devon stepped out of the bathroom and froze. His eyes widened and nostrils flared.

"What in the...?"

"Shhhhhh. Be cool. Don't panic," Damion said to his brother.

"What the fuck?!" Devon replied.

Devon sprung onto and then to the other side of the bed.

"Relax. Dev, it's me, your brother. Calm down. It's me, Damion."

Devon fiddled with the door locks, his hands shaking frantically.

"Bro, it's me!" Damion repeated as he ran over and held the door closed.

Devon ran to the window. He reached through the blinds to find the lock, then reconsidered the second-story drop. He then went to the corner, pressed his back into it, and shrank down onto the floor.

"Breathe, Devon. Just breathe."

Damion walked over to Devon.

"I'm alive, brother," he said in a soft voice. "I'm here. And I'm alive."

"Don't fucking touch me!" Devon slapped Damion's hand away.

Damion stood, turned, and took a seat in a chair on the far side of the room.

"Are you done?" he said to Devon. "Are you done being a little bitch?"

"Fuck you, Damo! What are you doing here?" Devon said. "You're supposed to be dead. How are you here right now, alive? Do you know we had a whole ceremony for you and everything? Mom was in pieces."

"I know," Damion replied. "I watched the whole thing online. Seeing her like that broke me up. But that was a beautiful send-off. I liked your little speech."

Devon, stone-faced, peered at Damion through narrowed eyes.

His breathing grew heavier and faster. He paced around the bed, opposite of Damion. He looked to the ceiling, rubbing his head, then leaned forward into the wall, palming it with both hands.

"Dev, you good, bro?"

Devon turned to face Damion.

"You are a disgusting, despicable human being. You know that? You have an insatiable need to always steal the spotlight—to be the center of attention. You live for it. And apparently, you are such a shit person that you'd even fake your own death for it. So, Damion, humor me: what's your story this time? Why did your family just have a memorial service for you? Why are you sitting in my apartment right now?"

"It's a long story," Damion started.

"You know what? I don't want to hear it—I don't care. It's always a long story. I don't know what you're into, all I know is I don't want any part of it. I want you to get out of my apartment. I've pretended you were dead for years. I was relieved when I thought you had actually died, because that meant I didn't have to pretend anymore. Now, go on. Leave. I'll be happy to go back to pretending."

"Dev, brother—"

"Go!" Devon shouted. "I don't have a brother. I want you to go away and stay away!"

"I'm not going anywhere," Damion said.

"Okay. Then I'll make you." Devon pulled his cell phone from his pocket.

Damion leaped over the bed and snatched the phone.

"Give it back!" Devon said, charging Damion.

The two landed on the bed, Devon on top, swinging wild, graceless slaps and punches.

Damion seized Devon's arms and, with a strong push of his legs, flipped them both. They landed hard onto the floor. Damion deftly pinned his brother.

"Get the fuck off me!" Devon yelled, unable to move.

"Shut up!" hissed Damion. He snatched a pillow from the bed, Devon's free hand futilely pummeling into his chest. Damion covered Devon's face with the pillow as he struggled.

After a few moments, Damion pulled the pillow back.

"Let me up," Devon gasped.

"Not until I know you're calm. Are you good?"

"Yeah. Let me up!"

"I need to hear you say, 'I'm good.'"

"Okay. I'm good. Now, get the fuck off of me."

Damion eased up and sat on the bed's edge.

Devon sat up on the floor, hugged his knees, and caught his breath. A minute later, he stood and started toward Damion.

"Aht, aht, aht," Damion said. "What are you doing?"

"What, am I your hostage now? I'm *going* to have a seat in the chair that I own. Is that okay with you?"

Devon took a seat in a chair across from Damion. He leaned forward toward him, elbows to knees.

"Well?" Devon said.

"Well, what?" Damion replied.

"Talk, asshole. I'm listening."

For the next hour, Damion related in detail his experiences over the last seven or so years. He talked about his time in Afghanistan—from working on the poo circuit to the death of his friend, Zapata. He talked about Jim and Jon and the opium runs. Then about his time in prison, Oni, and the attempt on his life.

Devon was literally on the edge of his seat, completely absorbed in the story.

"Wait," he interrupted. "How did you get in my apartment? How did you even find my apartment?"

"Well, it took me a few days in a shitty motel before I figured you were probably still driving my old car. Did you forget I installed a GPS way back when we were in high school? Nineteen of the last thirty days pinged at this location here in D.C. When I saw that, I knew you still had it, and I came straight here. Sure enough, there she was. And you have your name on the mailbox like an idiot. So, I just called the apartment manager, said I lost my key. A guy—Craig, I think—came a half-hour later to let me in. We *are* identical twins, remember? Although, you've picked up a potbelly, and you could stand to lift a dumbbell or two."

"So you impersonated me?!"

"Oh, don't act so high and mighty." Damion found a half-full bottle of cheap vodka and a couple of coffee mugs in the cabinet.

He poured them each a cup and gave one to Devon. He held it up and grinned.

"Here, drink with me, brother," he said to Devon.

Devon declined Damion's toast but took the shot.

"So, you were a drug dealer?" Devon asked.

"It's not like that," Damion replied. "I wasn't some street-level punk selling smack to junkies. We were sending raw medication ingredients to a legit pharmaceutical company."

"Oh, I'm sorry. You were an international drug trafficker. I stand corrected."

"I was just a spoke on a very large wheel—part of an enormous operation. They used me as a scapegoat."

"Whatever, Damo. Just tell me why you're here. What is it that you want from me?"

Damion leaned forward and put his hand on Devon's shoulder. Devon jerked away. Damion then sat back, clasping his hands together under his own chin, and closed his eyes.

"I need your help, brother. I got away with faking my death as far as the government is concerned, but if Damion Lee were to pop up on any radar, I could end up spending a long time behind bars."

"Okay, so, leave the country. Disappear. Don't pop up on any radar. You're a free man, nobody's looking for you. What do you need me for?"

"The problem is that I'm not quite sure the whole world has bought my story."

"What do you mean?"

"Remember Jim and Jon? Well, Keating Pharma, the company they work for, is very powerful, with pockets deeper than Farrakhan. Like I said, this is a big operation. I am a liability for them, and everybody up and down the supply line, including military and government brass—I'm a threat to them all. And if there's a chance they believe I might still be alive, they'll do whatever is necessary to eliminate that threat. They have the resources to reach out and touch just about anybody, anywhere. I told you what they did to my friend Zapata, right? And how they tried to poison me in prison? And what they did to the guy who gave me the poison? Get the picture?"

"And your bright idea was to lead them to me?" Devon popped to his feet, interlocked his fingers behind his head as he paced back and forth. "Why don't you just go back to the motel?"

Damion put his mug on the floor and leaned back in his chair.

"I can't go back to Strawberry Banks; it's not safe for me there. For fifty bucks, the motel manager will point anybody to my room. Listen." He leaned forward, grabbing Devon's shoulders. "You're my identical twin. I was thinking you could let me hold on to an ID. I figure I can share your life just for a little while until everything blows over. I'll spend most of my time here in the apartment, but at least I'll be able to go out and have a drink. Just a month or so until I can get my mind right—you know, work out a plan."

Devon brushed Damion's hands from his shoulders, then sat back in his chair. He threw up his hands and let out an incredulous sigh.

"I don't know why I'm even entertaining this conversation. The answer is no. No. No. *Hell no*. Damion, do you remember that day in Mama's kitchen years ago when I told you that you were getting close to the end of the line with me? I told you that if you ever got into any more trouble, that would be it. I said you would cease to be my brother. Do you remember that?"

Damion sat in silence.

"Well, I meant it then and I mean it now."

Damion hung his head and leaned forward, elbows to knees.

*"He is I. I am he,"* Damion recited.

"Oh, don't try to pull that 'I Am My Brother' shit on me," Devon said. "That has never meant anything to you."

*"How can you not see?"* Damion continued. *"No, I am not my brother's keeper. I am my brother. And my brother is me."*

"Get out of my apartment, Damion."

"Fuck, Dev! I need your help. You're the only person on Earth I can trust. Here, let me show you something."

Damion unlocked his phone and tossed it to Devon.

"What am I looking at?" Devon said.

"You're holding over forty million dollars in your hand. Ever heard of Bitcoin?"

"Yeah, of course," Devon replied. "Is this your account?"

"Every penny. I told you they paid me, but I didn't tell you how or how much. The market value has been doubling, tripling, and quadrupling over the years. Name your price. A million? Two? Five?"

Devon tossed Damion back his phone.

"Listen, I don't want your money and whatever trouble is attached to it."

Damion looked around the room. "Dev," he said, "you're driving a twenty-year-old beater. You're living in this shoebox. Your credit is trash, and you're okay eating day-old pizza from the floor. You may not *want* my money, but you need it."

"You ate it, too," Devon said.

"*I* just spent the past half-decade in Afghanistan and prison. *You* have no excuse."

Devon paused with pursed lips and a shrug.

"Touché," he replied. "Whatever. So, you're telling me you're a multimillionaire. You, Damion 'Fuck-Up For Life' Lee, a multimillionaire. I just assumed the government would've seized anything you made on your little drug runs."

"They can't seize what they can't find. As long as I have access to my digital wallet, and I'm the only one with the private key to unlock it, not even Uncle Sam can get his greedy fingers on it."

Devon pinched his chin between his thumb and index finger.

"I've put you and the family through hell over the years," Damion said. "This is my way to make it up to you. Let me do this one thing, and I promise after a few weeks, I'll be gone, and you will be rich."

"Damo, I appreciate your effort to redeem yourself, but like I said: I refuse to take dirty money from you or anyone else. I don't care how much it is. Regardless of what crock of shit your crooked friends told you, those drugs are making their way to the hood in Alphabet City where we grew up, and all over the country. And to know that my brother is behind that is disgraceful. You have sunken to a new low."

Damion turned around and looked through the blinds. Tears had begun to form in the corners of his eyes.

"Fine," he said, trying to hide his quavering voice. He began to grab his things.

Devon sat at the corner of the bed, arms crossed as he watched his brother. His expression started to soften, and he sighed as he rubbed his temples.

"Against every drop of better judgment in my body..." he started.

Damion snapped back around to face Devon. "Thank you! Thank you! Thank you!" he said.

"But you have one month—thirty days, Damo. No more. And I'm not taking your money. This is not a favor to *you*; I'm doing this because this is what Mama would want if she knew. It's what Dad would've wanted. They taught us to look out for each other. It's about brotherhood. You may not have learned that, but I did."

Damion approached Devon and extended his hand for a dap. "I knew you couldn't send your bro to the wolves."

"Wait," Devon said, not responding to Damion's hand nor his comment. "You said the muscle from the pharmaceutical company might be looking for you. I need to know how motivated they are. What are the odds they didn't buy the suicide story?"

"I'd say fifty-fifty. Jim and Jon popped up in Kansas and were poking around asking questions after I'd already left the hospital. I get the sense that they were just tying up loose ends. The nurse was solid, though. Super loyal and could sell fire in Hell. Plus, I paid her well."

"Hold up. What did these dudes look like? Greasy black hair? As big as a couple of refrigerators?"

"Sounds like them," Damion replied. "Why—have you seen them?"

Damion bit the knuckle of his index finger with a pensive expression.

"At your memorial ceremony—the church only allowed a handful of people there because of the coronavirus. They stuck out like two white guys at a Black funeral. They just stood in the back, looking around like a couple of Secret Service agents."

"Like I said," Damion replied, "I think they were just buttoning things up, making sure I was no longer a threat. But, again, I can't be a hundred percent."

They studied each other.

"You know, Damo, usually, when you're involved, people have to clutch their wallets. I've never known you to come bearing gifts. Tell me, just out of curiosity, how much were you willing to give me for letting you stay here?"

"You got student loans, right? And you need a reliable car? An upgrade from this shithole apartment?" Damion asked, fingering dust from the tattered, plastic Venetian blinds.

"Be careful. This *shithole* is where you're asking me to stay for a month."

"You're right. My bad," Damion replied. "I was willing to go as high as ten million."

Damion refreshed their mugs.

"Whew!" Devon said, shaking his head. "I can't lie: ten million dollars could clean a lot of slates."

"Well, you turned it down. So, the offer is off the table," Damion replied.

The two shared their first laugh of the night.

"Cheers."

"*Salud.*"

"By the way," Devon said, "earlier you mentioned I had bad credit. How did you know that?"

"Just a guess," Damion said, mug to mouth.

# TWENTY-FIVE

"Get outta bed, lazy head!" Damion pounded the mattress next to Devon's head. "'Member Mom used to say that?"

"What are you doing? Leave me alone," Devon said, swatting Damion's hand away.

"It's time to get up, Dev. If we're gonna be the same person, we have to look the same. It's time to work out. What, did you think I would become skinny with a potbelly like you? Think again, broham."

"It is *my* life that you want. Why shouldn't you look like me?" Devon rolled over.

Damion kneed him in the butt. "Wake up!"

"What in the actual fuck!"

"We're gonna have to work on how to curse proper, too," Damion said.

"That's 'properly,'" Devon replied.

"Huh?"

"I said 'properly.' You meant to use the adverb. 'How to curse *properly*' is what you should've said."

"Whatever, Dev. How 'bout you get outta bed, before I *properly* kick your adverb ass all over this shitty apartment?"

Devon checked his phone. "Damo, it's three o'clock. I'm going back to sleep."

Damion tossed one of Devon's sneakers, hitting him in the head. "I said let's go."

Devon threw it back aimlessly.

"Get dressed. And don't turn on the ceiling light; use the lamp."

"Why can't I use the big light?"

"The softer, the better. If someone's out there watching, a big, bright light could signal to them we're about to leave. Now, that's enough questions. Let's go."

Devon sat on the edge of the bed and rubbed the sleep from his eyes. Damion put on a pair of Devon's Saucony shoes.

"Not those. Those are my commuting shoes."

"'*Not those. Those are my commuting shoes,*'" Damion mocked his brother, continuing to tie the laces. "Get dressed."

They walked toward the back door. Damion had folded the olive green, wool blanket into a rectangle, the exact length and width of his pillow, which he had placed on top. He put them both neatly at the head of the bed.

Damion poked his head out first, his eyes cutting every direction. An orange cat scaled the fence. A lone drug-addicted prostitute speed-walked across the street and climbed into the passenger seat of an old Acura. The flicker of a barrel fire down the alley reflected off the brick walls of the other buildings while a group of men hovered around it to keep warm. Otherwise, the night was still. They moved through the alley to the corner of the block.

Damion grabbed the rusty railing of a sagging fence with one hand, and his ankle with the other. "Do what I do," he said.

After a series of stretches, Damion started jogging in place. Devon's feet barely left the ground.

"Get those knees up, Dev."

"The sun's not even up."

"What does that have to do with you picking up your legs?"

"I should be in bed right now."

"Mind over matter. If you don't mind it, it won't matter," Damion said, then jogged to the next corner.

Devon slugged on behind him.

•••

Damion popped off the bed when he heard keys jingling at the door. He checked the peephole, then unlocked it and let Devon inside.

"Hey, bro. I haven't seen you in a couple of days," Damion said. "I was worried. I thought you had been snatched up or something. Or were you avoiding Drill Sergeant Damo's boot camp?"

"I'm sorry. I didn't realize I needed to report my whereabouts to you. Is that part of the deal, too?"

"Someone's testy," Damion replied.

"My bad, man. I've just been taking it in the gut from everybody recently. If you think being on the lam is hard, try being a Black Republican."

"Wait. You're a Republican?"

"You mean to tell me you've had access to a television for over a week now and you haven't seen national news?" Devon picked up the remote and changed the channel from an old *The Fresh Prince of Bel Air* rerun to CNN, then to Fox News. Within a couple of minutes, one of his sound bites aired.

"I'm more of a local news guy," Damion replied. "Anyway, that was one helluva way to come out to your brother. You know," he said, holding back a chuckle, his hand on Devon's shoulder, "I always knew. I knew before you did. Did you tell Mama?"

"Listen, I take shit from people every day about it. I refuse to take it from you, too, Damion. And yes, she knows."

"I don't care either way. You know I don't do politics. I just remember what Mama always said about Republicans. What did she used to call it?"

"The Devil's politics," they said in unison, both laughing.

"So, where ya been the last coupla days—got a little girlfriend?"

Devon turned off the television and tossed the remote to the bed.

"None of your business?"

"Wait, don't tell me—you got a boyfriend? You know, growing up, I always knew that about you, too. Again, no judgement here."

"It's a girl, Damo—a woman."

"Whew," Damion said, dramatically swiping the back of his hand across his forehead. "I don't know if my little heart could handle two coming outs in one night."

"Beth—her name is Bethany. And yes. I've been sleeping at her place the last couple nights, because, contrary to what you might have thought, sleeping head-to-toe in the same bed with another grown man doesn't quite work for me. Your feet smell like spoiled milk, dude."

"Yeah, yeah. Don't try to change the subject. Beth...sounds like a white woman. So, tell me about Becky with the good hair."

"She's cool," Devon replied.

"Nah, I'm not accepting that. My bro, Dev, has a girlfriend. I never thought I'd see the day. You're gonna have to show me a picture or somethin'."

Devon opened his Instagram to her profile and held the phone to Damion's face. Damion snatched the phone and began scrolling.

"She's cute, bro. I can't lie. Nice little ass, too. Does Mama know about her?"

"What do you mean? Of course she knows."

"You know what I mean. Does she know Becky's a Becky?"

Devon reached for his phone, but Damion held him back with one hand, continuing to scroll with the other.

"If by 'Becky,' you mean 'white,' then no. She doesn't know. And frankly, I prefer it stays that way. I already know her views on the topic. And stop calling her Becky. It's derogatory and I don't like it."

"It's a what?"

"I don't like it. So, stop."

Damion tossed the phone and Devon caught it with his chest.

"Looks like I struck a raw nerve," Damion said. "But really—and I mean this with all sincerity—if your relationship with Beck...Bethany is that serious, I'm happy for you, brother, and I wish you all the best. Anyway, who am I to judge? I like the interracial stuff on Pornhub, myself."

"Thanks, man. I guess," Devon replied.

"But you do know that you're gonna have to introduce her to Mama at some point?"

"I'll cross that bridge when I get there."

"How did you get out of taking her to my memorial service? It sounds weird hearing myself say that."

"I told her it was a family reunion, and I wasn't ready to take that step yet."

"A family reunion?" Damion replied. "In January? In a pandemic? And she bought it?"

They both laughed.

"I didn't think that much into it," Devon replied.

"Whatever you do, just remember: no pillow talk about our little agreement. You could get us both killed."

"Of course."

Damion poured them each a cup of vodka. They tapped mugs and took sips.

"Do her parents know you're Black?" he asked.

"Yeah, but me being Black isn't a problem for them; their big issue is that I'm a Republican."

"Do they know that?" Damion asked.

"Yup. We all had dinner last Thursday. It was a shitshow."

# TWENTY-SIX

Damion sprang out of bed at the sound of banging at the door. Ducking low, he dug for the revolver in his bag, slipped on his Leavenworth sweatpants, and crept to the peephole.

"It's Becky. Fuck!" he whispered to himself.

"Devon," she called. "Don't be angry with me. I'm so sorry my parents were assholes to you the other night. Please—let me in. I know you're in there. I heard you moving around a second ago."

Her words were slurred.

"Let's talk about it tomorrow," Damion said. "Just go home. I'm not in the mood tonight."

"Come on, baby, I'm sorry. It's not my fault; I didn't know they would behave that way. I would've never knowingly put you in that situation."

"Not tonight, Beth. Let's just link up tomorrow, please."

"Makeba had better not be in there with you. I know you're seeing her. Is that bitch in there with you?"

Damion heard the sound of keys in the lock.

"Fuck!" He darted to the bed, put the gun in the nightstand, and grabbed a pillow.

The door swung open.

Stunned, Damion just stood there, holding the pillow to his bare chest.

Bethany looked around, then immediately dropped to her knees to check under the bed. Her ankles buckled as she pulled herself back to her feet. She then stumbled to the bathroom using the wall for support. She checked the shower and behind the door.

Her hair was in a messy bun. Black streaks of mascara extended from her eyes to her jawline. She was wearing one of Damion's old Army sweatshirts that Devon had taken as his own after the memorial service.

"Are you satisfied?" Damion asked.

"No," she replied. "Why haven't you been answering my calls, Devon?"

"The real question is: what are you doing here?" Damion replied.

"Did you forget you gave me your spares?"

"You should go, Becky. I just want to get some sleep."

She flopped onto the bed, holding her head in her hands, elbows on her knees.

"What did you just call me?" she asked, turning her head towards him.

"I called you Bethany—your name."

"The champagne must have gone to my head. I'm a little tipsy."

Damion pulled a tank top undershirt from the dresser drawer and pulled it over his head. Bethany perked up. She watched with bulged eyes.

"Either I really am toasted, or you got ripped in the last twenty-four hours," she said, moving in for closer inspection.

"Thanks," Damion said. "I think you could use some water." He sidestepped her and started for the refrigerator.

Bethany stood and followed him. As he went to open the refrigerator, she walked up behind him, pressing her body against his.

"Relax, Beth," Damion said, making his best efforts to peel her off.

She latched onto his chest.

"I know you've been working out recently," she said, "but I didn't realize your body would respond so quickly. Mmmm, yummy."

"I'm not in the mood tonight, babe," Damion said, pulling her hands from his pants.

"Listen, baby," she said, "I'm so sorry about my parents. Come on. Let me make it up to you."

Bethany led him out of the kitchen by the drawstring of his pants and tackled him to the bed. She mounted him, pinning his hands down. Damion put up little resistance.

"Keep it down over there! We have kids!" a neighbor yelled, while another banged on their ceiling with a broomstick.

•••

Bethany found herself in a hypnotic trance, arm dangling from the bedside, knuckles touching the wood floor.

"Get up, Beth," Damion said. "You have to go."

"Huh?" she replied.

"I need you to go home."

"Wha—why?" she said, coming out of her stupor.

"I have a meeting first thing, and I need to get ready for it," Damion replied. "Beth, get up!" He pounded the mattress next to her head.

In a daze, Beth dressed and collected her things, as if she were sleepwalking.

"I'll see you tomorrow, babe," Damion said.

She mumbled something unintelligible, while Damion, with a hand to the small of her back, ushered her to the door.

Damion pecked her on the cheek and sent her on her way.

"Hey, Beth."

"Huh?" she said, halfway down the stairs.

"I think your jeans are on backward."

# TWENTY-SEVEN

Whenever Damion left the apartment, he was vigilant—careful, almost to the point of paranoia.

The Army had taught him to notice every pattern in his environment, to look for inconsistencies. In Afghanistan, a spot of fresh, new concrete on an otherwise dilapidated stretch of road could be a sign that something treacherous lay beneath. Growing up in Alphabet City taught him to recognize when a person was up to no good by the mere look in his eye. He could tell a stranger's intentions by a wayward glance, a change in voice pitch, or the way they walked. Not having command of these skills was potentially deadly in Afghanistan and Alphabet City.

Every half hour before leaving the apartment, he did a window check, scanning outside for a different car, an odd person—anything out of place. Today was no different. Once he was satisfied, he slipped out of the back door and through the alley.

The pandemic made it easier for people to move about in relative anonymity. Damion couldn't care less about an airborne virus but welcomed the idea of something covering his face. He donned his mask, Devon's frayed Middle Georgia Law baseball cap, and a pair of cheap, plastic shades he'd picked up on the road. His Walmart backpack rested on the revolver he kept in the small of his back.

In an effort to minimize the chance of an engagement with the police, he often walked, leaving his car parked on a side street two blocks from the apartment. After walking a mile, he reached the grocery store. It had been years since he'd had a home-cooked meal, and he intended to remedy that today.

Damion inspected apples. He sampled grapes. He picked red onions and smelled green peppers.

He spotted a white man sniffing sunflowers in the floral section.

Damion looked around. There weren't any other white people in the market. In fact, besides a spattering of pioneering gentrifiers, the entire neighborhood was Black.

Damion examined a carton of eggs.

The man picked through collard greens on the far end.

Damion rounded the corner into the first aisle and perused wine labels. He selected two Pinots—a Noir and a Gris—and a Sauvignon blanc. The man appeared at the other end of the aisle where the sparkling wines were. Damion moved to the next aisle, where he opened the camera on his smartphone. Holding it to his face, he pretended to video-chat. The man, without a cart or handbasket, pulled and replaced boxes of pasta from the shelf. Damion snapped a photo.

The man moved with Damion, aisle by aisle, in a failed attempt at inconspicuousness.

He finally peeled away when Damion went for the registers to check out.

"I.D., sir."

"Come again?" Damion replied.

"I need to see your I.D.—for the wine," the cashier said through a plexiglass barrier.

"Oh, here ya go." He flashed Devon's old, expired Georgia driver's license. "Out of curiosity, what's the point of checking I.D. if people have to wear masks? You can't see their faces."

"Don't start with me," she replied. "I'm just doing my job."

Damion packed the groceries in his backpack and hand-carried a plastic bag with the eggs and apples.

The man exited ahead of Damion.

Damion kept him in sight as he returned his cart. He walked toward the far end of the parking lot.

"Shit!" he said, intentionally dropping the grocery bag as a decoy.

An apple rolled under a parked car and disappeared.

Damion ducked low, using the cars to obscure his movement as he picked up a jog. He had soon flanked the man, who had gone to investigate the spot between the cars where Damion had seemed to have disappeared.

Damion charged from behind and tackled him to the ground.

"Who the fuck are you?" Damion mounted the man and jammed his forearm into his Adam's apple.

Unable to breathe, the man tapped Damion's shoulder in desperation. Damion eased the pressure. The man wheezed and coughed.

"Why are you following me?"

"I'm a private eye," the man replied.

He was short. His salt and pepper hair was slicked back, and he wore a pair of perfectly circular wire glasses and a cardigan under a herringbone blazer.

"Who hired you?"

"I can't say."

"Last chance. Who hired you?!" Damion repeated, now gripping the man by the throat, his thumb buried into the man's pulse.

The man tapped Damion's thigh.

"Ms. Lewenberg," the man whimpered.

"Who is Ms. Loonber? Is she with Keating?"

"Lewenberg," the man replied, "your girlfriend. She hired me to see if you were cheating. Now, please let me up."

"Bethany hired you?"

"That *is* your girlfriend, right?" he replied. "Please, sir, I need to sit up. I'm having trouble breathing."

Damion showed the investigator the handle of his revolver. "Don't worry, sir. I won't hurt you as long as you do what I say. Now, where is your cell phone?" He frisked the man's pockets and dug it out. "I want you to call her right now and tell her to meet you at five, in front of her apartment. Don't mention anything about me being with you."

"Okay, okay. I just need to sit up, please."

Damion sat him up against the wheel of a Honda. He kept a palm pressed into the investigator's sternum.

The man unlocked the phone. Damion watched as he located her number.

"Put it on speakerphone," Damion demanded.

The man obeyed, and after a few rings, Bethany answered, "Good news, I hope."

"Yeah," the investigator replied. "But I can't say over the phone. Meet me in front of your apartment building at five."

"Can we make it five fifteen?"

The investigator looked to Damion, who gave a nod.

"See you then," the investigator said.

Damion handled the man from underneath the armpit, helping him to his feet. They found his car, a well-kept, fifteen-year-old Mercedes, and Damion took the passenger's side back seat.

"Residences at City Center," Damion said to the investigator, recalling the name of the apartments from when he had pinged the GPS history for the Mitsubishi. That was the only other place the car had shown up overnight other than Devon's apartment for several days each month.

"I'm not your taxi driver," the investigator said.

"You probably should consider being one," Damion replied, "because you suck as an investigator. How is it that you were supposed to be tailing me, but ended up getting tailed *by* me?"

"Ms. Lewenberg said you'd be an easy subject to track," he replied. "She told me you were a helpless nerd, not some ghetto ninja. Are you police, military, FBI, or something?"

"She said that? She said I was helpless?"

"You didn't hear that from me," the investigator replied.

Damion laughed. "Fucking Dev. His own girl thinks he's a pussy," he said to himself.

"Say what?" the investigator asked.

"Nothing. Just start driving." He flashed his gun in the rearview. The investigator grumbled, turned on the engine, and pulled out of the parking lot.

They double-parked in front of the luxury apartments, the most exclusive in the city, and Devon lay across the back seat. Within ten minutes, Bethany's Tesla pulled into the garage; she emerged on foot not long after. The inspector tapped the horn and waved her over.

He rolled down the window. "Hop in," the investigator said.

"Hey, babe," Damion said, popping upright when she shut the door.

"Holy fuck! Devon, you almost gave me a heart attack."

"I'm sorry about this," the investigator said. "He somehow made me, and then snuck up on me from behind."

"Listen, Beth, I'm not upset with you," Damion said. "Let's just go up to your apartment. We clearly have a lot to talk about."

"Hold on just a moment. I'm not leaving you with him unless I know you're safe. Do you know he has a gun?" the inspector said to Bethany.

"If I was gonna use it, I would've used it on you. We're good," Damion said.

"I need to hear *her* say it," the investigator said. "Do you feel safe leaving with him, Ms. Lewenberg?"

"I'll be fine, Archie," she said. "Thanks for everything."

"Again, I'm incredibly sorry about this, Ms. Lewenberg. I'll refund your deposit as soon as I get back to the office. And if it's not too much trouble, I'd appreciate a five-star rating."

"Let's go, Beth."

•••

Beth opened the door using an app on her phone. Damion entered behind her, making a beeline for her bar cart.

"Blue label. Nice," he said. He turned over two short glasses and poured. "Rocks?" he asked Bethany.

"Just a couple drops of water," she answered.

He paused to admire a metallic, life-sized statue of a man, swan diving from the fifteen-foot ceiling to the polished marble floor. Bethany explained that she had received it as a gift from the crown prince of the U.A.E. He'd had it removed from a display in the Dubai Mall and shipped to her.

She and Damion clinked glasses. Damion hopped onto the island. Bethany leaned against the wall, facing him. They each took sips, while studying each other.

"He's mighty fat," Damion said.

"Who's fat?" Bethany replied.

"That elephant over there in the corner."

"Do you have something to tell me?" Bethany asked.

"I think you're the one who has something to explain," Damion replied. "You put a P.I. on me?"

"Don't bullshit me. I know who you are, *Damion*."

Damion took a sip.

"How'd you find out?" he asked.

"I guess Archie, the private eye, wasn't all that incompetent, after all," she replied. "He dug it up and sent me an email this morning."

"He told me that you thought Devon was cheating," Damion said.

"I did. Well, I still do. When you rushed me out of your apartment last night, I suspected that you—or Devon—had another woman on the way. I called Archie from the car on my way home. Now I realize you just didn't want the real Devon to come home and catch us."

"How did you find an investigator on such short notice?"

"I'm from a family of means—let's just put it that way. But I didn't need Archie to tell me that you aren't your brother. I would've certainly figured it out today."

"What do you mean?" Damion asked.

"The way you handled Archie—Devon would never have been able to pull off what you did. Not his style. He's too docile."

Damion shot his drink and hopped down to refresh his glass. He paused to admire the view of the Capitol through Bethany's floor-to-ceiling panoramic glass windows.

"And he can't stand Scotch," she added. "Oh, and this. Alexa, turn on the T.V."

Damion turned around to see his brother in a split-screen CNN debate.

"It's live. He's been on T.V. all day. So, unless you're his doppelgänger, it looks like *you* have some explaining to do."

He and Bethany watched till the end of the segment.

"He's pretty good," Damion said.

"He's finally found his sea legs," Bethany replied.

"He doesn't look helpless to me."

"What do you mean?"

"Archie told me what you said about him."

"Old Archie has a tendency to take things out of context."

"You don't have to backpedal with me. I know my brother. And you're right. He's always been weak sauce. But I don't know this new 'Devon,'" Damion said, tipping his glass to the television. "Something's clearly taken ahold of him."

"Or *someone*," Bethany replied. "But what I don't understand is: why didn't he tell me he had a brother—a twin brother, at that? He's always said he was an only child."

"Have a seat," Damion said. He refreshed both their glasses. "My relationship with my brother is complicated. The long and short of it is that he's ashamed of me. And for good reason—I haven't exactly been a model citizen over the years, much less brother of the year."

Damion spent the next hour catching Bethany up on the last decade or so, taking creative liberties with certain facts, such as the circumstances of his military discharge, and omitting details relating to his imprisonment, his staged death, and his multimillionaire status.

Bethany clung to each word, entranced by his accent and cadence.

Their conversation was interrupted when Bethany's phone rang. "Speak of the devil," Bethany said, checking her smartwatch. "Excuse me for a sec."

Bethany walked into her bedroom to take the call.

•••

After speaking with Devon, Bethany opened the bedroom door to see Damion standing there, one hand on his hip, the other against the jamb. His presence startled her frozen.

"So, he really pretended like I never existed, huh?"

"Yup—just like he does with me when he and Makeba are doing God knows what."

Bethany looked Damion up, down, and up again, their eyes meeting and locking.

Damion lunged toward Bethany and lifted her by the waist. She wrapped her legs around his. They fell to the bed, rolled to the floor. Then to a chair, and back to the bed again.

•••

"I guess this counts as consent after the fact," Bethany said as she and Damion lay nude beneath her luxury Four Seasons bed sheets.

He pulled her in closer, burying his nose into her neck as they spooned. "What do you mean by that?" he replied.

"We were in murky water the other night when I thought you were your brother."

"Oh, please. You attacked me like a rabid pit bull. The Jaws of Life couldn't pull you off me. If anybody's consent was questionable, it was mine."

"Touché," she chuckled. "You know, it wasn't just the way you handled Archie, or you drinking the Scotch that gave your little secret away. I knew much earlier than that."

"Oh, yeah?"

"Yeah," she replied, turning to face him.

"Then what was it?"

"My wobbly legs told me when I almost took a tumble down the stairs in your building. That has never happened with Devon."

"Well, you know," Damion said with a smug chuckle.

Bethany checked her phone.

"I have to go," she said as she got out of bed.

"What's the rush?"

"I had just told Devon I'd meet up with him tonight. You know, right before you accosted me."

"Tonight? After what we just did? Either I didn't do my job right, or you're a machine."

"Oh, don't worry. I can assure you he and I won't be doing any of that. He's probably exhausted. I know I certainly am," she said planting a kiss between his eyes. "Devon has been doing interviews all day. If he does try anything, I'll just say Aunt Flow is in town. Besides, ever since he met Makeba, he hasn't had much interest in me."

"Makeba? Who's she?"

"She's just a friend of mine. At least I thought she was a friend. I think she and Devon have something going on."

"Nah, Dev is a lot of things, but he's not a cheater. I don't think he'd step out on you."

"Oh yeah? Then why is he always alone with her in her apartment? Why does she cook for him? You know he even slept overnight at her place?"

"Devon did that?" Damion replied with raised eyebrows. "So, are you leaving now to go confront him?"

"Oh, no. I'm smarter than that. I'm going to keep things status quo for the time being. I'll stay quiet and act normal. My best advantage right now is that he doesn't know that I know; I'll keep it that way until I'm ready to strike. I'll let him think I'm dumb. I'll lie low in the grass. And when the time is right, I'll pop up and bite his head off."

"Hold on, now. This is still my brother you're talking about."

"I don't mean literally, silly," Bethany replied. "I'm going to catch him in a bold-faced lie."

"That's what you'd better mean," Damion replied playfully. "Ahem, um, not that it's any surprise to me, but were you serious about having wobbly legs after leaving me last night? Am I that much better in bed than him?"

"Let's just say you two might be identical twins, but not everything about you is identical."

"Well, after years of not getting any, it's good to know that I still got it."

Bethany showered, changed, and went to the kitchen to pull two bottles of Perrier-Jouët from the wine refrigerator.

"I won't be back tonight," she said. "So, feel free to stay for a while. Oh, and no need to lock up. The door will lock automatically behind you."

# TWENTY-EIGHT

Jon stepped out of a taxi at the southeast end of Lake Jeanette. Jim had been waiting there on a park bench for ten minutes.

"Jim."

"Jon."

"Long time, no see, brother."

The two men gripped hands and embraced with the other arm.

"Can't say I'm happy to see your ugly mug," Jim said, patting Jon on the cheek.

"Same here. Good enough reason for us to clean this mess up so we can get back to our retirements as soon as possible. Whaddaya say?"

"They screwed the pooch on this, didn't they?" Jim said.

"Fucking idiots. We should've handled this in Afghanistan years ago."

"You know, this time four days ago, I was on Wet Betty off the coast of St. Tropez."

"Wet Betty. That your old lady?" Jon asked.

"She's my yacht," Jim replied.

"*Unsinkable II* is mine."

"*Unsinkable*? How original. But why 'II'? What happened to the—Oh. Clever."

"Well, I've settled down in Pattaya," Jon said.

"Thailand? Nice. I love it out there. Maybe I'll come check you out when this is all over."

"I'm freezing my nuts off," Jon said. "Let's get to work. The sooner we put a bow on this thing, the sooner we can get back to our lives."

•••

That afternoon, Jim and Jon arrived at St. John Hospital in uniform navy-blue suits, white shirts, and calf-length black, wool coats. The only difference between them was their tie patterns, though the same colors.

Winston Nightingale, Esquire, as Damion's attorney, had called ahead to the hospital for his room number and passed it along to Jim and Jon for their investigation.

•••

They walked fast. No one questioned their bona fides.

They filed into Damion's former room where they found Nurse Toni injecting medication into an I.V. of a man who appeared to be sleeping.

"Oh, hello. How may I help you?" she asked.

"I'm Special Agent Floyd, and this is Special Agent Mendelson," Jim said, "and we have a couple questions for you."

"Excuse me, agents, but as you can see, I'm treating a patient here. Can you wait outside? I'll be right with you."

Jim nodded to Jon, and they exited the room. Nurse Toni followed a minute later and led them into an empty room.

"How may I help you, gentlemen?"

Jim cleared his throat. "We're with the Federal Bureau of Prisons. Is the room we just left the one where Inmate BOP number 12041-906 was housed?"

"I'm sorry, sir, we treat everyone here as human beings, not numbers. I'm going to need a name for your inmate."

"Oh, pardon my partner's callousness," Jon said. "When you've been doing this job for as long as we have, it all becomes routine; sometimes you forget your couth. I'm sure you know what I mean, Nurse...I'm sorry, I missed your name."

"Antonia Montgomery, but everyone here just calls me 'Nurse Toni.' And no—I don't know what you mean."

"I'm certain you don't. You're too pretty to forget your manners like us ugly boneheads. We're looking for the room where an inmate by the name of 'Damion Lee' was cared for. This is it, correct?"

Pinching the bridge of her nose, Nurse Toni bowed her head and closed her eyes.

"That's correct," she answered, subdued. "I take it you are aware that Mr. Lee has passed away."

"We are, indeed," Jim said. "In fact, that's why we're here—to investigate the circumstances of his death."

Nurse Toni sat down on a gurney. "Pardon me, gents, but every chance a nurse gets to get off her feet, she takes it."

"Oh, by all means," Jim said.

"A Leavenworth City officer already conducted an investigation. Can't you just get a copy of his report?" she asked.

"We'll be reaching out to the city with a request for their report, too," Jon said. "We feds just like to do our own investigations. In our experience, small-town cops tend to do shoddy work."

"Listen, we know you're busy," Jim said. "We just have a few quick questions, and we'll be out of your hair. How does that sound?"

"Sure. Okay," Nurse Toni replied. "But, as you can see, I'm pretty busy."

"Okay, then. Let's get started. Were you the nurse in charge of taking care of Mr. Lee?" Jim asked.

"For the overnight shift, yes. I was. There were two others for the day and swing shifts, though."

"Were you here when Mr. Lee expired?"

"No. I wasn't."

"Our records show that he died sometime between three and seven o'clock in the morning," Jim said.

"That's my guess, too," Nurse Toni replied.

"Weren't you here during that time?"

"No. I was on shift. But I wasn't here in this room when he died. Wait, do I need an attorney?"

"Not at all," Jon replied. "These are standard questions. No foul play is suspected, and you are not under investigation."

Jim scribbled hard on a small notepad and flipped the page.

"Do you have the bottle of oxycodone Mr. Lee overdosed on?" he asked.

"Sure, but I can't release it to you unless you sign it out as evidence. There's a process for that."

"We won't be needing the bottle," Jon replied. "Maybe a coupla photos later, if that's okay?"

"You'll have to check with the front desk for that," she replied.

Jon checked his watch. "Just a couple more questions, and we'll be out of your hair."

"Were you the one who discovered him?" Jim asked.

"I was."

"Can you tell us what happened after?" Jon followed up.

"I got on the two military guards' case for not paying attention. And then, like I said, the Leavenworth cop showed up and did his investigation. He said it was open and shut. Then my assistant and I rolled Damion down to the morgue in the basement."

Jim looked at Jon. They both nodded.

"Well, Ms. Toni..."

"Nurse Toni," she interrupted.

"Oh, pardon me," Jim said with a polite chuckle. "*Nurse* Toni, I think that's all the questions we have for now. Can you give us a number we can reach you on if we have any more questions? And if you'd be so kind, would you point us to the morgue?"

•••

Jim and Jon convened in the hallway.

"Whaddaya think, brother?"

"My spidey senses are tinglin'."

"Mine, too."

"Nurse Toni seemed just a tad defensive. Did she not?"

"Oh, yeah. And did you notice the way she slipped up and called him Damion, instead of Mr. Lee? Almost sounds like he could've been more than just a patient."

"Good catch. Let's keep an eye on her."

The morgue was cold and dark, except for the motion-activated fluorescent lights. The walls, ceiling, and floors were white. There was a faint chemical smell. A small-framed, balding, middle-aged man with round, black glasses pored over an inch-thick stack of papers under a stainless-steel lamp.

"Ahem, excuse me," Jim said.

"Listen, I've told you guys everything I know," he said without looking up. "When I know something, so will you."

"We're special agents with the BOP," Jim said. "We just have a couple of questions about the body of a Mr. Damion Lee."

The morgue attendant looked up from his work.

"Oh, thank goodness," he said. "I thought you guys were here about another case. It's been driving me crazy. What did you say the name was again?"

"Damion—D-A-M-I-O-N—Lee. We'd just like to know what you have on him. He expired several days ago."

The attendant flipped through his papers.

"Damion Lee, you say? Ah, yes. Here we go. Mr. Lee's remains went off to the crematorium two days ago. They're pretty efficient over there, so, I'm sure he's in the wind by now—you know, if that's what his family did with his ashes. Some families scatter the ashes in the wind, some do it in the sea—but we don't have a sea nearby. Of course, we do have a river. Oh, and Lake Jeanette. Some families keep the remains in an urn on the mantle. You know, the most peculiar thing I've ever seen was a person who had their dead granny's ashes mixed into tattoo ink and—"

"We get the idea, Mr.—"

"Tandy, Andrea Tandy. My first name's Italian. Over there it's a man's name. It means the same as 'Andrew' here. I thought about going by 'Andrew' years ago, but I decided against it; it's a good discussion item."

"Ahem, thanks a lot, Mr. Tandy."

"Sorry about that," the attendant replied. "I tend to ramble when I see live people. It gets pretty lonely down here."

"And you're sure Mr. Lee is dead?" Jon asked.

"You see these papers here?" the attendant said, tapping the stack. He turned them around for both to inspect. "These are called the 'reaper papers'—the only list you don't want to be on. If he's listed here, he's most certainly in the Upper Room. That is, if you believe in that kinda thing. Because I know some people are atheists, and I certainly don't want to offend anybo—"

"Um, can we just see the list?" Jim interrupted. He flipped to the current week and dragged his index finger down the list of names, stopping at 'LEE, DAMION COREY' and tapping it for Jon to see.

"I think we have what we need, sir," Jim interrupted.

Jim and Jon started for the door.

"Oh, I almost forgot," Jim said, turning around. "When we first walked in, you said there was a case that was driving you crazy. Out of curiosity, do you mind telling us what that was about?"

"Oh, just this one guy—Mr. Walker Clement."

"What happened to Mr. Clement?" Jim asked.

"Well, his mom must've been clairvoyant when she named him, because his dead body seems to have just up and *walked* right on out of here."

"What do you mean?" Jim asked.

"He's missing. Can't find him anywhere," the attendant said.

Jim pulled out his notepad.

"When did he go missing?" Jon said.

"Four days ago," the attendant replied.

Jim and Jon shared a glance.

"Thanks for your help."

"You guys aren't leaving already, are you? Here, let me give you a tour. The space isn't big, but there's a lot to see. Ever seen real human kidneys? I've got three in the fridge right now. I can show y—"

"Th-thanks, Mr. Tandy, but we gotta be on our way."

Jim and Jon filed out.

•••

Jim and Jon convened in the stairwell outside the morgue to phone Winston.

"We're at a dead-end out here," Jim said to Winston. "They're saying the milk is expired, but we're not one hundred percent about that."

"I'm not understanding," Winston replied. "Is it handled or not?"

"We don't have confirmation," Jon replied, "but we're running down all our leads. There's a couple of people we're interested in. We'll let you know when we have something concrete."

"Well, you follow this thing wherever it takes you until you know for sure," Winston replied. "Is there going to be a send-off?"

"There's Facebook activity saying it's tomorrow afternoon in Georgia," Jim said.

"Well then, I hope you like peaches," Winston replied. "I'll send the jet. Pack up and head to the airport. I'll be in touch."

•••

"Welcome to our headquarters in beautiful Washington, D.C. How was your trip, fellas?" Winston flopped down into a space-age, ergonomic leather chair behind an oversized oak desk.

Jim and Jon sat opposite of each other at a twelve-foot conference table, perpendicular to Winston's desk.

"What new information do we have? And you can be candid," Winston said. "My office gets swept for bugs regularly."

"Okay then," Jim began. "Unfortunately, we still don't know for sure that he's dead. Although, at the memorial service, his mom certainly showed the pain of a mother who had just lost a son."

"Right," Jon added. "You can't fake that type of emotion."

"Do you think our guy has the guts to stage his own death and attempt a prison break?" Winston asked, thumb under his bottom lip.

"Damion was smart and ballsy, Mr. Nightingale," Jon said. "That's the reason we picked him to lead the operation over there in the first place."

"Okay," Winston replied, spinning around in his chair to his panoramic window to watch the K Street traffic. "Until we can verify conclusively that this guy has ceased to exist, we will operate under the working assumption that he is still alive."

"So, what about his twin brother?" Jim said.

"What about him?"

"Let's just say that if I were on the lam and needed a place to lie low, I might consider help from my brother."

"But then again," Jon added, "he is a multimillionaire. By this point, he could be in the wind with a new name and a new face."

"Yeah, but those things take time," Winston said. "He needs a place to collect himself. Plus, he can't show up in the world as 'Damion Lee,' because Damion Lee is dead. His social security number, bank account, passport—his whole identity—all died along with him. Anything related to his old identity is useless. He'll also find the Bitcoin to be useless, unless he can send it to an actual bank account and convert it to US dollars. Bottom line: he needs help, and some time to figure out how to get his new life started.

"Look, gentlemen," Winston said, spinning back around to face them. "If he's still alive, we only have a short window, maybe a couple of weeks, before we could potentially lose him for good."

"That wouldn't be so bad, right?" Jim said. "Out of sight, out of mind. As long as he has his money, he has no reason to rat us out. If you ask me, I say let 'em go."

"And I'd be inclined to agree with you if I believed money was his only motivation," Winston replied. "The last time he and I met, I got the sense that he was nearing his breaking point. He issued a veiled threat with a vengeful flavor to it. If revenge has become his motivation, no amount of money will keep him quiet. So, we must quiet him.

"Listen, guys, I'm the link between our little operation and Keating Pharma, and I assured them that we had this problem under control. Even if there's only a point zero one percent chance this guy could reemerge tomorrow, a year or ten years from now to tell his story, that's a risk I'm not comfortable with. I don't want to just *hope* he goes away and stays there; I have to know he's gone. We need to stamp out this little ember now before it becomes a raging wildfire."

"Even if he doesn't plan on squealing," Jon added, "there's the chance he could slip up and get a DUI or something. Cops'll run his prints. Game over. He'll take a deal and rat us out."

"There's that," Winston replied. "So, our bet is that he either has been, or will soon be in contact with his twin brother, Devon. That's where I want you two to focus. But to be safe, we'll also have his mom being tracked, along with a few other likely contacts."

A secretary entered and handed Winston a thick accordion folder. She whispered something so low that her lips barely moved. Winston nodded. He pressed a button and a projection screen lowered on the wall nearest the end of the conference table.

"That will be all, gentlemen," he said to Jim and Jon.

Three attorneys looking straight off of a Ralph Lauren runway filed into the office and stood along the wall.

"We'll be in touch," Jim said. He and Jon stood and started for the door.

"By the way, Mr. Nightingale," Jon said, "you wouldn't happen to have an address for us. Would you?"

"Figure it out," Winston replied.

# TWENTY-NINE

Devon collected his flashcards and put the stack on one of his three-inch-thick study books. Then he lifted his legs onto Makeba's couch and reclined, hugging one of the cushions.

Makeba sat on the carpet on the other side of the coffee table.

"Makeba, I can't tell you how much I appreciate you taking the time out to help me study for the bar."

"Oh, don't look at it as me doing you a favor. This is an investment. You're moving up in the world, and I might need you to hire me someday."

"Oh, please, Makeba. You went to Harvard for undergrad, and Howard, the Mecca of Black education, for law school. You'll write your own ticket."

"Be that as it may, a sista can still hedge her bets, can't she?" Makeba replied.

"In all seriousness, Makeba, I know my hours are always long, with the interviews and the campaign and all. You staying up so late to study with me—I mean, I've never had anyone do anything like that for me."

Makeba yawned and rubbed her eyes. "*In all seriousness,* when I call on you to return the favor, I don't want to hear no hemming and hawing, just 'when' and 'where.'"

"You got it," he replied. "You know, not even my evidence professor in law school could help me understand all these hearsay exceptions the way you do. I remember being in her office every other day, nagging her to death, only to come out knowing less than I did when I walked in."

"Just remember to focus on the policy reasoning behind the rule, and you'll at least be in the ballpark."

Devon's phone rang. He flipped it over, then he rolled his eyes, tilted his head back, and took a deep breath before answering.

"Hey, Beth."

"Are you still with Makeba? It's almost midnight."

"If you're asking me if I'm still studying for the bar exam, which is next month, the answer is yes," he replied.

"When do you plan on leaving?"

"When we're done."

"You don't have to be rude. I hope you're not putting on a performance to impress *her*."

"No one's performing. But you're right, babe. You don't deserve that. I'll be done very soon. If you want, I can come to your place after."

"That's my cue," Makeba whispered before disappearing to her bedroom.

"I'm actually about to hit the hay," Bethany said. "Let's just link up tomorrow if you find the time."

"So, you *don't* want me to come see you? That's a first."

"You can come if you'd like. I'm just tired. That's all."

"Okay...I'm wrapping up soon."

"Just make sure you call before you leave, so I can be looking out for you."

"Will do, babe."

"See you in a bit," Bethany said. "Love you."

"Be there soon," he replied, and ended the call.

Makeba stuck her head around the corner before re-entering the room. She returned to her spot on the carpet behind the coffee table.

"Have you noticed things have been weird between Beth and me?" she asked. "I think she hates me."

"What are you talking about? You're her idol. I think she wants to be you."

"Are you kidding me? Ever since that night we all went out for drinks, things have been off between her and me. She barely even looks in my direction, much less speaks to me. That girl hates my guts."

"No, she doesn't. Well, she doesn't hate all your guts. Maybe just a few inches of your large intestine."

The two laughed.

"Well, I'm glad you two are back on good terms, at least," Makeba said. "You had me worried for a moment there."

"That's not exactly an accurate statement," Devon said, kneading the cushion with his knuckles.

"What do you mean?"

"Things couldn't be rockier between us. With me working so much on the campaign, and now studying for the bar, it's like we barely know each other. We're not even intimate anymore. I know—TMI. But it's true."

Makeba gave him the side-eye and side-pucker combination. "You ain't gotta lie to kick it, Devon."

"What do you mean?"

"You know exactly what I mean," she replied. "I'm not a gossip, but since you brought it up, I have it on good authority that your and Beth's love life is doing just fine. You remember my friend Donita, right? The dentist who was at my chili night?"

"Yeah, what about her?"

"She said she saw you two hugged up last week in Georgetown, looking like the 2014 Kim and Ye."

"Your friend, *Donita,* needs to get her eyes checked. Beth and I haven't been out in a couple of weeks."

"Umm, okay. If you say so. I'm just saying you can be honest with me."

"I am being honest. Tell your friend to stop being messy and mind her business," he said.

"Okay. Okay. I believe you, geez. Don't bite my head off," Makeba replied. "Anyway, I've been meaning to ask you: how did you manage to convince your boss to run for that Senate seat after all? I thought you told me he was just using that as a ploy to get you to help him with the whole blackface scandal."

"What do you mean?" Devon replied. "I did what you said. I made him. I went on the radio and announced the run."

"I heard that," she replied. "But how did you convince him to go along with it?"

"I didn't. I just announced it, and he had no choice. He couldn't retract, because he'd lose support with his base. He couldn't fire me, because that would look bad on his part."

"Hold on. You're telling me that he said he wasn't running, and you nevertheless took it upon yourself to announce anyway? *Wow*. Bold, bold move. I'm impressed. I'm actually surprised that's not some sort of crime."

"I don't understand why this is such a shock to you," Damion replied. "It was your idea in the first place."

"What was my idea? That you go on a nationally syndicated radio show and announce that your boss, a member of Congress, is running for a U.S. Senate seat? And to do so against his will and without his permission? I told you to do nothing of the sort."

"Are you kidding me?" Devon replied. "What about *make him, make him*?" Devon said mockingly.

"Whoa, buddy, you so took *that* out of context. When I said 'make him,' I meant for you to use your logic. Appeal to his reason. Use your gift of persuasion to get him to run. I certainly didn't mean for you to push him out of the plane door while he was still asking questions about how to use the parachute."

"Well, you implied it."

"No. *You* inferred it."

"Well, in the future, you need to be clearer in your language," Devon replied. "I was operating on what I thought was sound strategic advice from a person whose political mind I trust and respect."

"Don't you dare try and put that on me," Makeba replied. "You have your own mind and your own free will."

She keyed in the passcode to her iPad, and pulled up a colorful map of Georgia.

"Anyway, I looked it up, and Grayton is barely popular in his own little House district. I haven't seen any polling numbers, but I'm willing to bet they'll show him getting trounced in a statewide Senate race."

"That's if you only count white Republican votes," Devon replied.

"Here, let me see that."

Makeba passed him the tablet.

"Look here," he continued, propping the tablet on the cushion in his lap, "Black people represented over fifty percent of all Democratic voters in Georgia in the last presidential election. Only thirty-three percent of the state is Black! That math ain't mathin'. And it's like that all over the country."

He expanded another map.

"In Michigan, twenty percent of all Democratic voters were Black. The Black population there is only fourteen percent. For Pennsylvania, Black people were twenty-one percent of the Dem vote, and only twelve percent of the population.

"If we could move a fraction of those voters over to the Republican side of the aisle in Georgia, my guy wins. And in the next election, the Democrats will fight like hell to regain those Black votes, while the Republicans will fight to retain us. They'll find out that empty gestures won't work. They'll need to show us what they've actually done to meet our needs since the last election. Bye-bye voter suppression laws. If we pull this off, we could scale this model nationwide.

"Can you imagine if we ran a slate of Black Republican Congressional candidates in dark blue districts—candidates who are not afraid to speak and act on the most urgent issues affecting the Black community? They would be untouchable."

Makeba paused in thought. "Sounds good in theory. But I don't know if I see it panning out like that in reality." She stood and started toward the kitchen. "I'm still in awe about that move of yours. It makes perfect sense now. This explains why you were the one making the announcement and not him."

"Now I feel like an idiot," Devon said, burying his face into the cushion.

"No," Makeba replied. "You shouldn't. It was a brilliant move. Risky as hell, but brilliant, nonetheless. In fact, it was so bold that I wish it *had been* my idea. Let's think about what it got you. One: it upped your profile. You were already in the clouds, now you're stratospheric—the young, Black guy who did the impossible, and revived the old, white Republican congressman after he touched the electric race fence. And now you're running his Senate campaign? That's big.

"And after the circus that was the last Republican administration, not to mention the white nationalist Capitol insurrection, the Republican Party must be licking their wounds, desperate for some new blood to help revive them, too. I wouldn't be surprised if they tried to get you on a congressional ticket in the near future."

"No chance. I would never run for anything," Devon replied. "I'm not interested in holding public office."

"The best statesmen aren't," Makeba replied. "Now, the other thing your daring little stunt achieved was showing every card in the congressman's stubby little hands. You know what he's holding, which puts you in charge. You are the most valuable person in the world to him right now. If he wins, it'll only be because of you; if you were to walk away right now, he not only certainly loses the Senate bid, but his House seat is vulnerable. You're the one pulling the strings, now. He's just a proxy."

"You should leave policy and be a political strategist," Devon said.

"I thought this was the interview," Makeba replied. "I want you to describe the look on his face when you finally met with him. What did he say? I want every detail."

# THIRTY

"I should probably leave before my brother gets here."

"No, stay, please. Just a few more minutes," Bethany replied. "I want to spend every millisecond I can with you."

"I know, baby. Me, too," Damion replied. "We're just walking too close to the edge. That's all."

"You're right," she replied with a mischievous grin. "It's so dangerous, but I can't stop doing it. You're just too damn irresistible." She rolled on top of him, forehead to forehead, her hair falling over his face like a tent. "Don't worry about him catching us. I told him to call when he's on his way. And he can't get on the elevator without the concierge calling me first."

"I can't believe this is happening. I've never been in love in my life, and then you come along—my brother's girlfriend—and I'm head over heels. Life is something, isn't it?"

"Yeah. And the weird thing about it, I don't feel guilty. Maybe I'm some sort of sociopath or something."

"We both are. I've screwed Devon over all our lives, and he finally breaks ties with me, as he should've. I convince him to take me back as his brother. He does. And I backstab him again. I'm such a shitty human being."

"You're not, baby. And neither am I. We just love each other. Some things are just out of our control, and love is at the top of that list.

Besides, Devon doesn't have the cleanest hands in all this either."

"Why do you say that?"

"First of all, he lied to me about not having a brother. And then, he disowned you. Who disowns their own twin brother? Besides, he's cheating on me with Makeba. He has the nerve to talk to me from her place. They're probably in bed together, too. So, trust me: Devon's no angel."

"I know. But it's still not right."

"But it feels right," Beth replied, nestling in closer.

"To be honest, when Devon told me he'd been going all these years without telling any of his new friends here that I existed, I thought he was just saying that out of anger. 'He could never deny the existence of his own brother,' I told myself."

Damion's eyes welled. Beth moved in closer, caressing his jawline.

"But when I met you that night—*his girlfriend*—and I realized it was true, it shook me. It cut me deep. I lied to myself that it didn't. But I was hurt. I still am. I mean nothing to him."

Tears began to flow. Beth wiped them with the corner of the sheet.

"Even at my memorial service, I could see it in his eyes. I could tell he was relieved, maybe even happy I was gone. He even told me that the stress I caused our dad sent him to an early grave."

Beth raised her head to connect with his eyes.

"I'm sorry. I must've missed something. 'Memorial service'? What do you mean, your 'memorial service'?"

"I'm sorry, babe," he said, pulling her back in. "I didn't tell you the whole story before. I didn't know if I could trust you. But now, besides this one nurse friend of mine, you're the only person on this earth who I can trust."

Damion filled Beth in on more of the details leading up to the staged suicide, this time leaving out the full scale of the drug operation and the enormity of his own wealth. She trailed her nail tips over his chest as he recounted.

"Such a liar," she said.

"I'm super sorry," Damion replied. "Like I said, I didn't know if I could trust you. You get that, right?"

"Not you. *Him*. He lied to me a few weeks ago, when he said he was at a family reunion. Based on what you're telling me now, he wasn't at a reunion. He was at his brother's funeral."

"And you bought it," Damion said with a chuckle. "Did you ever stop to think, who has a family reunion in January, during a pandemic?"

"I know," she replied, palming her face. "I was dubious, but I didn't have any proof to the contrary, so I went with it."

Bethany playfully popped onto her elbows and checked his pulse.

"So, let me get this straight. I have a dead man in my bed?"

"I'll bet you never thought a dead man could make you feel so alive. Did you?"

"I certainly didn't," she replied, kissing him on the clavicle. "I wish it could be like this forever."

"So do I. I hate all this sneaking around. I wish we could just be together out in the open."

"We tried that. Remember? Georgetown? Last week? I'm pretty sure one of Makeba's friends saw us."

"Everything good comes to an end. I just hate that it has to be so soon."

"Soon?"

"Yeah. My agreement with my brother is that I'll stay for only a month. That month is up in about a week."

"Where are you going to go?"

"I don't know yet. I'm working on getting a new identity. Maybe I'll drive down to Colombia and get some plastic surgery; I heard they have good surgeons down there."

"So, you weren't going to tell me? You were just going to up and leave?"

"Well, I'm telling you now."

Bethany rolled off Damion, facing away. He could hear her sniffling.

"It'll be okay," he said. He wrapped his arm over her shoulder and scooted in behind her.

"No. It won't be okay! I love you, Damion. You can't just come into my life and then disappear into thin air. I don't want to be without you."

She turned back over and rested her ear on his heart while he stared at the ceiling.

"What if I came with you?" she asked, breaking the silence.

"You're young, Beth. You have your whole life ahead of you. I'm the one who ruined mine. Besides, your parents have all the resources in the world to find you. And when they find you, they'll find me. That would never work."

"Okay. Then what if...?"

"What if, what?" Damion replied.

"Nothing."

"Say it."

"What if there was a way for you to stay and for us to be together? You know, out in the open?"

"What do you mean?"

"Well, you said it yourself: you mean nothing to him. He has discarded *you,* his own flesh and blood. He came here to Washington and created a new world, a new life for himself. A life in which you don't exist. Why should you care about him? Why should he exist in your new world?"

"What am I going to do—take out my own brother?"

Beth didn't respond. She turned over, her back against Damion.

"Beth?"

She began to cry again, then sob.

"Sweetheart." Damion wrapped himself tighter around her. "There isn't a strong enough word to express what I feel for you. Three weeks ago, I didn't even know you; now, I feel I can't live without you. I'd do anything if it meant you and I could be together. But surely you don't want me to ki—I can't even say it."

Beth turned back to face him. "Then I'll do it." She gripped him. "I'll do anything for you. Devon could never begin to fathom the love that we have for each other. He doesn't love anyone. He threw you away like garbage. And once he found someone better, he threw me away, too."

"Is that what this is about, Beth? Is all this because you think he left you for another woman? These things happen every day. It's not enough to—you don't even have proof."

"No, Damion. It's not about Makeba. It's not even about him. It's about us—you and me. And the two of us doing whatever it takes to be together. You love me more than anything in the world, right?"

"More than life itself," Damion replied.

"Then what does it matter whose life it is? I mean, think about it," she continued, "you two look exactly alike. And since he's started exercising, he's even starting to look fitter like you. You can become him, take over his life. You know everything about him. Is this really that far-fetched an idea?"

"Just hold on." Damion massaged his temples. "This is too much to process. I can't believe I'm having this discussion, much less actually thinking about it."

"Listen, Damion. I'm willing to give up everything for you. My family's wealth is immense. And because of Devon's politics, they said they'd cut me off financially if I didn't break up with him. I know my father. He does what he says. So, if you become Devon, and we continue to date, that's exactly what will happen. They'll cut me off. I'll be broke. But none of that will matter, because I'll be with you. You see? You're not the only one who will be sacrificing something."

Damion scratched his cheek and looked off.

"What is it?" Beth asked.

"Well, you wouldn't exactly be broke," he replied.

"I mean, sure, I can sell the things I already have," she said. "And then there's my checking and savings accounts. But all that amounts to maybe 450K, half a million if I sell the car. But that's only enough to get us started. We'll still have to manage on our own."

Damion got out of bed to find his phone in his pants pocket.

"No, Beth. What I mean is *we* won't be broke. I still have the money I made when I was in Afghanistan, the money from the runs, untraceable by the government. Over forty-million U.S. worth of Bitcoin, and it's rising almost every day with the market. I just need the legit bank account of a live person in order to convert the Bitcoin into real money."

He showed her the screen.

"And since your parents are high net worth gazillionaires," he continued, "having this kind of money flowing through your accounts wouldn't set off any alarm bells with the feds."

Beth eyes widened as she smiled. "Wait, is there anything else you failed to mention?"

"No, baby. You know everything now. You know all my secrets."

"I mean, it's not my parents' kind of money, but I think forty million will do just fine."

They both laughed and pulled each other closer, pausing to imagine the possibility of a new life together.

He found her eyes.

"You were really ready to give up everything for me, huh?"

"Everything and more," Beth replied.

They kissed.

"Not that this is something I'm even thinking about considering," Damion said, "but what would something like this even look like? I mean, how would we go about pulling it off?"

Just then, Beth's phone rang.

"Shit!" she said. "It's the concierge. Devon must be in the lobby. Idiot! I told him to call *before* he came. Get dressed quick, I'll stall with the concierge. You need to take the stairs down."

"No," Damion replied. "I don't want you to spend another night with him. Tell the concierge not to let him up."

Beth picked up Damion's shirt from the floor and pressed it into his chest.

"Get dressed, baby. Don't you worry, there's no way I can even think about doing anything with him. You have my heart. My whole heart. Plus, we need to act like everything is normal. He can't get any sense that something's up."

Beth checked the digital peephole from her phone.

"I'll call you tomorrow," she said. "We'll figure out a place to meet in person to hash out the details."

Beth stuck her head out of the apartment door and looked both ways. She jogged to the end of the hall and signaled for Damion to come out. He darted into the stairwell.

# THIRTY-ONE

"What's your location, brother?"

"I'm on the Southwest Waterfront," Jim replied. "I have eyes on the subject. Looks like our pal and his lady are having an intense chat at the end of the dock."

"You're shitting me! Are you sure it's him?"

"I'm fucking twenty meters away, staring a hole in the side of his head. It's him. I'm sure of it. Why? What do you see?"

"Believe it or not, I happen to have eyes on our pal, too. He's parked in his car near Thomas Circle."

"Wait. Are we talking about the same 'pal'?"

"We only have one 'pal', pal."

"Unbelievable," Jim said. "The asshole actually pulled it off. Do you know which one is which?"

"No, but I was considering buying them 'Thing One' and 'Thing Two' shirts so we can keep track," Jon said. "Wait, which *lady* do you see? Are we talking Gwyneth Paltrow or Halle Berry?"

"I don't get it."

"Swan or raven, ebony or ivory?

"I'm gonna need you to speak English, man."

"For God's sake, Jim—is the chick Black or white?"

"Don't bark at me. It's the white girl. Maybe we should've established code names like I suggested."

"You don't need a code name when there's only one—Hold on just one fucking minute, here," Jon said. "You won't believe who I'm seeing crossing over Thomas Circle right now. It's the other girlfriend—the Black one. Looks like she's about to hop in his car...Yup, she just did."

"Trippy. What, do they have some type of incestual interracial love triangle going on?

"It's four of them—that would make it a square. But never mind that. What we have here is interesting, but not our business," Jon said. "We have one mission. Let's just get it done so we can get back to our retirements."

"Well, whatever they're talking about on my end, it must be important," Jim said. "It's nineteen degrees out, and they're freezing their asses off on a boat dock, having a conversation they could just as soon have over the phone. I think they're planning a getaway. We need to act soon."

"Whaddaya say we rendezvous at the Firm at eighteen hundred hours to report what we know and get our marching orders?"

"Roger that."

"Out, here."

"Out, brother."

# THIRTY-TWO

Beth and Damion stood at the dock's edge.

"Look there." Damion pointed to several large, white birds on the water. "Those are called tundra swans. Did you know a group of swans are called a bevy, and a wedge when they're in flight?"

"No, I didn't, Damion. I did not know this information. I don't know what it is with you and birds."

"Well, I have to focus on something to keep my mind off of turning into an iceberg. You couldn't have picked a warmer place to do this, Beth? Like, I don't know, your apartment, maybe?"

"I'm supposed to be the sheltered, rich kid from California, and you're the big military commando man. Don't you guys in the Army go running in the cold?"

"That's different. When you're running, you're warm, because the blood is flowing and you're burning energy."

"We're about to plan a murder, Damion," Beth replied. "Do some push-ups or something. We can't afford to take any chances. Now that I think of it, we shouldn't have even said the things we said in my apartment last night. Who knows who might've been listening?"

"Okay," Damion said. "Let's get to it, then. What were you thinking?"

"I don't know. Maybe we can hire a hitman?"

"Good idea, Beth. Do you know any good ones?"

"Hey, listen, I'm not the only one with a brain here. The floor is open to your ideas, too, Damion."

"I'm sorry, babe. It's just—a hitman is just too risky. You could be contracting an FBI agent. Or, just as bad, the guy who does a sloppy job, and then all fingers point back to us."

"Okay. So, no hitman. What are you thinking?"

"I was thinking, is there another way? Can we just pay Devon to disappear or something? Killing him seems like the nuclear option."

"Stop it, Damion! We already discussed this. This is not the time for you to be having second thoughts. This is our only option if we want to be together. That is what you still want, right? For us to be together?"

"I do, but..."

"'But' nothing, then. This is our chance to make that happen. Our only chance."

Beth put her hands inside Damion's coat pockets with his. They interlocked fingers.

"Baby," she said, "this is the one hurdle we need to get over so that we can live together, free and happy. After this, we'll share a secret together. One that only you and I will know. It will bond us for life. Are you with me?"

Damion looked off into the Potomac. The sky had become light purple, as if snow was coming. A plane flew close overhead to land at nearby Reagan National Airport.

"Damion, baby, are you with me?"

"I'm with you, Beth."

"Are you sure?"

"Yes. I'm sure. What's your plan?" Damion asked.

"I don't know. You're the Army guy. Haven't you killed people before?"

"When I wasn't riding the shit truck around, I did logistics in the Army—a paper pusher. The only things I ever killed were nose hairs and trees."

"Well, whatever we do, he can't come back, dead or alive," Beth said.

Damion winced.

"Listen, Damion, you're going to have to pull it together."

"I know, Beth. It's just a little uncomfortable hearing you say it out loud."

"We already know what we have to do. The question is who's going to do it—you, me, or both of us?"

"I'll do it," Damion said. "I could never put you in a position to jeopardize your life. Mine is already fucked. So, if I get caught, I'm going back to prison either way. I'm willing to take that risk for you. You, on the other hand, are squeaky clean."

Beth smiled softly at him and gave his hands a tight squeeze. "I love you."

"I love you, too."

"Okay, enough of that," Damion said. "I'm freezing my nuts off. How about this? He gets home late every day from studying—or whatever he's doing—with Makeba. I have a revolver with the serial number shaved off. I'll pop out one night and do it. He won't see it coming. Quick, fast, and painless. And his apartment is in Anacostia, the roughest part of town, so no one will probably report the gunshot. I also have a car with bogus papers. We can put him inside it and burn it up, or push it in the river, or something."

"Archie had said you had a gun."

"Yeah. I keep it in the nightstand."

"Sexy. Like in the movies."

"Focus, Beth."

"Okay. Okay," she replied. "Your idea is good. But it's a lot—too many moving pieces. Also, and no offense, but Devon's not a regular Black dude. He's educated, works for Congress, has a clean record, and he's semi-famous. There's no way he could disappear that quietly. Two: I don't know how to dispose of a body, and I'm guessing you don't either. If we botch that part, and he's found, his murder would make national headlines. People will think it had something to do with him defending his boss for the blackface thing. The cops will put everything they've got on the case. Your plan could work, but it's too risky. Let's keep it in the parking lot, though. What else ya got?"

"We can bring him out here on the dock," Damion said. "He'll freeze to death in no time. They can bury him between the two of us."

"This is not the time for jokes," Bethany said. "We're planning a murder. He needs to disappear without a trace. And it needs to happen far away from here. I'm thinking international."

"International? Devon has never left the country. I'm betting he doesn't even have a passport."

"That shouldn't be a problem. My parents are billionaires. Billionaires don't operate by the same rules as everyone else. How about this?" she said. "When my parents came to town, they came in on a PJ."

"PJ?" Damion replied.

"Yes. A private jet. Devon couldn't lift his chin off the ground when he saw it; I mean, he gawked at the stupid thing. I can call and rent a similar plane. We have a beach house in the Cayman Islands that's empty most of the year, unless they loan it out to friends, which they seldom do. I don't even know if they remember they own it. I went down last year with some girlfriends, and I'm sure the key codes haven't changed."

"What about the passport? There will have to be some record that he was there, right?"

"That's the beauty of it all," Bethany replied. "The Caymans is an offshore financial haven for wealthy individuals, so everything about it is discreet. They do a good job of keeping secrets and looking the other way. Rich people fly in on their PJs all the time, and they never get stamped in or out of the country if they don't want to."

Damion rocked back and forth on his heels and began jogging in place.

"Can we walk and talk?" he said. "I need to get the blood circulating before I become an ice block."

The two turned and started off the dock, toward the street. Damion squinted and looked hard in the direction of a large man in a long, black coat on a park bench. The man stood and walked off.

"What's the matter?" Bethany asked.

"Nothing. I thought I saw something. That guy over there just seems out of place," he replied.

"You're just being paranoid."

"I'm just being careful. Anyway, back to the plan. So he and I fly to the Caymans; then what?"

"I don't know. Rent a boat or something. Go far out into the water and get him wasted. Then bop him over the head with a fire extinguisher and toss him overboard. You'd have to make sure you weigh him down with something heavy first. You know—like they do in the movies."

"I don't know the first thing about driving a boat," Damion replied.

"It's not socket rience. Just YouTube it."

"You mean 'rocket science'?"

"See. You're a smart guy. You've got this," Beth said. "It's settled, then. If we do this right, and we start posting together on Instagram soon after, no one will be looking for a dead body. We can move somewhere warm. People will think we eloped and got lost on my daddy's coin. What do you think about Cartagena?"

"I don't know where that is, but we can move to Hell if the winters are warmer than here."

"Okay, snowflake," she replied. "Let's get you somewhere warm. I'm parked at Seventh and Maine. Let's split up, and I'll meet you there."

# THIRTY-THREE

Winston blotted his sweat-soaked head with a towel, then wrapped it around his neck, tucking the ends into his UVA Law hoodie.

"Gentlemen," he said, "I take my workouts very seriously. It's the one time that I get to unplug from the stresses of the day. And I don't much care to have this time interrupted. Unless, of course, there's good news involved. So, my friends, I ask you: do you come bearing any of this good news?"

Winston wore a concealing smile. He hopped onto the conference table and swung his legs.

"We found him," Jim blurted.

"Okay. Good. Good. That's a start. And?"

"That's good news, right?" Jim asked.

"Is that all you have for me?" Winston asked.

"We know he's alive, and we know the places he might be," Jon said.

"I presume by your response that you do not mean he's in the trunk of your car, or, say, at the bottom of the Anacostia River. I further presume that our little problem still has a beating heart and a potentially flapping tongue. If, gentlemen, my presumption is correct, then what you have brought me is indeed news, but I'm afraid it falls somewhat shy of what qualifies as 'good' news. What you have just shared with me is what I call 'threshold news,'" Winston said.

"All we have to do now is catch up with him and finish the job," Jim said.

"Then I suggest you get out there and do that," Winston snapped, maintaining his smile.

"We're on it," Jon said. "The only thing is: we don't know which twin is which."

"And you came here because you want me to tell you? Maybe you should be paying me instead of the other way around."

"We were actually living quite nicely in retirement off the money we had already made. Couldn't you have found someone else for the job? I don't know about Jim here but I'm tired of being your flunky."

In one quick motion, Winston snatched his sweaty towel from his neck and snapped Jon across the face with it. "What did you just say to me?"

"Nothing," Jim said, stepping between the two. "We'll figure it out."

"No. No, you won't. You clearly came here so that I could do the thinking for you. So, here you go. Are you ready? Kill them both." Winston turned for the door. "Now go away. And don't come back until you have actual good news."

•••

Jim and Jon arrived early to stake out Devon's apartment. They looked on from one of the firm's unmarked utility fleet vans with no rear side windows and back windows that were opaque from the outside.

"Is that them?" Jon said.

"Well, I'll be damned. Sure looks like it."

"It's four in the morning. What are they doing out at this time?"

"From the looks of it, they're getting back from running or something," Jim replied.

"Well, let's go get them now and get it over with," Jon said.

"Wait, brother. Be patient. We have to take our time on this. We can't just run in there and pull them out. There could be cameras, or someone could spot us. We don't want to fuck this up."

Jim took a sip of coffee. "Here's what we do," he said. "If they're working out together, it's probably Damion's idea. And you know how the Army creates creatures of habit? That means they probably have a routine."

"Right," Jon replied. "And they come out at zero dark thirty to try and stay low profile. It almost worked, considering if it'd been half a minute later, we'd have missed them. So, what's your plan?"

"We come back each day for, say, a week or so," Jim replied. "And we hope they use the same running route. We'll just pick them both up somewhere on the route."

"A week? You don't think that's too long? Mr. Nightingale said we had a tight window. What if we miss it?"

"Fuck Winston Nightingale. He wasn't the one putting his neck on the line moving all that product in Afghanistan, and he damn sure ain't the one taking penitentiary chances out here. He's just the middleman—Keating Pharma's bitch boy. If we're gonna do this, we have to do it right. No sloppy rush job."

•••

On two of the next four days, Damion and Devon left the apartment through the back door at 3:15 and 3:10 a.m. They took the same route both mornings—through the alley, a left onto Seventeenth Street, a quick right on R, down the hill toward Anacostia High, then over the pedestrian overpass to Anacostia Park.

On the fifth day at 3:13, Damion waited in the patchy backyard at the foot of the stairs. Devon came outside seven minutes later. The twins used the rusted, sagging chain-link fence as support while they stretched. They started down the alley.

"There! That's our guy," Jim said to Jon. "Out in front, ya see there? That's Damion. The other brother must be the one lagging behind. You gotta figure a soldier would be faster than a lawyer."

Jim and Jon looked on from the back of the utility van. Jon pulled out a pair of cognac-colored leather driving gloves and started to put them on.

"What are you doing?" Jim asked.

"What do you mean?" Jon replied. "It's time to go get them. We've been watching them for a couple days now."

"No. Not yet, brother. It's too premature," Jim replied.

"Ah shit, man! Let's just get this thing over with right now so we can get back to our lives," Jon replied. "This is the perfect time. It's dark, and nobody's out but the crackheads and their dealers. And even if someone saw us, this is a Black neighborhood, and Black people don't snitch. It's a thing."

"Be that as it may," Jim said, "we didn't come all this way, move all that product, and make all that money just to get nabbed on a murder beef for snatching up these two idiots. And they're not even idiots; Damion's smart. He managed to break out of a maximum-security military prison. And the other one's sharp, too. I've watched him on television. We can't underestimate either of them, so let's take our time on this one. We're gonna do this by the numbers."

Jon tucked his gloves into his waistband.

"All right," he said. "But we're looking at them right now. It'd be too easy to pull up and toss them in the back of this van. I think we're pressing our luck if we wait any longer. We don't know if we'll get another opportunity like this."

"Just be patient, brother," Jim replied. "We took our time so far, and it yielded good results. Didn't it? Think about it: we now know their routine, their route, and we finally know which brother is which. What's another thing we've noticed over the last couple of days?"

Jon looked blank.

"Get your head in the game, brother," Jim said with a tap to his temple. "Each morning, Damion comes outside first, right? Devon has been at least five minutes behind him. So, tomorrow or the next day, we'll set up and wait in the alley between the two apartment buildings. We'll give ourselves a three-minute window. It shouldn't even take that long to knock him out and drag him into the van. By the time Devon wipes the crust from his eyes and comes outside, it'll be too late."

Jon opened his cigar case and lifted the false bottom to expose a handsome .357 caliber revolver with a polished wood handle.

"Mr. Nightingale gave us specific instructions to clip them both," Jon replied. "Why kidnap them and create unnecessary evidence? We can just pop them both in the alley and leave them there. I'm sure people around here hear gunshots all the time. And, like I said, Black people don't snitch anyway. Just two more thugs shot in the alley. We can even go as far as buying some crack from one of the dudes on the corner to sprinkle over their dead bodies. You know, like Chappelle said."

"How many times do I have to tell you?" Jim replied. "I don't give a shit what Nightingale says anymore. He's not here in the trenches with us. Is he? If we snatch and clip only Damion, then it's a no-crime crime; he's supposed to be dead anyway. If we clip the brother, too, then the cops will be looking for a murderer. If we clean it up, they'll be looking for a dead body and a murderer. And I should remind you that Devon's not your average five-baby-mama-havin', drug-dealin', menace-to-society homeboy; he has a squeaky-clean record. He's college-educated. He works for someone powerful. *And* he's on TV. The feds will be all over this, for sure."

"But don't you think Damion has already spilled the beans to his brother about us and the whole operation? I mean, he is hiding out at his place."

"I just can't imagine the nerd saying anything. If we snatch Damion, that square will be too spooked to say anything, afraid the same thing'd happen to him. Plus, what really did we tell Damion while we were over there? He only knew his little narrow part of the operation. He doesn't even know our real names. Sure, he might do some damage if he were alive to tell his story, but the nerd? Nah. Let's go at it my way and we can clean it up later with Nightingale."

"All right, then," Jon said, resigned. "We'll go with your plan. But, for the record, I still think it's a terrible idea to wait another day. If he slips away, it's on you."

# THIRTY-FOUR

"Get outta bed, lazy head!" Damion pounded the mattress next to Devon's head. Devon sprang up, unfazed, almost as if he'd been expecting it.

It was 3:07 a.m.

"Ready to get this workout in?" Devon said.

"Man, look who's finally found his groove. What's gotten into you?" Damion replied. "You're gonna make me have to dial our workout up a notch this morning."

"I don't know, man," Devon replied. "Ever since we started exercising, I just feel better. You know—stronger, more energetic. My mind is even clearer. And I like it."

"I call bullshit. I think you're trying to buff up to impress ol' girl."

"You mean Beth, my girlfriend?"

"Don't play dumb. I'm talking about the one helping you study for your lawyer test. You can be honest with me."

"What makes you say that?"

"Whatever, bro. I don't care, actually. If you like it, I love it," Damion replied. "Just get dressed. I'll be waiting for you in the back."

Devon found his sweats and running shoes. He pulled a knit cap over his ears and followed Damion outside. He stood at the top of the stairs and looked down at the area below. Damion was nowhere in sight.

"Damo!" he called in a breathy whisper, just low enough to not wake the neighbors. "Damion!" he called a little louder.

Devon made his way down the stairs and to the fence. His heart began to pound as panic set in. He bounded over the fence and darted another ten feet to where the alley met the street. His head snapped left to right.

A rustling sound came from behind. Devon turned. It was only a stray cat.

Just then, he saw the flicker of blue-white LED headlights on a black Cadillac Escalade, so clean it looked wet.

A loud whistle came from the driver's-side back window.

"Hurry up!" Damion said. "Get in, or we'll be late."

Devon jogged across the street to the SUV. He did a walk around, admiring the exterior trim. Then he climbed inside.

•••

"Don't say a word," Jim said to Jon. "Don't you say a goddamned word!"

"I told you we should've grabbed them both yesterday," Jon said. "Now, look at us."

Jim and Jon emerged from between the buildings. Jim picked up a jog.

"Just walk normal," Jon said. "You don't want to draw attention to us. It looks like a chauffeur—they drive slow, plus the streets are empty. We'll catch up to them."

They kept the Escalade in sight as it pulled off. Their van was across the street from where the Escalade was parked. Jim and Jon climbed in their van, did a U-turn, then bent the corner behind the SUV, following at a distance.

"Where are they going?"

"How the hell am I supposed to know?" Jim replied. "Just keep driving."

They trailed behind as the Escalade took Minnesota to Pennsylvania Avenue, then I-395 South toward Virginia. The early hour meant fewer cars were on the road. Jim and Jon kept far away to avoid being spotted.

"They're headed to the airport," Jon said.

"Do you really think they're flying anywhere dressed in gym clothes, with no luggage? Plus, planes aren't taking off at three thirty in the morning, anyway," Jim replied. "Just hang back, and don't lose 'em."

"Fuck that," Jon replied. "I listened to you yesterday, and look where that landed us. This is going down today. Right now. So I suggest you get ready."

Jon accelerated hard. Jim sighed and pulled a large, black pistol from under his seat. He inspected the chamber and charged it. The bolt slammed forward.

They caught up to the Escalade. Just as it had begun to turn onto the Reagan National Airport exit, Jon swerved the utility van around to the SUV's driver's side, then turned right to force it off the road. The Escalade broke hard, screeching to a halt. The van caught a patch of black ice and fishtailed. Its back whipped wide from one side to the other.

•••

"What the fuck is happening?" Damion said.

Damion, Devon, and their driver watched, stunned as Jim and Jon's van careened from shoulder to shoulder, then rolled over violently three times in front of them before landing in the tree line.

"Let's go! What are you doing?!" Damion said to the driver, pounding his headrest. "Drive! Drive! Drive!"

"But I could lose my job if I leave the scene of an accident," the driver said in a heavy Salvadoran Spanish accent.

"And you could lose your life if you stay put," Damion replied. "These guys could be dangerous. Look, you didn't cause this accident. So you won't get in any trouble. Just go!"

The driver zigzagged through the debris and continued toward the airport.

Damion turned around to look out the back window, and the upside-down van grew smaller. He didn't notice any signs of life.

Devon was silent. His back was cemented to the leather seat, his fingers leaving permanent imprints on the armrests.

"You good?" Damion asked. "Dev, are you all right?" He snapped his fingers in front of Devon's face.

"Damo, tell me that didn't just happen," he said, recovering from shock. "Were those the guys?"

"I can't say for sure. Either way, it's literally behind us now."

"Here's a better question: where are we going?"

"Can't you see?" Damion replied. "We're going to the airport."

"I see that, asshole. But why?"

The Escalade pulled over a one-way spike strip to a security guard shack. An officer stepped outside.

"Everybody, just be cool. I know you're still shook up," Damion said to Devon and the driver.

Damion rolled down his window and handed the officer Devon's congressional I.D. badge. The officer checked the name against a list on a clipboard. He looked around inside the SUV.

"He's my guest," Damion said to the officer, gesturing toward Devon.

The officer double-checked his list, and passed Damion back the I.D.

"One black SUV, three pax. Clear to pass," the officer said into a handheld radio clipped to his shoulder.

A tall black automatic gate opened.

"Did you just use my government I.D. to gain access to an airport?"

"Relax, bro," Damion replied. "Just chill out."

Damion tossed the I.D. into Devon's lap.

"I'm going to ask you this one last time, before I get out and call for the cops. What are we doing here, Damion?"

Just then, the Escalade pulled onto the tarmac, yards away from a navy-blue and white jet. It glistened under the airport lights.

Devon instantly forgot about the crash he'd just witnessed, and once again became hypnotized by the sight of the luxury private jet.

Damion got out of the SUV. "Let's go."

Devon snapped out of his spell for a moment. "Let's go where? We're not about to fly somewhere," he replied, still admiring the jet. "It's the middle of the week. I have to get into the office."

One of the plane's crew opened the Escalade's rear hatch.

"It's just us," Damion said to the man. "No luggage. Come on, bro, pick up your lip and let's roll. You can call out sick from the plane. We'll only be gone a coupla days."

"But I don't even have a wallet. All I have is my cell phone."

"That's all you'll need," Damion replied.

The door to the jet lowered to the ground. Devon's curiosity and the trappings of extravagance got the better of him.

As the two hopped out and started for the plane's stairs, the driver tapped the horn. "What? No tip?"

"No, thanks," Devon replied.

Damion waved the driver off while skipping to the top of the stairs in two bounds, Devon on his heels.

*"¡Caras de pija!"* the driver yelled before driving away.

•••

"This is insane," Devon said, running his fingertips over plush leather seats that were the color of peanut butter. "They're so soft."

He pressed a button on the cherry wood credenza, so glossy he could see his own reflection. A thirty-two-inch monitor rose from its seamlessly recessed setting.

Devon sat down in the seat across from Damion. He pressed a button on the armrest, and a table lowered between them.

A flight attendant greeted them with a warm smile. "Welcome to Emergence Executive Aviation Group, where 'Onward and Upward' is our motto. My name is Mika, and also aboard this flight is my colleague, Jasmin."

Mika, petite and in her early twenties, stunned them with her beauty. Her makeup accentuated her Asian facial features. She continued her welcome speech, and the twins continued to steal glances around the jet. They spotted the second flight attendant sliding open one of the twin chiller drawers and selecting a champagne bottle with white flowers painted on it, along with two crystal flutes from the adjoining cabinet.

Jasmin was wasting her time as a flight attendant. She belonged on a runway of the other sort. She owned her height with a pair of gold-studded black heels with red soles. The top of her head cleared the ceiling by barely an inch. There wasn't a single stray strand in her jet-black cornrows, the tips of which extended just beyond her elbows.

Devon gawked each time Jasmin passed by, nervously trying to smooth out his shirt and shorts. She greeted the brothers with as much warmth as Mika.

"I love your accent," Devon said. "Where's it from?"

"Copenhagen," Jasmin said. "And Seychelles."

"I thought Copenhagen was the chewing tobacco the white boys in the Army used. I didn't know it was a country," Damion said.

"It's not a country, dumbass," Devon replied, kicking Damion's feet under the table. "It's a city in Denmark, northern Europe."

"Either way, doesn't sound like a place that would have Black people," Damion said.

"Stop being rude, man," Devon said.

Jasmin removed the gold foil from the bottle and twisted open the wire cage, then the cork. There was a soft hissing sound instead of a pop.

"It's quite alright," she said, with the most pleasant of smiles. "He's correct. There aren't very many Africans in Denmark. My mom is from there; it's also where I grew up. And my father is from Seychelles, in Africa. But I live in Dubai now."

"Perrier-Jouët, my favorite," Devon said as Jasmin wet the glass, then finished the pour. "You're a woman after my own heart."

Damion took two more flutes from the credenza. "You girls aren't gonna let us drink alone. Are you?"

"They can't drink. They're working," Devon said.

"If you haven't noticed, you're not flying commercial. This is Emergence. Your pleasure is ours," Mika said.

Jasmin poured two more glasses. "Skål," she said, as they all tapped rims.

The captain entered the cabin.

"I don't care how private this flight is; if the pilot gets to drink, you can let me off right now," Devon said.

"Oh, heavens no," the captain said with a hearty belly laugh. "You all drink away. I just wanted to personally come back to welcome you two to Emergence for our nonstop flight to George Town, Cayman

Islands. I'm Captain Ogle. If you need anything, these young ladies will be happy to help you."

"The Cayman Islands?" Devon said. "But I don't have a—"

"Say," Damion interrupted, "how'd you guys come up with the name 'Emergence'? Sounds too much like 'emergency' to me. And at thirty thousand feet, an emergency is the last thing I want to think about."

"Don't mind my brother," Devon said to the captain. "He's a jerk. Nice meeting you, sir."

"You boys enjoy the flight accommodations," Captain Ogle said with a smile, and he turned for the cockpit. "Onward and upward!"

Damion turned to Devon. "Oh. So I'm your brother again?"

"The better question is: why are we on a private jet headed to the Cayman Islands?" Devon replied.

"Let's just say it's my way of showing gratitude for your hospitality over the last few weeks."

"Well, cheers to gratitude. I guess."

•••

The jet landed on a humid, 83-degree day. A pearl-colored version of the Escalade that had taken them to the airport in Virginia pulled up a few yards from the plane's exit.

As Damion and Devon went to bid their farewells, Jasmin stopped them. "Just a sec, please. We have something for you."

She presented them with a cedar box, then opened it to show two-dozen Cuban Romeo y Julietas.

"I'll smoke 'em with you, but I ain't touching that box right now," Damion said. "The last time someone gave me a box of cigars at an airport, things didn't work out too good for me."

"Enjoy your time on beautiful Grand Cayman," she said, handing Devon the box. "This is our gift to you."

Devon thanked her, and he and Damion started for the SUV.

"Wait." Damion turned back to Mika and Jasmin. "You guys wouldn't happen to be staying on the island for the whole three days, would you?"

"As a matter of fact, we are," Mika said.

"Well, you should come stay with us," Damion replied. "We've lined up a mansion on the water."

Devon looked at the ladies, then at Damion, then back at the ladies before palming his face.

"Over eight thousand square feet," Damion continued. "Panoramic, oceanfront view, infinity pool, gym, staff. It's gotta be better than wherever Emergence is putting you guys up."

The ladies exchanged looks.

"Don't worry. My brother and I are perfect gentlemen," Damion said. "Scout's honor."

"I'm game if you are," Mika said to Jasmin.

The twins got into the SUV, while the ladies went off to collect their things.

"I can't believe you convinced them to come with us," Devon whispered.

"Stick with me, kid. You'll learn something," Damion replied.

Mika and Jasmin soon joined them. They texted each other, giggling like schoolgirls in the back row.

An airport authority police car drove up and escorted the Escalade off the tarmac, bypassing customs and immigration. It turned around only after they had cleared airport grounds.

•••

No sooner than the four had crossed the threshold of the mansion's oversized door did Mika and Jasmin shed their flight attendant uniforms, both now wearing only mesh and lace bras and panties.

The ladies skipped across the marble, toward the twenty-five-foot wide, floor-to-ceiling windows, which opened up to a breathtaking southern view of the Caribbean Sea. The infinity swimming pool, made of black stone, gave the illusion that they dove into a pool of ink.

They frolicked about, splashing water on each other. Their underwear had become too restrictive. They tossed those onto the poolside.

"Are you guys gonna make us swim alone?" Mika called out to Damion and Devon.

Devon averted his eyes. "I'll catch up with you guys in a bit," he said to Damion.

"You've gotta be kidding me," Damion replied. "We have two of the finest women on this green earth in their birthday suits, asking us to join them in the pool, and your response is: 'I'll catch up with you'?"

"Go ahead, bro," Devon replied. "I'm just not up for it right now. Y'all have fun, though."

"This isn't about your little girlfriend, is it? Look, what happens on the island stays on the island. There's no way Beth will ever—"

"Oh, now you know her name?" Devon interjected.

"Of course I do. You only bit my head off about it. Anyway, how could she ever find out? Who knows? Maybe you'll find Ms. Copenhagen does it better than Beth ever could."

"You're wrong," Devon replied. "I'll know. And that's all that matters. I was just having fun on the plane, but this is different. I feel guilty even being here. Beth would never cheat on me."

Damion walked to the bar.

"Of course you want me to dog Beth out," Devon said. "It's clear you don't like her."

"How can I not like her? I don't even know her."

"Yeah, but you know she's white and you don't like that. You know, you're just like Mama on this, and all the other Black staffers who look at me sideways when Beth and I walk the halls. All of you need to get a grip."

"Negro, I served overseas in the Army with some solid people, and many of them were white. So it's not that. It's just a vibe I get from hearing you talk about her. I guess I just don't trust the chick. Can't put my finger on it; I just don't."

"You might feel differently if you ever met her, which you won't."

"All right. Calm down. It's not that serious."

Damion handed Devon a beer. They tapped bottlenecks.

"Suit yourself," Damion said. He took a swig, then started for the pool, still fully dressed.

"Onward and upward!" he yelled, running and tucking into a cannonball.

•••

The next morning, Devon found Damion poolside, reclined beneath a large shade. He blew a plume of cigar smoke into the air.

"This is how life is supposed to be lived, huh, brother?" he said to Devon.

"Sure beats February in D.C.," Devon replied. "I've never seen anything like this. That water doesn't even look real to me."

"Oh, it's real; we'll get out there a little later to see for ourselves. I rented a boat. I figure we can do a bit of fishing, call the chef in when we get back, and have him grill them up for us."

"Do you even know how to fish?" Devon asked.

"Nope. Don't know how to drive a boat either, but between the two of us, I'm sure we can figure it all out."

"I don't know about that."

Damion cut the end of a second cigar, lit it in his mouth, and handed it to Devon.

"Have a brotherhood smoke with me."

Devon took a pull and coughed the cigar onto the ground.

Damion erupted in laughter. "Easy, easy, bro. You're not supposed to inhale."

Devon's laughter merged into a series of more coughs. "It would've been nice if you'd told me that beforehand,"

Devon tried the cigar again. When he blew out, there was no smoke at all this time.

He looked around. "Where are the girls?"

"I broke them off some coins and sent them shopping. They should be away for a while. I figured we could get in some one-on-one bonding time today. You know, just us brothers, out on the open sea."

Devon had started to get the hang of the cigar. "I'm game, I guess."

"Those girls kept me up all night, anyway. They're like little bunny rabbits. They never got tired," Damion said.

"So I heard. I guess I'll just have to live vicariously through you," Devon replied with a chuckle.

The brothers took in the view and enjoyed the cigars.

•••

Damion had a pair of floral print, short-sleeved button-ups, khaki cargos, straw hats, and leather sandals delivered to the house later that day. Once they had changed, they headed out.

The Escalade was waiting for them outside. After a five-minute drive, they arrived at the dock, where their small cabin yacht, *The Usain Boat*, was waiting, fully stocked with food, spirits, and fishing tackle.

Damion signed the insurance paperwork in Devon's name. After a brief tutorial, he and Devon untied the lines and embarked into the deep blue.

There was barely a cloud in the sky. The gentle breeze paired well with the humidity.

"So, this is how the rich live, huh?" Devon said as they floated on the calm waters, nothing but sea in all directions.

Devon found a place to rest his cigar. He baited his hook, then dropped his line into the water. He glanced at his watch. "It's just after ten. If we're lucky enough to catch something in the next hour or so, we can grill it up right on the boat in time for lunch."

"Sounds good to me!"

Devon stood next to Damion, taking note of his fishing technique.

"Damo, do me a favor—just because I'm not taking your money, I know I can't stop you from taking care of Mama somehow. Just make sure you don't send her too much money at once, or it'll all go into the pastor's pockets."

Damion cut and lit his cigar. "That goes without saying,"

"So, Damo, level with me," Devon said. "It's just us two, and as far as the world knows, you're dead. There's no reason for ego."

"What's on your mind?" Damion replied.

"I just want to know why you were such a fuck-up as a kid. You put the family through hell."

"Honestly," Damion replied, ashing his cigar, "I know I was a handful. And don't think I don't regret all the stress I caused; I regret it all. When I was deployed overseas, and when I was in prison, I had a lot of time to think about my life—to trace back to the root of my anger and pain. And I'm pretty sure it was because I couldn't see."

"What do you mean 'you couldn't see?'" Devon replied. "You couldn't see Mama wailing every time she had to pick you up from the precinct?

You couldn't see the pain you caused Dad? Give me a break!"

"No, Dev, I mean, as a kid, I couldn't see. Like, literally, I could not see. I remember in third grade, I couldn't tell what Ms. Faxio was writing on the chalkboard. So, everybody thought I was stupid. The teachers made fun. The other kids picked on me. You even called me 'Dumbion.' 'Member that?"

Devon blinked fast multiple times with a perplexed look.

"I don't understand. Why didn't you say anything?" he replied. "You know Mama and Dad would've moved heaven and earth to get you a pair of glasses."

"How was I supposed to know my eyesight wasn't as good as everyone else's? I couldn't see through their eyes. By the time I'd figured it out, it was too late for me; I was so far behind in school. Plus, I had already gained a reputation as a thug. It wasn't until I joined the Army that I had my first eye test. They issued me these thick, ugly brown glasses they called 'BCGs,' for 'birth control glasses.' But I loved them. It was like I was seeing the world for the first time. And then the Army paid for the eye surgery. Now, I see better than twenty-twenty."

"Listen," Devon said. "I don't know what you went through back in the day. I just know what you've done to our family. You were given do-over after do-over, and each time, you blew it. So, tell me: what's your excuse for throwing your military career down the drain?

Damion stared into the blue.

"I don't know, Dev," he answered. "I guess, once you get used to trouble, trouble gets used to you. You know?"

"No, I don't know," Devon replied. "That's weak. And that's not how Mama and Dad raised us. Life is ten percent what happens to you, and ninety percent how you respond to it. Now, it seems you have one more chance. The world is giving you another chance. And I'm giving you *one more chance*. Everything else is up to you."

Devon held the rod handle steady against his navel with one hand and grabbed Damion by the shoulder with the other.

Damion reached over and wound back Devon's reel. "Here, I think you need to keep tension in the line."

"Dad would be proud of us," Devon said.

Damion paused. He thought about their father.

"*I am not my brother's keeper...*" he started the poem. Devon joined.

*...I know this may seem strange.*
*Though we have different names,*
*We are one and the same.*
*My shortfalls are his,*
*And his strengths, mine.*
*We ponder the same thoughts,*
*Because we share the same mind.*
*He is I. I am He.*
*How can you not see?*
*No, I am not my brother's keeper.*
*I AM MY BROTHER.*
*And my brother is me.*

"He sure would be proud," Damion said.

Damion started to laugh, then suddenly adopted a sober tone. He inhaled deeply.

"Devon, put your pole on the mount for a sec. I need to talk to you about something."

"Uh oh," Devon said, turning to see the seriousness in Damion's eyes. "What did you do?"

"You gotta know that I would never do anything to hurt you."

Devon gripped Damion at the shoulders.

"Relax, man. I need you to just listen."

"I said, what the fuck did you do, Damion?!" Devon asked again, attempting to shake the answer out of him.

"Calm down, okay. It's about Beth."

"Beth? Bethany, my girlfriend? What about her? What about Beth?" His eyes went wide. "Did you sleep with her?!"

Devon charged Damion backwards against the metal railing. Damion maneuvered his arms up under Devon's and outward to break his grip. He spun Devon around, bearhugging him from behind as

Devon struggled helplessly.

"Dev, stop it! Stop fighting. Yes, I slept with her, okay? And I'm sorry for that, but that's not what's important right now. I need you to listen to me. Beth is not who you think she is!"

After a short while, Damion could feel Devon getting weaker from exhaustion. He loosened his grip.

"Bethany is not who you think she is," he said, calmer now.

Devon's breathing was labored. "What are you talking about, Damion?" he managed to get out.

"Here, sit down." Damion tried to guide him over to the deck furniture.

Devon jerked away. "No."

"Plant your ass in the seat!"

Damion sat down on the couch near where their fishing poles were mounted. Devon followed begrudgingly and took a seat at the opposite end.

"Look, I know you hate me right now. I know I let you down again. But you have to know that what I did was in your best interest."

"How could screwing my girlfriend be in *my* best interest?"

"Hear me out, brother. She wants you dead, Dev."

"I don't understand," Devon said, peering through squinted eyes.

"She wants you dead. And she wants me to do it."

"Let me get this straight, Damo. My brother—my twin—and my girlfriend conspired to murder me?"

"Look, Dev," he said, placing his empty beer bottle on the deck. "I let you have your little MMA moment just now, but if I had really intended to kill you, trust me, you'd be shark bait right now. I never had plans on taking you out. You're my blood. Give me a little more credit."

"So why the trip? Why the boat?" Devon asked.

"I just needed to get you somewhere alone so I could let you know—so we could think this out. As you know, Bethany has resources. Who knows the types of bugs and tails she could've put on us? Getting you out here was my way to shake her. And maybe even bond with you. You know—like the time we stole off the UPS truck."

"Tell me you know that this is nothing like the time we stole off the UPS truck," Devon replied.

Damion stood and started for the cabin. "I'll be right back."

"Should I be saying my last prayers?" Devon asked.

Damion ignored him and returned with a bottle of Cîroc vodka and two Cayman Island souvenir shot glasses. He filled each. They overflowed onto the wood deck.

"Here." Damion handed Devon the drink. "We have a lot to unpack."

Damion finished in a swallow, then poured himself another. Devon shot half, then nursed the rest.

Damion started at the beginning. He explained how Bethany had initially come onto him in the apartment—that he had no choice, or he would've blown their cover. As he went on, he was careful to omit certain other explicit details, focusing on the murder plot.

Devon listened, much of the time his eyes closed, massaging his temples with the middle finger and thumb of the same hand.

"I still don't get it. Why does she want me dead?"

"I think it's pretty obvious, no?"

Devon opened his eyes.

"No—Makeba? You think Beth would go through all this because she thinks I'm dating someone else? Even if that is it, she couldn't have just keyed my car or something? She must be insane."

"If she can't have you, no one can."

"And she didn't think sleeping with my brother was enough?"

Devon looked away.

"Hey, maybe it wasn't a hundred percent about you. Maybe she hated Makeba for what she could do for you that she couldn't. I mean, you said ol' girl was helping you study for your test, right? And she cooked for you, and you guys spent all your free time together. Jealousy is a motherfucker. And for someone with unlimited coins like Beth, there's also no limit to what she might do for revenge. I guess this is just a rich girl's version of taking a baseball bat to your windshield."

"Well, that's one hell of a baseball bat."

"And what better way to get to me than to have my own brother—a man who doesn't exist—do it? It's quite brilliant, actually."

Damion and Devon sighed in unison.

"You saved my life, man. That woman is smart, conniving, and well-funded. Whether it was a staged drive-by or a dump truck that conveniently ran a red light, I was a goner. I'm glad she chose you."

"Me, too."

Devon took the bottle and filled both glasses.

"To brotherhood," Devon toasted. They each downed the shot in a single swallow.

Both winced and grunted.

"So, wait," Devon said. "I know good and well Beth—apparently homicidally jealous Beth—wouldn't put both you and me on a plane with two gorgeous women. In fact, I'm certain she would've specifically requested a couple of middle-aged men instead. Make that make sense."

"You hit that one on the head. She did basically that. But when she wasn't around, I dug through her purse and took a picture of the account number on her membership card, and I called them later to change it."

"Good thinkin'"

For the next few minutes, they sat in silence watching the birds circle above them.

"So, tell me about this Makeba chick. Is she cute?"

# THIRTY-FIVE

Jon had broken his wrist when it was caught in the steering wheel during the crash. Besides some scrapes and a minor concussion, Jim walked away unscathed.

The two had stalled Winston for three days, but his already thin patience had now expired completely. It was time for Jim and Jon to come clean that they'd lost Damion.

Their last-ditch plan was to split up and follow Beth and Makeba in hopes that they'd lead them to one or both of the twins. Given that it was Valentine's Day, the bet was a good one.

It was ten o'clock. Jon had spent the last two hours trailing Beth by car as she ran from downtown, D.C. to Rosslyn, Virginia and back. Sunday mornings were for long runs. He got out and stretched his legs while she ordered her coffee.

Makeba did only a grocery run before returning to her apartment.

Jim and Jon then each staked out Makeba's and Beth's apartment buildings. By eleven, there was still no sign of either twin.

Winston sent for them with a text: "HERE. NOW."

The summoning couldn't have come at a worse time, because, as Jon had started westbound on H Street, he spotted a silver Mitsubishi moving east. He couldn't make out the driver's face or the license plates but was fairly certain it was Devon's car because of the large muffler and transparent aftermarket taillights.

He whipped into a U-turn, not concerned about the accident he nearly caused and making little attempt to avoid being recognized by whoever was behind the wheel of the Mitsubishi.

Jon confirmed the plates. After circling Beth's block behind the Mitsubishi, it was clear the driver of the car was searching for parking. Jon double-parked near the main entrance to Beth's building and waited for either Damion or Devon to walk up.

As he was waiting, Jim sent him a text.

**Jim:** ETA?

**Jon:** I got eyes on. Stand by.

One of the twins crossed in front of Jon's car, barely a yard away, carrying a bouquet of sunflowers. Not yet used to the cast covering his wrist and arm, Jon attempted to snap a photo for proof to show to Nightingale, but fumbled his phone. By the time he recovered it from the floor, the twin was already inside.

He called Jim.

"I just spotted one of them walking into the swan's nest."

"'Swan's nest'?" Jim asked. "Oh, the *swan*. And the 'nest' is her—got it. Do you know which one it is?"

"Jesus, Jimmy, can *you* tell them apart? Anyway, it doesn't matter at this point. If it's not the one we want, he will certainly lead us to him.

Jon received a notification on his phone.

"Stand by," he said, placing Jim on hold. "Looks like we won't have to wait to be led to him."

Someone had tripped a spy sensor that the men had placed on the twins' apartment door while they were away.

"Good money," Jon said. "You're gonna have to go up and talk to Nightingale."

"Me? Alone?"

"Don't be a pussy. I need to stay here and sit on the subject, so, go buy us some more time. Forty-eight hours, tops. Tell him what happened, and that they're back in town now. Tell him about our early morning plan to get them both. And when you're done, I need you to get back to Southeast D.C. and sit on your guy."

"I thought we were just going after Damion. What happened to that?"

"Fuck it, we've been at this for way too long. Let's just clip them both so I can get back to my retirement. I don't care anymore at this point."

"Roger," Jim said.

"Oh, and try and get another utility van out of him."

"I'll see what I can do."

"Out."

"Out, here."

•••

Speaking through a mask, Devon pretended to be a flower delivery man and asked the elderly woman at the front desk to call Bethany Lewenberg down.

He chatted the nice lady up and minutes later, Bethany's head led her body out of the elevator and into her apartment building's lobby.

"Devon? Devon, you're alive!"

"I can't tell if you're surprised or happy to see me." he said with a grin.

"Surpr—I mean happy, of course!"

She went in for hug, her hands inside his unzipped coat to feel around for verification that it was Devon, not his brother.

"I haven't heard from you in days. Where have you been?"

"Well, the phone works both ways," he replied, feigning a smile. "Forget all that. I know things have been rocky between us, you know, with my work stuff, and studying for the bar and whatnot. But these are for you."

He handed her the half-dozen sunflowers.

"Happy Valentine's Day, Bethany. I know how much you like sunflowers. I told Makeba I would meet her later for a study sesh, but I figured I'd bring you these and we can walk around the corner for a couple of drinks and a bite first. Your choice, my treat."

"It's Valentine's Day and you're leaving me to—Never mind that. I'm just glad to have you back. I figured you needed some space, and I didn't want to take you off your track."

Her big smile disappeared the instant she put on her mask.

Walking out of the building and onto the sidewalk, Devon's eyes darted all around.

She lowered her mask under her nose to sniff the flowers.

"But I am curious. Where were you the last few days? Studying with Makeba?"

"No, Beth. I wasn't with *Makeba*. I just needed time to myself. It's been a stressful time for me. Can we just leave it at that?"

•••

It was hour thirty-nine of the additional forty-eight that Winston Nightingale had granted Jim and Jon to find and terminate the twins.

The men lay in wait beneath either side of the mouth of the footbridge that Damion and Devon used on their morning running route.

"I'm freezing my nuts off," Jon said. "Plus, I think a critter just ran over my leg. This is our second day out here. They're not coming. They didn't come yesterday; they're not coming today. How much longer do we have to stay?"

"Relax, brother," Jim said. "They'll be here. Just hang tight."

Suddenly, they started to hear footsteps and heavy breathing.

"Shhh," Jim said. "Hear that?"

The twins were approaching at a near sprint—so fast, Jim and Jon had little time to react, almost missing them.

Damion was out front, already onto the bridge. Devon trailed behind.

Jon—the only one who had brought his pistol—didn't think to reach for it. Instead, he sprung up and charged Devon with his cast arm, clotheslining him into a backflip.

Damion turned, rushed Jon, and latched onto his back, attempting a rear naked choke. But Jon was too strong. He drove Damion into a tree, leaving him gasping on the ground.

Devon managed to peel himself from the grown, charging Jon. He landed a well-aimed punt to Jon's testicles, collapsing him into a three-point stance.

Jim started after Devon, but he was too quick.

With only one hand, Jon raised Damion by the neck against the tree as easily as if he were made of cardboard. He pressed. Damion's body went limp.

Jim stopped chasing Devon. He approached Jon and Damion and pulled the .357 revolver from Jon's beltline and aimed it at Damion.

"Not yet!" Jon said to Jim. "We need him alive for now."

Jon released Damion, who then dropped to the grass in a slump.

"Damo!" Devon shouted as he ran to his brother. "Get up, Damo!"

"Help us!" Devon yelled to anyone in the neighborhood who could hear his cry.

But no one came.

Jim punched Devon in the back of the head, knocking him to the ground.

He and Jon each took a twin over the shoulder.

They hurled them onto the bed of the van and slammed the doors. Jim climbed in the back with them, while Jon drove.

Jim cocked the hammer on the revolver and aimed it at the twins.

"How goes it, old friend?"

"Go to hell!" Damion grunted.

"Go to hell, you say? Jon and I put more money into your ungrateful pockets than you or anyone you know ever would've seen in life, and now you want us to go to hell? You hear that, Jonny boy?"

"Who are these guys?" Devon asked Damion, still dazed and confused.

"We're the guys who made your brother here filthy rich. We're also the guys you two ran off the road a few days ago and left for dead. Ring a bell?" Jim said.

"You guys are the ones who tried to run *us* off the road," Damion said.

"That's one way to look at it," Jim replied. "Either way, we're the last guys you two will ever see. Though, I suggest you focus on me. My friend Jon isn't as easy on the eyes."

"Asshole," Jon said to Jim.

"Learn to take a joke, brother," Jon replied. "Now, back to business. When we were together in Afghanistan, we warned you that this was a life-or-death game. Did we not?"

Jon turned the van right onto Minnesota Avenue.

"And unfortunately, you chose the latter," Jim continued. "So here we are. Your fate is sealed now, boys. There's no way you two are getting out of this alive. But, I like you, Damion. I always have. So, I'll give you one last choice to make, for you and your brother."

"Oh, yeah?" Damion said. "What's that?"

"You don't have to thank me—no worries. I'm a big boy. You're not hurting my feelings one bit. Oh, by the way, did you ever learn what happened to your friend, Zapata? Such a shame."

"You are two sickos. You know that?!"

"This may be true. But we're compassionate, too. You see, we're giving you a choice your late friend didn't get," Jim said. "So you should feel fortunate. The choice is simple. Here goes it—"

Jim pulled a pistol from his waist and aimed it at Devon.

"Please," Damion said. "Kill me. Leave my brother. He has nothing to do with this! I brought him into it. He won't say a word. I promise. Isn't that right, Dev?"

"If you kill him, you'll have to kill me, too, or I won't rest until I hunt your asses down," Devon added.

"That one has some spunk," Jon said.

"He does," Jim said. "And that's honorable. But it won't help either of them right now. So, gentlemen, here's your choice: Fast?" He charged the pistol. "Or slow?"

"What's the catch?" Damion said.

"I'm glad you asked. When you left Afghanistan, your take from all the runs was, what? A couple million? Well, while you were in prison, Bitcoin has been booming. I'm sure you know. That means you should have somewhere in the ballpark of forty to fifty million stashed away. Now, that's a hell of a nest egg."

"It damn sure is," Devon said to Damion with surprise.

"I'm sure you know where this is going," Jim said. "Fast—you give us access to your Bitcoin wallet. Or slow—we torture you and your adorable twin brother here until you do. You see, Damion, my friend here and I were pulled out of retirement for this. You can damn sure bet we're gonna make it worth our while."

Jon turned right onto Good Hope Road toward Martin Luther King Avenue. After a few minutes of freeway driving, Damion smelled an unmistakable odor.

"Where are we?" he asked.

"Blue Plains Advanced Wastewater Treatment Plant," Jon replied. "Jim and I were feeling nostalgic about the good old days in Kandahar, and we figured you might be, too."

Jon parked in a brush-covered area on the back side of the facility grounds. He hopped out and cut a hole in the chain-link fence.

Jim escorted the twins out of the van and through the hole at gunpoint. They all followed Jon to a long set of metal stairs that led up the side of a sedimentation tank, an expansive cylinder full of sewage sludge and water.

"Bring back any memories?" Jon asked Damion. "I must admit, Jim, this was a nice touch—you outdid yourself with this idea."

At the top, the metal stairs turned into a footbridge that extended to the center of the tank. With the twins between Jim and Jon, the four walked onto it.

"Take a look below you," Jim said. "That there is tens of thousands of gallons of bubbling shit. That's like the Poo Pond to the twenty-fifth power. Who wants to take the first swim?"

Blue liquid spewed from Devon's mouth onto Damion's back and neck as he continued to dry heave.

"Someone drank his Gatorade too fast this morning," Jim said. "If you've been around this stuff as much as the three of us, it wouldn't bother you in the least bit."

Jon aimed his gun at Devon and thrust his casted forearm against his back, leaning him over the railing. "Now, I'm going to ask you again: fast, or slow."

"Okay! Okay!" Damion cried. "I'll give you the private key. Just let him go!"

Just then, a single shot rang out, hitting Jon in the torso. He spun around and over the railing. He flopped flat into the brown pool, spraying Jim and the twins.

"FBI!" shouted a man from the other end of the bridge. "Drop your gun!"

Jim looked down and saw Jon splashing and flopping helplessly. He placed his gun on the floor of the bridge.

Jon soon became lifeless, floating face down in the pool of sewage.

The agent directed Jim to come down first, then the twins.

"Antonio Jackson?" the agent said to Jim. "And I assume your pal, the swimmer, is Christopher Scott?"

Jim said nothing.

"You are under arrest for first-degree murder and conspiracy to commit murder of Omar Zapata, attempted murder of Damion and Devon Lee, and various international drug trafficking and kidnapping charges." The agent proceeded to read Jim his Miranda rights.

Once on the ground, a female agent called for medics to see to Damion and Devon as they sat on the edge of an ambulance bed.

"You guys could've shown up twenty minutes ago, before I got my nose bashed in and before both of us almost got killed," Devon said to the agent.

"Sorry about that, boys," she said. "We needed to make sure we secured the kidnapping charge first. But you two did an incredible job. You have no idea how wide this web reaches."

"As long as that web doesn't reach me and my brother here, I don't care where it goes," Damion replied.

After a perfunctory evaluation, the medic cleared Damion and Devon with a thumbs-up to the agent.

"We talked about your immunity deal on the phone," the agent said. "And the U.S. Attorney has authorized me to extend the deal to you both, not just you, Damion."

"What do you mean 'you both'?" Devon snapped. "I'm innocent in all this. I didn't commit one crime."

"I'm afraid you're wrong on that point, Mr. Lee," the agent replied. "At the very least, you harbored a federal fugitive. Oh, and by the way, when you departed and re-entered the United States, did you pass through immigration?"

Devon shot Damion a piercing look.

"And that's just off the top of my head," the agent continued. "I'm sure once we really start digging, there'll be a slew of charges we could throw your way. Some'll stick, and some won't. I understand you work for a member of Congress?"

Eyes wide, Devon massaged his temples.

"Having one of his main guys tangled up in an international drug bust won't be a good look. But don't worry," the agent said, her hand on Devon's shoulder, "you are not our target. We need you as much as you need us. As long as you hold up your end of the bargain and testify, both of you will be free as birds. It's up to you, though; you can either be criminals and spend the rest of your good years behind bars, or you can be heroes that toppled an international, intergovernmental drug conspiracy. Your choice."

"Can I get one of those masks?" Devon asked the medic, noticing the first news crew arriving at the scene. The medic passed him two white N95s.

"So," the agent continued, "if you don't mind, we'd like to get you down to the field office for a debriefing and to collect statements. Then we'll feed you and get you all the follow-up medical care you need."

"Sure thing," Devon said. "We just need to go back to our apartment first to get cleaned up. Is that okay?"

"Not a problem," the agent said. "I'll have my colleague drive you. He'll be waiting outside to take you to our office when you're done. Feel free to shower, and take all the time you need."

Damion and Devon shuffled to a black SUV with U.S. Government plates.

•••

Devon unlocked the door to his apartment.

"Crappy morning, eh," Damion said as they entered the apartment.

"Don't you think it's a little too soon for wisecracks?"

The door swung shut. They then heard a metallic click and froze in their place. They slowly looked at each other with wide eyes, then turned around.

"Beth, what are you doing?!" Devon said. "Why are you aiming a gun at me?"

Bethany said nothing. She just swayed side to side. Her eyes were bloodshot, and her hair frizzy and disheveled.

"I overestimated you, Damion. You're not as strong as I thought you were," she said, hands trembling. "I thought your love for me was stronger. I guess I was mistaken. We had a plan, and you couldn't pull it off. So, I'm here to do it for you. For us."

Damion stepped toward Bethany.

"Stop right there, Damion!" she said. "I need to know. I need to know if we're still doing this. Will we still be together? Or is it over?" Bethany began to cry.

Damion inched closer. "Of course, baby. Just you and me, just like we planned. Fuck him. He's never been a brother to me. He's always hated me. He means nothing to me. The only reason I didn't get rid of him on the boat is because a witness showed up."

"Beth," Devon said. "Please drop the gun. I'm sorry. I'm sorry for everything. Whatever I did, I'm sorry."

"Shut up, Devon," Beth snapped. "All you care about is that bitch Makeba. Do you think she's better than me? You think she's prettier? Smarter?"

"No," Devon said. "I love you."

"Quiet!" she said. "You're a liar! I know you've been sleeping with her."

"I haven't. You have to believe me, Beth, she's just helping me with the bar. That's it."

"I told you I didn't like it, Devon. I told you I didn't want you being with her."

"Beth, baby."

"Not another word."

"But sweetheart—"

"I said shut up!"

She thrust the gun in Devon's direction, firing a single shot, as if she was throwing the bullet out of the barrel. She immediately dropped the gun and covered her ears, an instinctual response to the painful, deafening sound of gunfire in a small space. Damion lunged onto her and gained control of the revolver.

"Dev, you okay?!" he yelled, pinning Bethany down with his body.

Devon had dived in the space between the bed and wall. He frantically checked his body for wounds. "I think I'm good, man. It just sounds like a smoke detector is going off in my head."

The bullet she'd fired had landed in the floor, nearly an arm's length away from where Devon was standing.

Damion stood Bethany up, restraining her with her arm folded behind her back.

"You'd better be glad she's a hippie chick from Cali, and not one of those backwoods Georgia girls. Otherwise, you'd be a goner," Damion said.

"You're damn sure right about that," Devon replied.

The twins laughed.

"Wait," Bethany said, "how are you two laughing about this? Did Damion tell you that he and I have been seeing each other for weeks?"

"He told me all about it right after we caught the biggest fish on the planet," Devon said. "Did you really think he'd betray his own blood?"

The apartment door crashed open and into the wall behind it. The agent who had driven Damion and Devon home barged in with his service weapon drawn.

"Late again," Damion said.

"That woman just took a shot at us," Devon said, pointing at Bethany with both his hands above his head.

"I'll take it from here," the agent said.

# THIRTY-SIX

Devon spooned a scoop of chili onto a saltine. "Thanks for making this for me again, Makeba. You need to start a restaurant."

"Anything for you. With your girlfriend on her way to prison, I figured it's the least I can do."

Devon shoved the cracker into his mouth and dabbed the corners with a napkin.

"Ex, you mean. My ex-girlfriend is headed to prison, exactly where she belongs," he said with a mouthful. "I had two attempts on my life in one morning."

Makeba refreshed his wine glass. "Well, you know what they say: people give bread to pigeons and hunt eagles."

"You're saying all the right words this afternoon, Makeba."

She sat at the other end of the couch and lifted his ankles onto her lap.

"I know it's probably too early to tell, but what do you think will happen now? I mean, how big is this thing?"

"You mean how far does the web reach? Not sure. The feds didn't tell us much, but if what Damo told me was true, it reaches far and wide. I heard they were investigating a company called Keating Pharmaceuticals. There's top military brass involved, too. And Damo's lawyer also seems to be in the mix. At the very least, I think he'll be disbarred. There's even talk that this might've been a political hit job—

that Beth and her parents were part of some fringe liberal scheme to take me out."

"Now *that* would make better sense," Makeba replied. "I mean, you're cute and all, but it's hard to believe Beth would've risked everything for just that—no offense—even if she thought you were cheating. Think about it, she was at the table at Off the Record when you were talking all that Black political empowerment, policy over party stuff, right? Well, you were harmless back then, but not anymore. Now, you're in a position to actually make some of those things happen. You're not just dangerous, you're potentially transformative."

Devon stared at Makeba with wide eyes.

"I guess I need to get Grayton to get back my security detail, huh?"

"Umm, ya think?"

Devon's phone rang. He took the call in Makeba's hallway.

"Devon, Randy here. Glad I could reach ya."

"What's up?"

"I know things have been turbulent for you recently, but we got a call from the Keep and Bear Association—you know, the Second Amendment group. If you're up to it, they're looking for a keynote address from our office for their hundred and fiftieth. We were hoping you could do it."

"Me? I don't know the first thing about guns. Why can't *you* draft the speech for the congressman? Weren't you a Marine back in the day? Hell, I've seen Grayton talk off the cuff a million times about guns. He knows this space. It's low-hanging fruit for him. This'll be a friendly crowd."

"You're not understanding me, Devon," Randy replied. "No one's asking you to draft the speech—well, they are, but they also want you to *do* the speech—as in deliver it. From your mouth."

"I don't think I'm the right person for it. I mean, I'm Republican, but I'm not *their* type of Republican, if you know what I mean. Plus, I have the bar exam in exactly ten days; I need to study. When is this thing, anyway?"

"Saturday morning. You'll have a couple days to prepare."

"Saturday? Yeah, it's a 'no' for me, man," Devon replied. "They're gonna have to pick somebody else."

"Are you sure? Because the congressman and I talked it over, and we both agree that you should have free rein to give the speech your way, in your own words. No input from us. After all, it's only because of you that we made it through that other thing. And now we have a real shot at taking that Senate seat in November."

"I just need some time away from it all. No can do."

Randy sighed.

"Alrighty then. Just do me a favor and chew on it overnight. Would ya? I told them I'd have an answer first thing in the morning. Deal?"

"Okay, but it'll be a 'no' tomorrow, too."

Devon went back into Makeba's living room and flopped onto the sectional, on the opposite end of her.

"I was ear hustling. Did I hear someone wants you to give a speech?"

"Yeah. It's Keep and Bear. But there's no way I'm doing that; that crowd would eat me alive and suck the marrow from my bones."

"That sounds like you're scared, just like you were scared when you told me about the spokesperson job in the first place. And look what you did with that. If you don't want to do it because you're tired, overwhelmed, or just plain don't want to do it, then don't. But if you don't want to do it because you're scared, well then—"

Makeba picked up her iPad. She typed in a search and handed the tablet to Devon.

"What's this?" he asked.

"Ever heard of it?"

"'What, to the Slave, is the Fourth of July'?" he read the title aloud.

"It's a speech Frederick Douglass delivered in 1852," Makeba said. "He lambasted an audience of six hundred white northerners about the gross inadequacy of their efforts to end slavery. In *1852*. During slavery. Even though he delivered it in the north, he was far from safe. Back then, he was regarded as *the* most dangerous Black man in the country. He was being hunted by men who wanted to return him to the south to die as a slave."

Devon sat up and began to read:

> *What, to the American slave, is your Fourth of July? I answer: a day that reveals to him, more than all other*

> *days in the year, the gross injustice and cruelty to which he is the constant victim.*

"Did I mention he said that in 1852?" Makeba asked.

"A couple times already," Devon replied.

"I'm just saying, Uncle Freddie wasn't scared." She took another sip of her Pinot noir and looked away.

Devon pressed a throw pillow against his face and let out a frustrated growl. "Why do you do this to me, Makeba?"

"Do what?" she said, brows raised as she took another sip.

"You know exactly what you're doing."

She placed the glass on the coffee table and raised her feet to the couch.

"How many times am I going to have to tell you this? They're using you, Devon. Their party is in shambles. After a failed presidency, getting shellacked at the polls, and an attempted coup, they need some new blood to take the party in a new direction. They're using you for that. So, use them back.

"When's this thing again? Saturday? That's February twentieth. That also happens to be the day Frederick Douglass died. I'm not saying it's a sign, but it's a sign."

Makeba reached for Devon's hand and pulled him to her.

"Come here, baby," she said.

Devon hesitated, then scooted towards her and raised his feet. He rested his back to her chest, his head on her shoulder.

"I know you have a lot going on right now. I do," she said. "But God has put you in this position for a reason. You have to do the work."

Devon nestled in closer. The smell of her hair calmed him.

"Did you just call me 'baby'?" he asked, playfully.

"Oh, hush!" she replied with a giggle.

•••

The sun awakened them the next morning, Makeba clinging to Devon from behind, arms clasped around his chest, her legs wrapping his hips.

His phone rang.

"What's the word?" Randy asked.

"I'll do it," Devon replied.

"Good deal. I'll get you locked in."

# THIRTY-SEVEN

Mama Lee gripped Uncle Butch's fingers at the middle knuckles. He absorbed the pain with a wince. She breathed fast and deep, almost to the point of hyperventilation. Her face and neck sheened, then droplets formed.

"Take your time and breathe, sis," Uncle Butch said to her. "Just breathe."

"The Lord is my shepherd. I shall not want..." she started. Uncle Butch joined her in prayer.

A soft, southern woman's voice came over the P.A. system: "At this time, please make sure your seat backs and tray tables are in their full upright positions and that your seat belt is correctly fastened."

At sixty, Mama Lee had never been on an airplane.

The flight from Hartsfield-Jackson to Reagan National was one hour and forty-four minutes.

Mama Lee didn't drink, but Uncle Butch convinced her to take the edge off, reasoning that turning water into wine was Jesus' first miracle. He ordered her a sweet red, which she took with ice. By thirty thousand feet, both Mama Lee and Uncle Butch had passed out.

The landing jolted them to attention.

"Jesus Christ!" Mama Lee exclaimed. She looked around to the unfazed faces of her fellow passengers. She then lifted the window shade, exhaling into a prayer when she realized they had touched down.

Her knees shook so badly that a flight attendant offered a wheelchair as they deplaned. She declined. Uncle Butch just helped her along until her footing was steady.

Once they reached baggage claim, Uncle Butch broke off to hunt for their luggage on the carousel. In the meantime, Mama Lee admired the floor-to-ceiling windows that stretched all the way down the airport halls, and the reflective, golden arches that decorated the ceiling.

A man bumped into Mama Lee while lifting a child onto his shoulders.

"I suppose folks don't excuse themselves in these parts," she said, loudly enough for the man to hear. "Bless his heart."

The man turned back, flung up a halfhearted hand, and continued on his way.

She shrugged with a mutter, then scanned the crowd for Butch.

Another bump from behind.

"Now, I don't know how folks do things in Washington, D.C., but in Georgia..." she started, pausing before turning around to confront the offender.

"'Scuse me, ma'am."

Mama Lee froze, not yet meeting the face belonging to the voice. But it was unmistakable to her.

She breathed into both palms and began to weep.

Her legs gave way. Damion caught her and brought her back to her feet.

Damion embraced Mama Lee over the shoulders, one hand cradling the back of her head.

"I knew it!" she cried. "I prayed it, and I knew it. God is an awesome God!"

Damion and Mama Lee hugged in the center of the walkway, ignoring the other travelers with their rolling luggage passing all around them.

Uncle Butch watched, then broke them up with gentle pats to their backs.

"Here, son," he said to Damion. "Grab these two." He used his knee to push a pair of hard, leather, chest-like bags with no wheels.

Damion grunted, heaving the luggage. "Glad to know you packed our old house in these bags."

•••

"First time in D.C.?" the Uber driver asked as he helped Damion and Uncle Butch load the luggage into the back of the black Chevy Suburban.

"It's been quite a while for me," Uncle Butch answered.

Uncle Butch helped Mama Lee into the back seat. Damion climbed in and sat beside her, and Uncle Butch sat in the front.

Mama Lee marveled at the sight of the Jefferson Memorial, then the Washington Monument, and then the U.S. Capitol in the distance.

Damion noticed old debris on the highway shoulder and the broken tree from when Jim and Jon had chased him and Devon a few weeks prior. He averted his eyes.

"I still can't believe it," Mama Lee said. "I have my son back."

"You never lost me, Mama," Damion replied.

"I couldn't believe it when I saw you on the news," she said. "And for something *good*! I can't begin to imagine what you've been through over these last few years—war, prison, taking down a drug cartel."

"We have a lot to catch up on, Mama."

"Just know I'm proud of you." Mama Lee reached for his hand. The creases around her eyes deepened. Her eyes welled but did not run.

Damion gripped her hand slightly firmer, closed his eyes, and leaned his head back against the headrest.

"You know, Mama, that's the first time I ever remember hearing you say that."

"I've always been proud to have you as my son. I've never been ashamed of you. Even when you were out in the streets acting a fool, I never let anyone talk bad about you, not even the folks at church. You've just broken my heart over and over, because I knew you weren't living up to your potential. But *I am* proud of you. And I love you and your brother more than life itself."

They shared a smile and continued holding hands in silence, while Uncle Butch snapped photos and quizzed the driver about his D.C. knowledge.

They took the Fourteenth Street exit into downtown. Minutes later, they pulled in front of a large building with columns and ornate carvings.

"Is this our hotel?" Mama Lee asked Damion. "Doesn't look like one."

"No, Mama. This is the venue, where Dev's speaking today."

"I can't go in there like this," she replied. "I look a mess. I need to go freshen up."

"No time, Mama. He goes on at three. It's three on the dot now. And you look beautiful."

# THIRTY-EIGHT

Devon looked over the crowd. The only other Black people he could see were a security guard and ushers.

The physical attendance was roughly double the number that Frederick Douglass had addressed in 1852. But Douglass didn't have social media back then. Among all the social media livestreams and conservative television news crews, Devon was set to address millions.

The organization's president spoke first, rendering Devon a long, flattering introduction, which Devon tuned out completely. When it was his turn, Devon cleared his throat, adjusted the microphone, and began:

> Mr. President, friends, and fellow citizens:
>
> I stand here today humbled by the circumstances in which I currently find myself. Here on a stage in Washington, D.C.'s Constitution Hall, I'm optimistic about the possibilities—about our potential as a nation, if we choose to continuously endeavor to achieve it. For it is this very structure in which we all are present that, in 1939, Marian Anderson, a Black woman, and renowned opera singer, was refused to perform before an integrated audience.
>
> Now, look at me, less than one hundred years later.

To be sure, I am no Marian Anderson. I could never fill her shoes. But I look around, and I see a crowd of people, not many of whom look like me, just as she would have seen over eighty years ago if she had been allowed to take the stage. So, that begs the question: how far have we really come?

Nonetheless, it is with distinct honor and gratitude that I have this opportunity to address this august body on your 150th anniversary. I commend you all for the way in which you have fervently defended your Second Amendment right to keep and bear arms over the years.

**Devon paused. He shifted his weight and looked up, then back at the crowd.**

Fellow citizens, pardon me. Allow me to ask, why am I called upon to speak here today?

Yes, I am human. Just like you. I am American, as are you. And, sure, we are all presumably Republican.

But make no mistake, we are not the same.

We are no more the same than Donald Trump is the same as Frederick Douglass, who, by the way, was a Black Republican like me.

The careful listener noticed that I earlier referred to the Amendment that is at the core of this organization's purpose as "yours," not "ours." This is because, just as many other protections, benefits, and privileges in this country, the Second Amendment does not apply to people who look like me.

Please allow me to tell you the story of one Mr. Philando Castile, a thirty-two-year-old Black man from Minnesota. You might have heard of him. An officer stopped his car, because he and his girlfriend quote: "looked like people who were involved in a robbery." Something about him having a wide-set nose. Did I mention their four-year-old daughter was in the back seat?

Well, that officer killed Mr. Castile that night—shot him seven times, two of the rounds piercing his heart, in front of his daughter and her mother. You see, Mr. Castile told the officer that he had a licensed gun on his person. And he did. But when he went for his license and registration, the officer decided that was threat enough to take Mr. Castile's life.

That officer stole Mr. Castile from the people who loved him. He traumatized Mr. Castile's precious little daughter, and her mother. And whatever came of the officer? You know the answer to that question: after being charged five months after the killing, 'not guilty' was the verdict.

I watched and read the news in horror. And from the premier gun rights organization in this country, we heard nothing. No denouncement. No message of support for Mr. Castile's family. Nothing.

The message? It's clear what the message is. It's that all people have the right to keep and bear arms in this country. That is, unless you're Black.

You achieve this by allowing strict gun laws in urban areas, where many Black people happen to live. So, law-abiding Black people can't defend themselves against criminals. You achieve this by over-policing Blacks, trumping up charges and pinning felonies on us, because, of course, felons can't carry guns. And if we manage to avoid all your traps, get a license to carry, and do all the right things, your cops still get to shoot us down in the streets. And they get to do it with impunity.

And it's not just guns. This is the story of Black Americans when it comes to housing, education, healthcare—you name the issue.

The greatest trick this party has played on Black

people is convincing us that we don't belong.

You weaponize racist rhetoric. You stoke the flames of hatred and bigotry. You go to great lengths to say to us: "This is not your party." And the ones who don't directly take part in this sit quietly and allow it to happen.

So, it's no small wonder why my mother calls this party the Devil's Politics. It's clear why Black Americans run away from you.

But our repulsion to the Republican Party doesn't faze you in the least bit. Does it? In fact, it has been your design to keep us away. To ensure we only play on one side of the basketball court in a full-court game.

The Democrats don't tell Black people: "Vote for us, because..." They say only "vote." Because the party for which we vote is a foregone conclusion. Republicans, on the other hand, try to suppress our vote, for the same reason.

And when a Black person is murdered in the streets, both Republicans and Democrats alike are just fine seeing "Black Lives Matter" painted on streets, as long as lawmakers don't actually have to do anything. Sure, you'll give us a holiday, or let us take down a few statues. But I'll take statutes over statues. Where are the policies?

You enjoy the same rights and privileges that you don't want us to have. So, no, we are not the same. You are Trump Republicans, McConnell Republicans, Reagan Republicans.

I'm a Douglass Republican.

Because, while you and I agree in principle on many issues, we both know that those issues impact Black Americans differently. Therefore, you and I are a world apart.

The last president brought this party and this country to its knees. And when you look at the electoral

> map, it's clear how the party lost. Black people. Black people turned out in record numbers to vote against Donald Trump. In the final hours, the voting districts that mattered were all Black. Places like Milwaukee. Black. Philly. Black. Fulton County, Georgia. Black.
>
> You see, if the Republican Party wants to rebuild, you will need black people, just like Black people need participation on both sides of the aisle to see any meaningful progress in this incredible nation.
>
> So court our votes. Run us on your ballots. Elect us. Speak out when we're wronged.
>
> Because we belong, too.
>
> Congratulations on your 150th anniversary. And continue to enjoy your Second Amendment.

The crowd was still and silent. You could hear only the barrage of camera shutters. Devon turned and walked off the stage without staying to accept his speaker gift from the Keep and Bear president.

"Wooooo! That's my brother right there!" shouted Damion.

"Oh, glory be to God. Great job, son!" yelled Mama Lee.

Damion, Makeba, and Mama Lee's applause filled the entire concert hall. At that moment, their approval was the only approval that mattered to Devon.

They all met him at the foot of the stage stairs. Devon pulled Makeba in by the waist. And they kissed.

"Who managed to get you out of Macon?" Devon said to Mama Lee.

"When I found out this knucklehead son of mine was alive and here, I was on the first thing smokin'."

Mama Lee embraced Devon with one of those long hugs where you rock side to side. "And Makeba is so beautiful. She's a keeper. I'm so proud of you," she whispered into his ear.

"Let's get out of here," Devon said. "We all have a lot of catching up to do."

The four of them started for the exit.

A call came to Devon's phone. It was Congressman Grayton. He put both phones on "Do Not Disturb."

He stepped around a reporter and her cameraman.

"Mr. Lee, you seem to have a lot of ideas about the direction of the Republican Party. Do you think you're the one to lead it? Do you see yourself running for office? The House, maybe?"

Without stopping, Devon turned to the camera: "If the Republican Party can use me, I can sure use it."

# ACKNOWLEDGEMENTS

Through sheer serendipity, a pattern developed that was impossible for me to ignore during the crafting of this novel. Of the dozen or so people who helped me to mold this project into the best version of itself, all but one were women.

Therefore, I thought it necessary to highlight this and to honor and thank them for walking beside me, specifically while writing the book, and in life generally.

At the front of the line is my mother, Clarice Coward. You loved me, prayed for me, and encouraged me to go find everything that was meant for me in this world. Without your permission to join the Army when I was seventeen, I would not have had the experiences I needed to conceive this novel in the first place. You and my sister, Andrea Rivers, supported me from the home front, while I deployed to Middle East combat zones every three to five years over the last two decades.

To my daughter, Audrey, and niece, Drew, you both played relatively peacefully together with your Barbies while I created at my dining room table.

I love you all.

And now, to my fellow bohemians who had a direct hand in *The Devil's Politics*:

To my dear friend, Melanie Meek, it initially took some pressure for me to extract your candid opinions (you're so diplomatic). But once the gates opened, the feedback flooded out. You read as I wrote, checking the Google Docs shared folder daily for my updates. We quibbled often, and I locked you out of the document often. But I let you back in every time. Your feedback was invaluable. I couldn't have done it without you.

Similarly, I must thank my friend Chinyere Nwosu. Chi Chi, you, too, were around from the beginning of my work. You read daily. We chatted daily. Who am I kidding? You entertained my ramblings for hours, multiple times per day, about this book. When I was discouraged and took a pause from writing, it was your enthusiastic interest that got me back behind the keyboard. Thank you for your valuable input.

Silvia Kerali, you are one of my closest friends. You took time from your busy schedule to read my manuscript. You challenged me intellectually to rethink and rework critical pieces of the novel. You advised me on pre- and post-publication marketing strategies. I value and appreciate you.

Krystal Robinson, your attachment to some characters and strong disdain for others gave me the confidence to know that I was working with something special. Your often humorous review of my chapters relieved my self-imposed writer's tension.

To one of my best friends, Farrah Saint-Surrin, while I spent the first year of the pandemic working on my passion project, you were busy working at the center of America's disease response efforts. Yet, you found time to talk to me about my ideas for the novel. Your feedback resulted in a significant change to the cover art.

Thank you, Malek Naz Freidouni, for shooting the perfect headshot over two days to accommodate my pickiness. You're a true professional.

My friend, D. Watkins, thank you for the advance read, and for the most humbling of compliments to display on the cover.

Finally, and equally as important, I must thank Di Angelo Publications.

Ashley Crantas, with each round of edits, you dared me to go harder. You pushed me to show, not tell. Your sharp editorial eye caught inconsistencies and character development deficiencies. You were patient and communicative. Under Elizabeth Geeslin Zinn's editorial leadership, you, Kim James, Jessica Warren, Willy Rowberry, and Stephanie Yoxen transformed *The Devil's Politics*, elevating the project to the professional level of art it has become.

And to Sequoia Schmidt, thank you for giving me this enormous opportunity to introduce into the public discourse my third-rail ideas concerning race and politics.

www.ingramcontent.com/pod-product-compliance
Lightning Source LLC
Chambersburg PA
CBHW030526310726
48979CB00010B/1812/J

* 9 7 8 1 9 5 5 6 9 0 0 3 4 *